Acclai
JACQUELYN MITCHARD
and
A THEORY OF RELATIVITY

"Mitchard's canvas in *A Theory of Relativity* is peopled with parents, lovers, lawyers, farmers, and children who have convictions and questions about what it means to be family. . . . This family saga is filled with trademark Mitchard humor and is, to date, her best."

Jane Hamilton

"Mitchard . . . offers another slam dunk here . . . these characters are wonderfully human and their wrenching situation is skillfully unfurled."

Library Journal (*Starred Review*)

"A nuanced, captivating story that is striking in its authenticity. Emotionally richer than her first novel, yet devoid of heavy-handed sentiment, *A Theory of Relativity* is no less compelling. . . . Mitchard is a gifted creator of characters. All the players in this drama (and there are many) are multifaceted, superbly crafted gems, rendered all the more human for their imperfections. . . . It is Mitchard's considerable talent in rendering the complexity of human emotion that will touch her readers."

San Diego Union-Tribune

"Few are her equal in illuminating the personal stake
we all have in the daily business of living."
People Magazine

"Gripping fiction on a par with her Oprah pick, *The Deep End of
the Ocean*. Once again, she excels in rendering domestic scenes
and family relationships, while providing a suspenseful story
that tugs at the heartstrings . . . pushes all the right buttons."
Publishers Weekly (*Starred Review*)

"Mitchard . . . brings literary finesse, wisdom, and deep
emotion to this believable and remarkably involving tale."
Booklist

"Jacquelyn Mitchard knows more than most about the
complexities and ambiguities of what makes family.
She explores this territory with humor and compassion
and an infallible sense of story. *A Theory of Relativity* is a
smart, funny, and deeply compassionate novel about
how we go on in the face of loss and grief."
Anne D. LeClaire, author of *Entering Normal*

"Written with a deft hand and born of personal experience . . .
packed with smart observations and segueing smoothly from
one plot twist to the next . . . Mitchard shines."
Kansas City Star

"*A Theory of Relativity* is Jacquelyn Mitchard at her best,
at work with her most provocative themes,
especially the profound matters of identity
that become bound up in our love for a child."
Scott Turow

"Mitchard is excellent at making the most spare moments
exceedingly meaningful and moving."
Associated Press

"Mitchard is a lovely writer with a
deft knack for characterization."
Baltimore Sun

"A writer fluent in the language of family."
Entertainment Weekly

"Ms. Mitchard is blessed with a surplus of talent."
Kaye Gibbons

"A great summer read."
Wisconsin State Journal

By Jacquelyn Mitchard

Fiction

No Time to Wave Goodbye
Still Summer
Cage of Stars
The Breakdown Lane
Christmas, Present
Twelve Times Blessed
A Theory of Relativity
The Most Wanted
The Deep End of the Ocean

Nonfiction

The Rest of Us

JACQUELYN MITCHARD

A THEORY *of* RELATIVITY

wm

WILLIAM MORROW

An Imprint of HarperCollins*Publishers*

This book is a work of fiction. Actual places, people, and references to legal cases are mentioned for the sake of authenticity of the narrative, but all the characters, their circumstances and motivations, are products of the author's imagination. Tall Trees is a loving composite of many Wisconsin towns, and any resemblance between its residents and actual people is coincidental.

A hardcover edition of this book was published in 2001 by HarperCollins Publishers.

A THEORY OF RELATIVITY. Copyright © 2001 by Jacquelyn Mitchard. All rights reserved. Printed in the United States of America. No part of this book may be used or reproduced in any manner whatsoever without written permission except in the case of brief quotations embodied in critical articles and reviews. For information address HarperCollins Publishers, 10 East 53rd Street, New York, NY 10022.

HarperCollins books may be purchased for educational, business, or sales promotional use. For information please write: Special Markets Department, HarperCollins Publishers, 10 East 53rd Street, New York, NY 10022.

Library of Congress Cataloging-in-Publication Data is available upon request.

ISBN 978-0-06-083693-1

11 12 13 14 15   ID/RRD   10 9 8 7 6 5 4 3 2 1

For Christopher and for Maria Christopher
And for Moochie

Acknowledgments

Mere gratitude is all I have to give to those whose knowledge and generosity made possible the telling of this story.

For sharing his understanding of science and students, I thank Greg Boyer. For their understanding of legal and psychological issues of child custody, I am grateful to Marlene Porter, Richard Auerbach, Greg Lyons, Elizabeth Vander-Werf, and Cindy Jensen. Brenda O'Donnell and Adrian Lund of the Insurance Institute of Highway Safety offered facts, as did Greg Siborski, Marilyn Chohaney, M.D., and Michael Brownstein of the National Institutes of Health. Artists Lora Donahue and Annette Turow lent expertise on their medium and its teaching. For painstaking legal research, I thank Clarice Dewey. For her research assistance, editing advice, and enduring friendship, I owe a great debt to Patricia Kelly.

Daniel Moeser is a wise and devoted judge and a kind friend. Franny Van Nevel, to whom I tell each story I write, gave me more of the bones of this tale than she will ever realize. My beloved brother, Bobby, his pal John, and my longtime friend, fellow writer Brian Hewitt, taught me golf enough for a gimme. For insights into the natural world of central Wisconsin, I thank Andy Johnston and my son Robert Allegretti.

My friends Anne D. LeClaire and Barbara Grossman were readers of exemplary wisdom. During a harrowing passage, my agent of eighteen years and friend forever, Jane Gelfman, was my confidante and compass. Jennifer Hershey edited this book with light and firm hands; Cathy Hemming published it with verve and idealism. The cover designer, Roberto De Vicq De Cumptich, gave this story its magnificent face.

To my daily friends and family, especially my endlessly resourceful assistant, Pamela English, my right hand, Jill DeYoung, and the Nora of my life, Karen Smith, my constant love and loyalty. To my daughters, Maria, Francie, and Jocelyn, and my sons, Rob, Daniel, and Martin—thanks for sparing and forgiving me. To Joyce M. and Joyce S., Laurie, Karen T., Sam, Peg, Emily, Hillary, Sandy Mitchard, Stacey, Jane H., Patty, Artie, Larry, Pam, Mikey, Anna, Alyssa, Bryan, and the rest of my posse, three cheers and a hug. Special thanks to my godson and the namesake of Gordon McKenna.

And for special grace, I thank Rosie, Bob, and Scott.

How swiftly the strained honey
of afternoon light
flows into darkness

and the closed bud shrugs off
its special mystery
in order to break into blossom

as if what exists, exists
so that it can be lost
and become precious.

—LISEL MUELLER, "In Passing"

The chief merit of the name "relativity" is in reminding us that a
scientist is unavoidably a participant in the system he is studying.
. . . In short, would the laws of nature be the same for everyone,
regardless of his place and motion?

—NIGEL CALDER, *Einstein's Universe*

"My goodness. My gracious!" they shouted. "MY WORD!"
It's something brand new!
IT'S AN ELEPHANT-BIRD!!
—DR. SEUSS, *Horton Hatches the Egg*

CHAPTER one

*T*hey died instantly.

Or close enough.

Gordon, of course, knew that "instantly," in this context, didn't mean what it seemed to suggest: Several minutes would have passed inside the car after the impact, while the final tick and swoosh of Ray's and Georgia's heart-sent blood swept a pointless circuit, while muscles contracted loyally at the behest of a last volley of neurological commands. But there would have been no awareness, or only a few twilight seconds—and no memory.

Most of the others in Tall Trees, the McKenna family and their friends, didn't know as much about the biology involved or care to. Small town people, they were accustomed to having something to be grateful for, even death no more physically complex than a power failure. It seemed to many a source of comfort. And as the months unfurled, comfort of any sort was in short supply.

Even Gordon had to admit he was relieved. Couldn't it have been worse, much, much worse?

It could have been. This, Gordon decided, in those few breathless, shocky moments as he prepared to leave his school classroom and drive to the scene of the accident at Lost Tribe Creek, would be his mantra. He would not yowl

and quake at this abrupt conclusion to the year of living cat-
astrophically. He would not let himself come unglued. Dread
tapped at his gut, like an unwelcome salesman tapping insistently at the window—*Your sister is dead; your sister really
is dead!* But Gordon breathed in and out, spoke to himself of
focus.

He would be the one who remained analytical. Looking at
the facts straight on was both his nature and his calling. He
could do that best of anyone in his family. It would be the
way he would protect himself and his parents.

He was, of course, frightened. All the signs. The trem-
bling legs. The fluttering pulse. It had begun the moment he
heard Sheriff Larsen's voice.

"Gordon," said the sheriff, "what are you doing, son?"

What was he *doing*?

An old friend of his father's calling him in the middle of a
weekday, at school, though by rights he should not even
have been there, the term having ended for summer break
two weeks earlier, asking him what he was doing? Something was up, something bad; he could not imagine what;
everything bad had already happened.

Gordon felt a burning the size of a pinprick deep in his
abdomen.

"I'm cleaning, um, my classroom," he'd answered finally,
uneasily. "Throwing out the moldy agar dishes. Reading all
the love letters the kids left in the lab trays. Science teacher
fun."

"Good," Sheriff Larsen said. "Good." His voice had always reminded Gordon of Ronald Reagan's. "So . . . so, you
alone there?"

Gordon had been alone and relishing the solitude. The
days when Georgia went to the University of Minnesota for
her chemotherapy were the only times the McKennas felt
they had permission to do ordinary tasks—get haircuts, return library books—things that felt shameful and selfish
when Georgia was home and miserable. He had almost not

answered the phone. For it would surely have been his mother with another bulletin about the afternoon's accomplishments of his year-old niece, Keefer:—She'd held her own spoon! She'd said "Moo!" Gordon loved Keefer and thought her exceedingly bright, but this was becoming like *CNN Headline News.*

"What's up?" he'd asked Dale Larsen.

And as the older man spoke—an accident, a very bad accident, no survivors, should he cruise by there and pick Gordon up—the level of shock built until Gordon's chest seemed to have room to contain his heart or his lungs, but not both. This was normal, was probably a kind of hypotensive shock. Fear, he reminded himself, was, like anything else, only a thought. Hadn't he mastered that a year ago, when they'd learned that Georgia, Gordon's only sister, just twenty-six years old, a triumphant wife and exultant new mother, had cancer, stage four, Do-Not-Pass-Go cancer? Hadn't he watched her suffer an endless year of days, mourned and mopped and propped and wished for her release and flogged himself for the wishing?

It was over. She had been released.

And Ray, Georgia's husband, Gordon's longtime friend, his sweet-souled frat buddy from Jupiter, Florida, a lumbering athlete with a physicist's brain and the heart of a child. . . . Ray was dead, too. Gordon had to recalibrate. Ray had told Gordon more than once during the illness, *Bo, I can't live without her.* Gordon had sensed it had been more than just a manner of speaking. So perhaps Ray had felt gratitude, too, in the last conscious instant of his life. The mind was capable of firing off dozens of impressions in fractions of seconds.

And so it had proved with his own mind. Gordon decided he would not call his mother. He would give her these few last moments of innocent play with Keefer. Nor would he call his Aunt Nora. She was as brave as a bear, but for all her homespun daffiness Gordon could never quite believe that the same twentieth century that had produced his own parents had also produced Aunt Nora. Nora had told Gordon not long ago she didn't need to know all the whys and wherefores, that she would ask Georgia about it someday, in heaven.

But heaven, Gordon thought, as he carefully parked his car a prudent distance up on the dry shoulder of the road, had been only a concept when Nora made that statement. Now, that kingdom had come. Nora would be shattered.

It would be he, he realized, at twenty-four the youngest but one of his cousins, who would have to provide the strong shoulder, the steadying hand.

But everything he saw looked odd, looked unsettling.

For everything looked like any other day. Gordon first thought that he had come to the wrong place. Or that this had all been a mistake. A prank. Where was Dale Larsen, after all? There was no sign of the familiar police cruiser. Merry, frank summer afternoon sunlight glistened on the river birches. And there was the insistent, melodramatic call of a grosbeak—a call Gordon could never listen to, not even at this moment, without thinking of his mother saying it sounded just like a robin who'd taken acting lessons. Cars bristling with bikes and camping gear boomed past. Gordon felt himself to be the only thing in the landscape at all out of the ordinary.

Even the rupture in the aluminum railing, a swinging wing, looked innocuous, fender-bender quality. He looked to the bank beyond. A half-dozen members of the Trempeauleau County Fire Department stood gazing into the shallow stream, doing, apparently, nothing. The car must have flown . . . the wreck must be over there. A county ambulance parked a few yards up the bank was not running, though the doors yawned wide.

He leaned over, and looked down and across the stream.

He could see it then.

The metallic stack of angles that was all that was left of his father's beloved vintage car nuzzled shyly nose down in its nest of sand, river boulders, and concrete, encircled by a rainbow fan of slick oil and blood, with glass everywhere, more glass than it seemed a car could have contained, on the banks, among the water-sudsed boulders, in the trees. And more, webs and strands of red and beige, in the water, in the willow branches. Gordon could never recall the next moments except as fractured vignettes, sequenced with periods of blindness, like slides shown in a darkened room. Vaulting the rail, he'd slip-walked down the hot grassy slope, past the policemen, an eerie dream-walk that felt in every exterior sense so normal that it could have been any sunny summer day of his childhood, a day he'd wakened feeling lucky that he lived on the verge of the big woods, where other kids only got to go for vacations. Sliding, nearly falling, recovering his footing, finally he was abreast of the car.

In the creek was a concrete abutment, a kind of dam meant to keep spring floodwaters off the road. The car had apparently smacked into the leftmost edge of it. The hood was bent back against what had been the front seat the way a child bends bread for a jelly sandwich. Nothing could have been extracted living.

The windows had popped outward and what Gordon could see through the collapsed driver's side opening looked at first something like the sea wasps he saw when he dived deep, delicate parachute-like membranes veined with maroon and blue and golden threads. . . . Ray . . . oh Ray, and what the side pillar of the windshield had done. Ray. He could not focus on what bobbed on the shallow stream at the corner of his field of vision, the long strip of purple fabric embroidered with gold stars, his sister's shirt.

Gordon began to cry.

Two of the officers ambled over, reached out, and in the stiff-limbed fashion of men of his father's generation, patted his back, and Gordon fought down the strong desire to hide his face against their barrel chests and sob. Stay here, they said, an octave of basso voices, no one voice seeming to issue from any one man, no, son, don't go any closer, nothing you can do for them now. Then Dale Larsen came mincing down the hill in the delicate, balletic way of some big older men, and his presence—representative of the safe, decent, obscenely unchanged atmosphere—triggered a collapse. Sheriff Larsen was part of the stable world. Gordon had once leched for Larsen's daughter, the hot, wild girl who looked like Joan Jett, who'd been Homecoming Queen in Georgia's year. Stephanie. How could he have forgotten her name even for a moment? Stephanie. Gordon grabbed two fistfuls of the sheriff's starched blue shirt and clung. And in a gesture Gordon would always think of as encompassing both a terrible intimacy and a terrible restraint, Dale Larsen reached up and lightly covered Gordon's hands with his own huge, dry paws.

"What we've got to do now is even harder, son," he'd said. "We've got to go see your folks."

Larsen led him back up the bank, and the perceptions that came to Gordon were again those of a child. Gordon was glad that Dad would never see the ruin of his cherished 1957 Bel-Air convertible, a big-bodied cream-colored dream with bright red seats, the honeymoon car, chosen in part, Mark McKenna once told his son—in a rare moment of blazing candor—for that big cushy backseat. Purchased from its only other owner, a university professor who was leaving the country, it had been kept like a trophy, yearly bathed in oils and glazes, swaddled during the winter in its own blanket, taken out occasionally for a spin, as Georgia and Ray had taken it today. It was, for Dad, a chariot of youth that trailed back to the time a tall, quiet guy had found himself courting an exotic dark-haired art major who grew up in an apartment on Chicago's Gold Coast. Shown old pictures of his parents during those early days, Gordon thought they looked like movie stars, impossibly young and startlingly handsome, flirting with the camera.

Oh, Mom, Gordon thought. Oh Mom, oh Mom.

Sheriff Larsen was talking, murmuring, about a cell-phone Samaritan who'd happened along, headed up from Janesville to Burnt Church Lake for a fishing weekend with his two little boys. The man had wheeled onto the shoulder of the road only to roust the children, who'd slipped out of their seat belts and were beating on each other with life preservers.

"Poor guy," Dale Larsen said. "It was his little kid, couldn't have been more than six, he saw the car, and he said, 'Daddy, there's . . .'"

"What?" Gordon asked. Suddenly, he sat down hard on the roadside. He'd had to.

"Nothing," Dale said. "It was just that the foliage was all piled around the vehicle . . . it was hard to see. The daddy thought at first it was one of those derelicts people shove off the road, on account of the car being so old and all. The guy was crying when we got here. He was holding both his boys in one arm so they couldn't look down, crying on the phone to his ex-wife, he said. Shook up."

"He saw the bodies . . . the kid did."

"No, Gordon. Just the . . ."

"The blood . . ."

"Well. Leave it alone, son. Just know, that there was nothing . . . the medics tried. They got the jaws of life, and they were going in. But they were gone . . ."

"I know. I know they tried their best."

"It had probably been hours. The way the car was, no one would have noticed it."

"They . . . Ray and . . . my sister . . . left really early. I was over at my mom's. Georgia put the baby in bed with me and said, 'Kiss me, so you don't . . .' Had he smelled of Georgia's scent, the Sugar Cookie cologne they sold at the Soap Bubble? He had a brief, gauzy impression of the cologne washing over him. *Kiss me, so you don't miss me.* The limp, dampish bundle of Keefer, in her terry-cloth footie suit, placed between Gordon and the wall.

"What?"

"No, just a thing my sister . . . my mom always said it to us, when we left for school. Just, it was how she said good-bye; I wasn't even awake yet."

"Oh. Anyhow, are you . . . can you get up, son? But take all the time you need. I could use a breather myself." The big man, his eyes ringed and sad as a hound's, was pouring sweat.

"I'm ready."

"We should go see your folks, then. Ed Dean . . . my deputy called your uncle Mike. I'm guessing Mike went to get your dad at Medi-Sun." Larsen drew a deep breath. "Gordon, you know I'm sorry from the bottom of my heart. Your folks, and Georgia, especially Georgia, meant a great deal to us. I know this is a helluva note. You've all had a time of it. And this isn't going to make things any—"

"It's okay," Gordon said. "Really, if you think about it one way, it makes things simpler for us."

The sheriff fell silent so long Gordon at first believed the man had not heard him, but when he glanced up, he saw with a sinking heart, the familiar look . . . he'd seen it a hundred times before. He'd gone ahead and done it, cut to the chase when other people were getting used to the scenery. Done it, meaning nothing by it, nothing but a leadfooted attempt at assurance.

"You mean," Sheriff Larsen ventured, "that it's easier on . . . on Georgia."

"Yes," Gordon agreed gratefully. "This way . . . it's just. We would have had to watch her . . . die."

But then Gordon realized—and he had to work at this a bit, his mind struggling to get around it as a small child struggles to hold a fat pencil—Ray's death made things simple in other ways, as well. Ways that even he could never say openly, could barely even permit himself to think. Georgia *would* have died soon in any case; but Ray would have lived on. And probably sooner rather than later, he'd have taken Keefer and moved to the edge of some southland golf club.

He'd want to be near his own parents, so they could look after her during the endless summer Ray spent out on his minor pro golf tour. Ray might even have remarried—he was younger than Georgia, Gordon's age. And eventually, the McKennas' daily immersion in Keefer, since the day of her birth, would dwindle to Christmas visits and thank-you notes markered in a childish hand. They would have lost Keefer as surely as they had lost Georgia, in a breathtaking one-two punch.

But now, the latter half of the punch was pulled. For Ray's and Georgia's will specified that the McKennas, he and his parents, would care for Keefer. If anything should ever happen.

And anything had.

What he had meant to say, and he had almost said it, was that losing Ray meant not losing Keefer.

Okay, it was horrible. It was shitty. It was cold and harsh.

But it was true, wasn't it?

Life is not a lab, he heard his sister's voice say. Gordie, you are the most well-educated doorknob I have ever known. You always manage to have all the facts and still miss the point.

The facts, he had always retorted, were the point.

And the facts, Gordie thought, as he got into his own car to follow the sheriff's cruiser to his parents' home on Cleveland Avenue, meant he would have to be, now, right now, a father. And so he would have to give an account of this day to Keefer to explain why her own parents could not raise her. He would have to take painstaking care to tell it true, just as his parents had told him the unvarnished truth—he would have, honestly, preferred a little varnish—about his own origin. Keefer would be, Gordon realized, an adopted child, too, as he and Georgia had been. And she would, as Gordon did, tend to date her origins not from conception but from inclusion. She was only a baby, after all. She would never remember this time. Gordon had himself always felt that before his parents claimed him, he'd existed in limbo, between lives.

He prized his story, the story his parents told him over and over. How you came to be ours. And Georgia had prized her story even more. His sister, exotically enough, had been the birth child of a Hungarian medical student stranded pregnant in the United States. His own story was humbler, a teenage cashier's vague recollection of tanned biceps, a moonlit night, and the guy who ran the Tilt o'Whirl. His mother had once told Gordon, who remained rueful about the comment for years, that when they'd heard of Georgia's existence, "We thought we hit the genetic jackpot! Since the mother was both Hungarian, like my family, like Grammy and Grandpa Kiss, and a medical student, we'd have a baby who'd look like me and be smart like Daddy!"

But Gordon had been the one who earned a bachelor's in environmental science. Georgia, who could play chess at four and read the newspaper headlines at five, whizzed through high school without ever studying for a test or ever earning anything less than a C, perpetually running for something, some school office or club, making Lorraine paint posters, buying jelly beans for the whole student body on election day. Mark had predicted that he would walk into the parking lot at Medi-Sun one morning and find his daughter shaking hands: "I'm Georgia McKenna, your senator . . ." But Georgia had summoned up no greater ambition than managing a soap boutique in Tall Trees, two blocks from the house where she'd grown up.

And here, Keefer would grow up. Keefer's story, beginning with this day, would include radiant, intentional parents snatched away by a grotesque twist of fate, which was horrible.

But it would be told her by the remains of her birth family, which was a plus.

They would have to explain to Keefer about that collision of forfeit and gift, the truth of all adoptions.

Gordon would want her to know that not even his grief over losing his sister and Ray meant that he would ever be anything but happy to have her. He did love her so. Being around Keefer had made these past months bearable. That, and . . . well, he shouldn't even think this, but . . . having his sister back. Half the time he was terrified and horrified by her illness, but half the time he was . . . happy. Happy in her company, which he'd missed since she'd gone ahead, zoomed into full-fledged adulthood, leaving him feeling like some absurd, overgrown kid. He'd enjoyed sitting up late with her when she couldn't sleep, while Ray was out on the circuit or snoring like a rhino on the twin bed that had been shoved to one side to make room for Georgia's massive hospital contraption, watching *Twilight Zone* reruns, even playing charades. *You can't always do* Rainman, *Gordie. It's like running the play up the middle. The other team catches on after a while.*

He wouldn't have chosen this. But here it was.

He would take it as it came.

People would say he was being too . . . methodical or something. They would say he shouldn't even be thinking of the future at a time like this. They always said that. And it was always bullshit.

Well, he'd tried slowing down to the polite pace, and he had no talent for it. Georgia loved to tell the story of Gordie's first attempt at heroic sensitivity. Her name was Taylor, and for the first semester of college, a mere whiff of her Vanilla Bean sun lotion was a ticket to his instant erection. But fall melted into winter and then spring, and he'd got eyes for this peppery little New Yorker in his water-quality engineering lab, and that meant facing the inevitable kiss-off confrontation over caffeine. It seemed to Gordon an amazement of life: One day Taylor's sleeping bag on Cocoa Beach was all he'd ever hoped of heaven, and the next day, it was like finishing off a pound of fudge. You just knew you would have to have time to forget the taste before you'd touch the stuff again. With what seemed to him great care, Gordon had explained to Taylor that he had hoped theirs would turn out to be a great year-long relationship, but instead, it had turned out to be a great three-month relationship. There was nothing wrong with them, nothing wrong with her, or with him. There was no reason to be sorry for the times they'd spent together; he would always remember them. She would always show up in his dreams, he said (and he'd liked this part), in Technicolor, and with the smell of vanilla. And in an instant, Taylor one-handed her heavy book bag across the table, knocking over his cup, burning the hell out of his thigh. . . . What? Why?

Don't you get it, Gordo, Georgia had asked him, back then, when he'd whined over the phone about the general unreasonableness of women, *don't you get that you could have chosen a more sensitive way?*

Gordon couldn't believe it; that *had* been the sensitive way. The unvarnished truth would have been to tell Taylor that leaving him notes sealed with kitten stickers and insisting that the whorl of hair on the crown of a human head was an exact mirror of the solar system were things he could ignore only before the first full month they'd been sleeping together.

No, no, no! Georgia had said. *No one could ever meet your standards and still keep you from getting bored.* She told him that his intolerance for other people's little quirks and weaknesses was really not integrity. It was a birth defect, a mental block that only tripped other people.

It had been only one dumb conversation. One of hundreds of impromptu brother-sister rants. But dying young, and leaving in her wake a raveled mess of intentions, Georgia had made all her words last words, and all her words prophetic . . .

It would finally come to him, long after the court proceedings were over, that he had—in innocence? in arrogance?—honestly thought that life could be lived like an experiment conducted in keeping with scientific method, that a certain set of results could be obtained and, once obtained, repeated. And it was not possible. Or it was possible only if you were a hermit. If your life was lived in contact with anyone else, contact changed the nature of the experiment. The uncontrolled variable intruded, the pressure of the human hand behind the instruments.

The day of the accident, the drive home from the bridge, would be the last time Gordon would be confident, stupidly confident, that he was well on the way to managing the most horrific surprise his life would likely ever offer.

In court just a few months after the accident, the facts, that which Gordon had always relied on as his best defense, would be turned to work against him. And they would seem poised to work against him decisively, elegantly, just as Georgia's leukocytes, her body's sworn defenders, had turned collaborators with her illness, doing just what cells should do, but more avidly, with more precision. The judge would suggest an interpretation of law that no one could argue was not literally true, but which might have the power to blight both the future and also the past for Gordon and his family. Love, like fear, might only be a thought, but love had blinkered Gordon. He had not seen it coming.

CHAPTER *two*

$\mathcal{A}$nother half hour, and Nora Nordstrom would have been gone by the time the sheriff's car pulled up to the curb on Cleveland Avenue. She'd have made the turn off County Q onto Spirit Lake Road and been more than halfway home. Her sister-in-law Lorraine would have been alone when Dale Larsen came up that walk with the burden of his terrible news, Gordon trailing right behind him.

The Lord, Nora had to think, not without a shudder, works in mysterious ways. But some of the things he revealed were not wonders.

There was only one kind of grief that was unendurable, a child dying who was old enough to know what dying was. Nora had lost a baby boy born two months too soon, years before her eldest son. He'd lived only two days, and though she could still feel the leaflike weight of him in her arms, she still kept a white crocheted blanket she'd swaddled him in while he took his few, excruciatingly slow and shuddering breaths, she had known even then that she was young and strong enough to be able to convert this death to a sad memory instead of a tragedy. Nora imagined that the transition back between worlds had been inconsiderable, the only loss being her own. As for Georgia's death, Nora feared that if she let herself think about anything but helping console her brother and Lorraine and Gordie, her rage would burn down these walls.

When she saw the police car, her first, silly thought was, there'll be no berries boxed this afternoon. A police car never meant anything good. Lorraine, carrying Keefer, came into the hall where Nora was already standing, her big straw carryall at her feet.

"Lorraine," the sheriff said, "may I come inside?"

"Of course, Dale," Lorraine told him, pushing open the screen, admitting the sheriff into the gloom of the hall. She said then, "Look, I know it's Mark. He had a heart attack, didn't he? I know he'll make it. He's been jogging every day for fifteen years—"

"It's not Mark," the sheriff said. "Afternoon, Nora." He nodded, and carefully, as if it hurt him, removed his broad-brimmed hat. "Gordie's right here, he's just fine, and Mike is bringing Mark home from the plant. Mark is just fine."

"Georgia's in the hospital," Lorraine said, her voice dull as a nickel dropping. "She had a seizure. Keefer Kathryn," she nuzzled the baby. "Your mama loves you with all her heart."

"Lorraine," the sheriff said.

"Mommy," Gordon put in. His face was raw looking, blotched. "Let Aunt Nora take Keefer for a minute." Lorraine obeyed, mutely opening her arms, eyes wide.

"There's been an accident, Lorraine," Dale Larsen said gently, reaching out to take Lorraine's elbow when she swayed. "The car . . . Mark's old car. Maybe the brakes went out. It was at Lost Tribe crick. They went through the guardrail. The car flew over to the opposite bank."

"Where are they?" Lorraine asked. "Was Ray hurt?"

"Both Ray and Georgia were killed instantly, Lorraine. They never felt a thing. They never knew what happened."

Lorraine moaned and her head rolled back on her shoulders, that wild mop of hair unraveling. She looked to Nora like one of those Greek or Roman women in the paintings they put on the overhead projector back in high school, mourning fallen legions on the battlefield. Nora opened her arms and Gordie snuggled against her. "I saw the car," he said.

"Are you sure there wasn't a mistake?" Nora asked, thinking of the time her middle boy, Dan, was supposed to have been out with his friends at one of those drinking parties at Two Chimneys, and someone heard over their home scanner there was a wreck, and she and Hayes about went crazy until they found Dan asleep in the backyard hammock. "Are you sure it was them?"

Georgia? she thought, scanning the sunny distance for some hint of connection to her niece, to her niece's consciousness. Georgia? Georgia, of all the seven McKenna clan children, the only girl, her auntie's special angel, from the time she was a demanding, headstrong little girl in corkscrew curls to the luminous bride blowing an air kiss at Nora while she walked down the aisle, her train like a mermaid's shining, luxuriant tail.

"The car was completely destroyed," the sheriff said. "That car . . . you couldn't take the Chevy for anyone else's car."

"We brought her home in that car," Lorraine said dreamily. "It was our lucky car. You know? We felt like, Georgia being born made us young all over again. It was kind of old even then, and I had my station wagon, which was probably a lot safer . . ."

"I'm going to put Keefer down," Nora said, but she didn't move, just stood there.

"Georgia was three days old. We'd never seen anything so tiny and perfect. Mark asked me if human babies had their eyes open when they were born! As if she was a kitten! People didn't really use car seats so much then. But we got one, because we were afraid that if we didn't do everything to the letter the social worker would take her back or something. Mark said she looked like an egg in a cup. But we got about one mile away from the foster parents' house and I reached back and took her out. I knew it was dangerous, and she was fast asleep; but I wanted to *bring her home in my arms . . .*"

Nora and the sheriff exchanged frowns. It would have been a relief if Lorraine had screamed or cried or even collapsed on the floor. Keefer whined, "Mama!" As if she knew.

Nora caught herself remembering. That sunny summer morning Mark and Lorraine had driven by the farm on the way home with the new baby, in that big, fancy sports car, she and Hayes just jumped in their truck and followed them back to town. It was like a parade, from the library to the University of Wisconsin Extension office, to the mechanic, the diner, Lorraine's school, the Chaptmans', the Soderbergs', the Reillys', the Upchurches'. Adopting a baby was not so commonplace then. People hardly knew how to stop themselves from blurting things like, she's so beautiful, why didn't her mother want her? They just let you have her? Is she all right?

Nora was still lost in that anguishing recollection of approving smiles, blessing hands, honeyed sunshine, when her brother Mike came peeling around the corner of First and Cleveland and drove his truck up onto the curb, he and Mark—both of them skinny as cranes—loping up over the lawn, Mark, his big hands helplessly spread, reaching first for his wife, then his sister, and Mike angry, *what the hell had happened? Wasn't enough grief for one family, enough?*

All at once, the phone started to ring, and over the next hour, the first wave of friends began hitting the front porch like soldiers landing on a beach. Nora ended up never going home at all, just sending word to Hayes and her daughter-in-law Bradie to turn off the soup she'd set to simmer that morning and leave it out for the fieldworkers to eat that night. She felt a twinge of guilt, glad the answering machine picked up, instead of her husband. She'd been spending so much time in town since Georgia's illness that Hayes was beginning to grouse. On a truck farm this far north, hours of sunlight and warmth were gold, pure gold.

But she and Bradie had made the season's last strawberry pies that morning, and Georgia had loved strawberry pie all her life. Even in the weeks before her wedding, when she was living on Grapenuts to squeeze into the wasp-waisted antique wedding gown from one of those Southern belle Nye relatives, Georgia could still not refuse her aunt's strawberry pies. Tonight, the latest round of chemo would have kicked in and the vomiting would have begun. Nora had wanted Georgia to be able to enjoy one piece of pie before she would have to spend the next two days trying to swallow tea from a spoon.

"I'm only doing chemo because of Keefer, Auntie," Georgia had told her. "If I get better, I really think it's going to be from the minerals and the juices. The body really can heal itself. My mother-in-law is right about that. I know what they put in me at the hospital is just poison." Nora held her tongue when Georgia, yellow, exhausted, gagged as she tried to swallow the oat-straw and cypress-bark tea Diane Nye sent up in freezer bags from Florida. It was all poison.

If dying in Georgia's stead would have been worth trying, Nora would eagerly have done that. Since her from-a-passing-cloud, tumble-down birth, Georgia had been Nora's pet, and when Keefer was born, Nora did the same thing she'd done for Georgia, sat right down in the middle of planting, no apologies to Hayes or any of them, and smocked a little gray cotton dress with ladybugs on the bodice, the whole thing no bigger than one of her husband's handkerchiefs. And Georgia, tired as she was—so tired she could sleep right through the baby's crying, and of course, at least then, nobody knew why—her niece drove all the way out to put some pretty soap in Nora's mailbox as a thank-you.

The hours marched past and Nora's exhaustion took on a plodding rhythm. She brewed so many pots she thought the coffeemaker would blow up, and scribbled so many phone messages from relatives about their plane flights and rides they needed from the airport that her hand got a cramp. She was grateful only that the work distracted her. All Nora's boys left work and came, and so did Ray's cousins, Craig and Delia, from Madison, who hadn't seen Keefer since they'd stood godparents for her last fall. Mark's and Nora's cousins drove down from the Cities. Nora filled an envelope back with so many ranks of four-digit flight numbers they began to read like a code she could make no sense of at all. One of Ray's sisters would fly from Tampa that night. Could she meet someone else in Madison and share a car? And could they hold off on making any more phone calls until she had time to inform her parents? Ray's other sister was on a cruise in Alaska. Could she make it home in time? Nora had to call Fidelis Hill and even the Half Moon Motel to find places for everyone to stay once she'd calculated that the farm couldn't hold them all. In her bustling about, she'd pass Lorraine and Mark at the kitchen table. Mark got up occasionally to walk out onto the porch and stretch his legs, but Lorraine never moved. Even her eyes did not move. Nora would think, well, they're all right for now, they're together. Dale Larsen came back for a second time, with his wife, and Nora almost didn't know him in his civilian clothes, a red open-necked golf shirt and beige slacks; it was like being a girl and seeing the intern priest at the pool swimming with the youth group, his whole body white but for the notched little band of tan where his clerical collar stopped. Sheila, the sheriff's wife, bless her soul, brought puppets she'd made for the children's hospital in the Cities and set to playing castle with Keefer.

This numb bustling around was what sustained people after a tragedy. Nora was thankful for it.

Nora had earlier overheard Gordie snort to his dad, "One more word about 'arrangements' and 'at peace' and I'm going to throw up . . ." but the arrangements weren't to care for the dead (the dead, Nora believed, could take care of themselves) but to keep the living reminded they were living. And she relished the presence of all her family under one roof. The way the McKennas had circled the wagons since Georgia's illness was the way families ought to behave even in ordinary times, to Nora's way of thinking. From Thanksgiving on, Gordon virtually lived at his parents' house, especially with Georgia's own husband gone on that Knockers Tour, or whatever it was called, half the time, even on Christmas Day. Nora personally did not think that the dramatic way he finally did come home, giving up his greatest match in the last minutes, all those pictures in all the papers that said, "Georgia on His Mind," made up for it. But Georgia loved Ray. And it was all over now.

Sometime toward sundown, the phone stopped ringing as if it had run out of breath, and Nora decided to tidy things up for Lorraine. She went into Georgia's room with an old pillowcase, because somehow a bag from Wilton's Grocery didn't seem quite respectful, and began stripping the bedding, with its lambswool pads underneath the sheets to cushion her poor bony bottom. She rolled up the pressure socks into little balls and swept the stack of pill bottles into a Tupperware box she thought she'd maybe put discreetly on Mark and Lorraine's bureau—she was no doctor, and though she'd tossed all Pop's meds when he died, she didn't know whether this was the procedure to use in every case. She pushed the portable IV pole into a closet, and began stacking up the papers, pamphlets with titles like *Facing Cancer in a Young Person*.

There was a stack of spiral notebooks with dates written on the cover in thick marker, the way girls used to etch their boyfriends' names on school folders. Nora knew what they were—the sort of running journal of letters Ray and Georgia mailed back and forth while he was on the road. It had been Georgia's ambition, she'd told Nora, for their marriage to be "a long conversation that never stops, like my parents' is." The books, she'd said, would be a record, something to read when they were old, when all their disagreements would seem silly. He'd write an entry and mail it off; she'd write an entry and mail it back. Nora opened to one, in Georgia's small, elegant hand, "The thing I miss most is sleeping skin to skin . . ."

Nora closed the book.

She'd only heard them have one argument, over the hours of tapes Georgia had insisted on recording for Keefer. Tapes of Georgia reading aloud or singing the lullabies she crooned rocking Keefer to sleep, old songs such as "You Are My Sunshine" and that old Irish song about wild mountain thyme and the blooming heather. The video camera on its tripod was still set up in the corner, pointed at the bed. She had seen Georgia walking the baby, while Georgia could still walk on her own, back and forth in front of the camera's lens in her stroller, or sitting Keefer up on her shoulders, the baby, still far too little then to really manage this, slumped over the top of her mother's head like a rag doll. Hayes and Ray had rigged up a little holster for the remote, so Georgia didn't even have to sit up to turn the camcorder on, whenever she felt strong enough to talk. Once, over everyone's objections, Gordie had insisted on playing one back to see if the system was working at all, and that was when they'd realized Georgia had been making tapes even in the middle of the night. It had been spooky—Georgia, in a dark room, her face in the glow of the bedside lamp thin and somehow hot, like a paper lantern, holding up a children's book, as if she were on a TV show, "Go to sleep, little bird, little bird . . ." Georgia had exploded in a rage one day when Ray insisted she rest, after a bout of retching. She didn't want to sleep. Her face sheened in cold sweat, she'd cried out, "I'm right in the middle of *Green Eggs and Ham!*" (People a county over could hear it; Hayes used to say Georgia missed her vocation as a hog caller.) "These are her memories, Ray! How can you ask me to stop making her memories? What good is another bloody hour of sleep going to do me?"

I do not like them, Sam, I am.

All right, thought Nora, as she lay herself down on the bed where Georgia had lain.

She said, out loud, "Fuck it."

Nora let the sobs take her and shake her, let pictures of her niece roll up in front of her mind. She allowed loss to pound her, and also the guilt, for the fool she'd been twenty years ago, when she'd believed that people who took in Korean orphans and such were saints, but that an adopted child could never really be kin. She saw five-year-old Georgia, hands on hips, telling Nora, "I find the smell of cow shit depressing." She saw Georgia roaring with laughter when the fancy pressure canner Hayes gave Nora for Christmas exploded, spewing blackberry jam from hell to Sunday. She saw Georgia's quiet rapture—she couldn't have been more than ten—the first time she made a tidy French embroidery knot. Nora had shared with Georgia all the homely things she'd have shared with the daughter she'd never had, things people didn't really do anymore unless they were rich and read Martha Stewart. Georgia hadn't wanted a high-powered career. She'd wanted a home and family.

She certainly hadn't gotten that from Lorraine. No offense. The same old Belgian woman who cleaned house for the monks had come to clean Lorraine's house every week, even back in the days when having a "cleaning lady," if a woman wasn't bedridden, was unheard of in Tall Trees. But Lorraine had her teaching and her painting, and she did things for the children, but not the things ordinary moms did. Nora used to marvel at the built-in closets filled with neatly stored and labeled costumes from Georgia's plays, the shelves of polished trophies Gordie brought home. One of the only real jokes Nora and Lorraine had ever shared had been when Georgia had chicken pox, and Nora had dropped by one night to bring cookies. "Wait!" Lorraine suddenly cried, in the middle of their joint effort to count Georgia's spots. "I have to get something out of the oven!" And she'd taken out a cookie sheet, but instead of cookies, well, there were bright sculpted clay figures of Lady, and the Tramp, and the Siamese cats, all just perfect. Georgia clapped her hands—what child wouldn't? A mother who was their own toy shop. Lorraine had looked at Nora perfectly seriously, and, pointing at the oven, said, "I used to wonder what this thing was for when we first moved, then I figured it out."

And Lorraine had always been sharp as a pin, clothes ordered from the Spiegel catalogue, not purchased for the bowling banquet from Gloria's Finer Designs, which even Nora, whose clothes ran to new Levi's and old Levi's, knew were anything but.

To tell the truth, Nora thought heavily, as the heaving in her breast subsided and she sat up on the bed, she liked Lorraine better now, in the disarray that had claimed her since Georgia got sick, than she ever had when Lorraine was such a powerhouse she never had time to sit down even for a piece of coffee cake. They were cut of different bolts, as Hayes put it. The first time Mark brought her home, she'd swept in as if she were some highly colored exotic bird Mark had captured. Thirty years ago, she couldn't imagine how Lorraine would fit in, in Tall Trees—well, the Tall Trees they'd grown up in, anyway, before part of town became a sort of northern suburb grown up to house executives and workers at the big Medi-Sun plant. There'd always been mom-and-pop-type tourists, and there were more swanky ones now that the monks had converted Fidelis Hill into a ski resort. At the same time, original Tall Trees people still called acreage after the farmers who'd owned it, years after the farms were made into subdivisions. They might buy their paper toweling at the big Sam's, which looked like an alien installation glowing in the darkness of the pines at the junction of Q and the interstate, but they would buy meat at

Wilton's. If you turned off the radio, you could pretend it was 1955.

But Lorraine had found her fit. She'd made her place as a teacher, and sold her huge paintings, which always looked to Nora like a cross between giant flowers and sexy highway maps. And Mark was kind of a minor celebrity on account of having been the county extension agent for so many years, answering callers' questions on Larry Miller's public radio show about why you often saw a small bird chasing a big bird or how mole rats were different from shrews.

Given that Georgia was adopted, it was peculiar how similar she was to Lorraine. Two little women with big hands and hips and masses of ringlety hair so dark it was almost purple in the sun. Nora's son Marty (the rascal) said Georgia and Lorraine had the "uni-brow," and it swept over eyes so black the pediatrician thought Georgia had a congenital cataract when she was born.

Lately, Lorraine had withered along with her child, as if eating when Georgia could not was a sin. She didn't trouble with the pretty auburn highlights anymore, her scraggled hair long, streaked white, witchlike, skewered with what looked like a hatpin. The house was going seedy. Whenever Nora came by, she thought how she'd once envied that plushy emerald lawn and stately redbrick foursquare with its white awnings, the awnings alone a badge, to Nora, of ease and education. It was still cleaner than her own farmhouse could ever be, where dried mud and flies made a batter as customary as the bread and butter at the supper table. But Mark had planted no annuals this year; the hedges were parched and stringy, shoots like angry fingers blocking the picture window.

How much of Lorraine's life Nora had envied. That special current between her and Mark, for one thing, which was nothing like the stately companionability of her and Hayes. There were times when Nora felt as though she and Hayes were more like brother and sister than she and Mark were.

For a time, Nora had thought that Lorraine's having two careers and a marriage that looked from the outside more like a courtship, was the reason Mark and Lorraine never had kids.

Then had come that one Christmas Nora would never forget. Dinner was just over, and the men were groaning, too stuffed to move, and Lorraine, for once, got up with the rest of the women to help clear.

Debbie had been pregnant then with Matt, and they'd got to telling stories about labor, as women will do, and Debbie had told about some woman from her office at Wisconsin Bell who got so big her stretch marks literally tore open, and Lorraine said, "I couldn't bear that. I couldn't bear to be torn up like that . . ."

And it just spilled out. Nora had said, "Well, I guess you're going to have that flat tummy of yours all your life . . . I mean, I know your art is like a child, in a sense . . ."

Lorraine had given Nora a look that could've set paper on fire.

"Is that what you-all think?" Lorraine asked, her jaw cast tightly to one side, "that I don't want a baby because I have a *job*?"

"It's none of our business," Debbie put in, handing Nora a dish to dry. But Lorraine tore out of that kitchen—"Now you've done it," Debbie said—and then she was back, towing her husband, "Tell them, Mark. Tell them. Tell them why we don't have a baby."

Nora and Debbie were so embarrassed they wanted the linoleum to open and swallow them up. But Lorraine bullied it all out of him. How many years they'd tried to conceive a child. How they'd tried all the medical things. How they'd almost drifted past the age when they could hope to adopt one. How Lorraine wanted to adopt a baby who was blind or ill or already in first grade. "Tell them how you feel about that, Mark," Lorraine said, in that honeyed voice of hers that could make a cuss sound like a Valentine, words that no man should have had to put up with from his wife. "Tell your family what you think."

And Mark said it. "I just don't think I could ever really love a child who wasn't mine."

Not that Nora blamed him. Not one bit. Hayes, when she'd told him about it, said the same thing. A man wanted his name carried on, and that was that.

But then, months after they'd all forgotten about it (except for Nora, who could still burn with embarrassment at night before bed when she thought of what she'd asked), there was Georgia, like a sun shower from a blue sky. Mark ended up thinking the sun rose and set on her. But even after Gordie came—and despite the many weekends he'd spent on the farm with her own boys and the hopes Nora had that they'd all moved into territory with a shared border—Mark and Lorraine and their children still mostly kept themselves to themselves, as if the four of them made their own country.

All that unease vanished, however, with the first phone call, from Mark, his voice saying that Georgia was ill. Nora had made more visits to Cleveland Avenue in the past year than in the past decade.

It was when she reached down to pick up a get-well card that Nora found Georgia's Florida State sweatshirt, the one she'd begun wearing over her nightgowns because she was always so cold. "Look at me, Auntie," she'd said one day, shrugging her shoulders lost inside the folds of cloth, "I'm a skinny girl. I'm more pretty and slim than I've ever been in my life, without even trying. When I go out, people who don't know say, 'Gosh, I wish I'd been that thin when my baby was ten months old . . .' If I wasn't practically dying, I'd be totally happy." Nora pressed the shirt against her face. Even the sour taint of the air in this closed room couldn't erase Georgia's brisk scent, crisp and sassy as a pine needle crushed in your hand.

Feeling like a disobedient child, Nora dropped the straps of her own overalls, raised up her yellow blouse and laid that sweatshirt against her skin, smoothing it down like wallpaper, tucking it down into her cotton underwear. She could simply ask Mark if she could keep it, but she would not take the chance. She would walk right out and put it in the back of her truck along with Keefer's overnight things and the little gray flannel pallet the baby slept on, because Georgia would never use a crib; she said they were cages. Who knew when Lorraine would be up to having the baby back here?

When she suddenly heard Gordon's voice from the kitchen, raised, she jumped, and glanced at the videotape camera, as if she'd been caught stealing on a bank monitor.

"Well, it's true, Mom," Gordon was saying, "The only way the body can experience pain is through a neurological response, and the way that the accident was . . . the car was firm but people's bones and skulls are more fragile. There was huge gravitational force."

"Look at all these cakes," Lorraine said, as if Gordon hadn't said anything at all, "There are four cakes here. What, do people just have a cake sitting around in case somebody dies?"

Nora crept closer to the hall, where she could hear more clearly.

"Mom," Gordon persisted, "what I mean is that the way Georgia would have died from the cancer would have been a lot worse. Peaceful deaths aren't really peaceful. Your lungs fill up. It's like drowning in your own body. But think about on TV, how a gazelle looks when a lion grabs it," he said, words coming faster, "You know, at the last moment, the deer just lets go? That's when the endorphins kick in—it means 'endogenous morphine,' Mom, your body's own morphine, and so even the worst kind of bleeding or bruising, well, you probably feel pretty good during the last seconds."

"Shut up, Gordon, honey, just shut up," said Lorraine quietly.

"Lor," Mark put in quietly. "Leave him alone. He's only trying to help . . ." Nora peeked around the edge of the door.

Her sister-in-law sat huddled in a shawl, a line of untouched plates of pie and cups of coffee arranged on the table before her, with the two men standing, leaning toward her, both of them so tall and her so little. It struck Nora that they often appeared that way, leaning down to Lorraine as she told them what was what; it reminded Nora of one of those funny photos you saw once in a while in the *Country Journal*. A bantam hen set unawares on a clutch of Canadian goose eggs, and when they hatched, there'd be this tiny little mother with huge chicks four times her size toddling along behind her.

"I know he is, Mark," Lorraine said. "But he doesn't think." She scanned the counters again. "Look at all this food. Who's going to eat it? I'm glad I don't have to. I don't ever have to eat again if I don't want to. I don't have to keep my strength up anymore."

"Yes, you do, Lor," Mark said.

"No, I don't," Lorraine answered. "Well, you take it home, Gordie."

"I don't eat cake," he said. Gordie, Nora thought, was a health nut.

"Well, someone will eat it. Maybe Mike or Matt. Maybe cousin Delia. She doesn't look like she ever missed a meal."

"Lor!" Mark chided.

"Well, it's just so . . . isn't it? It's disrespectful. People chowing down like it's their last meal."

"It's what people do," Mark said softly.

"All I meant was," Gordon began again, "if you just think about it the way it really is, if she would have died at home, it would have been better for us, but not for her. That's all I meant."

Lorraine's voice, when she replied, made Nora's neck prickle. "I warn you, Gordon. You're the one who doesn't get it. The way it *really* is. This is your sister! Your only . . . my only . . ."

"Your only . . . what?"

"My only daughter."

"I thought you were going to say, my only child."

"I would never say that. And Gordie, for God's sake, this is not about you, so just, just shut up, honey!" And Lorraine was up, knocking over cups in her flight, brushing past Nora, her shawl cloaking her head to toe, her dark shape triangular, like bats' wings, dark on dark. Nora expelled the breath she had been holding. She could barely see Gordon's blond head in the cage of his clean hands, where he sat slumped at the table, his elbows soaked by the rivulets of dripping coffee, his knees blocked by overturned chairs. Mark stood beside him, his hand extended, not quite touching Gordon's shoulder.

"It's okay, son," Mark said.

"Make her come back, Dad," Gordon said.

"She will," said Mark.

Patting the bulge at her waist where the sweatshirt lay, Nora pictured her niece up there, still tethered to earth like a kite, unable to comfort her loved ones or stop them from turning on one another. Nora recalled that priests always used the child's name in the context of sainthood at a baptism, even if it was Saint Tiffany or Saint Justin. Nora said a prayer to Georgia. *I'm going to need your help,* she said. She hoped it was not blasphemy, especially at a time like this.

Diane Nye hoped she did not look as stupid as she felt, because she felt stupid enough for three people, and the size of three people, with a purple foam rubber harness strapped around her middle and purple foam slippers strapped onto each foot, churning her legs up and down in the deep end of the pool at Sandpiper. This water aerobics class had been Shelby's idea. Shelby, Diane's herbalist and best friend, though probably not much older than Diane herself, was starting menopause and starting to pack on the pounds. She'd cajoled Diane into at least trying the class with her, pleading she'd otherwise be the only lady there under sixty.

Diane owed it to her friend, whose floral teas had banished Diane's migraines three years before and who was now concocting everything in her power to help save Georgia.

Shelby, whose face was ruddy with effort, glanced over at Diane, and Diane tried to smile. But she kept feeling as though at any moment she was going to tip over like a duck diving and end up with those absurd slippers waving in the air.

This was a little much. Diane liked a walk, and tennis, but she had never gone for that Ironwoman crap, and she never would. She knew Shelby was trying to hold back time, so that she might still have a baby with that really sweet (and much younger) guy of hers. But she thought Shelby ought to be looking to freeze-dry some of her eggs before she ran out of them instead of lifting weights and churning up the club pool.

"Okay, now let's stride!" called the instructor, miming giant steps on the edge of the pool. The teacher was no older than Diane's children, and had one of those peekaboo little navels, the kind Diane had been proud to display like a tiny smile above her hip huggers even after she'd had Raymond Junior and Alison. Of course, she'd been only twenty-one after those first two, with skin that snapped back like a Spandex leotard. It was Caroline, who weighed ten pounds, who stretched Diane's poor tummy to such a size her belly button still looked like a shut eye winking. Well. Couldn't hurt, Diane sighed, trying to synchronize her arms and legs to sluice through the water like one of those big old skinny bugs that skated over the pond at her grandpa's horse farm when she was a little girl.

At first, Diane thought it was the heat or all this damned flailing around that made her think she saw her daughter, Caro, standing with her mouth open and her hands pasted against the glass of the clubhouse grill. But, no, it was Caro, and she was crying.

Diane went still in the water, then awkwardly rowed herself over to the ladder, hauling herself up even though the foam-rubber belt felt like a huge purple sponge. Big Ray, she'd thought first, he's had heatstroke or palpitations. Merciful God, the man couldn't stuff himself with cheeseburgers and martinis and then go out in this heat and play nine more holes . . . then, she'd thought, oh, no, oh, it's Georgia. Georgia's had a seizure again. Georgia's dead. As she walked toward Caro, Diane had a last, irritating notion. Caro should still have been at work. It had to be Caro's husband Leland. Some new fart-witted nonsense from Leland, like the time he'd gone off to New Mexico to turn himself into a he-man by drumming with the Indians. Then Caro had disappeared and come running out the door of the ladies' locker room and said the thing that would break open Diane's world like a boot to a melon.

She'd been shaking Caro, shaking her daughter's shoulders hard, her clenched fingers digging wet ridges into her daughter's silk blazer, when Shelby pulled her off; but Diane, as if watching from a distance, kept on yelling, "You shut up! Stop it! Raymond's dead? *Raymond*'s dead?"

"Mama, it's true, Mama! They were in a car accident!"

"I don't believe you!"

"It's true, Mama."

"What do you mean?" Caroline had never had the sense God gave an angleworm.

"Diane, honey," Shelby said. "Come on. We'll phone. Someone get Mrs. Nye a drink, please."

The instructor had scurried over with a paper cup full of water, which Shelby regarded with disdain. "I mean, get Mrs. Nye a drink, please. A drink."

Diane was sitting there, holding a glass of red wine, staring down at those ridiculous rubber duck feet, while someone took off on a golf cart to get Big Ray, when Caro said in a baby voice, "Mama, my brother loved Georgia so. At least they're together."

And Diane, who did not care at that moment whether God

forgave her, said, "Caroline. They never should have been together in the first place. If Georgia hadn't talked my boy into moving to that frozen hellhole, he'd be here with us now. He'd be . . . warm and safe, and where he belonged . . . he'd have had the life he was supposed to have. All this"—Diane gestured, the wine sloshing over the rim of the glass, red splashes staining the concrete of the pool deck—"was his life. My baby. They took it all away."

CHAPTER *three*

$\mathscr{I}$t was a produce counter, but instead of lettuce and apples there were pills, all shapes, sizes, and smells, her child's garden of pharmacology.

Lorraine knelt on the floor in Georgia's bedroom, her elbows on the card table they'd set up to display all the translucent orange bottles with their childproof white chef's-hat tops. There were shy pink pills to suppress Georgia's normal, young-woman's hormone functions. Businesslike-scored white tablets—Lorraine thought of them as little nurses—to soothe the nausea. Pale blue footballs for anxiety. And then the big pills, the gulls and eagles that sent the neurological system soaring, capsules with serious beads of shiny amber and red. Those for sleep were lawyerly mauve and blue, sleek and seductive as miniature guns. Those for mood were more cheerful and squat, dental hygienists in kelly green.

Lorraine sighed.

Even the big-gun pills didn't deliver her anymore. Her liver must have the density of a submarine. In college, Lorraine had inhaled enough dope to stagger a hippo and then unnerved her friends by asking, "Now what?" She had wanted to get noddy and giggly, but nothing ever pushed her over the edge.

And yet, not long after Georgia's first surgery, Lorraine

had begun hopefully abusing her daughter's medications, just a little. It had been almost a reflex, a logical if asinine response to an emotional pain so fierce it seemed to cry out for medical intervention—two Percocet for you, sweetie, and one for me.

The pills had indeed been kindly. After no more than fifteen minutes came a heady wave, leaving Lorraine floating on what felt, unexamined, like well-being. Soon, she was doing it twice a day. The hospice nurses and the University of Minnesota doctors, bless their hearts, threw drugs at Georgia. They didn't pay any attention to numbers and dosage this far down into the valley. It was a free-for-all, a Mardi Gras of pills. And yet, after a few months, the pills no longer lifted Lorraine up onto the lap of the awaited surge. But she still used them. They had the power to move truths into the next room.

On the morning after Georgia died, Lorraine had solemnly assured one of the nurses (one who happened to have once been a student of Lorraine's, and would never have suspected kindly, grammatical Mrs. McKenna of anything bad) that she had flushed all those pills down the toilet. But Mrs. McKenna had no intention of doing any flushing. She had taken the bottles out of the Tupperware box, where someone had thrown them all ajumble, and lined them up in comfortable ranks on the card table. There was morphine here, and Nembutal, serious blot-out medicine for someone so inclined. Lorraine was going to guard Georgia's pills. In the middle of the first night after the crash, she'd gone wandering in the dark to find a few for sleep and nearly sobbed when she could not locate them. They were options, not to be wasted, she'd thought, with growing panic, as she first carefully then with abandon opened and tossed the boxes of pressure bandages, bins of syringes; and then finally, she'd found them, plunging her hand in the dark into the rubber box where the pill bottles clicked like nestled beetles.

She didn't intend to commit suicide with them.

Suicide seemed an awfully dramatic, athletic kind of thing to do.

But she was relieved that living was something she was no longer strictly required to do.

Any living she did from now on would be extra credit.

People would tell her to be strong. But she'd already been strong. She had lifted her dying, leaking, groaning little girl out of her sweat-and-pee-soaked bed. She had stayed awake for eighteen-hour stretches, lying or pacing on the carpeted floor, listening to the thump-hiss of the oxygen apparatus and Georgia's moans. Freezing one set of washcloths, soaking another set in hot water and oil, Rhuli for the lips, bag balm for the bedsores. She had left school for a month of "compassionate" leave (after twenty-two years of service, that meant "unpaid") and so had learned to use rice creatively and to forget phone numbers of friends she'd known for twenty-five years. For a year, she had not picked up a brush except to paint cat whiskers on Keefer's cupid mouth, not ventured beyond the baby and pajama department of any store for six months, learned to live on four hours a night of sleep, though that had been the one constant she'd craved in quantity as sustenance her entire life, gotten glasses to be able to read *Wuthering Heights* in the dark so as not to assault Georgia's light-sensitive eyes, watched the beloved flesh of her daughter mutate from exquisite to china pale to clay, and smiled and sang . . . be strong?

What about those books she'd been discreetly slipped by Natalie Chaptman? By Karen Wright and Nina Upchurch? Hope and healing books. Live a full life after loss? Come to terms? Understand that bad things happened to good people?

What would Lorraine's seventh-graders say to that?

In your dreams.

I'm so sure.

I don't think so.

Not.

No hardened adult could ever talk so jaded as they: My

world, your problem. Talk to the hand 'cause the mind don't understand.

Right they were. They had the balls not to be fooled. Adults were not mature, they were chickenshit and full of pretense. Not kids.

At first, when Mark called her from the oncologist's office— it had just been a precaution by the obstetrician, to "rule things out"—she had wanted for Georgia to die. Right away. Before she got home. Lorraine had copied articles from the library, from the books about rational suicide, recipes for pill cocktails. Mark had had to take Georgia to work and the doctor, because Lorraine could not bear to look at her beautiful child. A copy of the *Golf Week* photo, the one from the feature story about up-and-comers on the minor tours, the ones with real PGA hopes, with Georgia crisp and slim wearing the obligatory chinos and loafers, gazing proudly at her Ray, was still propped on the mantel. And she had been sick then! It hadn't been nursing that let her "get in shape" so quickly after Keefer's birth. After that photo and the interview tension that went with it, Georgia had slept fourteen hours. That had been the beginning of the end. Weight had continued to peel off, and then the tenderness under Georgia's arm, first attributed to a blocked milk duct, had worsened.

Not until months later, when Georgia was finally too sick to work, too sick to be alone, and Ray was away, did Lorraine finally take over. Neither Mark nor Gordie could do the personal things. And it had been, to Lorraine's surprise, like having a baby again.

Two babies, Georgia and Keefer.

Lorraine loved it. For the first time in decades she hadn't been running off to her studio or to a conference or to get just one more phone call in before running out the door. She spooned applesauce into Georgia's mouth. She cut up washcloths and froze them, as she had when Georgia was a baby and teething, to soothe the sores that pitted Georgia's mouth. After Christmas, Lorraine's prayers changed. She began to ask the Lord to allow Georgia to simply stay, disabled if she had to be, just as she was. Lorraine would adjust. Mark would adjust. Ray would find a way. They would be like those families Lorraine would see in the street sometimes lifting a child into a motorized wheelchair. She would wrench away her gaze thinking, how can they do it? But it had become second nature.

It had become a life.

A life, at least preferable to a death.

Twenty-four hours from now, Lorraine would have to iron a blouse. Unroll new stockings from a package, and put on makeup. Look dignified and smoothed for a ceremony that would end with lowering her little girl into the ground and covering her with dirt. Do that, and then think about it and all the lovely years and unlovely months before it, until she got dementia.

So.

She didn't have to die, but she didn't have to really live, either. She had the option of neglecting herself to the point of consequence, and it made her feel free.

She had a job. She'd had a job. She could no more do it than be a shepherd or run the honey wagon for Septic King. She'd loved her job, her small art shows, working with other teachers. Could she go back to school? Teach? Teach girls whose every gesture—even the absent tucking of a strand of hair behind one ear while reading—would make her shriek and keen for her daughter? Could she even go through the motions?

Think of Gordon, Nora would say. Think of Mark.

Think of Keefer.

She would not think of Keefer.

She would think of Gordon. But not protectively. Gordon adored her, but he was self-sufficient, even self-absorbed. He had copious things to keep him occupied, and with Keefer, he'd have things to occupy him without end. He'd had a markless life to this point. Co-valedictorian. The hal-

lowed Florida State golf team. The credit for that was all
Gordie's, but true, he'd been raised by parents so grateful to
have him and so determined to prove it, that they'd gone
forth into family life with missionary zeal. The high school
principal, Hart Rooney, had once confided to Lorraine that
her kids were so great he would never have suspected they
were adopted. Lorraine had never spoken to the man again.

Mark, well . . . she could not imagine ever again being his
life's most amiable companion. Mark would be lonely and
bemused. But Lorraine was not responsible for him. She
would no longer be able to tantalize him and surprise him,
lead him on the lively chase for her approval that she had
somehow been able to play for more than thirty years. Could
she ever attend another Medi-Sun Christmas banquet, accept
her stocking full of SuperC and B-Blasts with the smile all
Mark's coworkers told him was visible from Saturn? Mark
would . . . oh, Mark would undertake good works, in Georgia's name.

Perhaps he would remarry.

In any case, Mark was making a bore of himself. In bed
these past nights, he'd softly explained his boring intention
to "process" Georgia's and Ray's death, like a kind of amino
acid or cheese spread.

Mark wanted to understand the deaths, Nora to beatify
them, Gordon to explain the mechanics. The Nyes, judging
from Lorraine's one brief conversation with Ray's mother,
Diane, wanted someone to sue. Who knew what Lorraine's
own sister would have to say when she arrived in her neurologist's wife's Mercedes? Judy Reilly was on the Internet,
researching getaway vacations for Lorraine and Mark.
Karen Wright was embroidering a pall for the casket, with
butterflies.

Butterflies.

Bullshit.

Only Lorraine wanted simply not to know.

She'd had an intestinal exam once, in which the doctor

had used a curious sedative to put her in a gauzy state neither quite in nor out of consciousness. The drug apparently did not deaden what would have been considerable pain, but it made the brain unable to recall the sensation for more than a few seconds—which was virtually the same as not experiencing the pain at all. Wouldn't it be fine to have a home line of that stuff, piped into the house like natural gas or water?

Just that morning, Lorraine had become dizzy and fallen getting out of the shower. She had no idea why. Perhaps the water had been too hot. Her ankle had collapsed with a huge, wayward, biting sprong, bringing her down hard on her hip on the ceramic tile. As she sat there, fascinated, dripping, the thing swelled, darkened. Sick-making as the pain was, Lorraine's first thought was gratitude.

I won't be able to attend the wake. I won't be able to walk to the funeral.

"I won't be able to attend the funeral," she'd called from the bathroom. Mark suggested quietly that her unsteadiness might have something to do with all those painkillers and tranquilizers.

How had he known? Finding his own shoes was like a big-game hunt for Mark.

Lorraine shouted, "That's ridiculous. Those silly things have no more effect on me than Ludens cough drops."

Mark winced. She felt nearly sorry for him. She never yelled at Mark. She could not remember more than half a dozen times in their lives that she'd raised her voice.

Eventually, Lorraine's basic good health and an ice pack swamped her best intentions. The swelling subsided. There was no permanent damage. She could stand, although gingerly. She would be able to lean on Mark's arm and no one would think anything of it. She would have to perform the whole ballet. To stay home would have invited more of those doleful half-smiles, more self-indemnifying sympathy. Let's be ever so sorry for the McKennas, or next time, it could be us. She would have to come home from the wake, and sometime in the following week, wash a load of her daughter's underpants and nightgowns, which still lay in the bottom of the clothes hamper, while Georgia herself lay in a cool room at Chaptmans. A few days later, Lorraine would fold the nightgowns and put the best away for Keefer to keep, while Georgia lay across the street under a blanket of earth.

"If only I'd knocked myself on the head instead of on the ankle," she'd told Mark. He was staring, puzzled, at the lint roller, which was fuzzy and had apparently lost its tacky properties. His navy blue suit hung on the back of a door. Lorraine took the lint roller from him and peeled back the tape. He brightened, grateful.

Mark wanted to be grateful. He was glad, he said, that the ordeal was over. He seemed to think they'd summited. To Lorraine's fury, he had said, "At least it's not you." And when she looked at him, saying nothing, his words had lost velocity, as if her look had pressed on some critical valve. Was he saying he would not have died in Georgia's stead? He would not have wanted Lorraine to die in Georgia's stead? Simply that he could not bear this without his wife's comfort? Was he made of wood? Had he no more tact than a drill bit?

Did he not think being dead would be so much easier than being marooned on this narrow peninsula of leftover years?

Twenty, certainly. Thirty maybe.

The self she no longer wanted still had a mind of its own. She had already caught herself noticing the milky luxury of the opening peonies. The air smelled good, poppy-baked, in the early morning. Oblivious as a queen, summer paraded its natural excesses, and, like a starving person set down in a marketplace, Lorraine was diverted. She still wanted her coffee. She still couldn't feel clean unless she flossed. Even the morphine, which Lorraine graduated to the morning after the accident—hoping to go drifting like a Beatle through gardens of chuckling flowers—only made her have an awful dream. Georgia, aged ten or eleven, was perched naked on a burning mountain, screaming for her mother, while Lorraine tried to make herself climb onto hot, rolling, sliding charcoal bricks, driven back by fear each time. *Jump, Georgia,* she would cry, but Georgia would simply go on screaming, as if she had not heard.

The real-life Georgia had never screamed. Winced, a little, but tried to hide it, pretending she'd been clearing her throat. She'd been stubbornly, stupidly optimistic: *I'm feeling stronger today, Little Mom. I think Keefer said "Grandma." She'll be talking by Christmas. This time, she's really going to know about Santa Claus! I can't wait!!* Only a single time had she cried out, when her feet flexed helplessly and her hands splayed during the first seizure: "I'm scared, Mommy! I'm so scared. Does this mean I'm going to die right this minute?"

After the morphine dream, Lorraine had not wanted to sleep again.

But sleep was the only thing that snapped closed her mind's perpetually paging photo album.

Georgia at five.

Bold as the storybook child raised by wolves, tanned everywhere but chin and elbow creases, from her miniature athlete's legs to the unselfconscious ellipse of her perfect belly, she threw off her clothes and ran screaming into Hat Lake. A sprite, a savage. Georgia sitting in the naughty chair straight-backed for three hours. "I'm not going to talk to you, Daddy," she would tell Mark, "until you behave." It had been Mark who'd finally broken, whispering words of caution and penitence into her soft little shoulder.

Georgia at six, dark and elfin, saying in her curiously deep voice, "You're too little to be a mommy; why are you so little?"

"I just quit growing in seventh grade," Lorraine had told her. She still lied about her height, giving it as five feet two on her driver's license when she wouldn't have topped five feet stretched on a rack. "You're not so big yourself, short stuff."

"I'm going to be bigger than you, Mom. In, like, a week."

"I don't think so. I'm a lot older than you."

"Are you very old, Mom?"

"Real old."

"Are you going to die soon?"

"No. Not soon at all," Lorraine would tell her, thinking, panicky, I have to do regular breast self-exams from now on, I'm going back to the gym . . .

"Because I don't want to die."

"What, honey?"

"When you die, I have to die."

"No, you won't."

"Yes, I will."

"You'll be a big grown-up lady with lots of babies of your own, and the last thing you'll want to do is die. You'll be sad, but you'll go on and you'll remember me . . ."

"No, I'll die, too."

"No, you won't. Stop this, Georgia. And anyway, Georgia, I promise I won't die until you're all ready for me to die . . ." Why did I smoke for ten years, Lorraine would think, at times like those; I didn't even like it. Why did I let my aunt Clara give me diet pills? Why don't I take vitamin E and B12 every day? And C? And eat green peppers like potato chips? People in my family don't die young, she'd thought. Holidays at her mother's looked like the gathering of a coven. I'll be one of them, she'd thought. I can promise.

"Are you sure you're not going to die, Little Mom?"

"I'm sure, I promise."

"Do you promise, you'll always be my Mommy Dolphin?"

"Yes, I will."

"You'll always be my Mommy Dinosaur?"

"I promise."

"You'll always be my Mommy Koala, and bring me euca-lyptus leaves?"

"Always." This, as the two of them cuddled in a nest of old comforters, munching graham crackers they imagined as leaves.

Georgia at twelve, with a pout like a shelf that Lorraine's mother, Grandma Lena, said the birds would poop on. Georgia, shoving in Lorraine's face a library book on the adopted adolescent, "It's all here. You just wanted to replace the perfect baby you couldn't have. Nice try."

Lorraine had followed Georgia to her locked bedroom door that day, putting her mouth against the crack, opening her memory wide to receive some vestigial wisdom, something to say that all her teachers training might have somehow instilled in her angry, fearful mother's brain. How could anything comfort a child who felt like an understudy in the drama of her own family's history?

"Georgia," she'd said finally. "You're my child. I only love you."

Silence.

"I love the mother who gave birth to you. I love the father who made her pregnant. I would let them come to live at our house if they would promise not to take you away."

Silence.

"Of course, you replaced the baby I couldn't have. You didn't only replace her, you . . . erased her. She never existed. When you were little, I . . . people would sometimes think I'd given birth to you because we looked alike. At first, I got a kick out of that. I did want to feel like everyone else. But after a while, it bothered me. It was like I was letting people pretend it was better that you looked as though you came from me. I wished you were blond, like Gordie, and six feet tall, so you would know for sure I didn't have to pretend that you came from my body to love you. I just love you, not some facsimile of me."

A tremor had overtaken her voice, and she'd imagined Georgia's contempt, then Georgia's rage. She was in there doing something awful, sawing her wrists, swallowing a whole bottle of Tylenol, making a rope of sheets. "Georgia!" she'd shouted, "Come out here. I'm going to go get a screwdriver and take off this lock!" And she would have, but as she turned to go, the door opened a crack, so that Lorraine could see the glow of the weird black light inside, and Georgia extended one hand, which her mother had taken, without a word, the two of them standing there until both their palms were hot and their wrists weary.

Lorraine thought, I would take that. I would be happy with heaven if it were only that one hand. I would go to church every day and stifle all my doubts and forbid my bitterness.

Georgia at fourteen.

Quick-marched up the walk at two in the morning by Dale Larsen, after having slid on the downspout to run to a hideous, dangerous midnight beer bash in the woods. Lorraine dragging Georgia up the stairs, growling through clenched teeth that they were going to have to move to Canada, slapping her on the butt and the arms and the back of the head all the way up to her bedroom, to the pillow dummy Georgia had made to suggest her innocent, sleeping shape. Who were the parents of these other kids? Alkies? Third-shifters? Didn't they value their children's lives? When Georgia told her, proudly—"*Life* is something you know nothing about, Mother"—that she was the only eighth-grader allowed, the rest of the crowd were seniors in high school or dropouts who worked at the lumberyard or the trout farm, dangerous barn-burner boys in tight jeans, Lorraine thought she would have to wear disguises in town to hide her shame and swollen eyes. It was with a rueful, shameful comfort that Lorraine realized, after high school began, that Dale Larsen's own Stephanie was even worse, the international poster child for bad influences.

As he made his way up the walk after the accident, Dale must have thought of those long-ago days. Lorraine climbed up onto the bed, propping herself against the adjustable headboard where Georgia's religious medal, with its swords and dragons, hung from a tack on a shred of red ribbon. Lorraine's tears were so great in volume she felt she must be dissolving from within. If she stepped onto a scale, she would find herself pounds lighter, the way she and her sister Daphne would be when they were girls, after hours of running around the school's track in rubber suits.

Gordon had been easier. Lorraine sometimes thought she had taken Gordon for granted. Like many second children, he'd chosen the role of compliant child, if only to ensure his share of the attention. Georgia ruled. Vixen, Lorraine's father called her. Critical of Gordie, doting, bullying, forgiving, impressionable, sarcastic. He'd worshiped her. Had Lorraine ever wished she'd had two Gordies, two hardworking, calm children, who let her sleep nights—both as babies and as young adults? Lorraine and Mark had never worried about him, even when he'd dived and climbed under and over the earth with EnviroTreks. Gordie knew himself. He knew his measure, how genial he was, how good-looking, how graceful. He didn't rock the boat. Georgia was ever bemoaning something—her weight, her hair, hiding her brains one day, bragging about them the next. Lorraine had despaired of her daughter ever finding equilibrium.

Had she ever regretted Georgia? Had a stray ribbon of that regret found its way on high, like a banner drawn by a small plane? Lorraine had done her own reading, when Georgia entered her hellcat phase, and no matter what Lorraine said, Georgia had a comeback: "I don't hate you just because adopted kids are supposed to have identity problems, Mom," Georgia had once told her—her expression had been so blank that Lorraine's first impulse, to laugh, curdled in her mouth—"I hate you personally." Lorraine couldn't count the nights she'd shaken Mark awake, Mark—who could have slept through the demolition of the roof—and insisted on being cradled, begging for reassurance about their daughter.

She's a smart girl, Mark murmured, over and over. *She's too smart to go too far.*

Georgia graduated with honors. Then, despite all those high test scores, Georgia stayed home, working at The Soap Bubble, dating boys who would be farmers or salesmen, taking marketing classes at Woodruff Tech. A change had taken place. Georgia had forgiven her parents. Only when she was older, almost too old to fit in, when she was sure she could shelter under the wing of the little brother she'd bossed, had she followed Gordie to Florida State and met Ray. The grown Georgia was just like the baby Georgia reborn, a wistful young woman who liked baking smells and presents wrapped with cloth ribbon, who collected fairy-tale books, who made Lorraine laugh by holding her mother on her lap, who helped Nora with canning.

It seemed, when she'd moved back home as a married woman, that she'd almost never been away. Georgia and Lorraine had fallen in silly, sticky, cards-for-no-reason, mother-and-daughter love. Taller by three inches than her mother, Georgia had again been her baby dinosaur . . . the frothy wedding, the textbook birth, Georgia clinging to Ray's forearm on one side and her mother's sleeve on the other, Gordon, wide-eyed, choosing that moment to proclaim that he would never again have unprotected sex, Georgia's unwonted sensitivity, "I wish you could have given birth to me, Little Mama, because I feel so bad that you never got to have this feeling of . . . being the creator," her sweet expansiveness dissolving Lorraine's surprising envy.

Georgia had been shy, that was all. As Keefer was shy. It had been fear that turned her angry. Fear of the big world.

The violation of this! Gordie might insist that there was no fairness or justice in nature, but Lorraine had been sure, until now, that there was. She had never, as an adult, doubted it, just as she had not doubted her ability to hear her children's requests when they were still too young to talk. She'd put away her art-school disaffection and run to catch up with God. Why, then, had she and Mark, when time had already run out, been given the chance to raise a child so perfect—

her very bilateral symmetry, digits in order, one almond eye spaced either side of a forceful nose, made Lorraine want to fall to her knees—and then had that chance revoked?

How would Keefer, the puree of Georgia and Ray, turn out? She had already been dragged through so much change. They had all tried to shield her. The Nyes had taken her for a full week after Georgia's first chemo (the baby had come back drinking from a sippee cup, and Lorraine felt reproached for her laziness in letting her keep her bottle). But how could the best efforts of anyone give Keefer the babyhood she'd deserved? Ray could not have stayed at home full-time; the hospital bills alone would have sunk them. The baby could not have been away from Georgia, and Georgia could never have summoned the energy to take care of Keefer on her own. Thank God for Gordon's predictable job, his stripped-down personal life and inexhaustible reserves of disposable time, his courage in taking leave even as a rookie teacher. Gordie, Lorraine believed, had given Georgia the best possible experience that her destruction could have permitted.

It must have been so hard for him.

Lorraine would have to equip Gordon with some sort of basic skills for raising Keefer before she could . . . before she could, what? Die? Degrade? Though Gordon had become proficient at teasing Keefer into her sweet potatoes and out of her nastiest diapers, his role in the baby's life still had consisted mainly of chasing her around the living room on all fours, growling like a bear.

But Gordon would be able to manage. Eventually. Gordon would have to manage. He would have to grow up faster. He would have to figure out that time was real and that he could not say whatever came into his head as soon as he thought it.

Lorraine noticed that she could no longer see her feet tucked against her headboard. The day had slipped past her window, the room into dimness as she lay necklaced in her tears.

There, she'd thought. A day and a night and another day and another night evaporated. Georgia was decisively among the dead now, not the living, every minute drawing her further from her mother . . . Lorraine had done not a single thing but sit up and lie down, sit up and lie down and use the bathroom and refuse phone calls, even from Natalie Chaptman, though Natalie was the closest thing Lorraine had to a best friend, if she didn't count Mark. But Natalie's husband was the funeral director, and Lorraine could not bring herself to have a conversation with someone holding a phone in a building where her daughter's and son-in-law's bodies lay. When the telephone rang yet again, she was in the midst of calling out to Mark to say she was asleep when he walked into the room.

"It was Diane and Big Ray; they're coming over now."

"Now?"

"Lor, they want to see us. They want to see Keefer."

"She's at Nora's."

"Nora's on her way here. She's bringing Keefer. Diane and Ray want to take her in the pool at their hotel."

"I suppose that's all right."

"I told them it would be fine."

"I don't think she'll go to them."

"I think she will . . ." Mark sat down on the bed, then lay down, tucking Lorraine's head under his chin, pulling her over onto his chest. "Are you . . . do you want to get up and change, or anything?"

"Why, Mark? Do I look like a slob?" The first time they'd met her, Diane had just come in off the tennis court. "I hate this weather," she'd said to Lorraine. "I hate to perspire. And it's worse if you work out. I'm a bad Southerner, for sure," she'd said, and extended one perfectly French-manicured hand, silky as talcum powder. When Lorraine complimented her on her skirted shorts, Diane confided, "Honey, I have to buy them in the girls department at Neiman-Marcus. The missy sizes just fall right off me. . . ."

Over Mark's exasperated protests, Lorraine had spent the evening at the hotel in Jupiter, throwing away her own clothes.

Now, as he looked her over where she lay on the bed, Mark said to Lorraine, "I don't think you look like a slob, sweetie. But you might want to put on something that's not quite so . . ."

"So what?"

"Well, wrinkled."

"Okay," Lorraine sighed. She walked into their closet and turned on the light, offended by the sight of so many brightly colored articles of clothing, so many inanimate things that outlasted people. She pulled out her most comfortable jeans and a white shirt that was . . . well, not very wrinkled. She then reached for a soft jersey pin-striped dress, underwear, and stockings, laying out her clothes in the order she would put them on, as she had since she was a child, bra, pants, slip . . . Mark interrupted her.

"I don't think you need to get that dressed up for the Nyes."

"I'm not. I'll just put on jeans. This is . . . it's for tomorrow night."

"Oh."

"I just didn't want to have to go back into the closet twice, Mark. Sweetie, I can't explain. I'm too tired to explain." Lorraine slipped a white button-down shirt over her head, to avoid undoing the buttons, then pulled her hair back into a semblance of its customary bun. The doorbell rang.

Nora was there, Keefer squirming in her arms. "Nora," Lorraine said, "you know you don't have to knock."

"I know," Nora said uneasily. "Just, things feel funny now."

"Nana, Nana," Keefer leaped into Lorraine's water-weak arms, furiously pat-patting her grandmother's back. "Mama, Mama. Kipper Mama?" In four words, the baby's dilemma. *Where was Keefer's Mama?*

How was Lorraine to explain?

"She was up all night," Nora told them softly. "It's as if she senses it. Bradie got her to play with Dan's drums a little. We took her to the barn to see the kitties . . ."

"Kitties," said Keefer, her thumb tucked securely in the far back left corner of her mouth, fingers splayed against her temple. "Nana, Mama?"

"I told her Mommy and Daddy had gone away," Nora said, wriggling her discomfort as Mark pillowed his head on the door frame and sighed, "I know it's stupid. What else could I say?"

"Well," Lorraine sat down heavily on the hall bench, "I guess we'll just tell her the truth. I guess we'll tell her the truth until she gets it. That's what Gordon thinks . . ."

"We can tell her that Mommy's in a better place and she's not sick anymore."

"I don't want her to hate Georgia for going to a better place without her," Lorraine disagreed, "She'll think they went to Disney World."

Keefer had fallen asleep by the time the Nyes arrived. Diane enfolded all of them in her thin arms; she looked incongruously bronzed and neat; her earrings matched her lapel pin.

"Diane, we're so sorry . . ." Mark began. "This is so bad and unexpected for you."

"We're all in this together now," Big Ray put in, in a comforting rumble. "We have to stand up tall for this little one here."

"Do you want something to eat?" Nora asked.

"We have all the food in America," Lorraine added.

"We can't eat," Diane said.

They all found chairs in the living room, and sat staring at one another through the shadows. No one moved to turn on a light. Diane fumbled in her huge kidney-shaped leather bag. "I brought a photo from before Christmas," she said. Keefer and Ray, bare feet oversized in the foreground, laughing faces in the background, sitting on a knoll at Sand-piper Reserve, the golf course where the older Nyes lived.

"This is incredibly thoughtful of you to bring us this," Lorraine said. "Thank you, Diane."

"My baby," Diane said, her thumb caressing Ray's sun-hallowed head. "Does anyone know how this happened?"

"We won't know anything for a while, I guess," Mark told her.

"It was accidental," Nora put in. They all turned to look at her.

"You remember my sister," Mark said, "Nora Nordstrom. I don't know why I didn't think to introduce . . . I hardly know what I'm thinking. I don't know if I am thinking . . ."

"We didn't get to say good-bye," Diane went on.

"Mother, now," Ray got up and settled himself around his wife, and Lorraine felt a moment's envy. People always treated women like Diane as if they needed taking care of, like babies. For once, Lorraine would like to be treated as if she were a baby.

"None of us got to say good-bye," Mark told her, astounding Lorraine. This had to be the second or third longest conversation Mark had ever willingly conducted with anyone outside his immediate family. And there was something else in it, a sharpness. Did Mark feel the same way she felt about Diane? "Really, if we'd had a chance, what would we have said, anyway? They knew how much we loved them."

"At least we can be thankful they didn't bring the baby along," Big Ray said.

"They wouldn't have. It was the old car," Mark murmured.

"We want to take Keefer for the night," Diane said, "let you folks get some rest. My daughters are here, and the grandbabies, the two little boys. They just love her to death. They're only three and four, Brent and Brooks, they have no idea . . ."

"They're all in the pool right now," Ray said, "I don't know how Ali and her husband got back from their cruise so fast, but thank the Lord. Caroline is doing all right but Alison's been having a hard time; she and Ray were only fifteen months apart. We raised them like twins, same outfits . . ."

"We all loved Ray," Mark said. "Ray loved Georgia so much."

"Where's Gordon?" Diane asked, "Why isn't he here? Is he here yet?"

"Oh, he's in town. He lives here, Diane. That's probably half of why she wanted to move back to Wisconsin, Gordie being here. I don't know where he is right now, but I think, I don't know," Lorraine said, "I think he went to Ray and Georgia's . . . house, to find . . . pictures . . . I guess to try to write the things he wants to say . . . tomorrow. . . ."

"Big Ray will give our son's eulogy," Diane said suddenly. "Of course."

"And we are going to have a memorial service for him at the clubhouse. So many of the players want to come. They have something planned for Keefer. I think for a scholarship. You all come, if you'd like."

"Well," Lorraine said, "it kind of will depend on the baby."

"She's been so stressed," Mark explained. "We want to give her a little time to adjust."

"This won't be for a few weeks," Ray said soothingly. "She'll be all settled in by then."

Settled in, Lorraine thought?

"I talked to Alison and Caroline, just a little," Diane said. "You know, Caroline and her hubby don't have any of their own yet; they're such career kids. But Alison's thinking it over. She's going to talk to Andy over dinner . . ."

"Think over what?"

"The baby. We have to decide, not that we want to bring this up now, but, well, Lorraine, you know, I'm only in my forties, how old are you?"

"I'm fifty-nine," Lorraine said.

"So, you're almost in your sixties . . ."

"I'm actually just turning fifty-nine, but, sure, that's right . . ."

"Are you retired?"

"I still teach. I imagine for a few more years."

"And Mark?"

"I have my job at the plant. I head up the lab," Mark said. "What I'll do when I retire, it just doesn't seem like such a big concern right now. But I'll have to do something. Or I'll just use myself up—"

"Well," Diane went on, "what we thought was, since I don't work outside, we'll have to think it over . . . I'm not thinking very well right now. But I do know we want Keefer to know both sides of her family."

"We do, too," Lorraine agreed. "We know that's what the kids wanted, when they wrote the will . . ." Ray and Diane exchanged glances. Or did she imagine it? "But we have to just take this one day at a time. This is all so shocking."

"You can't even imagine," Diane said. "This was my first-born, my firstborn son."

"And she was our only daughter," Mark said, "We know, Diane. We've lived with this for almost a year. Georgia was our firstborn."

"I thought Georgia was adopted," Diane asked Mark.

"She was. And she was still our firstborn."

"And the baby is all we have left," Diane said. "All we have of Raymond."

"And Georgia," Mark said.

"We have to think of Baby," Diane said.

"I think we should leave it to the wishes of Georgia and Ray," Mark said forcefully, with so much unaccustomed volume that Lorraine, who had lost track of the conversation after revealing her age, jumped, disturbing Keefer, who whined and shifted position.

"Baba," Keefer sighed.

"She wants her juice ba, Nora."

"It's right here," Nora said, rooting in the bag. Lorraine settled Keefer, sucking, into the curve of her arm.

"She's back on the bottle," Diane shook her head.

"Just once in a while," Lorraine hurried to explain, thinking, why should I feel guilty? "Just mainly when she goes in a car . . ."

"Oh," Diane said, smoothing her short, layered blond hair.

"I think we should leave it to Georgia and Ray, because they provided for Keefer in their wills," Mark explained. "We have copies of them. We'll get you copies of them."

"Okay," the Nyes said, in unison, and then Diane added, "We aren't going to go right back home. We'll stay a few days . . . after . . . after . . . can you imagine this? We're all sitting here talking about this? About Raymond? Not only Georgia?"

"It seems impossible," Mark said.

"But we all want this little girl to feel all safe," Big Ray added.

"Can we take her now?" Diane stood up.

"I hope she doesn't fuss," Lorraine said. "She's very shy."

Diane reached out for the baby, who shuddered and then relaxed, her auburn curls damp on her forehead. Lorraine felt a pang; she did not usually think that Keefer resembled Georgia, because she was so big and so fair, but the curve of Keefer's dangling leg was exactly Georgia's, the strong, prominent calf muscles, the big thighs that had driven her daughter mad.

Georgia! Lorraine thought, and the baby screamed.

She sat up in Diane's arms as if someone had stolen upon her and given her an injection, her mouth gaping, the tears coursing like individual crystals, each perfectly formed. "Nana!" she screamed, gasping.

"Yes, darling girl," Diane shifted Keefer so that her head was facing Ray, over Diane's shoulder, but Keefer fought, with her considerable strength, kicking Diane in the stomach as hard as she could with her boxy little sandaled feet.

"Nana!"

"Oh Diane, I'm so sorry, I think she means me," Lorraine whispered, making to take the baby.

"She'll be fine, let's get going," said Big Ray.

"Do you need her diaper bag?" Nora held the bag out wordlessly. Diane refused the offer with a toss of her blond head, turning to Keefer. "Shall we get this little missy here an ice cream cone?" Diane asked. The baby had writhed until her torso was nearly at a level with Diane's knees. She was sweating and reaching out both hands to Lorraine.

"Maybe we can bring her over later," Mark suggested.

"Nana!" Keefer sobbed. "Dory!"

"She's saying, 'Gordie,'" Lorraine explained, trying to master her voice.

Diane capped the baby's churning overheated head with one hand. "It's okay, Keefer Kathryn. Nana is here. It's Grandma Diane. Keefer. Keefer."

Both McKennas were sweating, though the room was cool.

"Keefer Kathryn, let's go see Brooksie!"

"Maybe if you just called her Keefer . . ." Mark suggested. "They . . . we never used her middle name."

"Though it's a lovely name," Lorraine put in, "a lovely old-fashioned name."

"My mother's name," Diane said. "We kind of pushed for her to be named Kathryn, so she could be called Kitty, like mother . . . but it *was* sweet how they picked Keefer . . ."

"It's kind of after Georgia, in a sense," Mark said. "When he was a baby, Gordon couldn't say her name, so he used her middle name . . ."

"I know the story," Diane said. "Sweet."

Ray said evenly, "Let's get a move on, Mother. Come on, kiddo."

"Okay, Keefer," Lorraine bent to lay her cheek on the baby's cheek, trying to ignore Keefer's distraught attempt to grab at her shoulders, her collar, to climb off Diane like an anguished monkey. "Kiss me, so you don't miss me, Keefer. You'll come right home soon." To Diane, she said, "I'm sorry, Diane. You can appreciate how hard this is . . ."

But Keefer's screams redoubled as the Nyes, each supporting whatever appendage of her little body they could grab, hurried down the walk. Bob and Mary Dwors, the old couple who lived next door, stood up from their rosebushes to watch helplessly, exchanging shrugs with Lorraine and Mark.

"I know she'll be okay," Nora said, from the kitchen, because no one else had the strength to speak. They had forgotten Nora was there, but Lorraine suddenly smelled coffee brewing. Nora would consume coffee in hell, Lorraine thought. "I just hate to see her have to go through this. It's like she thinks she's being taken away from us forever."

Mark slammed the door. "I cannot for the life of me figure out why I feel the way I do about Diane."

"Why did she say it was worse for them than for us . . . I mean, for you?" Nora held a mug out to Mark.

"For us," Mark patted his sister's arm, and Lorraine could feel her sister-in-law's involuntary start of satisfaction. It made her generous.

"Mark, she's just lost her only son," Lorraine said. "She's not a bad person. She's just not used to bad things."

"I don't think she's a bad person," Mark said, watching Diane lurch into the backseat with Keefer. "I just think she always gets what she wants. And Ray did, too."

The room seemed to empty of all sound. Mark's good opinion of almost everyone verged on the fatuous. Even the most sluggish clock-watcher at Medi-Sun was "a good kid." Alone among the brass, Mark had urged that the bookkeeper who embezzled ten thousand dollars to put a down payment on a double-wide be given a chance to keep her job and pay the company back over time.

Now, glowering, he added, "And they didn't even take the car seat."

"It's only two miles to Fidelis Hill," Lorraine comforted, amazed by his anger. "It's not worth it. She hates the car seat."

"And what if someone sees them, Lorraine. There have been enough car wrecks this week, Lorraine. And both of them are probably . . . their blood pressure is soaring. Ray looks like he's on the verge of a stroke half the time anyhow. The man must be sixty pounds overweight."

"Well then," said Lorraine, "run out and stop them, then."

Mark rubbed his chin. Though he would later not recall having said the precise words, he told Lorraine and Nora, "Nothing would stop her."

And it would be at that moment that something in Lorraine, some interior body that had lain supine, put its hands firmly on the arms of the chair and stood up.

CHAPTER *four*

*H*e felt like a thief entering the condominium.

He felt like a thief stealing into a tomb.

Hesitantly, Gordon made his way down the hall, keeping close to the walls, unwilling to leave marks in the thick carpeting. The place was stifling, hot air motionless and thick with smell. Gordon sniffed—lactobacillus. One of Keefer's bottles, probably, moldering under the couch. Ray had not slept here for weeks. It would not have occurred to him, passing through, to crack the windows or to keep the air conditioner turned on low. What had made Ray an athlete was his absolute inability to think of more than one thing at one time. Their friend Carl Jurgen used to say of Ray that all guys who play golf keep looking for the zone, the place where concentration is so utter that their swing wouldn't falter if they stepped on a rake. "But Ray's there all the time, not just when he plays golf," Jurgen complained.

Gordon was looking for clues, something to add to the words he had already written, which were clumsy and expected: "Today, we come here to say good-bye to Georgia O'Keeffe McKenna Nye, a long and remarkable name for a remarkable person who did not live long enough to grow into it. And to her husband, my brother-in-law, Raymond Nye, Junior, not such an unusual name, but simply a wonderful person (crossed out), he was simply one of the world's great guys. We come to say that these two great (crossed out) wonderful (crossed out) . . . good and gentle people, who were blessings in our lives and in their own lives . . ."

Gordon wasn't a graceful writer at the best of times. How could he provide eloquence on demand now?

Georgia had bailed out his butt on every term paper he'd written in high school, and most of college. He'd done everything but dress in drag to take her finals in Chemistry for Poets. Georgia would not have stood for this hokey, half-hearted stumbling around. She would have demanded *drama*! Lights, casket, organ music, poetry! That she was not here, helping him out right now, was to Gordon proof that there was no afterlife.

The hall closet door stood half opened. Keefer's tiny yellow rubber ducky boots tucked into Georgia's red clogs, the huge old cardigan Aunt Nora had knitted, a horror of psychedelic pastels, which his sister loyally continued to wear, calling it "my matching sweater," Ray's wall of caps, each with the band expanded to the last possible notch. His brother-in-law's head was so huge Jurgen once said that his golf cap looked like a thumbtack on a pumpkin. All ordinary objects were transformed into relics. One of Keefer's politically correct wooden toys held down a stack of printouts about the Thisacillin or Thatamyicin doctors were eager to put into Georgia's veins. Next to the toy was his sister's tinkly ankle bracelet with bells, the one she used to wear with her swimsuit. Gordon remembered her asking, in a voice slurred with morphine syrups, for Ray to bring it to her parents' house, because the sound would comfort the baby.

A cup that had contained coffee and . . . here it was, the milk that had gone bad . . . stood beside Ray's datebook. The open entry, June 3, was for Georgia's chemo. Slightly queasy, Gordon flipped ahead a few days. Block-printed across the spaces for a whole week later in the month were

the words "Call lawyer." That, and a note for September reminding Ray to schedule Keefer's eighteen-month checkup,
were the only entries. A litter of indistinct faxes from the
Knockouts Tour were folded and stuck in a back pocket,
along with a fast-food game card scribbled with what looked
to be a shopping list: Garlic capsules, juice, molasses . . .
Ray's mom was the South's lay minister of health food. Un-
opened bottles of herbal drops still lined the windowsill in
Georgia's old bedroom at his parents' house, names more
appropriate to a picnic than a war on cancer: dandelion, this-
tle, wild clover.

Gordon tried not to look at the hall gallery. He'd only a
few hours left before the whole engine of mourning was set
in motion. Once he saw the inside of Chaptmans Funeral
Home, Gordon knew that any remnant of ability to concentrate would be torn away. He didn't need distractions now.

There was Georgia in her gown with the twenty-two-foot
train. Tim Upchurch had called it the Atchison, Topeka, and
Santa Maria. It was not one of the formal wedding portraits,
but a candid, and Georgia loved it more than any of the others. In the photo, also, was Ray's cousin Delia, who lived in
Madison; she'd grown up with Ray nearly as a sibling and
had made Ray's move to the North bearable, and she had
also been Georgia's matron of honor and was Keefer's god-
mother. She was quite the Bible-thumping pill, if Gordon recalled correctly—everything that could go wrong with a
woman who was resolutely blond, resolutely Christian, and
from Tampa. He could recall only one thing Georgia had
ever said about Delia, "I like her. She really believes what
she says." In the photo, Delia was reverently holding up the
end of the languid net of lace, holy beatitude in her face, but
her teenage kid from her previous marriage—what was the
kid's name, Alyssa? Alexandra?—was peeking through the
huge fountain of bronze leaves and stands of creamy Japanese lilacs and bearded irises like some kind of wacky altar

ornament, her plush red hair wild and her face a map of pure hellion glee.

Gordon thought idly, nastily, all that holiness did not evidently preclude divorce . . . but that was lousy. He barely knew Delia. Maybe she was a widow.

One space over, a photo of Ray and Georgia in the pool at their first apartment, that place in Titusville. ("Titsville," Georgia had written, just after learning she was expecting a baby. "I'm the only woman in this whole complex under five feet ten and over a hundred and thirty pounds. You have to be an aerobics instructor or they won't let you sign a lease.") And the next shot, Ray holding newborn Keefer triumphantly overhead in one of his massive hands, as if she were the Stanley Cup.

Then, Georgia's framed collage: "Why You Are Keefer" (picture of the baby, in a felt bonnet sewn to look like a sunflower, with an arrow from that to a toddler picture of Gordon, grinning toothlessly, Georgia with one fat arm around him in a headlock. "Once There Was a Little Boy Who Could Not Say His Sister's First Name." How, Gordon now tried to remember, had he ever ended up calling Georgia "Keefie," and not just when he was a tot, but until . . . what, sixth grade or so, when she threatened to belt him if he didn't stop it? He still sometimes slipped up, especially after the baby was born, calling both of them "Keefie." Gordon put one of his hands over his eyes and jammed Ray's day calendar into his back pocket.

This place. You couldn't breathe. The air was greenhouse quality.

That morning, awakening fully dressed on top of his comforter, Gordon had written in his spiral notebook, "Party girl, rowdy girl, dutiful daughter, rebellious daughter, perfect sister, sister tormentor, best friend, generous, and idealistic," and "Georgia took no prisoners. It took the magic of Raymond Nye, Junior, to accomplish the transformation. But if

Ray was here, and I wish he were here, he'd tell you that he knew just who was boss." It sounded like some awful roast at the Elks Club.

He should be making Georgia sound like Albert Einstein and Mother Teresa, but how could he pretend his sister had meant very much to the world in general? She hadn't. She'd had no time to redeem her life. All she'd done was love Ray and reproduce and help her brother out and make their folks happy . . . the only loss Gordon could truly feel was his own.

They would never again stand behind Dad's back and mimic the way he stuck his knees up like a heron when he walked. Georgia would never again send Gordon his Christmas present two weeks early, because she just couldn't wait, and then call him and make him open it while she was still on the phone. They would never again get stoned and have to wait so long for a table at Fast Eddie's that they'd start eating from the bus trays. Georgia would never again hear her baby say "Keefer."

He could not say these things—people were already impossibly sad. This whole ceremonial attempt was a physical effort, like hauling up a lobster pot, hand over hand, and just as deceptive. Water was so much heavier than anything you could swallow and see through had a right to be. Carl Jurgen used to complain about it, the summer that he and Ray and Gordon spent living alone in the Evans Scholars house, running the pots for the tiny old man who owned Leo's Sea Subs.

The thought that came to him, as he stood poised between staying longer and getting the hell out of there, would have sounded overblown if not suspicious to anyone else, but Georgia would have understood it. And maybe Ray would have, too. Georgia had probably been the real reason that his bond with his two dozen dearly and temporarily beloved girlfriends had never deepened beyond the well-rehearsed routine of date at the symphony, Italian dinner, first sex, regular sex, camping trip, denouement. Georgia had taken up more room in his life than a sister should have taken. Even good old loyal Lindsay Snow had rounded on him once and said, angrily, "You dote on every word she says!"

He hadn't doted on every word Georgia had said. But her phone number in Florida was the only number besides his parents' he'd ever committed to memory. He and Georgia had, of course, gone through that teenage stage when the esteem of peers had been paramount; but she, and a few others, were most of what Gordon required in the way of intimacies. Tim Upchurch and Pat Chaptman were as close to him as cousins, closer than his own cousins were. Then there was Jurgen, and of course, Ray. But there had never seemed to be any good reason to try to explain himself to a woman, or to discuss intellectual puzzles with anyone but his father, or emotional puzzles with anyone but Georgia.

There had never been a need to discuss anything with his mother. She read his mind.

All his time had been consumed by taking care of Georgia or Keefer. Those nights he stole for Lindsay, he'd had to all but literally bite his tongue to keep from asking whether they could skip the preliminaries and go to bed. It was true that Gordon had begun investigating a tempting offer from Tortoise Tours, a new outfit that took families on tours to places like the Galapagos. He'd joined a ski and climbing club in Wausau and endured the chatter because the women were succulent to look at if not to listen to. And he'd been out, with Lindsay or Tim or one of the girls Tim called his aqua-bunnies, on most weekend nights. But stupid as it was, he always felt safer when he came home to a blinking answering machine light. He always called back. Georgia always talked to him, even if he woke her up. Half the time, he'd just drive over there. Sometimes, the birds were talking by the time they fell asleep.

Gordon had rationalized, when Georgia got really ill, that the time he spent sponging her and helping her make her tapes and reading *Wuthering Heights* to her would compensate for the scattered days they would have shared over the course of forty more years—a sprinkling of holidays, a family trip or two. Why had he not taken better care to think of what he'd say when this time came. Why had he not asked Georgia for help? Would she have delighted in the sly mischief of writing her own memorial? Part of him thought so. Would the effort, with its bald admission of defeat, have been so unbearably poignant the two of them could never have borne it?

And yet, Gordon's memories of his sister were all her version. Georgia was custodian of boxes of blackmail-quality photographs from childhood. Gordon had a single eighteen-by-twenty frame of family snaps, chosen (by Georgia) to represent their lives together, and a shoebox full of semi-seductive photos taken of or by girlfriends. It also contained a college graduation card that read, "Way to Go!! Who Says Hard Work Doesn't Pay Off?" with a laminated fourth-grade science test, grade D-plus. Any stories he couldn't tell to his mother, he'd taken to Georgia. About the ER intern in Colorado who treated his broken tailbone and ended up taking him home with her for a week, about the girl he taught who thought animals with split hooves had roots.

Gordon ventured into their bedroom. Georgia's wedding dress, in its heavy-duty plastic bag, took up the space of three men's parkas. On a shelf, under a couple of half-used rolls of Christmas wrapping paper, Gordon uncovered an oversized, full-color book of photos, "Compromise and Positions: A Hot Guide for Cool Couples." Absently, he opened and closed drawers. Georgia's nursing bras. The big old Knockouts promotional T-shirts she slept in. Ray's boxer shorts, the size of small backpacker tents . . . Christ, he'd been a big guy. For a crystalline instant, he could see Ray on the fourth tee at Pelican Point, waiting for him and Jurgen, hacky-sacking the ball with his driver, bouncing it around, never letting it drop, Ray's excruciatingly slow, metronomically precise swing—Tempo Ramundo, they called him, recalling Ray Floyd—the shot cleaving the exact middle of the sky. "That's no balota," Jurgen would say, clasping his hands as if in prayer, "thass a bullet."

The horrible pity of trespass swamped him—the dead had no privacy. When he was old, he would burn his every intimate scrap and document. Which would probably amount to that same shoebox full of photos. He pictured himself, a bent, silver-haired man in cargo shorts, poking a tiny bonfire.

Helplessly, he thought of Georgia and how she'd been unable to keep her hands out of the back of Ray's tuxedo pants even during the reception, of Ray shaking him awake the morning after his and Georgia's second date, "You and me got to have a word, Bo. Did she call you?"

"Ray, it's nine A.M."

"But did she call you yet? About me?"

"Didn't you just come from there?" And then the realization. Sleep parting for amusement. "Did you spend the night there?" Ray shaking his head, shaking Gordon's shoulder, shaking off his prying, a blush spreading up from his jaw, possessing his whole face.

"We sat up all night. On the beach. I never felt like this before. This is the real one, Bo," he said. "I want you to sit up here and tell me everything about her. All the TV shows she used to like. What she's scared of, like bugs or snakes. Like, what's her favorite color and was there, you know, was there a guy before me that she really, you know . . ." At their wedding, leaning over to whisper to him, as they waited for the opening notes, "I love her more than my own life, Bo." At the end of the reception, Georgia running back in blue jeans to kiss him good-bye, him standing there rumpled, resentful, drunk and blinking under the sudden lights that signaled the party was over, her cheerful *kiss me so you don't miss me* . . .

Just before Gordon took his month's family leave from school, he'd awakened one night at his parents' house. It had been a cold spring weekend when Ray was home, but scheduled to take off early the following morning for Atlanta, so Gordon had slept over in anticipation of watching the baby while his mother took Georgia to the doctor. In the middle of the night, alarmed by noises from the hall, Gordon stumbled out to find Ray, carrying a blanket-bundled Georgia in his arms, his foot wedging the front door open.

Gordon blurted, "Is she sick? Are you taking her to the hospital?"

"No, no," Ray smiled, genial and calm. "We're just taking a drive."

"A drive?"

"She can't sleep. And it's the anniversary of when we got engaged, Bo. Two years since the night she said yes. We're going to drive out to Hat Lake and look at the stars . . . maybe fool around. We're still newlyweds, after all . . ." Gordon took in Georgia's thin arm, bruised from her endless blood draws, dangling from a fold of the blanket, her dozy smile, and was struck speechless. There was so much he could respect, but not understand.

His last long conversation with Georgia had been a fight. It had been . . . Thursday. No, the previous weekend. Certainly since the little stroke that had put her in the hospital for a week, an ominous marker that the end was closing in. She'd been cranky, short tempered, who wouldn't have been? Coughing and puffing—it was in her lungs, now, the doctor said, in her bones, and Gordon had thought, only Georgia would consider telling him off as being a good use of her last breaths. She'd started in, did he realize what other people would give to be like him? She had said he was like a people savant, memorizing the human phone book at first glance. He got dates out of wrong numbers, from picking up packages people dropped in parking lots. A girl had written him thanking him for taking her virginity. People stuck to him the way Sargasso stuck to turtle grass at the beach. *Man, woman, and dog, they fall in love with you*, she'd said, *and*

*you take them for granted. You don't work for it. What you're
good at is being loved . . .*

"You have a thousand friends, Georgia," he'd said.

"But I had to work for them. I figure forty beers per one
friend. Twenty pounds per dozen."

"I work at it too. I'm nice to people."

"You let people be nice to you. You work out, so people
will have something nice to look at. You have experiences,
so you can tell people about them. That's your big gift to the
world, Gordie. You are your gift . . ." She'd paused, breathing so deeply and slowly Gordon thought she'd fallen
asleep. "You have to make Keefer be just like you."

He'd thought, I didn't hear that. He and Georgia were dog
and cat—he, active, agile, more competitive at everything
than skilled at anything, she the laziest nonmale he'd ever
known, who had never walked anywhere she could drive,
who called him Pectoralisaurus. Georgia hated pain so much
she wouldn't even get a back rub. For the past two hundred
days and loose change, the grit she had summoned in her
suffering had amazed him.

"You hope Keefer is like me?"

"I hope she's like you. It's all easy for you."

"This isn't easy for me."

"Easier for you than me," she'd said.

"No, not really."

She'd turned her wasted face against the pillow and
smiled at him. "I didn't mean that. I know it isn't."

"I think she'll be like Ray," Gordon had said.

"Well, she won't," his sister replied. "That's not my
wish." Georgia let her eyes drift to one of the prints Lorraine
had framed for her in childhood, an early O'Keeffe, a pansy
so luxuriant it seemed the very paper would be velvety to the
touch. "I don't want her to be the kind of person who cares
so much about love that she can't let go. It was her . . ."
Georgia sighed. Talking was a breathtaking task for her.

"Her?"

"Her, Georgia O'Keeffe her. She said, um, don't be the kind of person who loves, because it will . . . chew you up and swallow you whole. I wish for her to be good at being loved. Can you do that one thing? Can you make her like that?"

What had she meant?

Was there something wrong with him? Was he too into himself? He was a teacher, for Pete's sake. Teachers were altruistic. He contributed to every environmental cause on the globe. He was not selfish. Or was he? Why did he prefer to let all his interactions skim instead of sink in? That wasn't true. He and Tim had been friends for fifteen years. He and Lindsay . . . well. Would he want to infect Keefer with a vaccine against caring too much? But otherwise, he'd have been engaged ten times already.

Okay . . . some of it was bullshit. He'd cultivated a shy, wistful demeanor for the purpose of breaking up with girls. Tim called it the Velvet Cad. He'd make dreamy open-ended remarks about his basic immaturity, about the real possibility of his moving to Australia. He'd mastered a shrug . . . slow, expressive, as if redolent of regret over his own inability to commit. He left a door slightly open. He might become more seasoned with time. . . . It worked like hypnosis. Women who should have wanted to burn him in effigy were magically content to remain his friends. That was a great relief. Why shouldn't it be? He valued those women, even more so after they'd let him go, when his memories of them were rinsed of the jittery tedium of long dinners, TV shows endured entwined on a series of couches, hair spray against his cheek. What he loved to remember were their bodies all so different, soft or taut, mounded or convex, rolling and bobbing, rising and falling, nipples spreading like the secret stained hearts of flowers, so many varieties of poppies and lilies. He loved them all, still, in retrospect. How could he fail to be genuinely happy when he saw them again? Why would they ever think that his smile, his welcome, even his physical affection, in the moment, meant he wanted them to share, again, more than memories? But they always thought that. And he always had to be a thug again, a person who carefully returned only the third phone call, and then breezily.

He wasn't a thug.

He was a thug.

For Christ's sake, he was young!

He should never have moved back here. Why had he moved back here? EnviroTreks had been like a floating Shangri-la of nonchalant sex, easy fitness, learning, and teaching . . . why had he come home? His mother had written him about the job opening at the high school. Why? He had wanted to come home for the baby's birth; why hadn't he just sent a fruit basket?

There was nothing wrong with him. He had his friends, his beautiful old 1972 Fender that he was finally learning to play, his students, the occasional bright bulb among the mumbling throng of turnips. He was not lonely.

That was what was wrong with him.

He would be lonely . . . now.

Eager to close up this place, to run, Gordon riffled through her desk, her bookshelf, and her jewelry armoire, finding another copy of her will stuck in a folder of scrawled notes, notes that, so far as he could tell, dealt with Georgia's suspicion that Keefer had allergies. A pamphlet from an agency in Boston called Families United. He had never heard of it. He snatched these up. This place. You couldn't breathe. The air was greenhouse quality.

Why did he care so much, in point of fact, what he said at the funeral? Who'd be taking notes? The only things he was now able to think of were so poignant he would not be able to make his mouth say them without crying. ("She said yes, Bo! Can you believe that? You got to be my best man. I'm so happy I could shit.") They would be vulgar or meaningless.

Except to the two people who would never hear Gordon say them.

Damn Georgia.

She and Ray had an entire life that had nothing to do with him, but she had also not wanted to surrender her eminence in her brother's landscape. She had been as selfish as he.

She had been.

She'd wanted the gratitude. Honor thy sister, who rescues you on a regular basis from the otherwise swift and direct results of your own slack-witted tendencies. Remember the First Date Recipe, for angel hair and broccoli, she'd be saying.

She hadn't done it all for gratitude.

She had loved him and tried to color in his blank spots, out of love.

He was thankful she'd come home. He was thankful he'd come home. What if she'd died in Florida? She'd grown to hate the South as much as Ray loved it. ("Sex on the Beach," she wrote to her brother once, referring to a cocktail popular at the time in local bars, "is a real oxymoron. When I watch *Here to Eternity,* all I can think about is the sand in her crotch.") Even Ray could not have convinced Georgia to raise her baby there. Gordon imagined how it would be now, if all of them had had to troop down there to bring Keefer and all of her paraphernalia home.

He locked the door behind him and drove the few blocks to his own apartment. His lair. His slum. Opening the door, throwing himself down on his couch, he imagined Georgia saying, *remember the time you wanted to impress somebody but you couldn't get home and I cleaned the whole place and even put my CDs in the player, even though I was eight months pregnant?*

That was one thing he could say. Marriage had remade her. Domesticated the girl who often purchased her outfit on the way to a party and dressed in the car. She became this sweetheart who not only cooked, but baked sourdough from a

Nye family starter, who not only cleaned, but hand-covered a whole wall with quilted textile. She'd taken an interest in remodeling, her brother as well as her condo. Gordon, who'd never in his life owned more than two pairs of shoes, and one of those for running, who bought and wore out the identical four pairs of Lands' End corduroys each year, was taken shopping for real slacks, Italian loafers, and a pillow-top mattress that sat on an actual frame, instead of on the floor. She'd made him feel like a hobo, a parody bachelor with his single set of silverware, his guitar, his bike propped against his scuba tank in his living room, and his unframed blowups of his underwater photos of Cod Hole at the Great Barrier Reef thumbtacked to the wall.

He had never really thanked her. In fact, he'd pretended he was the one doing her a favor, letting her work out her hormonal excesses, in Ray's absences, on her poor single-guy brother.

But, he now realized, those few months after both of them had moved back to Tall Trees, before Keefer was born and new life collided with new peril, that had been the time when they had finally come parallel, after a lifetime in which one had pulled ahead and glanced back, and then the other overtook and surged ahead. They had been eye to eye, and so close.

It had almost made him forgive her growing up, so all at once, so without him.

And now she had gone on ahead, without him, again.

His phone rang. Gordon realized he had nearly fallen asleep.

He let it ring through to the machine. There were twenty-three unplayed messages on the tape, a few that he'd heard come in. Women. His cousin Dan. A couple from students, which touched him deeply, and three from Tim, who seemed to think he should come over or Gordon would kill himself. "Hey," said his own slow voice, picking up, his before voice, ready for anything. "Depending on who you are, leave a message for either Gordon or Mr. McKenna, and don't make it your life story." Lindsay's voice filled the room with its urgency.

"Gordon? Gordo? It's me. I guess you're not there, but if you need me . . ."

Lindsay could help me write this, he thought. Lindsay and Georgia had been friends since they were children. He picked up the phone, and said nothing. "Gordo? Is that you?"

There was no one who could help him. He put the receiver back in its cradle and let himself drift again.

His father had slept twelve hours straight after identifying Ray and Georgia.

Gordon had offered to do it in his stead, but after an hour of thinking it over, Mark had gone alone to the morgue.

All he had seen, he told Gordon, and told him reluctantly, was a close-up color photo of Georgia's left hand, with its green diamond engagement ring, pale and unmarked except by the big sickle-shaped scar she'd gotten when they were little, fighting over a croquet mallet, breaking it in half. Then, softly lit behind a plateglass window, they'd shown him the side of Ray's face that was most intact. The rest of Ray's head and body had been layered in clean sheets. "But you could see that it wasn't shaped properly," Mark admitted. "I really tried not to look very much, because I didn't want to remember it. I don't think we should ever tell Keefer this."

He dreamed of Lindsay kneeling next to the bed, her long red hair down, tickling his cheek.

It was Lindsay. She was there. Where was he? Gordon realized he had, finally, desperately, fallen asleep, and that outside, the sun was low. He sat up, streaming sweat, chilled.

"Did I miss it?" he asked. "How did you get in here?"

Lindsay sat back on her heels, her sleeveless peach-colored summer dress settling like a parachute over her knees. "I got the key from your mom," she said. "You didn't answer the phone. It scared the hell out of her, Gordon, if you must know. And me, too."

She'd brought him food. Ham and Swiss, macaroni salad, a smoothie. He ate thankfully, voraciously, and for once, her solicitude made him feel only grateful, not leashed. He showered while she sat on the closed toilet seat and read the obituary aloud to him; she told him it would be okay to wear a T-shirt and a linen jacket for the viewing, that his father would not have the presence of mind to notice Gordon was not wearing a tie. After all, she told him, everyone knew he had only one suit, and that was for the funeral. And when he was dressed, Lindsay drove, though it crossed his mind that her driving would put them back here, alone together, sometime later that night, unless he fotched an excuse about having to ride home with his parents, which would keep him out of bed with Lindsay, which was where he should stay, and he was graceless to even think about that, but she looked wonderful, familiarly wonderful, and he could not help but notice the pure white strip of her bra through the open sleeve of her dress. He wondered how much of what he felt for Lindsay was born of her constancy, the reflection of her devotion to him. He would figure that out, once and for all. He would put it on his mental to-do list, at the top.

When they crested the hill outside of town where Chaptmans was set up on a small parklike verge near where the woods thickened toward Tomahawk, he was astounded: Cars were lined up for half a mile on both sides of the highway. There were two news trucks with their portable satellite dishes like upturned hockey masks. Lindsay had to brake for people crossing the road purposefully, hurriedly, as if to an auction or a concert, an event where being first in was of the essence.

Gordon made a pillow of his folded arms against the dash and hid his face.

"What?" Lindsay cried, reaching for his hand. "Are you

feeling sick?" He shook his head, not trusting his voice. "Are you surprised . . . didn't you think so many people loved her?"

No, he thought, squeezing her hand, her good reliable hand, as he would later that night hold her cool naked waist in his two hands, feel her tiny breasts with their startling large nipples like echinacea flowers crushed against his chest, unable in his grief and gratitude to even regret starting up again what he knew he should not start up again . . . no, he thought. I just didn't think it would ever get this far.

That it would get this far so fast, so fast that he could not stop tumbling long enough to find a place to stand and make an analysis, dreads and doubts breaking free like pebbles from a fragile rock face.

After this night, he wouldn't be able to rely on his sister to fill in his gaps. He'd have to return all his life's ignored phone calls, or he would be alone. Alone with his parents and Keefer, in a life he had never planned.

He would grow up perforce. He would never be able to entertain an offer from Tortoise Tours for a sabbatical year, or even a summer. Not until he was old. He would never hang out with his students, still able to whip the Frisbee farther, still able to do more pull-ups on the door frame. He'd have things to do, even more and more urgent things than he'd had before. He'd have to rush home from school, the way Chris Ebbets and Mary Hermanson and every other . . . parent he knew did.

He would never be free again. It was monstrously selfish, but he had imagined that he would get back to his old ways after Georgia's death. He had longed for those ways.

But he would not get his life back. It had not been on suspension. It had been over the day his sister became ill.

Worse, more wrenching, he would not have wanted it back if he could have claimed it.

It had been a stupid life. A life he'd treasured mostly in

the retelling. His audience was gone. His audience was mortally distracted.

He might be happy again; he might feel joy when Keefer learned to walk. He might fall in love. He would certainly fall in love. But his would never, never again be an unadulterated happiness, a boy's happiness. It would always be crossed with this.

Gordon had not realized how much he had cherished himself as a person who could sometimes feel truly carefree.

Georgia would have understood this, because though she had never been truly carefree, she had cherished it in him. She had never actually said those words, so with his mind, he made her say them, in her own voice. He could still remember her voice. He could.

I cherished it, she said, *in you.*

She added, because Georgia would not have left on a sappy note, *otherwise I would never have put up with you.*

As he and Lindsay got out of the car, a woman swamped him in the vigor of her bruin hug. Delia. He had not recognized her. And her kid, now almost old enough to be one of his students. He was all but overwhelmed by Delia's hug, the damp mug of her heavy perfume. When Delia released him, the kid put out her hand in a dignified way, "I'm Alex," she said. "I was in the wedding? I'm sorry about your sister. Georgia was a cool person." Gordon felt moved to pat her head, but she was too old for that. He squeezed her hand instead.

As they turned into the hedges that bordered the door, a man motioned to Gordon, shamefaced. There was something about the man he recognized. A friend of his dad's? No, a student's dad. Was the kid's name . . . Jules? But the man was apologizing, already, "I know I shouldn't even talk to you at a time like this, and I shouldn't even talk to you about this anyhow, it is probably inappropriate. I . . . it's that I met with your sister and her husband . . ."

"I have to go inside right now," Gordon said tenderly, aware of Lindsay gently tugging his arm. He could see his mother, just inside the foyer, her arms around his aunt Daphne.

"I'm a lawyer," the man told him, "and this is my card. And I need to talk with Mr. Nye's parents, about the will. The notes I have made. Nothing was finalized. We were going to have an appointment to do that on Friday. With the parents. I was helping Ray prepare . . . his . . . their . . . and I have no idea how this is all going to turn out, but I'm assuming your family will be able to reach some kind of concordance . . . but I wanted to talk with you, too, just as a . . . courtesy, a private courtesy, because you were a good teacher to my son . . ."

"Jules," said Gordon.

"Julius," the man repeated, "my son. He goes to Platteville now. He plays basketball. He's never going to be a Rhodes scholar, you know? But he's going to major in science. Maybe teach, coach?"

"I have my sister's will," Gordon explained. "Ray and Georgia went over all of it with me."

"They revoked that will," said the man, "weeks ago."

Gordon turned to Lindsay. He said, "Don't tell my mom."

CHAPTER *five*

$\mathcal{D}$ale Larsen leaned against the back wall of the church, a position in which he could watch without feeling that his uniform would seem an intrusion. It was a duty he normally liked, the funerals. Heading up the line of mourners' cars, the silver cruiser freshly polished, its blue light silently and authoritatively rotating on slow beam, on what amounted to a last journey, past the hospital and the school, past the park, the pool, the creek, the Wild Rose and Soderberg's Electronics Repair and Noon Buffet, past places that had contained the impressions of a life; it was a way of showing respect.

It was not an easy duty, not a day off by any means. Dale held grief in high esteem.

Even at his age, he had less real fear of wrassling a drunk to the pavement than of encountering grief, grief so wild it seemed even the longest string of seasons would never ease it. There was the time when the Redmonds' toddlers were killed by that pitiable drunk Collins. The Redmonds had been on their way to the Smart Mart to buy microwave popcorn, and Collins—woozling from two beds and three bars—had been on his way from bad to worse. Or the awful funeral of David Abel, who'd just gotten a full-ride scholarship to Madison when he'd rolled his Jeep five times on the way home from a beer bash at Two Chimneys. Debbie Abel's only child. And three other boys, all good boys.

His daughter, Stephanie, had been at that party. She could easily have been in the car. Stephanie, during the time in her life when she wouldn't have recognized a set of car keys sober. Stephanie, or Georgia, though Georgia never took the most dangerous chances.

Larsen let his eyes rest briefly on the pallbearers, Kip Sweeney and Pat Chaptman and the youngest of all those Upchurch sons, a rascal, Tim or Tom. The tall boy with the mane of white-blond hair, who had a Southern accent, was Ray's pal, from Florida. And there was a cousin, Craig. . . . the sheriff remembered him vaguely as the godfather of Keefer. And Gordie. Gordie had helped carry his sister's and his brother-in-law's domed coffins. He looked like a kid dressed for graduation in his sober gray suit.

How could a family absorb so many blows?

Father Victor Barry was normally so spry, Larsen used to tell his wife the priest was like an advertisement for good health through celibacy. But today his ritual movements were abstracted and slow; he looked his eighty years. Father was talking about the procession of ironies. "We expected loss," he said, referring to Georgia's illness. "But what we face here today is unexpected, and so devastating. A child has lost both her parents. Two families have lost their children. This is a magnitude we had not imagined. 'Lord, my grief is so great I cannot stand.' How can we see such a terrible event as proceeding from a merciful God? The truth is, we cannot and we must not. If the Lord is here, and I believe the Lord is here, he is here to console all of us, as a loving parent consoles a child when that child is hurt, despite all the parents' best intentions to protect . . ."

Father Barry glanced down at Lorraine, who had averted her face. The baby had climbed into her lap and fallen asleep with her thumb upside down in her mouth. "Blessed are the sorrowful, for they shall be comforted . . . Let us offer our silent prayers, first, for the comfort we seek."

Stephanie was there, with Sheila and their youngest daughter, Trina. She was whispering to that sweet kid who tended bar at the Wild Rose, Katie Savage, the tiniest and most effective bouncer in America. He could guess the text of her whispering. Stephanie was pregnant, but so newly nothing showed; and she had last night assured her father this did indeed mean she and Devon, the boy she lived with, were getting married. Devon's family *would* have to be one of two Puerto Rican families in all of northwest Wisconsin—Stephanie would always be different, no matter how hard she had to look for a lever to move the world. But he was a good boy. Everyone loved him.

His grandchild would be a Salazar.

Stephanie.

When she finally got her degree, she'd do art therapy, she'd said. Stephanie had been through so much counseling she probably didn't feel comfortable outside one of those gray-and-rose offices with all the latest magazines.

Stephanie as a senior had more pierces in her ears than hairs on her gracefully paisley-dyed head. Georgia had quieted down after the Abel tragedy, but Stephanie was still going strong, finding strawberry pickers and rodeo cowboys to bring home. In her combat boots and the secondhand waitress uniforms left open to reveal lacy, black, industrial-strength bras, Stephanie had looked like a venereal disease waiting to happen. Dale could read the looks on the faces of the other Rotary guys when they passed him on the street. And the boys from the Booster Club, who were the ones who voted to elect a Homecoming Queen, had banded together for a spiteful spoof and elected Stephanie, even though Georgia—pep squad captain, student council secretary four years running, hospital volunteer, B-plus student, and hot party girl besides—was the logical choice. Stephanie, baffled, resentful, had vowed to wreak revenge by wearing a black sheer negligee with nothing underneath. And then, Georgia breezed in on Saturday and announced they were going shopping. There had been days of many phone calls, many bags rustling in and out of the Larsen house on Merrill Street, trips out to Nora Nordstrom's farm for sewing assistance.

On the evening of the dance, no one, not even Dale's wife, had been allowed into Stephanie's room. And then, the two of them had emerged, Georgia disheveled and rosy, in cutoffs and a T-shirt. ("I'll change later," she'd told Sheila, "I'm not the queen.")

Stephanie had looked like the young Audrey Hepburn. She wore not one bauble save a dot pearl in each ear, and the midnight-blue, ankle-length strapless dress was wound around her stick slenderness like a sugar cone around pink sherbet.

"We got it in a secondhand store!" Georgia had exulted, "Isn't it wonderful? Isn't it perfect? It cost . . . like thirty bucks! And look at this! Look!" The tiara was slipped down over Stephanie's scant, sleek cap of hair, colored back to its own sweet otter brown. "We made it! We got this bridal thing and pulled all the fake flowers off, so Steph won't have to wear that tacky rhinestone thing the school sticks on people's heads! She could be a French girl! Isn't she gorgeous?"

"She's . . . she's perfect," Dale had breathed, and Sheila had not been able to say a thing through her tears.

Things had been better after that. People had stood back in awe of the new Stephanie, and she had responded. She'd begun affecting big sunglasses and Dale's white shirts over thrift-store pedal pushers, a decade before those pants came back into fashion. She'd taken honors in art.

Dale Larsen knew for a fact that a reporter from the *Messenger* had found out all about the fantastic circumstances of the Homecoming Queen vote and tried to get Georgia and Stephanie to talk about it.

He knew also that Georgia had refused. In a way he would not ever want to have to explain, Dale felt he owed Georgia his daughter's life.

Father Barry's eyes were reddening. He spoke of Georgia's own baptism, the wedding, Keefer's christening, all solemnized at this very altar where two coffins now lay, head to head. "I will not be able to give you the answers that will satisfy your hungry hearts. Indeed, my possible answers do not satisfy me. I remember Georgia telling me before the baptism that though her own middle name was spelled with two *f*s, like the name of the great prairie artist, her baby's was not. 'Father,' she told me, 'the second *f* was silent.' Ill as she was, even then, she had a glad heart to share with me."

Just after the baptism, Dale Larsen remembered, had come that big charity golf event, for cancer research, the one Andy North came all the way up here to Lake in the Woods to attend. The human-interest stories in the *Messenger*, about hereditary risk, about breast self-exams. By then the Larsens and McKennas had drifted apart, what with Georgia and Stephanie already grown. They'd drifted from a connection that for a short time felt like a lifeline in dark water, but was later almost shameful, something to be forgotten. Dale still asked Mark to sit in on his poker circle once in a while, though Mark was possibly the most daft cardplayer Dale had ever encountered. But that was all.

Since that day at the bridge, Dale had not slept well. He'd even thought that it was time to take his twenty and open a bait shop. His wife told him he'd been crying in his sleep, talking aloud, telling Georgia and Stephanie to get their butts home. For two nights running, he'd gone back out, after his customary rounds in the squad, to look in on Trina, their youngest, who was nineteen, and had just gotten one of those tiny little efficiencies in the hundred-year-old building that housed Wilton's and Gloria's Finer Designs. After a dozen years, few walls in Tall Trees were opaque to him. He knew which doors were opened each Monday by dapper managers and closed on wives with split lips and amethyst cheekbones. He knew which young father would be in jail but for the shame of the fifteen-year-old running back on the Wildwood team whose mother found the two of them in a sleeping bag out at Two Chimneys. He knew that the old bachelor, Hal Fry, had poisoned the Leahys' collie, that the Weldons' girl had given birth to a baby one night in the family bathroom, a baby he and his deputy had whisked to a Wausau hospital. The town was a body to him, and he its monitor. There was a knowing, a sense as sure as the vision in a doctor's fingers, about which domestic strife should be brought to law and which left alone.

Dozens of times, he'd popped his lights off to slide past the house on Cleveland Avenue. He had been able to tell how everyone was doing inside, during the months of Georgia's illness, from the patterns of the lights. A light burning in Georgia's room was ordinary. If there were lights on in the kitchen, Lorraine was sitting up. If Mark's reading lamp was on, it was a bad night all around. He counted the ambulance calls, the family cars parked overnight in numb defiance of even-odd regulation. He had not known what he could do, except watch.

"I once knew this little girl," Father Barry was saying, "who had to do a reading in church. She'd memorized the Twenty-third Psalm. And she got up, all confidence, and she began, 'The Lord is my shepherd . . .' And she was stuck. She tried again. 'The Lord is my shepherd . . .' And she couldn't remember another thing. And so she just looked out at the congregation and said, 'Well, that's enough for now.'

"And that, I think, is going to have to be the way we all approach this . . ."

Gordon had taken Father Barry's place at the altar and was adjusting the microphone.

Lorraine was alarmed at the sight of her son. Gordon looked ghastly, the skin rubbed red under his eyes the only color in his face, his blond hair childlike with the wet tooth marks of the comb. She was reminded of him as an eight-year-old, after a fall from that tree fort, the snapped raw bone of one forearm shining in the sinister light of the emergency room. ("Aren't you the little heartbreaker?" the nurse cooed, and Georgia, bored by all the flustered attention her brother was receiving, snapped, "No, he's a little arm breaker.")

Gordon began steadily, "I'm here to talk about Georgia O'Keeffe McKenna Nye, my . . . my sister . . . who was a good person. And I'm going to start by reading from the journal I kept during her sickness, just one part. It won't take too long." He opened a green spiral notebook. "It says, 'I am beginning this journal, diary or document or whatever it may be while sitting at Georgia's bedside at the University of Minnesota Clark Medical Center on the morning of April 3. Ray is on the other side. He is on this tiny little cot, and his big feet are hanging over the end, and he is trying to gather a few minutes of sleep in the respite that has been provided by Georgia's last injection of morphine. Timmy Upchurch is out in the visitors lounge on a couch.' Tim"—Gordon looked up, and searched the pews—"Tim was there all the time for us. Anyway. It goes on, 'I can hear Georgia's labored lungs, attempting to draw in breath around the irresistible impulse to cough. She coughs approximately every ten to fifteen minutes. I have had to watch in pseudosecrecy and pretend to agree with her when she says, "I feel better today" partly because of our parents. She is not a naive person, but this bitch of a disease has overcome all her cynical wit. I see her sneak a whimper. But the patented Georgia smile stays in place. All she wants is to get home and get Keefer back in her arms. She does not want Keefer to see her here. She thinks it would scare her baby. I do not think anything about Georgia scares Keefer. I do not think Keefer can see anything but Georgia's smile. When we came in here, before Ray came home, the nurse in the ER asked me if Georgia's teeth were caps, because they are so perfect. Georgia is the bravest woman I have ever met. I think she must be one of the bravest women in the world.'"

Gordon laid the notebook down.

"I don't think my sister was a remarkable person to the whole world. She didn't have time for that. But she was a remarkable person to me. She was a remarkable wife to Ray, putting up with him being on the road all the time when other wives might have complained about that. She was very proud of him. We were very proud of her."

Diane Nye sneaked one eyeful of Lorraine. She had to look at something, or she would scream.

Nothing about Lorraine except the gray-striped suit that wasn't quite a suit and her gray kid gloves—gloves! in June!—looked any different from the other day. Lorraine was wearing not one speck of makeup, and she had done her hair in the dark. It was so disrespectful, Diane thought, staring hard at the open hymnal in her lap.

And it was awful of her to notice. Ungracious, unkind. Georgia was their child. They must feel everything she felt, everything they were able to feel. But they could not feel the ineluctable coring out of self that howled inside Diane. Even Big Ray could not fully enter the loss of a mother who had built the flesh of her child, carried a baby in her body, next to her heart, felt him flicker, move and then grow . . . there was no genius that exceeded the capacity to make a person. This death was a crime against creation. But Keefer Kathryn, their consolation, looked so sweet in the white dress embroidered with daisies she and Ray had bought for her, and the little white patent shoes. Baby had refused to wear the matching headband; four times Diane had slipped it on her head, and four times Keefer had pulled it roughly off and told Diane, "No no!" She was finally so exasperated that Diane started to tell Baby to wear the pretty hat for Mommy, but Big Ray interrupted her. He was right. He was wise sometimes. She could, Diane knew, get all caught up in appearances sometimes. Shelby said it was a way of keeping things tidy on the outside so she didn't have to mess with the inside. And Shelby was probably right.

"They just don't dress her up, Mother," Ray had said. Well, Diane thought, oh well. Big deal. These poor people had other things on their mind than fussing over Baby's wardrobe. Diane should have come up here when Georgia got sick. She should have, but Lorraine had been so rigid, so defensive; the McKennas had roped Georgia off to such a degree even Raymond felt excluded. Still, they had done . . . the impossible. She had to give them that. Diane could not conceive it; imagine her lithe, clean Alison corroding, drooping.

Keefer *was*, however, wild as a jackrabbit. Big Ray had carried Keefer into the church, and they all sat down in the first row, but as soon as Keefer saw Lorraine, she had gone scooting across the aisle and into Lorraine's lap. She'd run right in front of the pallbearers bringing in the coffin. Look at Keefer Kathryn, Diane thought. She was the picture of Raymond as a baby, big and rosy and strong. Georgia might not even have been part of the mix. Raymond could have had his pick; the phone rang off the hook, girls who'd been pageant queens, journalists, Rainy Kittredge was a model . . . and Diane had even thought, God forgive her for it, at least he would have the chance to start a new life after . . . it was over.

Georgia had not wanted to mix with the other players' wives, and she expected Raymond to stay home and play Scrabble with her when his parents knew that there were places he ought to be seen for the good of his career. He had, after all, chosen to delay his career, to finish college, to stay with Georgia, though he could have left and turned pro, and it simply meant that he had more to prove. It was as if Georgia thought of Raymond's gift as a job you could leave at the end of the day. And moving up here, that had been the last straw. It had thrown Raymond off, just entirely thrown him.

She and Ray personally believed that Raymond would have placed in the top three, for sure the top ten on the Knockout two years or more earlier if Georgia had not been so hot to have a baby right off the bat. When he told them, Raymond had just given them that moony smile and said, just happened, Mama, meant to be. And then Georgia wore Raymond out telling him she had to be with her mother after the baby came.

Tour players did not live in Wisconsin. They did not live in three-tavern burgs with the only course run by some Catholic cult or other, the fairways hard and bald as an alligator park.

Now, her son would lie in this cold ground.

Diane could not protect him any longer. She wanted to beat her fists against these ugly walls, this church that looked like a hunting lodge only missing a moose head, beat her fists against these square, fat people with their flat, backward voices and their dark, ugly clothes. He'd been so alone here. She'd heard it in his voice.

Since they had first seen the miracle in Raymond, when he was six or seven, they had protected him, the way you protect a rare orchid cutting. The neurological illness that had first sent Diane to Shelby, the migraines and the shooting pains in her hips and legs that meant Big Ray had to lift her into the bath some mornings, Raymond knew nothing of this. He had known nothing of Big Ray's midlife crazies, his "executive assistant," that battleship butt from Apalachicola, the nights she and Shelby spent driving down on South Street, watching from the playground shelter until Big Ray's Lincoln came nosing into that woman's apartment parking lot, jumping out, snapping pictures with that little disposable camera, her running off to Caroline's house and drinking a whole bottle of Nyquil, Raymond Jr. knew none of that. And he shouldn't have known. He'd had a gift and a gift meant the responsibility to put that gift first.

Gordon was holding his hand up as if to ask for the patience of the crowd. Diane could see the tears.

He was only a boy.

This was not Gordon's fault. Gordon had loved the game of golf. He had loved Ray. And it had not been Georgia's fault, either. There was good in Georgia. Delia and Georgia had grown so close. Delia had purchased the herbs Shelby couldn't send, the hexaphosphate and Inositol. Delia and Craig had come visiting, trying to re-create those beach picnics they all used to have back in Florida, trying to raise Georgia's spirits.

There was Lorraine standing now, jouncing the baby, nodding to Gordon. This church was so hot and stinking with incense Diane felt as though she had a dirty sponge pressed against her face. If Raymond hadn't called them, heartsick, just last month, confessed it all to them, they'd never have known how pressured he'd felt by Georgia and Lorraine and Mark to name a guardian for Keefer, to name the McKennas as guardians for Keefer. It was as if Keefer were not a Nye, as if none of them even existed in her life. If Big Ray hadn't helped Raymond find his own lawyer, they actually might have lost Keefer, too. It was the only thing that kept Diane going. Baby was their little sunshine. She had brightened right up once they'd got back to the hotel, after that terrible mess at the McKennas. She looked exactly like Brent and Brooks.

"The last thing my sister said to me might sound dumb," Gordon finally continued, "but it was something our mother always said, like, give me a kiss . . . that doesn't matter. Basically, she was saying if you take the time to love someone when you should, you won't miss that person so much. I think we will miss Georgia all our lives, though, because she was one of the mainstays of our lives, as was Ray. And what I want to ask from all of you is for you to help all of us raise Keefer Kathryn Nye to remember her mother and her father, too."

* * *

Tim hated himself for thinking something like this in the middle of his best friend's total breakdown, but he could not stop looking at Lindsay.

Lindsay Snow was so fucking hot, Tim Upchurch would have tiptoed over new tar on the Fourth of July to put his hand on the small of her back and walk out onto a dance floor with her. He would have been willing to be fired from his job, just to touch his lips to the palm of her hand, would gratefully have dislocated a knee to unsnap her bra and release the smell of her contained breasts. He spent whole hours at his desk imagining leaning over a tub, rinsing Lindsay's long red hair with lavender water spilled from a pitcher. He would bring her herbal tea when she had her period. He would cue up the CD in his car to her favorite Abba song—he knew what it was, too—every time she slid in next to him. He would worship her. He would never make her get up and get him a beer.

And there she was staring up at Gordon like Gordon was Tom Cruise crossed with Jesus Christ. Even crying made her look fucking beautiful. She was just this red-haired goddess, was all, and he had to act like a brother to her because she was his best friend's girl, *although* she was only his best friend's girl when his best friend wasn't on the tail trail of some gymnastics instructor or rocket scientist or folk-dancing kindergarten teacher or flagger on the highway who would be looking at him in exactly the same way within twelve hours.

Being Gordon McKenna's best friend was an exercise in masochism. In any normal situation, Tim was no slouch. He'd had his share, from blasted gropes and insti-fucks in senior year to the long, symphonic tango with Cara, that exchange student from Italy, with whom he'd done stuff he thought people ended up in jail for; but walking into the Wild Rose with Gordon was like being the invisible man. Have you met my friend, he wanted to ask women between sixteen and forty, and then try to talk to the ones who were left over. They went to a strip joint in Madison—were they even eighteen? And the cutest girl of all leaned over, stark naked except for an American flag vest, and dropped a note in Gordo's lap; she got off work at ten. What was it about Gordo? It wasn't just looks, though Gordon's looks were gleaming. Gordo could get the same effect from sticking his head out the window when he drove that took Tim twenty minutes in front of the mirror. Gordo could only bench one-eighty, and Tim could bench two-twenty, but Gordo was built like an equilateral triangle and Tim like a life preserver. Gordo, blond as a Viking, tanned; Tim got freckles bigger than chicken pox. When Gordon danced, he went into a trance like the beat was being poured into his head; he danced away from the women he was with, and they followed him.

Was that it? The general what-the-fuckness of Gordon, the aphrodisiac quality that he would be totally happy whether anyone else was there or not? The offhand way Gordo stayed right in the moment, while Tim was already worrying, as he got dressed for the first date, how it was going to affect his job next week or next month when he realized that the woman didn't like him as much as he liked her? Tim didn't ordinarily mind. Gordon was the readiest friend he ever had. He had the best ideas. Gordo figured out how to mount a camcorder in the vent above the girls' shower and record a solid four hours of great nudity, and when Tim suggested maybe they were perverts, Gordo told him, "Church, this isn't voyeurism, it's pornography. Voyeurism is a mental illness, but pornography is protected by the First Amendment to the Constitution."

Calling Gordo was like checking in with some force of nature. There was always something absurd to do, like the six weeks shearing Christmas trees down in Wautoma, hot as hell and caked with sticky sap, playing softball with the migrant kids who worked on the potato farms and all the other kids who came by bus from miles around to shear trees—a keg at second, which meant you had to chug whenever you rounded the bases, and after that they'd go back to work, with goddamn machetes no less! Streaking with Jessica and Libby Dickensen in the woods behind Fidelis Hill—Gordon had the gift for clothing removal with women—and the Colorado camping trip when they'd jumped eighty feet into the river like Sundance and the Kid, the spring-break nights in Florida, blasted on ganj like no other dope he'd ever had, bumping down the beach in Jurgen's umpty-million-dollar convertible, he wouldn't have traded his adventures with Gordo. He loved the McKennas. It was a goddamned wickedness, what had happened to Georgia, the sister that Tim, afflicted with four brothers, had never had. She was as good as any guy to talk to.

If only he didn't have it so bad for Lindsay. Worse since Gordo had come home and gotten back together with her and Tim had to spend time with the new Lin, this sharp-dressed, peaceful, curvy woman that Tim could no longer even pretend was the skinny-legged girl who'd grown up practically in his backyard, so shy she'd always worn a big T-shirt over her bathing suit.

Sweet Christ, Tim prayed, let me stop feeling like I want to burst my pants around Lindsay Snow. Let me be a good friend to my buddy when he needs me.

In the few moments that remained before he would need to raise himself from this pew and speak, Ray Nye, Sr., was attempting to compose himself. A pulse in his neck was pounding as if it would tear through the cloth of his shirt. He was thinking of his child's hands, those magnificent hands, he now imagined, closed softly over Raymond, Jr., huge chest beneath that shiny lid. He was thinking of Raymond at seven, so brawny he'd outgrown the cut-down set of clubs his father had given him at kindergarten graduation. Even at seven, the Vaden grip, which took most youngsters years to master, was as natural to him as breathing.

He had not been in favor of the marriage. He would admit it. They were too young, and Raymond's game too fragile. When they had come to him, he'd tried to suggest they get established first, even offered to stake Georgia in that business idea she'd had, a service that would redecorate people's houses with the furnishings they already had. He'd reminded them that life wasn't a big race. But he remembered also that he and Diane, the two of them all of nineteen years old, wouldn't be talked out of it either. And though there had been a moment, long ago, when that had seemed a mistake, he could not imagine life without his Diane sparkling at his side.

Just before the two of them moved, Big Ray had come upon Georgia sitting on a hill behind the house at Sandpiper, watching Raymond hit two-irons, then five-irons. He hadn't been surprised five hours later, coming home from the office to grab a bite, to see Raymond still at it: His son's zone had been astonishing. Even as a baby, when they'd laid him down to sleep, he'd fallen asleep in less than a minute, and slept twelve hours. He'd come down late to the Christmas tree once, because he'd wanted to finish his Hardy Boys book.

What was astonishing, that day at Sandpiper, was that Georgia was still there, too, and when Big Ray had come closer, he'd seen she was crying. It was on his lips to ask, What's wrong, honey? Is the baby all right? But then Georgia had whispered to him, she was not sad, she was just moved. By Raymond's hands. That he had the hands of a Michelangelo.

And Big Ray had known then that the girl understood. That she was the best wife his son could have found, and that he was a fool to doubt his son's judgment, which had never been anything but on the nose.

Stiffly, the blood roaring in his ears, Raymond Nye, Sr., lifted his feet and made himself walk to the lectern. He touched Gordon lightly on the shoulder and took Gordon's place at the lectern.

"I'm not much at Bible quoting, not since Sunday school. So you'll forgive me if I don't quite get it all right. But this," said Ray, opening his big hand as if to sprinkle something soft over the domed sheen of the coffin, "is my beloved son, with whom I am well pleased."

He rattled a sheaf of papers and held up a copy of *Life* magazine, with Katie Couric on the cover. "Perhaps some of you read, just a few months ago, about Ray in this publication. I don't have it here because I'm full of myself, but because I'm full of pride for my son, who brought us much joy in his short life.

"My son played golf. Oh, he did a lot of other things, too. He majored in mathematics. He could figure out and make sense of things I couldn't even read without getting a headache. He had a ton of friends, some of them, like Carl Jurgen right here and Gordie, they were like sons to us, too. Our house was always full of boys and cleats and golf clubs; they ate like condemned men . . ." Big Ray paused, and swallowed. "But in golf, my son was among the top young players of his generation. Now, you can say that Ray Nye, Junior, was not Davis Love, the third. He was not Phil Mickelson. And I would say to you, yes, he was not those men, who are prodigies. But if you can imagine several hundred men who, out of all the men who love the game in America, have the hands and the heart to become touring pros, then our son was among that tenth of a tenth of a tenth of a percent . . ." Ray sighed and scraped his hair. "And he was coming on. Last year, and this year, he was this close in winnings to that six days of torture at Doral, the qualifying school, to earn one of those slots on the biggest, richest golf tour in the world. He was coming on, but slowly. You see, our son did everything very slowly. You would hear about it in the stories written about it. 'Slow but Sure, but Nye Will Not Be Denied,' they would say. His backswing was so slow you would think he'd forgotten in the middle what he was doing. But he never forgot.

"Now, I don't know how much you Northerners"—there was a soft burble of laughter—"really know about golf. But there is no such thing as a perfect game. Arnold Palmer played a perfect game once, he says, but then he woke up." Laughter stopped him again. "Only three times in the history of the PGA has a player broken sixty. David Duval did it. Al Geiberger did it. But you just can't be perfect. There's going to be a mistake. You're not going to have five pars and thirteen birdies. It's not human.

"Nonetheless, all players are striving for that perfect game. And I believe that my son did achieve a perfect game. It was during the event recounted in this publication, in *Life* magazine, under the headline 'Georgia on His Mind.' At the end of the day last April, my son, Ray, was tied for the lead at six under in the . . . well, in the most important event of his career, when he learned from the McKennas here that his wife, who was terribly ill, had had a seizure. And Ray knew what that meant. It meant that if he waited, even another day, his wife might not be, she might not be . . . conscious to see him again.

"And so he left Coachman's Hill in Charlotte, North Carolina, my friends. He laid down his club and went to the airport, and he told the reporters that there would be many rounds of golf to play, but only once could he play the most important role in his life, as a husband in need and as a father . . . it says it all here in this magazine. But it doesn't really express what it meant for a young man who played golf to give up that moment, which was the biggest moment in his professional life. He didn't even think about it. That was Ray.

"Georgia got better. But not very much better. It turned out that Ray didn't really need to make that sacrifice, giving up what would have been a tremendous amount of money he could have used to care for his baby, giving up the certainty of making that next step. But I stand here today to tell you that I am glad he did it. Even though it meant . . . it meant this . . . it finally meant that he would not have those other days to reach for medal play. Even though coming back here, and of course his mother and his sisters and I are brokenhearted that Ray lies here today, instead of sitting beside us, beside the little girl it was his right and his joy to raise . . ."

Lorraine had to look away. Big Ray was chewing on his sorrow, trying hard to swallow. She looked down at sleeping Keefer, her four limbs confidently sprawled, and observed how little time she had really spent watching her granddaughter sleep. Asleep, her blue eyes hidden, she looked exactly like Georgia.

As Big Ray cleared his throat once, then again, Lorraine heard Mark wince. "So," Ray finally went on, "no matter what has happened, I am glad Raymond, Junior, did this, because he achieved in life what no player of golf can ever achieve on the course. He achieved a perfect game. And I am proud of him. And I thank you for being proud of him, too." Diane cried out and stretched out her hands.

They all bent their heads and tried to be still and tried to ignore the tumult of suppressed coughs and cries that rose on the left, on the right, from the rear of the church, as if instruments in an orchestra were being hastily tuned. Those who were Catholic placed a finger to their foreheads, wings, and hearts; those who were not gathered their sport coats and purses and the printed programs they did not want to keep but could not bear to leave behind, programs that would end up on kitchen counters and telephone stands throughout the town and throughout the state for weeks, finally scribbled on with times for baseball registrations, dates of dental appointments, and baby-sitters' telephone numbers. They turned in hundreds as one body.

Then, the thin, tenor throat of the organ surprised them and they looked up, expecting to see Mrs. Wilton at the keyboard. But instead, there sat Carl Jurgen, blue-white in his linen slacks and shirt, bathed in a funnel of sunlight, playing that old jazz, "Georgia."

CHAPTER six

"*D*id you notice Carl Jurgen didn't have a suitcase," Tim was saying. "He's like a spy in a movie or something."

Gordon didn't reply. He had to tug himself from a trance state even to understand what Upchurch had said. They were sitting in Church's Maxima on one of the embryonic roads in Wood Violet Hollow, the new subdivision that was Tim's pride and obsession—he being, as he would often offer, apropos of nothing, the second-youngest public works director in the nation. After dropping Jurgen off at the airport, Tim had stopped for a couple of double cheeseburgers with everything. The smell of the burgers and the sound of Tim's energetic munching made Gordon's stomach quake.

"I don't know how that works," Gordon admitted. "I know he changed his clothes two or three times. He was wearing linen pants at the funeral."

"Linen pants. Right. They'd have been up around my knees after the first hour. Where'd he iron them?"

"I have no idea," Gordon said. "I don't even own an iron. Could you open a window while you eat that, Church? Or better yet, eat it in . . . Canada or someplace? I'm going to hurl, here."

Church bit into his burger unperturbed. A spurt of mayonnaise coated his lower lip. "Maybe the clothes thing is from being born rich," he went on. "Maybe they have shrunken clothes like those capsules little kids have. You just put them in water and they grow up into dinosaurs. Only these would grow up and be sport coats. The rich are different from us, Gordo."

They sank into a silence that must have seemed companionable to Tim, but was excruciating for Gordon. It wasn't that he minded the quiet. He'd heard enough voices in the past two days to last him the rest of his life. But a welter of competing thoughts and narratives were slugging it out in the back of his mind, nagging him to get home, not to his own place, but to Cleveland Avenue.

Church was chattering on about the latest installment in the environmentally challenged history of the subdivision, which owed its name to a tiny circle of land, a bowl of tender blue flowers that legend described as an ancient buffalo wallow. Then the members of the Red Stick tribe had turned up, anxious, to the point of litigation, to halt the whole project until it could be determined if a strangely table-shaped rise was a Woodland Peoples' burial cairn. The desperate developer then offered to name the subdivision "Indian Burial Mound Place." One of Gordon's only honest laughs of the past year had been Tim's account of his diplomatic reaction, when he'd gently asked the developer, *How long has it been since you've seen any . . . horror movies?*

"I think I'd better get home soon," Gordon suggested softly. "My folks probably need me. We were gone all night. I just feel like I was in a play . . . a production of some kind and now it's over. Like it was a show we put on for other people."

Gordon thought briefly of the news report they'd watched yesterday, as if TV coverage were a staple of everyone's family tragedy. Jane Hampton of WINN-TV in Madison intoned sadly, "We first met little Keefer Nye last year when we covered a touching event. The forces of big-time athletics and small town love joined in a huge benefit to raise funds to fight cancer, which was claiming the life of Keefer's twenty-six-year-old mother, Georgia McKenna Nye, whose husband, Ray, was an up-and-coming pro golfer on the Knockout Tour. Today, there is news almost too sad to imagine. Keefer Nye has lost both her mother and her father." The sports guy, Mike Albert, weighed in, almost joshing, "Keefer is lucky in that she has two sets of loving grandparents still living, and maybe she'll grow up to play on the LPGA . . ."

"Got any aspirin, Church?"

Tim shook his head, chewing. Gordon was fairly certain he was well into stage one of a bastard hangover. This sitting around was aimless, but it seemed somehow necessary, an obligatory pause before everyone turned away and plunged into the flume of everyday life. There were two conversations that stood out in his mind from the night before. He cudgeled them in his mind, and they only deepened his impatience.

The first was something Delia Cady, Ray's cousin, had said at an impromptu dinner with the younger people.

Gordon had, by then, sunk into a stupor he'd hoped would be taken as the effects of shock, and so at first, he hadn't realized that Delia's comments about Ray's absolute faith in eternal life were directed at him.

"And I know Georgia felt the same way," Delia had said, brushing back the skillful rigid structure of dark ringlets that framed her large, pale face. "That's right, isn't it, Gordon?"

"I don't know," Gordon had said, itching with discomfort as the rest fell silent. "I mean, I don't know whether she believed in that."

"She was your sister," Delia chided. "We discussed it many times. She felt certain that God was directing her course."

"God was her copilot," Tim put in, his attempt at lightness landing with a leaden plop in the hush.

"We just never discussed religion," Gordon had explained. "I know she was more religious than I am . . ."

"I wonder if she'll be raised . . . Catholic," Delia said.

"Do you mean Keefer?"

She'd nodded. "You know, the Nyes aren't."

"My folks are, though," Gordon said. "Socially, at least."

"There's a lot more to it than smells and bells and holidays," Delia went on. "It's a big responsibility, one of the most important things about raising a child."

"I think . . . well, we haven't got that far yet, Delia," Gordon had said wearily, and he remembered wondering as he spoke, were the McKennas somehow behind the game?

He'd assumed, of course, especially after learning of the annulled will, that there would have to be some sort of conference about Keefer. But the McKennas were her designated guardians. Everyone knew that. He hadn't discussed the lawyer's message with his parents, hesitating out of deference to their grief. He'd been angry, in fact, that his attention to his own grief had been diverted by ridiculous speculation. But as he listened to Delia, he'd been forced into more speculating: Had his parents been holding back also, out of respect for him? Did all three of them know things they weren't telling one another?

The second conversation had happened that morning, with Carl Jurgen, during the dizzy dawn of a long night. A drinking conclave had followed the dinner. It started with at least two of the Upchurch brothers (Gordon's memory blurred), Pat Chaptman, Kip Sweeney, Lindsay, and Stephanie Larsen and her boyfriend, along with great quantities of cranberry juice and vodka and Triple Sec that dwindled to vodka alone. By the wee hours, the crowd also had dwindled, leaving only Gordon, Tim, Jurgen, and Kip.

Jurgen had been talking quietly with Tim, making it clear he intended to sleep that night at Tim's apartment, and Tim—though he'd met Jurgen only once before, on a visit to Florida—was going along with the plan as if it had been his own invitation, as if they'd been brothers for life. That was Jurgen's effect on people, a wonder to Gordon as long as he'd known him. People said he, Gordon, took things lightly, but Carl had nerves of steel, or of silk.

Sometime during the night, in a befuddled way, Gordon had decided that Jurgen would be someone to confide in. Jurgen was, after all, almost a lawyer, one of the few of his friends from college who hadn't been math or science grinds.

And so he had waited. He had waited, trying to do his part in recalling, for the Tall Trees bunch, the impossible rapture of their Southern college days and nights, which seemed at this point, in alcohol-fueled retrospect, like an endless sunlit kiss on a white beach that stretched on forever.

"Tonight," Jurgen said then—with elegance out of keeping with the pie tins rubbled with two roach ends and the butts of Kip's Camels, and flies drowning in the pool of cranberry juice that had jelled on the cable spool Tim used for a coffee table—"Despite all . . . this revelry, which is probably unseemly, we are all a little older than we should be. So let's remember when we were young." He'd added, "For my beloved pal, Ray Nye, Junior."

And Jurgen went on, his recall for place and words so much more acute than Gordon's own. He'd told them all about the sandwich guy they'd tortured with their weekend raids on his marquee—by Sunday morning, "Meatball Subs" read "Bust Me Balls," "Hot Dog and Fries" ended up "Sand Ho Got Fried." About using Carl's lawyer father's credit card to charge cases of Hula Girl at the Sunoco station, the weary guy behind the counter deadpanning, "Regular or unleaded?" slapping the charge slip right on top of the sweating beer cans. They'd traded stories of adventures that led up to the fall when Georgia had come to Florida State. For Gordon, a Northerner utterly infatuated with the languor of the South, life had then been perfect. With new friends, Georgia had taken on the role of unofficial little sister to the

Evans Scholars, organizing softball matches and dress-up dances. The first Thanksgiving after, as Jurgen put it, "Georgia conquered Florida," there'd been a big golf tournament. And so a dozen of them couldn't go home for the holiday.

Georgia had cooked a dinner, and in lieu of a blessing, had sung, in her sweet alto, the old Louis Armstrong song, "What a Wonderful World," whereupon strong men sobbed and rushed from the table to call their mothers.

It was on the tide of those memories, at dawn, when pink flossy clouds were shredding overhead, that Gordon had asked Carl to join him on the balcony at Tim's place, finally able to give voice to his troubles.

"I guess, you know, we haven't had a chance to work everything out, about my niece," he'd begun. "But I guess we'll take care of her all together. The three of us. Me, mostly, I guess."

"I've been thinking about that," Jurgen said solemnly, and Gordon's neck prickled. "I can't imagine raising a baby alone."

"I can't imagine raising a baby at all. But it's Keefer. I have to."

"Do you want to?"

"It's Keefer."

"Big Ray and Diane," Jurgen said thoughtfully, "are they okay with this?"

The thought of that student's dad, Mr. . . . Liotis, lawyer Liotis, rapped at Gordon's chest.

He wanted to ask Jurgen, did the last will stand in force even if the principals revoked it? Did they have to work out all these complexities immediately, and for all time? His words stalled in his mouth. Georgia seemed to be receding, fast, away from him down a long passage, like a vanishing train.

"My sister and Ray named us guardians," he'd ventured. "That's what they both wanted."

"Us," Jurgen repeated.

"Didn't the Nyes talk about it?"

"Yes, they did," Jurgen acknowledged.

"What, do you feel okay telling me what they said?"

"All they said was, they were meeting with Ray's lawyer. Friday. Tomorrow. Today, I guess, by now. And I assumed this had something to do with their estate."

"They didn't have much of an estate, Carl, and it's all Keefer's, I mean, whatever we can get for the condo, or whatever . . . it will pay for her college and all."

"They had insurance. I assume any responsible parent, with, I'm sorry, a very ill spouse, would be very careful about that."

"I, you know, I just hadn't thought of it."

"No one would, in your circumstances."

"Do you think that the Nyes . . . ?"

"What?"

"Well, do you think they would consider wanting custody of Keefer?"

"I think they would consider that, yes."

"Do you think that would be . . . ?"

"I'm in a sort of place, here, Gordo. Ray was my best friend all my life. I've known the Nyes since I was in first grade. And two finer people never walked on land. They love that little girl. And your mom and dad are equally good people."

"And they've been with the baby, every day of her life, practically."

"It's a tough one. I'm sure the Nyes want the very best for Keefer." Something in his tone alerted Gordon. Implied a contest. Will there be sides, Gordon thought? Will Jurgen be on mine? South versus North? Friendship versus history?

"I know they do. I know they do," he'd finally managed, stupidly.

"I'm sure good people can work this all out. You know, Georgia was in her way a great beauty, Gordo. I got to know her well in the time they lived down there, when you were off in the jungles with the earthy folk. She had a mouth on her, but what a sweet soul. Yep, I'm sure you all can work this out."

Was he sure? Gordon sneaked a look at Jurgen's angular jaw. His friend looked placid, serene. Then Jurgen sighed. "I'm pulling for . . . well, for all of you."

All of you, Gordon's mind repeated. Jurgen had to have an agenda here. The ties were deep and tangled. Jurgen, Gordon happened to know, had availed himself of Alison Nye's virginity one fiercely hot night on the carpet of the ninth green at Sandpiper, though it had not been an enduring relationship, and Alison had married Andy several years later. At Georgia's wedding, the fact that Gordon had been Ray's best man, had been a sore point with Jurgen.

But what significance could any of this have now, Gordon thought? Here, now, when they'd all grown up and Ray and Georgia were dead and he was sweating and nauseated, in the dawn of his grief, in a car in Tall Trees in the middle of a dusty field with Tim—Gordon noticed now—asleep in the driver's seat?

Gordon nudged him. "Isn't it Friday? Don't you have to go to work or something?"

"Three days compassionate leave," Tim snorted, wakening. "I told my boss it was a relative."

"We're not your relatives," Gordon said.

"Same as."

"We . . . appreciate all you did."

"*De nada.*"

"I have to get home, now, Church. For real. My folks need me. And I need aspirin and peanut butter toast."

"Absolutely," Tim said.

Cleveland Avenue was as quiet as a Sunday morning. I'm a teacher, Gordon thought, I should be sleeping. There are three great things about teaching, said the fridge magnet his mother had given him—June, July, and August. Tim parked the car. For a moment, both of them dozed against the seat, Coltrane's "A Love Supreme" gently vibrating from Tim's very good speakers through their arms and butts.

"Your mom is yelling on the lawn, Gordo," Tim said sleepily.

Gordon jerked into consciousness. Horse-smelling sweat poured down his chin. The air conditioner was blasting.

His mom was indeed standing on the lawn, in her T-shirt and boxer shorts, her mouth snapping soundlessly. Gordon thought of a nutcracker. He rolled down the passenger-side window.

"—don! Now!" Lorraine scolded.

To his shame, Gordon spotted the identical Dwors leaning out their porch window next door. He waved.

"I need you to come in right now, Gordon," she said, "Right now. Hi, Tim." As if they were children and she were helping them out of the car, Lorraine began fumbling at the door handle.

"Take it easy, Mom," Gordon struggled to open the door from his side. His Grandma Lena would always do this. You could never open the car door for her because she'd be wrestling with the handle on the inside all the while you were trying from the outside. "Let it alone, Mom! I can't get out if you're messing with it."

Finally, Tim was gone and Gordon and Lorraine stood face-to-face on the lawn.

"They have five hundred thousand dollars!" she practically yelled.

"Who?"

"The kids! Ray and Georgia! They have five hundred thousand dollars, and the insurance investigator just called me . . . they think it was a suicide!"

"Let's go inside, Mom. Who's here?"

"Your father. Nora."

"Okay, okay, let's just settle down . . ."

Nora and Mark were seated at the kitchen table. Each of

them had a clean tablet and a sharpened number 2 pencil and a telephone book.

"We have to call a lawyer," Lorraine told him. "Do you have any ideas?"

"Well, I know one we can't call," Gordon said. He leaned over and kissed his aunt's soft forehead, and then, after thinking about it for an instant, kissed his father's cheek.

It took him the better part of an hour to explain about Julius Liotis's father, about Jurgen's revelation about the Nyes' meeting with the lawyer, about the revoked will. The process was halting, because Nora or Lorraine would interrupt about every fifteen seconds—"No!" or "That's impossible!"—so that he could not complete a sentence. They hadn't suspected a thing.

"Why would they change their will?" Nora asked.

"I have no idea, I only know what the lawyer said," Gordon replied. "And Carl said they were meeting with the lawyer . . . today."

"Son, did he say that they had signed a new will?"

"He said he was helping them prepare it. I assume so."

"So they have a will," Mark sighed, "that we don't know about."

"Diane Nye has convinced them to give her the baby," Lorraine muttered. She had raked her hair into dreadlocks, the effect some of Gordon's students achieved with dish soap.

"But, Lor, wouldn't you do the same thing?" Mark asked.

"No"—Lorraine turned on her husband savagely—"I would not try to take a baby away from the only people she knows best and loves! I would not try to get control of all that baby's money!"

"Lorraine!" Mark admonished her, "We don't know anything about that."

"Why would they think the children committed suicide?" Nora asked.

"Well, Auntie," Gordon began, "cars are . . . car accidents

are a common method people . . . use to try to cover up a suicide."

"Like Porter Avery."

They all lapsed into silence, thinking of the farmer neighbor of the Nordstroms who had crushed himself with gruesome creativity under his own tractor. A cardinal whistled outside the open window, and they all jumped at the grinding of a truck's gears.

"It's garbage day!" Mark announced. "I completely forgot it!"

"Don't you dare go get out those cans." Lorraine warned her husband.

"It's going to smell, Lor; there's a bunch of that food in it."

"I'll do it," Nora offered.

"No, I will," Gordon interrupted.

Lorraine erupted, "Let the fucking cans sit! All of you! Am I the only one here who realizes we have to make a plan of some kind or Keefer is going to have a Southern accent?"

Gordon had never heard his mother say "fuck." He would not have imagined she knew how.

The telephone rang, but no one answered. They all listened as Diane Nye's soft, lilting voice spoke into the answering tape. "We have a little appointment about ten, Lorraine. And then we thought we'd take Baby up to the inn to visit with the grandkids. I think they're going home tonight. Is that okay? Okay. And then we can make arrangements for Keefer coming back home with us—home to Jupiter, I mean. For Raymond's memorial. And, of course, you are invited. Are you all doing okay? I slept a little. Thank your doctor for me." After the funeral, Diane had suffered a migraine, and Eve Holly, from Pine Grove Medical, who'd been in attendance, had given her an injection. "Okay. Well, 'bye all."

They all watched the telephone as if it were a mad dog about to spring. Keefer wandered out into the kitchen, her diaper slung low like plumbers' pants, her pink Elmo shirt

pulled up over her belly, the terry-cloth frog she both cuddled and chewed under one arm.

"Dory!" she beamed, and climbed into Gordon's lap, a
warm spreading squish of pee immediately dampening his
thighs. "Moobie?"

"She's saying 'movie,'" Lorraine explained.

"I know what she's saying, Mom," Gordon said sharply.
"It's because we watched *Wizard of Oz* last week."

Nora busied herself with the moosh of soaked Cheerios in
the mermaid bowl that Keefer demanded every morning for
breakfast and, stripping the baby of her weighty diaper,
swept her into her high chair. "Wed poon!" Keefer intoned,
ominously.

"She's saying she wants her red spoon, Mom," Gordon
snapped.

But Lorraine was leafing through the telephone book.
Gordon caught sight of the page headings: Abortion, Adoption. "Do we need an estate lawyer, Mark? Or an adoption
lawyer?"

"Well," Nora said mildly, "Bradie's older sister is infertile,
from endometriosis. And she's adopting a baby girl from
China, did you know that? And I know they went through an
agency in Morehouse. So I'll just call her, is all . . ." Nora
gathered up her pad and removed herself to Mark's tiny sun-
porch office.

"It's actually pretty obvious why they would consider it a
suicide, Mom," Gordon began.

"It's an insult," Lorraine replied.

"No, it's pretty obvious. Ray was very depressed. It was
more than Georgia. He had just given up the biggest victory—"

"Oh, Christ, if I hear one more word about the miracle at
Coachman's Hill I'm going to throw up," Lorraine said. "Ray
Nye should have quit the goddamned tour the minute she got
sick, Gordon."

"They had to have the income, Mom."

"I know that. But that wasn't his only motivation. His . . . work distracted him. He couldn't face all this. He counted on us. He knew we would take care of our child. How often did you see Diane and Big Ray here cleaning up the . . . taking care of your sister? Diane didn't come here once. Diane sent her tree bark crap in the mail, and it was surface mail, Gordon. She didn't even FedEx it."

"Mom, wait—"

"I mean it! Now here they come, talking about baby, baby, baby, like she doesn't have a name—"

"That's just a Southern phrase—"

"And their son, the great hero."

"Mom, Ray loved Georgia."

"Ray loved Georgia, and Ray went on with his life, Gordon! We quit our lives! I took time off school, and you took time off, and your dad barely went to work, and Mike and Nora, we all stopped our lives, Gordon. Even Lindsay and Tim interrupted their lives—"

"How could we have done anything else, Mom?"

"That's the point! And now, they want Keefer because she's their genetic link to Ray."

"That stinks, Mom."

"Okay, okay, it stinks. But I don't have to be rational, Gordon. My child is dead. Your father's child and mine is lying across the street under the ground." Gordon thought, suddenly, Not your only child, Mom, but dismissed it. "And we have to figure out a way to keep what's left of our family together."

Nora came back beaming. She held up her notepad, triumphant, a good girl who had finished her homework before the rest of the class. "I found it!" she told them, "I got the name of Amber Dugan's agency. It's Adoption Alliance—"

"A . . . Aardvark," Mark said. They stared at him, and he continued, flustered, "That's why everyone does that. You know. A-One Auto Body. They want to be the first in the phone book."

"Thanks, Mark," Lorraine said.

"Anyhow, I got the name of the lawyer, too. Greg Katt. In Merill."

"Let's get calling," Lorraine whispered. "They're going to be here in . . . what time is it?"

"Wait a minute." Gordon, nauseated and baffled, panted, "Wait a minute. Can't we all just talk this over? With the Nyes?"

"We have to find out how to secure custody of Keefer," Lorraine explained, slowly, as if explaining to a middle-school child how to hold a pencil for shading. "We have to take the first step, before they do."

"But as of right now, we already have custody of Keefer. I'm worried about it, too, Mom. I've been thinking about it twenty-four-seven. But I don't think we have to get out the big guns yet."

"Gordon, your father and I are almost sixty years old. Do you think a court is going to give us a toddler to raise? We're not going to live forever," Lorraine said, and then stopped, and went on more gently. "I don't mean we're going to die anytime soon. But we're not wealthy people, honey, not like Big Ray, who builds all those instant communities, every one with its own golf course, they'll be golfing on the ocean floor next—"

"Mommy, you're not saying this has anything to do with needing . . . the baby's money?" Gordon glanced at Keefer, who grinned at him madly, poking the air in his direction with her spoon, as if to say, howsa about that? He felt his eyes start to burn and fill, "I mean needing the money to bring her up and stuff . . ."

"I mean, Gordon, that a . . . well, a court is not going to just say, here, let's give this little baby to an old school-teacher and her husband who sells vitamins." She glanced at Mark. "Sweetie, I'm sorry, but you know what I mean. When they could give her to this rich developer and his preppie wife who had their first child when they were thirteen."

"Stop exaggerating, Mom. You just hate Diane," Gordon said. "That's half of what this is about."

"It's more than that," said Lorraine.

"It really is more than that," Mark added, "though we're probably biased—"

"Don't go all fair and balanced on us, Mark," Lorraine told him through clenched teeth.

Gordon was aghast. His mother and father were fighting. Comets would collide with the earth. The last time he had seen his parents fight was the time Mark let Gordon sleep over at Davey Ober's house, where Davey's two brothers shot crows with their .22s. Lorraine had come roaring up the Obers' driveway and all but hauled Gordon out by the arm, grinning at Mrs. Ober and nattering about some family function they'd forgotten, tossing him into the front seat, practically breaking his tooth with the seat belt, zooming home down Q, up First and onto Cleveland Avenue, yelling at Mark, *don't you ever, ever let him go to a house where there are unlocked guns!*

Georgia had come out and sat beside him, *I figure you're grounded for two weeks,* she'd said, *maybe more,* smiling. And he'd realized, right then, how his parents had found out about the Ober kids' guns in the first place. Still, he hadn't been grounded. Lorraine had come swooping out onto the porch, clasping him to her, telling him, I only have one Gordie, while Georgia watched in disgust.

"You always knew you were the one, didn't you?" his mother asked now.

"I was the one?"

"To adopt Keefer?"

He had known, of course. He had known. But he had known in theory. He had known in fact. But not in huge, present, demanding fact.

"Keefer has to have a real parent of her own, not just grandparents," Lorraine said, sounding, to Gordon, faint and far off.

"I don't know if I'm ready, Mom."

"I don't know if you're ready, either," Lorraine sighed.

"He's ready," Nora put in. "Gordie, it's not like you're going to be alone. We're all here. And Georgia will help you." Gordon looked into his aunt's good, faded blue eyes and did not have the heart to speak one syllable about the afterlife, or lack thereof. "Listen. I wasn't going to say this right now," Nora went on, "but I called that adoption agency, too. The social worker is sending the paperwork overnight, all the forms, the medical forms and such, and she said they can start the home study right away."

"You have to move." Lorraine began scribbling on her own notepad, "The Wiltons have that pretty flat, the third story of the big Victorian, on First. Their daughter teaches first grade, Judy. She must be forty now. She lives on the second floor. Helen Wilton says it's a beautiful place, only one bedroom, but really spacious, not like your—"

"Dump," Gordon finished for her.

"Bachelor pad," Lorraine said primly.

"I'm not going to move," Gordon said stubbornly. "I just got my place fixed up." Oh, Georgia, he thought, all I was going to do was get my posters framed.

"It's not that fixed up, Gordie," his mother told him dryly. "And there's not enough room for a family."

A family. She was right. Where would Keefer sleep? On the sofa? Under the sofa?

"So anyhow," Nora went on, "the social worker will come out Tuesday—is that okay, Gordie? It's not too soon, is it?"

It's all too soon, he thought.

Nora went on, "I don't think you can move by Tuesday, Gordie, but Hayes and Rob and the boys and I will help you spruce the place up."

"Did you tell them everything?" Lorraine asked Nora.

"You mean, about Georgia and Ray and all? The lady knew. She saw it on TV."

"I mean, about Ray and Diane."

"I told her the truth, Lorraine," Nora said stoutly. "I told her we were going to adopt a baby. She's going to come out to see Gordon at one in the afternoon."

Lorraine reached across the table and caught Nora's big rough hand in her delicate small one. "You're God, Nora," she said.

Gordon pulled Keefer onto his lap. Close enough, he thought.

CHAPTER *seven*

On the day that would have been Georgia and Ray's second wedding anniversary, Lorraine and Mark walked down the narrow folding step from an eight-seater plane onto the tarmac at the Jupiter Municipal Airport, after a patchwork of flights from Wausau to Milwaukee, Milwaukee to Tampa.

The heat was paralyzing. The skin of Lorraine's face seemed to shrink a size with the initial blast of it. How did people live?

"Air-conditioning," Mark told her. "They don't go outside for six months of the year. But neither do we, Lor. The other way around." Actually, Mark admitted, the heat felt good to him. He'd been cold for weeks.

They sat in the baggage-claim area, Lorraine feeling like a sparrow in the peacock pen. For Tall Trees, her manner of dress was unique, understated, urban. But in Florida, all the women, and the men, Lorraine now remembered—from the times they'd visited first Gordie and Georgia, and then Ray and Georgia—seemed to vie with one another to do the best impersonation of a tropical fruit drink. "Teal is the new beige here," she said to Mark.

"Hmmmm," he replied, with not even a pantomime of interest. Lorraine felt a quirt of anger. Why did she have to be the one to bother with the up-tempo chat? It was not only he who could not ignore that just twenty-four months ago at this very hour—twenty-four months comprising an afternoon of life, no more, especially once life spilled over into the plain of middle age—they had been seated in the front pew at Our Lady of the Lake, watching Georgia dash away tears, promising to honor and cherish Raymond, her husband, for all their lives. Crying and then laughing as Georgia, after their twenty-second kiss, sneaked a peek over Ray's back at the green diamond, gift to the firstborn son from Diane's mother, Kathryn, who sat nodding and smiling on the other side of the aisle, her burnished, lineless face a twin of Diane's own.

The green diamond now lay gleaming in Lorraine's bedside table drawer, slipped from Georgia's finger by Bud Chaptman, pressed into Lorraine's hand by a sobbing Natalie at the little supper following the funeral.

For Keefer.

Why had Lorraine suddenly had to take on the role of activator, motivator, cheerleader for the bunch of them? Mark had slept sixteen hours a day for the past week, and it had been Lorraine who had sworn to give up . . . she'd gently layered her arsenal of pills among her underthings in her carry-on bag that morning as if she were crating eggs. Keeping her grief at arm's length took a pharmaceutical hit squad. When would she be able to lie down and keen?

On Monday, there had been the first lawyer's appointment, which had gone beautifully. Greg Katt's wife had been one of Lorraine's former students. Katt's quick enthusiasm reassured them all. Gordon should be able to petition to adopt Keefer under that section of Wisconsin law that provided for immediate family. Commonly referred to as "stepparent" adoption, it also applied to any close family member, parent, aunt, uncle, sister, brother. Lorraine was bathed in relief. The home study could be streamlined down from the daunting two-inch-thick packet of forms they'd received on the previous Saturday because, Katt explained, the presumption of fitness to parent was weighted heavily in favor of the family the minor child already knew and loved. Greg Katt had Xeroxed the McKennas' copy of the only will and testament the three of them knew of and promised to speak to both the lawyer who'd prepared the first will—someone Lorraine didn't know named Stacey Sweeney—and to Attorney Liotis, Ray's new lawyer, that week.

"Passions run high at a time like this," he'd told them, tapping his tented fingers, "but try not to worry. The first thing I'm going to do is file a petition for temporary guardianship for you and Mark. That only makes sense. And if the Nyes file, too, where are they? Well, you are here and she is here. And it's first come, first served, that is, first filer gets the petition heard first. This should be no problem. Any judge will realize a family needs time to sort things out. You intend to give the Nyes the same access to your granddaughter as they would have had if their son had survived, do you not?" They'd all nodded. "I don't see a huge, huge problem here. Unless one of the Nye siblings who is married comes forward, I don't see a problem. And even then, there would be the issue of Keefer's comfort. Her comfort, psychologically speaking, that is." He'd asked about visiting—how often had Caroline and Alison come to spend time with Keefer? How often had they visited Tall Trees? Were they primary caregivers for Keefer during her time spent in Florida?

Lorraine and Mark had given the best answers they could summon. Lorraine was forced to reckon how much of the past year's life had gone on above her head, in the unexplored stratosphere of life outside Georgia's illness. Gordon remembered only the visits of Keefer's godparents, Ray's cousin Delia and her husband, Craig, who had driven up from Madison a dozen times or more, often bringing along Delia's daughter, Alex, the red-haired teenager who'd brought Keefer all her old Barbies. "Well," Katt told them, "Wisconsin law pays very close attention to what is referred to as the best interests of the child. And everything here suggests that the best interests of a child who has endured such a difficult . . . transition in her little life is to stay right where she feels safe."

And on Tuesday, Katt had filed. And the judge had agreed to a temporary order, with circumstances to be reviewed in ninety days.

They had her. Legally at least. Lorraine considered writing to the Nyes, but decided it would be indelicate. And dangerous. After all, Keefer was in Florida at the moment. The Nyes were in physical possession. Mark said possession was nine-tenths of the law. Lorraine convinced herself that waiting to explain about the order could wait until Ray's parents had withstood their son's memorial . . . and until Keefer was in the backseat of their rental car, on the way to the airport.

On Wednesday, when Cindy Rogan from Adoption Alliance had come to interview Gordon at his suddenly country-antique–decorated apartment, Lorraine and Mark had been shanghaied by the investigator from Northern Mutual, who'd spent two hours grilling them about Ray's emotional state. The representative had been one of those men so petite it seemed impossible he could purchase suits in the men's department, a stereotypically parched and tidy insurance man, with a mustache that wasn't worth his trouble. He'd informed them that Ray had paid premiums for three months on the policy in question, paid regularly and on time, he'd sighed, as if this were a source of profound regret! And he'd further told them that the company would endeavor to conduct a reenactment of the crash, which the McKennas could attend if they chose.

"Why would we do that?" Mark had asked him.

But Gordon had felt confident during the interview, Lorraine heard that night from Lindsay Snow, who'd dropped by Gordon's house immediately after work. The social worker would have to come back when Keefer was home, to observe her interaction with Gordon.

There was one hitch. It was a good thing, Lindsay diplomatically told Lorraine, that Gordon was moving, because Cindy Rogan had expressed concern about the busy street. So Lorraine had spent the entire next morning trying to track down Helen Wilton to follow through on her idea of getting Gordon moved into the Victorian, to convince her that she didn't really want to rent to that photographer who was going to document the archaeological dig at Wood Violet Hollow. A man who'd only be around a few months? Gordon would be a more stable tenant, Lorraine sweetly assured Helen. It would be years before he'd be able to afford a house of his own. Helen was dubious, as the photographer was single and about the same age as her very single daughter, Judy. But Gordon was so strong. He could help out with maintenance around the place. And he was such a polite boy. And the baby. . . . Finally, Helen relented. It only remained for Lorraine to talk Gordon's landlord into breaking his lease, which should be breezy, since he was one of Dale Larsen's longtime deputies.

For Keefer. That was why Lorraine had pushed herself to limits she had not imagined she possessed, wheedled and plotted and strategized even though a single thought of Georgia, a chance glance at her graduation portrait on the turn of the stairs, could bend Lorraine double, make her cover her ears as if agony had an intolerable sound. For Keefer. For Keefer.

They had not seen Keefer for a week. Big Ray and Diane had shown up with a little two-wheeled suitcase stuffed with new outfits—"Just summer togs, Lorraine," Diane had explained. "She'd melt down there in those dungaree things." And though the tears had begun when Lorraine handed Keefer to her other grandmother, Diane had wisely kept up a monologue about Baby's very own swimming pool, a pool outside, where it was nice out all the time! Finally, tentatively, Keefer had waved bye-bye. Relinquishing her doused the pilot light. Neither of them spoke, but their bed beckoned, a void as cool and neutral as a snow field. This is what they would become, Lorraine thought, as they lay down, Mark's right arm automatically opening to enclose her shoulder, old people lying expectant in the motionless museum of their past, sinking into a suspended state, a voluntary hibernation. Gordon would return to the unintentionally self-seeking life of a young single man, grooming his life, his work, his pleasure. Keefer. Keefer. Lorraine's longing for the delectable curve of Keefer's rear end frightened her into the first long, black, sodden sleep since the crash. Gordon woke them. "She's already gone, isn't she?" His good-natured face was slack. Lorraine moved over, and he lay down next to them. They'd all lain there until it was dark outside, safe to get up, and then for some reason, they had all spent three hours cleaning the house, afterward deciding to drive over to the condo to see what furniture of Georgia's and Ray's was useful and anonymous enough to transfer to Gordon's new digs.

The locks had been changed.

Lorraine, furious, had wanted to call the Nyes at that moment, from the nearest pay phone. But Gordon swung himself up onto the second floor terrace and pushed in a window. They'd made piles: towels, silverware, Georgia's beautiful, heavy, enameled cookware. And then they'd boxed all Ray's hats to send to his parents, except one, his Evans Scholars hat, which Gordon asked to keep. Lorraine had called Masterlock the next morning at 7:00 A.M. and had the locks changed again.

An hour after Mark and Lorraine's flight landed, they were still waiting, Mark impatiently insisting that they rent a car, since clearly the promised ride was not forthcoming. But just as they gathered their things and headed for the rental-car booths, one of the Nye girls' husbands, Leland, showed up, waving and shaking his head.

"I have to apologize, folks," he said. "Everything between here and Texas is torn up for the highway renovation. Big

Ray and Diane are going to have my hide. Did you guys have to wait long?"

"Oh, no," Mark said, "we've just been people-watching."

Into the land of palms and Porsches they'd gone, Leland thoughtfully dialing up talk radio to simulate conversation. He told them that Keefer was berry brown; Caroline swore the baby could swim. Leland would take them to Caroline's house right now, where Keefer was playing. Everyone else was at the club, absorbed in last-minute details for the memorial. How long would they be staying? Mark dithered; he'd thought they might drive around a bit, perhaps up to the campus to see Ray and Gordon's old fraternity. Perhaps to Cape Canaveral, where a shuttle launch was scheduled for Saturday; he could not conceal, Lorraine thought ruefully, the wisp of excitement in his voice. She wondered if there might ever be a grandfathers-in-space program. "Well, that's great," Leland smiled, slipping a pair of pearly sunglasses from the glove box. "Keefer is going to love having you guys around."

Mark and Lorraine exchanged glances. Mark took Lorraine's hand.

When Leland swung open the car door for them in front of a Spanish-style house on a boulevard shaded by sentry rows of cypress, Lorraine stopped on the lawn to listen. She could hear Keefer. "Birdie! Birdie up!"

"That's a sentence," she'd whispered to Mark.

Leland offered to drop their luggage at Silver Shoals, where the McKennas had reserved their room, despite Big Ray's protests that they had nothing but space at their place. "Do you need to get back to the office?" Lorraine asked. She had no idea what Leland did, but his car and his clothing did not hint at carpentry.

"Actually, no," Leland dipped his head. "I'm living at my alumnae club right this minute. Caroline and I are trying to figure some things out. It's been . . . well, we'd planned this before Ray died, but it's been a real hard time for her. Goes without saying I just love the Nyes, every one of them," he went on, "and family's family."

"We're sorry," Mark said.

"Oh, golly, there's worse things. Caro's just the best friend I've got. We'll be just fine."

And then Keefer, with Caroline close behind, was running barefoot down the lawn, tumbling into a half-somersault, up without missing a beat. Mark was as unashamedly fervent as Lorraine had ever seen him, covering the baby's wrists and elbows and forehead with kisses. Mark had not wept from joy since . . . Gordon was born. They all sat in Caroline's meticulous, subzero sunroom, drinking mint tea, marveling over the parade of toys Keefer carried, one after another, to her grandmother's lap for inspection.

"Have you seen my folks yet?" Caroline asked brightly.

"Leland just brought us here, and I guess we can take a taxi? To the hotel," Lorraine told her, "I could use a bath, and maybe we can take Keefer swimming. I know you have so much to do."

"Well, she's had her share of swimming! That's not going to be a novel experience," Caroline told them.

"We're sorry," Lorraine began. There was an awkward pause. "Leland told us. About your marriage troubles. That you'd parted, at least for a little while . . ."

"It's okay, it's really okay. It's been coming for, like, ever. And after . . . Ray died, and Georgia died, I just decided it was time for me to start living my life as if my life wasn't going to last forever. I'm twenty-one and I've only ever done what I was told! It was like I had three lives—one for me, one for Leland's parents, one for my parents, but every time I cut the pie, my slice got smaller."

Neither of the McKennas could respond. Keefer, however, said, "Birdie?"

"I have a finch," Caroline explained, "and it's her best friend right now. You know, she's so wonderful. She's like a cuddly little koala bear. She's exactly like Ray, those legs! She's just the image of his baby pictures. And who she really looks like is my dad's mom. I don't think Grandma Nye was still alive when Ray and Georgia got married."

"I don't think so," Lorraine said.

"Makes me want my own someday," Caroline went on easily, as Lorraine without warning found herself sweating in the frigid room. "But not right now! I need a life first. I've been married to Lee since I was born, and we are clearly not going to ever have a child."

"Perhaps it can be worked out," Lorraine said. "Being newly married is so hard. You're not quite a dating couple and not quite a family yet."

"He's gay, though, that's the thing of it."

"Oh," Lorraine said.

"He's a great gay husband. I felt like I was being dressed by my own in-house Versace. But he is a gay guy. And his parents would sooner eat glass than admit it and my parents would sooner eat poisoned glass. But Ray knew. Ray told me, get out, girl! And now I don't have my big brother to stick up for me. Mother and Father are taking it hard, but I just can't pretend anymore. Anyhow, now they've got little peachie here to fuss over and worry about. I'm done being the baby."

"Have, Caroline, I hope you don't mind my asking, but have your parents made plans . . . about Keefer?" Mark asked.

"Just totally made that room into F.A.O. Schwarz is all. She's got a slide into her bed, don't you, Sugar? A slide into her crib. She can't climb up it. It's completely child safe—"

"At their house?"

"Well, Andy and Ali can't decide. Frankly, I think Ali has her hands full with the monsters—"

"We'll just get a taxi over to the hotel now," Lorraine said abruptly.

"Don't you want something to drink or eat?"

"I just want a hot bath, a cool bath," Lorraine said, absently gathering up from the floor whatever seemed to belong to Keefer. "You know how it is when you travel? You just feel grimy. Is her dipe bag here anywhere, Caroline?"

"Mother's been putting her on the potty."

"She's fifteen months old!"

"She does a great job!"

Keefer grinned.

"Can we use your phone?"

"Oh, I'll drive you over. We have family counseling at four. This has been so"—Caroline's face crumpled—"We just never imagined. Losing Ray. Ray was our hero. And I don't know if I should say this, but . . . you know, this was their wedding day."

Lorraine stood up. "I know when my daughter's wedding day was."

"I didn't mean it that way."

"I'm sure you . . . I know. We're all on edge. So, now, Caroline, the memorial is at noon tomorrow?"

"It is, but Mother expects you for dinner tonight."

"You know, Caroline, we can't. I just . . . don't feel well," Lorraine said. "And we want to get reacquainted with Keefer. Spend some time with her."

"Mother and Father really appreciate everything you've done. For Keefer. And what Gordie has done," she looked up, shaking back her blond curls. "Is Gordie single?"

"He's engaged," Lorraine said. "Not really. Not formally. But you met Lindsay." Mark stared at her. "They've been sweethearts forever."

"He's great," Caroline said, "hot."

"He's hot all right." Lorraine smiled. "So, okay, we'll see you tomorrow." She scooped Keefer up, and pull-up pants and juice bottles tumbled. Mark scrambled to retrieve them. "Just leave them, Mark," Lorraine whispered, as Caroline went to retrieve her car keys. "Let's get out of here."

Mark settled Keefer in her car seat in the back of Caroline's Mustang. With his knees folded under his chin in the backseat, Mark looked like a marionette. Once at the hotel, Lorraine threw open the passenger door in the crushed-shell circle drive, and hauled Keefer out, seat and all. Keefer looked up plaintively, "Birdie?"

" 'Bye, 'bye, Kathryn," Caroline said, brushing the baby's outstretched hand with her lips. "Keefer Kathryn."

Mark and Lorraine stood in the blazing sun, Keefer struggling in her seat. Mark took the seat from his wife and they stepped, blinking, into the lobby gloom, where two-story waterfalls made Lorraine feel she had to shout to be heard. "Let's get in the room," she called to Mark.

He returned a moment later, looking sheepish. "It's been paid for," he said, "for as long as we wish to stay." They rode up silently, beside a silent bellman, in a glass cage.

Keefer trampolined on the king-sized bed while Lorraine rummaged for a phone book. "I doubt whether we can get a flight out of here tonight. But we can drive to Tampa. We can drive anywhere, really . . ."

Mark put his hand over the phone cradle, depressing the lever. "Wait, Lor, I know what you're thinking. I'm thinking the same thing. But we have to go to the memorial service."

"Why? Why? They'll have us restrained by Republican bodyguards."

"It's not a joke, Lor."

"I'm not joking, Mark."

"Let's get a good night's sleep and decide tomorrow. Let's call Gordie."

"I'm not leaving this room."

"Let's get some food."

Mark chewed on lackluster ribs, but Lorraine ignored her shrimp cocktail. Gordon was not at home. They did not leave the room, or set up a crib. Keefer slept between them, savoring her sideways thumb. In the morning, they dressed Keefer in the white dress with the daisies, which looked cleaner than it had when Diane unwrapped it from its tissue paper in Tall Trees. Perhaps it was a duplicate, Lorraine thought. The phone rang, and a car came. Lorraine scrutinized the interior locks. The parking lot at the Nyes' club, Sandpiper Reserve, was crowded, and knots of identical young men, all blond, all wearing red ties, rocked heel to heel, restlessly, in the sun. Inside, interlocking circles of white roses around a smaller circle of red buds, at least four feet tall, stood at the entrance to the ballroom. "Happy Trails, Raymundo," the ribbon read, "from your pals at Knockers."

"I didn't think . . . it's so obvious," Mark said.

"They're not known for taste, they're known for . . . fun," Lorraine answered. She had never openly acknowledged her discomfort with her son-in-law's tour sponsor, a restaurant chain neither she nor Mark had ever visited, which specialized in the Knockouts, bikinied servers in knee-high black leather skates. But it was a big tour, as big as the Nike tour.

Spotting them from across the huge polished floor, Carl Jurgen came gliding over to welcome them. Diane Nye followed him, subdued in a black skirt and white long-sleeved blouse, her artfully cropped hair flattened and, to Lorraine's shock, displaying yellowed roots. "I look like hell," Diane read Lorraine's mind. "But for us, this is the worst. This is the end. This is when I have to admit he's never going to walk in the back door and pick me up . . ."

Drowned in pity and regret, Lorraine opened her arms, and Diane let herself be held. "Do you ever think you're going to lose your mind, Lorraine? I mean, really lose it? Just melt away?"

"Every day."

"What do you do?"

I think of Keefer, Lorraine thought, I remember Keefer. I remember Gordon. "I try to think of the future, because I can't bear to think of the happy past," she said.

"There's no God, Lorraine," Diane said.

"I wonder myself. But I want to think so."

"Do you take antidepressants?" Diane asked.

"Not yet," Lorraine murmured, thinking of her stash.

"There's no God, or God is insane," Diane went on. "Hi, Mark." He touched Diane's arm. "Hi, darlin' baby girl. God might have needed one of them. But both of them? Raymond was . . . he was a gift to the whole world."

"He was a decent, good kid," Lorraine agreed, thinking, Gordon was right. People of goodwill can compromise. She did not envision ever being Diane's friend precisely, but they could share, bind a warp of sharing around their love for Keefer.

"Can you have dinner with us after this?" Diane asked. "I mean, just the four of us? So that we can really talk?"

"Of course," Lorraine said. "Of course, we will."

"Big Ray and I really want to talk to you, grandparent to grandparent. We want to make this work. We want you to be an important part of Baby's life, always." Diane looked into Lorraine's eyes. In the center of Diane's eye, Lorraine imagined she could see an egg yolk, expanding and contracting. "If only you didn't live at the damn North Pole! Pardon my French. But we want her to . . . grow up with all . . . well, you understand, Lorraine. You want the best for her, too. I know you do."

A drizzle of guitar notes urged people to take their seats. Huge and solemn in his gray suit, Big Ray nodded to the McKennas and motioned to Diane. Into Lorraine's ear, Mark said evenly, "I want you to listen to me. I don't want you to flip out. I heard what she said. I know what she said. Now, I am going to leave this room quietly, and you take Keefer up there and sit down, and when I come back, I promise you I will have made arrangements for us to go home. I promise, Lorraine."

Lorraine's heart tumbled in her chest. She showed her teeth to Mark, to the room. She knelt to pick up the baby. The guitarist was playing something sad and Spanish. Then they all heard the faraway sound of a bagpipe, its burr closer and closer, and a young man in Blackwatch plaid strode slowly into the room. He faced the crowd and played the song Ray and Georgia had chosen for their wedding procession, an old ballad called "Wild Mountain Thyme." Her eyes streaming, Lorraine went to sit beside Diane, placing Keefer between them.

Carl Jurgen rose to speak. "All of you here today knew Ray Nye as well as he knew himself. You knew him on the playing field, in school, in the house where he grew up and where his parents still live. I had thought to be older when I spoke at the memorial of my best friend. I thought perhaps it would be Ray who spoke of me. But what I will say here will be the truth, and brief. Ray Nye, Junior, was a phenomenon. He could drink every night, of course I'm not saying he did, Ray and Diane, but he could drink every night, and come home and walk through the Scholars house, tutoring Gordie when he hit the wall on differential equations, reminding me how Locke differed from Hume. I never observed Ray study, and yet, he breathed in knowledge and shared it. He would have given you the shirt off his back, which would have been big enough for you to live in, and the answers on his test paper . . . though, of course"—Jurgen smiled whitely—"of course, he never did. Ray believed it all belonged to everyone.

"And because I believe he is looking down on me, I am going to tell one tiny tale out of school. When Ray and I were sophomores, we believed our fathers did not support us in the fashion we wanted to become accustomed to. And so, up we would go, to Pelican Point, and hang around on the green, stubbing putts, for many hours, until along would come some fellows . . . and Ray could spot these fellows, perhaps because he was, in his own way, so trustful of human nature. We are college students, Ray would tell these fellows—men from Plum, Pennsylvania, or Iron River, Michigan—and we play a little. And we would start, stiff-legged in our earnestness. Now anyone who has ever seen Ray Nye play golf knows he did swing slowly. To watch him swing was to think, this is impossible, this ball is going to dribble off the tee like mustard onto an old man's tie.

"And indeed, that's what we'd do at first. Diane, close your ears if you can't bear this . . ." But Diane was smiling, as was Alison, who'd slipped into the seat beside her mother with her two combed and Eton-suited tots, "We would hit the ball out into the road, and take the distance and the penalty stroke. We would tee off into a tree. And it would be we who would at some point suggest six-point Scotch . . ."

How long, Lorraine thought, had Mark been gone? Did anyone notice, in the blazing charm of this boy's presence?

"I'm not playing well, Ray would admit, and this was not a falsehood. He was not playing well.

"It was on the fifth tee, I would stand back in awe, that Ray would gently, ever so gently, suggest that he and his buddy must catch up, that the fifty cents a point could be a dollar. Was that okay with me? My job was to shake my head, no, ever so emphatically, but by then, Mr. Plum and Mr. Iron River were in the thrall of competition. They didn't need much pushing. And Ray would stand up then, and take about a ten-minute backswing, and send the ball three hundred yards, no more—Pelican Point was a par four, three hundred and twenty off the tee—and it always seemed that we would play downwind . . . and there he would be, putting for the eagle. And he would say, God bless his heart, I'm feeling looser now, should we double?

"Ray Nye, Junior, never had to hustle golf, just as he never had to study to get a score of ninety-seven while the rest of us sweated our gentlemen's Cs. He would not have to hustle heaven, because he was heaven's draft choice."

The smell caught Lorraine's nose at the exact moment that Diane, her face upturned in rapture at Carl's closing words, twitched and turned and grimaced delicately. Keefer's tiny face was red with concentration, her chubby knees tucked up in her folding chair.

Whispering some foolish words of apology, Lorraine

scooped the baby up and carried her, reeking, toward the ballroom door, chanting, thank you, Keefer, thank you. Mark was standing in the arch, just to the left of the giant floral boobs, and they ran. It did not seem to Lorraine that they stopped running for nine hours, until they turned the key in the lock of their house in Tall Trees and saw the message light on their answering machine blinking, blinking red in the dark.

CHAPTER *eight*

The spot at Spirit Lake was their own. They had claimed it, how long before? Eight years? More? For both of them, that long-ago night had been the first time, and it was over before it started, Lindsay comforting him past her own pain and the blood they'd had to wash off her white sweater, past his hideous embarrassment, *it's okay, Gordie, really, it's okay, I wanted it, I wanted to.* He had never been able to think of that except as "innocent," as guileless and tender as a childhood Christmas. He had been, well, not even sixteen, she two years older, the one "good girl" who'd stuck with Georgia as she'd begun her cheerful descent into disorderly conduct. Before that, the sum total of his sexual experience had been one quick handful of Annie Toffer's sweatered boob on the pool table at Tim's ninth-grade birthday party with Mrs. Upchurch fifty feet away in the kitchen preparing Sloppy Joes. As a junior, Lindsay had been sociologically well beyond his reach. "But she wants you," his sister had assured him, and Georgia had come along with the two of them, to throw his parents off the scent.

The movie they'd gone to see was some Swedish thing with subtitles, which, Georgia had convinced their mother, Gordon needed to see for his World Geography class. Just before they entered the theater, by a prearrangement that

Gordon pretended not to notice, Georgia ditched them to join her fellow nail-heads at the mall. Partly because it was boring, partly because of the hot friction of their entwined hands, Lindsay and Gordon had not stayed for the end.

When Lindsay agreed with Gordon's suggestion of a walk at Spirit Lake, he froze, stabbed in the leg by the Empire-State–size erection. The most he'd expected was the excuse to put his arm around her in the blue moonlight. Tim's entirely theoretical opinion was that the best technique for the kiss was to open with a dry lipper, no tongue, and then, if all went well, settle down and explore.

But their first kiss had gone well indeed, and it had been Lindsay, like every other girl he'd ever loved, who upped the stakes, who nudged his shirt out of his pants, so that his softest skin made contact with her softest skin, and there had been no turning back. There had been no condom, either, which had given Gordon a bad . . . oh, sixty-five seconds or so, since everyone knew it was impossible for a girl to get pregnant the first time. He'd known as much about human biology, at the time, as he'd known about quarterly income taxes.

The giddy grin that split his face didn't escape Tim's notice the next day at church youth group. "Don't tell me, McKenna," he'd grimaced. "Don't tell me. I know you did. I can't believe you did. Christallfuckingmighty, you did, didn't you?"

Gordon was sure dozens of strolling couples, toddlers with buckets and shovels, old people with binoculars, teens with six-packs and blunts in their pockets tromped all over this tiny and sexually sacred spit of sand that made a pocket harbor. But he and Lindsay had never, not once, encountered another soul on their visits. Lindsay called that magic. Gordon called it luck. As teenagers, they'd done it there as naked as people could get and still have skin, backward and forward, mouth to breast, mouth to thigh. The first time Lindsay had put her lips to him, he'd exploded all over her chest and the layers of their clothing beneath them. (Another sweater. Another furtive purchase of Shout stain remover from the Smart-Mart, more scrubbing.) As they grew older and realized they might actually live long enough for another try, they'd thrown a sleeping bag over themselves, or left their tops on, saving the Cadillac screw for borrowed beds.

Now they had apartments. They were grown people, well into the fifth or sixth resurrection of their whatever-ship, and still, they came to the lake. Today, it was the Fourth of July, so early in the morning that even the birds still sounded confused.

And though Gordon didn't feel dismal, precisely, it crossed his mind that their place might never be theirs again, in this way.

He had felt older by orders of magnitude in just the few weeks since the inevitability of death and legal struggle and fatherhood settled in. Try, he'd told himself. Glory in each bachelor day left. Each day that Keefer lived at his folks' and he could get up and lazily shuffle off to his run, read the newspaper front to back, play pickup with Church and the guys in the VFW parking lot; each of those days should be a vacation in a room at the top of the universe.

But the ominous opening chords of everlasting responsibility wouldn't be silenced. His mother had played for him the message that Diane Nye left on the answering machine after they'd fled Ray's memorial—a move that in Gordon's opinion had been a bit hysterical. Diane had been smooth, but clearly enraged. "We're sorry you had to leave so quickly, Lorraine," she'd said, "but we'll see you soon. What we would have told you, if we'd had the chance, is that Big Ray is going part-time, and Delia and Craig found us a nice little place in Madison so I can come for the summer. At least for the summer . . ." Big Ray's voice, unintelligible, boomed in the background. "And we're going to file for permanent custody—I don't care, Ray—it's no secret, and you know that was what Raymond wanted, and Georgia, too, we have the notes Mr. Liotis prepared for the will they were going to complete . . . she's a Nye, Lorraine. You know that . . ." More muttering, and then Diane's sharp, "I said I don't care, Ray. Anyhow, you folks take care, and kiss our baby for us."

His mom must have played the message ten times, searching for signs and portents in the inflections. Lorraine had been doing the Grandma Lena stuff big time these past days. Don't put a hat on the bed, Gordie, it's bad luck. Don't open the window, Gordie, when those birds are in the crab apple tree. When a bird flies into the house it means someone in the family will fly out. She was driving him around the bend. His only comfort lay in seeing that the "case" seemed to ease some of the lethargy that had possessed his mother since Georgia's death. Her desperate energy at least made her behave more like the mother he knew.

It was she, in fact, who did most of the communicating with Greg Katt. Gordon didn't feel old or mature enough to "have" a lawyer any more than he would have felt "having" an estate planner.

In fact, he probably needed an estate planner. But whatever. So far as Gordon could tell, all the worry was misplaced. Now that the cards were on the table, it was clear that all the Nyes could really do was delay the inevitable. Gordon would be Keefer's father by September. Madison condo or no, the Nyes, to Keefer, were older acquaintances from far away. The first will was the only will that had ever been signed, and it would have sway. Even when Katt phoned to tell Gordon and his parents that Delia and Craig Cady were making noises about filing a competing petition to adopt Keefer, Katt was quick to point out that this was actually good news. Friends, even if technically second cousins to a child, were not immediate family.

Flurries of documents began drifting down.

The Nyes filed, in Dane County, a petition for permanent

guardianship. But Katt said the Nyes were not residents, so the McKennas' petition, filed first, had precedence. Point, counterpoint.

Of course, Katt would have to motor on down there for a hearing . . . even meaningless petitions needed to be heard, and a hearing was one of those things lawyers never did for free. . . . Some driving, some paying, and things stayed just as they were.

Next, the Cadys turned up with their request to adopt Keefer. Gordon had felt a tick of concern: He'd only just had his home study; he hadn't even had a chance to file! But, Katt reminded Gordon and his parents, at least Gordon *had* a home study. That showed intent. Once an uncle stepped forward, and he had, already, done everything except formally step forward, all those other appeals would fade into expensive, mute irrelevance. Advantage, McKennas.

Katt had called him one night directly, bypassing Lorraine and Mark. Gordon had known instantly, from the sound of the line, that it was not someone he knew. The only person who owned a cell phone who called him regularly was Church, and Tim's cell phone (county-provided) was such an exalted product Gordon could never tell it wasn't a land line. By contrast, Katt's cell phone made him sound like the blub-voices during underwater knife fights on *Sea Hunt*, voices he and Georgia would imitate, in their rubber blow-up pool, making a game of trying to guess what the other person was saying with a submerged head.

Katt had asked about Gordon's relationship with the elder Nyes. What was it like?

"Well," Gordon said slowly, "first it was fine, and now it's lousy."

"I don't mean how do you feel about them, Gordon," Katt replied. Gordon could hear the thwap of paper; what, did Katt have a desk in the car?

Would he have objections, Katt continued, that he hadn't had before, to Ray and Diane maintaining a normal grandparent bond with Keefer? After everything was said and done? Katt would understand, fully understand, if Gordon had reservations—on the other hand, those assurances of the willingness to "be open" on Keefer's behalf would strengthen their position in the eyes of the court.

Gordon, appalled, stammered first no, then yes, then how the hell should he know . . . if they were going to act like monsters, they sure as hell couldn't be around her. But if they were going to be the nice people they had been before, if things settled down once everyone began to recover from their losses . . . "We'd have to wait and see whether things could get back to normal," he said. We who, he thought? He was talking the way celebrities talked, referring to himself in the plural.

"Things will never be exactly normal," Katt reminded him.

"I mean, normal for the way things are now."

"Well, sure."

"Then, yes, I could see them having some . . . contact with her." Gordon felt again huge, regnant, an impostor, as if he were a guy who'd worked weekends doing ten-minute lubes and woke up one morning to learn he'd inherited the whole dealership and people were humbly approaching him, calling him boss. It was hard for him to even imagine himself with the words "access" and "reasonable visitation" in his mouth . . . shouldn't someone be calling his father? Or his mother? But Gordon swallowed on no saliva and kept his voice level as he assured Katt that, yes, theoretically— theoretically!—he'd want Keefer to have access to all her family. Katt said softly, "We'll see, we'll see." And when he put the phone down, Gordon wondered, had he really meant it? Could this breach—deepening as precipitously as a sink-hole, sucking down family ties that had seemed immutable, as ruptured roads and houses and stores and telephone polls seem immutable—could it ever be filled in and covered over?

Could he trust—ever trust—Ray and Diane and Delia and her husband with Keefer?

Had he ever really trusted them with Keefer? Had he really—it stopped him physically, in the middle of the room, like a poke in the chest—given Ray his full due as Keefer's father? It had been Gordon who'd done so many of the paternal chores. Had he thought of himself, long before Georgia died, as her father? As her surrogate father?

Bills began to arrive. Perusing the first month's statements, Gordon decided that Katt, who'd spent fifteen minutes on a letter from the lawyer who prepared Ray and Georgia's original will, was indeed a very slow reader. There were all these hearings, and the cost of a co-counsel expert in adoption—"She's a big gun. From Madison," Katt told them, "and even if we don't really need her, it's better to have her on our side, huh?" This could run into a little money, Katt warned. Not huge money. About the amount it would cost a couple to adopt a child, the lawyer supposed.

Gordon had some savings. He assumed that his parents had plenty of money. He'd not thought about his parents in economic terms—not since they'd point-blank refused to buy him a motorcycle—any more than he'd wondered how packages of socks and underwear had ended up in his dresser drawers when he was a kid or how checks in envelopes carefully marked "Tuition" and "Fees" and "Books" were tucked into his college duffels. Money was not going to be a big problem. If it were, they'd have told him by now. Gordon would need to submit to a psychological evaluation beyond Cindy Rogan's cheerful home study. But not to worry about that, Katt said, it was just standard practice, to rule out any issues. A court-appointed private psychologist would do it for the county. Katt had set it for . . . days from now. July whatever, sometime.

Big deal. Gordon was more worried about the physical for the home study. About the AIDS test. There had been an

AIDS test for the teaching job, and it was fine, of course. But one test didn't mean anything considering that night more than two years ago. In the Galápagos—Christ, he hardly remembered it. The girl, a bewitching United Nations of a woman, black and Asian and green-eyed, the dance floor in that tumbledown hut beach bar, the ziggety music, the superoctane brew that tasted like Tang and fueled him so he was walking on Jupiter. The condom hadn't broken. He knew that. But it had been some kind of hellacious Third World condom, and she'd put it on with her teeth . . . God. He couldn't die. He couldn't die on Keefer. Not even twenty years from now. He'd lain awake on his bed, listening to Keefer sing to herself, on one of only two nights she'd consented to lie down alone for more than fifteen minutes, thinking about AIDS and ebola and all the sweltering, ferally gorgeous places he'd let himself be thrown around in, getting cut and scraped and insect bitten and sunburned when he hadn't thought of being a father to his little leaflet, his orphaned baby. Like a psycho, he'd gone and picked up Keefer and rocked her in front of the window until he was dizzily sleepy and she was wide awake.

All these things were so . . . boring. They were always in the way, like box turtles in the road that could neither be rolled over nor hurried.

He was afraid of getting to be like his mother, throwing salt over her shoulder.

He caught himself thinking of stupid shit he hadn't thought about in years, about his grandma McKenna's brother, awful Harold, asking Lorraine, right in front of him—okay, Gordon had been a kid, but not a deaf kid—if there'd been "insanity in the family of that boy you got."

Not until now, had been his mother's frosty answer.

What had he done to provoke his great-uncle's remark? Some dumb kid thing, he and Pat Chaptman's invention of the Barbie guillotine or something. A mean old man taking out his own stuff on a kid. He still saw it as a teacher. Adults, in all their power, could dish out heavy grief. His teacher acquaintances did it all the time, dividing the town up into "house parents" and "trailer parents." They thought the kids didn't know, but the kids knew everything.

When he was little, he'd ridden his bike through the Wildflower Trailer Park, imagining every weary blonde he saw perched smoking on pull-down metal steps to be his birth mother. Not that he'd had any profound interest in her. His folks had made sure he knew the girl's name—Heather. She'd only been fifteen or so when he made his appearance. When Gordon was still a toddler, Lorraine had told him, Heather's trail went cold somewhere in Milwaukee. They'd done their best, Lorraine apologized, especially given that adoptions that took place in the sixties were supposed to have been "sealed" for reasons of pretense that held sway in a much less frank time. As if he cared. He didn't care. It didn't occupy him. Except to piss him off when someone drew attention to it. The occasional questions, in middle school, *You mean Mrs. McKenna's not your real mother? Who is, then? Olivia Newton-John*, he'd said to that lousy Reilly brat, Ryan. *Get out,* Reilly gasped, *for real?* Ryan Reilly had the brains of a mailbox. *No,* Gordon said, *the truth is, it was really your mother.*

His first fistfight over that.

Gordon could not ever have foreseen how something like adoption, something so ordinary to him, could have become this boiling, festering focus in his adult life. And not even his adoption, or Georgia's. Georgia had gone through the usual TV-movie silliness, imagining her birth mother as a famous Harvard researcher using all the scientific detective skills at her command to find her lost child, intent on bestowing a cache of jewels passed from generation to generation since Marie Vetsera. But they had never shared aching conversations about "who they were." Had he been afraid to delve? Had he been afraid to insult his parents? Or just . . . who cared?

The current wrangling had nothing to do with him and Keefer. He and Keefer were as comfy as a boy with his puppy. He stood her on the counter and held her little hands while he played the Mambo Kings. They flew the shark kite out his bedroom window. She cried the first time she'd run full tilt into the screen coming in from the terrace, but then let him know, endless times after that, using her few words and her fluent little chimp sign language, that she wanted him to close the screen so she could run into it and then fall down on her padded bottom, the two of them belly-laughing like drunks at the Wild Rose. She curled her arms around his neck and held on to fistfuls of his hair when they sauntered through Wilton's Market, him feeling all the eyes on him. Yeah, I'm with the shortie. I'm her pop. She ate Pad-Thai from his outstretched index finger, making him feel for all the world like a mother bird. They mooed at every cow they passed and said goodnight to Georgia's wedding photo when Keefer slept at his place. He'd started having her sleep over, at his mother's urging, just one night a week. But soon they were up to three, the goal being that by the hearing, it would be Grandma's and Grandpa's house that felt like a fun place to visit and Gordon's apartment in the Victorian that felt like home. He'd been intimidated at first by all the directions that accompanied her—wipe butt front to back, eyes from the outer corner in, hold on to the little wisp of hair close to the scalp and comb hair knots from the middle of each strand down, shoot Tylenol into the cheek (and then wipe it off his shirt when it spewed back out). It was all stuff he'd done before, but as an assistant, with his mother or Georgia the managing director. Now he was on his own. He'd mastered the gag when he opened one of the truly terrifying clay-yellow diapers—-how could a person have two entirely different kinds of bowel movements, pebbles and a mass of mush, in one diaper?—and was grateful for the many hours he'd spent dissecting ripe dogfish shark carcasses. He'd overcome the impulse to burst into tears himself whenever she cried, which was a good thing, since she cried often. First came what Mark called the "boo-boo face," a pout so heartbreakingly fetching Gordon couldn't believe Keefer hadn't practiced in the mirror. And then, once the tears started coursing, she'd pop open the snaps on his shirts and press one wet cheek against his neck. He would be utterly powerless. He would feel as huge as Atlas, at the same time. "Baa," she would say, when she kissed him good-bye, "Baa." He first thought she was reminding him to include her juice bottle in her pack, but he gradually got that she was trying to mimic the sound adults made when they blew kisses.

Hour by hour, his barely twenty-pound niece was rearranging huge chunks of his life. Increasingly, when Keefer stayed at his parents', Gordon would find an excuse to call and talk to her on the phone, as though it were not insane to talk on the phone to a baby—"Is she still there? Hello? Keefster? Is that you?" She made spitting noises and pressed the buttons. But when his mother took over and said, "She's smiling really big now, Gordie," he would become too choked to say anything. It was like the feeling he used to have as a teenager when he imagined himself doing the NBC commentary for his own stardom: *Fans of the tournament all over the world are turning their sights on Scotland tonight and asking, who is this Gordon McKenna, a science teacher from Wisconsin . . . And the Nobel prize for biochemistry goes to . . . Gordon Cooper McKenna!*

It was absurd. If he were a woman, he would have considered it hormonal.

Nothing had tickled him more than the terrific bedroom he'd figured out for Keefer at the new apartment. There was a huge walk-in closet off his own bedroom, which he would never have enough clothing to fill. Shopping with Lindsay one night for a shower curtain, he'd come across this big sheepskin dog bed at the Sam's Club—a dog bed for a Shetland pony, by the size of it, and it fit right in to one corner of the walk-in. With her Barbies and her embroidered "Queen of Almost Everything" blanket, she would be set, Gordon supposed. It was dark and cool in there, even when the rest of the apartment baked under that peaked roof. He had never actually tried putting her down in the bed—by the time Keefer gave up, he was so shot that they usually fell asleep together on the floor, with the TV still on.

Up until then, Delia and Craig had made only a few day trips, driving all the way from Madison to take Keefer to the McDonald's for an hour. And then, suddenly, they phoned to request a sleep-over visit.

Agree, Katt advised—in custody, victory goes to those who share.

Their manner, when they showed up, was so off, so beyond the expected awkwardness, that he should have sensed the double cross. By then, their custody petition would have already been prepared. Should he have known? Gordon would later be sure that he'd concocted as many cues and clues as he'd ignored.

You should have known, he'd think later, in Georgia's exasperated voice.

"It's better we not talk, Gordie," Delia told him apologetically, when he carried Keefer out onto his parents' lawn. Mark and Lorraine sat like matched mannequins on the porch swing. They didn't want to use the new sheepskin bed. They had a handmade crib that had once belonged to Alexis. Mark reminded them that Ray and Georgia had never put the baby in a crib. Craig said Keefer would adjust—babies belonged in cribs.

There had been nothing anyone could do.

The worst moment came when Gordon tried to peel Keefer's tenuous little fingers from his neck one by one, and Keefer began to pant and then to sob, "Dory, no no! Dory no!" Nora had driven up by then and was frantically offering everyone coffee, and Lorraine simply jumped up and walked straight backed into the house.

But Mark, and Gordon admired this, came down on the steps and stared steadily, piercingly, at the Cadys, as first Delia, then Craig tried to settle Keefer, who was by then well into one of her full-blown fits, shrieking as though someone were trying to filet her. In the end it was the kid, Alex, Delia's teenager with hair the color of brass pumpkins, who coaxed Keefer into her arms with soothing promises of introducing her to their two baby kitties, one white, one black.

To her credit, Delia was red faced, striking at the corners of her eyes, appealing to Gordon with her gaze, shrugging and shaking her head. Craig had gripped the wheel and squinted straight ahead as though he were trying to find an exit on the Santa Monica freeway.

Once they'd pulled away, Gordon didn't fight his impulse to charge inside and crack open a beer. Lorraine was loading the dishwasher so fiercely she broke a cup. Nora was deep in her coffee, a ski hill of Kleenex at her elbow.

"All babies this age have stranger anxiety," Nora remarked. "You did, Gordie."

"She can sense something," Lorraine said.

"She cannot sense something, Lor," Mark put in, "other than how we feel, is all. I'm sure she'll be laughing in no time."

"That little girl of theirs is a cutie," Nora said.

"Clearly the brains of the outfit," Lorraine muttered darkly.

Of course, in hindsight, it would all seem ludicrously civil.

Why had they been so foolish as to assume that the Cadys would bring the baby back at all? Diane was batty. Delia was no better. What if Diane had simply taken off for Tampa International? Or for the West Fucking Indies? It could have taken them years, literally years, to get Keefer back. People did it all the time . . . that guy in California hid his daughter from his ex-wife for seventeen years! And in the same state!

That doctor who skipped to the Netherlands with her son . . . American law could foam at the mouth, but what would it really avail if the relatives were ready and willing to give up their lives for the purpose and go to prison if they were caught? Why hadn't they even talked about the risk? Because they, themselves, weren't the kind of people who flew off to the Netherlands? Not the kind of people whose family disagreements ended up in tabloid publications? At least not then, not at that point. Mark would have considered such suspicions impolite if nothing else. They were still the kind of people who could at least pretend that good manners and goodwill would triumph in the end.

Later, as fall came on, legal things would begin to slam together so quickly that this one midsummer evening would seem like a plateau of boundless innocence. Gordon had been stupidly grateful for the short break from Keefer to give him the chance to move all his last traps into the new place.

The predominant sense Gordon had, that night when they were all left standing in the blue gold of vanilla-scented gloaming by the vibernum bushes on Cleveland Avenue, was pity for his parents. It was obvious that they couldn't bear too many more wet Kleenex evenings. When they'd all sat down dutifully to consume Nora's colloidal coffee, he had seen Mark and Lorraine, for the first time, as old, deserving of safekeeping. How, he would wonder, had he changed? A handful of weeks ago, he'd been a golden lad whose youth was so striking even beside his same-age cousins, with their growing guts and their company shirts. All at once, he would feel like the parent of everybody.

The first night without Keefer, Gordon fell gratefully into bed and slept twelve hours straight. The second night, he and Church had gone out to play pool. He'd scratched a dozen. He couldn't think. It was sleep deprivation. Muzzy from the beers they consumed, he came home alone, listened to two of Lindsay's three messages, decided it was too late to call back, relished the silence, went to work on his feet with the pumice, did some hammer curls, and then was gripped by such an abrupt forlornness that he rummaged around for Keefer's "Queen of Almost Everything" blanket and folded it under his head as a pillow. And still, he couldn't sleep for shit.

He'd been up for an hour the next morning, when Lindsay showed up for their dawn picnic. She was dressed in a diaphanous white peasant blouse, which Gordon could see right through, over a scrap of bra he could see right through as well. "You look . . . delicious," he'd told her. "You look like an edible flower."

"Other edibles first," Lindsay grinned, unpacking one of her incredible picnics, cheese and avocado sandwiches and champagne with orange juice. They ate a few bites, and then they stripped, stopping to fold their clothes like the old married people Gordon sometimes felt they had become. They waded into the brackish bathwater of Spirit Lake, rinsing, play-fighting, and dunking, until Gordon could no longer pretend to ignore the way her nipples had puckered, each a kiss for him. He held his breath and slipped under to tease open her cool red bush and lick at her as she first wriggled, made as if to push him away. And then her smooth legs, mottled with freckles like sparrows' eggs, opened gratefully. They stumbled out then, he lay on sand already warm and forgiving from yesterday's sun, and Lindsay slid on top and onto him in one supple motion. Digging in her knees, she rocked him, clenched him, milked him, until the fumbling interlude to search the picnic basket for the condom, which Lindsay always brought; and when he was finished, he spilled champagne on her belly from thirst more than lust and tongued her for as long as his dry lips would bear, and then she rode his thumb until she collapsed with a sigh. They never came together, always took turns. Lindsay was too focused on Gordon's pleasure while he was inside her to let go, no matter how he cajoled her. She was as considerate and quiet and docile in sex as she was in everything else. That didn't bother Gordon. He loved their sex as he loved other mild pleasures in life, as he loved sleeping outside or his aunt Nora's cherry applesauce. Screwing Lindsay was like wrapping himself in sun-dried towels; afterward, he felt cleaner.

But there were times when, eyes closed, he would catch himself recalling the exquisite timing of Liza the stripper, his first after Lindsay, his premiere experience of pure wenching, the summer after he got out of high school, when he and Lindsay had "agreed" to see other people. Liza also was older, twenty-two, but she lived with her mother, and their entire relationship took place either on the Union Terrace at the university or in the backseat of his car on the many Friday nights he drove to Madison to watch her dance naked in front of fifty other men, lunatic with the knowledge that only he, among all of them, would actually get to do what every one of them was fantasizing. In Lindsay's arms, he would replay his and Liza's simultaneous yesses and no's and hoarse shouts, her small hands first tickling, then clenching, then slamming the flesh of his butt, both of them lost in feral fucking of their own, as if they were conjoined only by accident. But, alas, Liza called mail-order clothing catalogues "magazines" and read them carefully. Gordon privately feared what they said was true. It was either one or the other; the action in a girl was distributed wholly either heads or tails.

Having brushed off most of the sand and pulled on their shirts, Lindsay and Gordon ate, drank, and watched the sun rise weightily, so plushy orange it looked three-dimensional. The mist that gave the lake its name twirled and eddied. Lindsay looked tired; she had to work today at the Soap

Bubble, where she had, after a long and much-discussed bout of guilt, accepted the post of acting manager when Georgia became too ill to work. She'd told Gordon she'd overcome most of her initial nervousness, got pages of compliments from the owner on her color sense and customer skills. She thought the post would now be permanent, which was great, since she would now not have to consider option two, going back for a master's in marketing. Lindsay could never imagine leaving Tall Trees, her parents, or her married sister. Her final two years at UW-Stevens Point had been an agony of homesickness.

Today, the town would be filled with vacationers from cabins on Big Heart Lake; there would be a Main Street sidewalk sale, a beer tent, and pony rides before the fireworks. The traffic in soap would be brisk, Lindsay told Gordon, especially the new stuff they had, which was sawed off a huge block and sold in chunks, soap embedded with stars or spangles. He thought, as he often did, how Lindsay's looked like a big cat's face, huge Russian cheekbones, green eyes with nearly invisible long lashes tawny as the sunburned grass around the lake. When she wore makeup and twisted up her bushy red hair, which she rarely ever did, she looked like another woman, an actress or a model. Men turned their heads and clutched at their hearts in admiring pantomime, and Lindsay never noticed. Her heart was at rest with Gordon. Why wasn't his? He watched as she smiled, shut-eyed, into the sun, and noticed fine crinkles at her eye corners. It stabbed him, how long she had waited for him, how much she had forgiven.

"The sun," she said, "it's so gorgeous."

"Do you know why it looks like that?"

"Well, it's morning."

"No, why it's so big."

"Because it's big."

"It's an optical illusion, Lins. Your eye sees it as big because of what's around it on the horizon, the trees and the telephone poles. You don't see those when it's high in the sky."

"If it's a trick of the eye, how come you can't make it not happen?"

"You can't tell yourself no to see water on the road when it's hot out, even if there's no water there, can you?"

Lindsay poured her quarter-inch of champagne, still cold, on his foot. "Why can't you just let the sun be the sun, Gordie? It's just beautiful, is all."

"Why can't you still think it's beautiful and understand it? Isn't it more interesting?"

"Not really."

Why, Gordon thought, did he torment her?

At any rate, that effectively ended the picnic. As if on cue, a cloud slid over the sun, and they both reached for their chinos. Gordon noticed they were dressed like ten-year-old twins—beige slacks, white shirts.

"I have to get to the store," Lindsay said. "I'll drop you off. Is Keefer coming home today?"

"Later on."

"Just two nights with them?"

"Just two. She's only sixteen months old."

"Do you know how smart she is, Gordie?" Lindsay was busily packing up. The formed plastic plates were dirty, but Lindsay still nested them, one inside the other, and put the glasses in their elastic holders. "The other day, I counted how many words she can say. It's, like, fifteen. If you count the doggie sound and the cow sound. Dory and Nana and Nona and Papa, and when she sees me, she says 'Bunny.'"

"She thinks you look like a rabbit."

"Cut it out," but Lindsay smiled.

"It's the ears," Gordon said, leaning up to kiss her. "No, really, she's trying to say your name. And she says 'plane' and 'uh-oh.' She says 'uh-oh' a lot, when she's destroying my house . . ."

"You're crazy about her."

"She gets all those smarts from . . . my sister. Georgia was the smart one."

"I can't talk about . . . I can't talk about Georgia." Huge, round tears quivered, then spilled. "I think of her all day. There are still laminated signs on the wall at the store . . . in her handwriting. Can you imagine how that is for me? Don't make me cry. I have to work. Do I look okay?"

"Perfect."

"Really."

"You can see your nipples through that shirt. You might want to consider a turtleneck."

"I'll change," Lindsay beamed, delighted at a hint of jealousy from him. "You're going to be a great father, Gordie."

"I hope so."

"And you're not alone. You have, for example, me."

"You're a pretty virgin mother yourself, Lins."

"You make me sound like Saint Mary."

"Hardly."

"I think I'm a good . . . mother. And I'm no virgin. Thanks to you."

"Me and David Robb and . . . what was that guy's name with the old Silver Cloud?"

"My life according to my boyfriends' cars . . ."

"What was his name?"

"Wesley Tanco."

"See? You could have been Mrs. Tanco."

"I never did."

"What?"

"I never . . . slept with them."

"Come on, Lins. I don't care."

"I know you don't care, but I didn't."

"Surely, you went out with that Tanco guy for like . . . a year or something."

"But we only fooled around."

"Well, at least that was something . . ."

"It wasn't . . . what we do."

"What are you trying to say?"

"That I've only ever done it with you."

"That's . . . wow, Lins. You didn't have to tell me that."

"What's that supposed to mean? Aren't you glad?"

"Sure I'm . . ." Gordon stopped himself. Was he glad? Was he proud? Was he claiming some sort of pledge he hadn't made? "Of course, I'm glad, I guess. But it wouldn't matter. I mean, we're here now. It's us now."

"Is it?"

"What?"

"Us now? Are we together?"

"Either that or I was just raped by some wood nymph out there."

"You know what I mean."

He did, and he would rather have had dental surgery than start the discussion now, before he knew where he wanted it to go. Please, he thought. Not now. The whole dilemma of him and Lindsay was like the secretary desk that had belonged to his grandma McKenna. Gordon had kept the desk in the same place for five years, moving it from one flop to the next, setting it up with all the sandpaper and stain laid out on newspaper next to it, as if he were about to start refinishing it at any moment. The last time he'd checked, the stain had congealed. He might never get around to actually doing it. And still, he could not imagine parting with the desk. It belonged to him.

He should end this now.

He didn't want to end it.

He didn't want to begin it.

Why couldn't they just live in the moment? For the moment? Why was it always necessary to give up the luscious mouthfuls of now, which the possibility of their passing only made sweeter, because they couldn't be frozen and sealed in a package marked "Forever Fresh"?

"Lins," he said, "I don't know who I am or where I am right now. I don't know what the future holds for me, or for us. I know I'm going to be with Keefer, but I don't know anything else. And I know I'm here with you right now, and it's where I want to be."

"What am I to you?"

"Jesus, Lindsay. You're my friend. I love you. You know that. I'd do anything in the world for you." That was not a lie. He'd do anything in the world, at this moment, for example, to teleport Lindsay to work before he could say something they'd both regret.

"I don't want to be your friend."

"Too late," said Gordon, but he knew exactly what she meant. At least he owed her that much, and it wasn't fair to play stupid. "I know, I know. You don't want to be only my friend. In that context, it's kind of insulting. I just can't say for sure, well, in one year, we're going to do this or do that . . ."

"I'm not asking for you to say that we're going to do anything—"

"But you are asking, what does this mean?"

"And the answer?"

"I don't know that any better than you do, Lins. And, anyway, that's not all my choice, is it? That's up to both of us." He wanted badly to believe that. He wasn't some goddamned spoiled martinet, who wanted all the princesses of the kingdom driven before him . . . he was a father! Almost! If Keefer were grown, he wouldn't want a man to call all the shots for her. What if Keefer one day loved someone as Lindsay loved him? Some spoiled, grabby bastard?

But that was different. Keefer was his child.

Or was it different? Lindsay was a beloved child. What would gimlet-eyed Al Snow, an actuary with an actuary's soul, say if he knew not only how freely Lindsay had offered the peach, but how thoughtlessly he had gobbled, then got the taste for a pear, or a navel orange . . .

Lindsay allowed her great eyes to go wider, as if something within had slackened. He had to move. He heaved himself out of her car on First Street, suddenly worn out, suddenly annoyed that he'd gotten up at five in the morning on a holiday; she put a hand out and stopped him. "Now, don't worry," she said.

"About what?"

"About . . . the evaluation. That's just a few days from now, Gordie. It's like . . . next week."

"You don't have to remind me," he'd said sharply.

Did they all think him a dunce? His mother would remind him at the fireworks that night as well. He'd been cuddling Keefer, who, to his delight, had scrambled off his father's lap and onto Gordon's when the first rocket exploded. Gordon wrapped her in his cotton sweater, and thought of the previous year, when he'd handed his tiny niece out the upstairs window to Georgia, and then climbed out after her, so they could watch the fireworks from the roof. Ray'd been gone, to some tournament in Mississippi or Alabama, wuffling around on some wretched, groomed piece of reclaimed swamp.

Gordon's mother had gone bananas. What if they dropped the baby? Lorraine didn't know that they were Alpinists of the roof, that they'd flicked dozens of ashes from dozens of butts into the gutters. He'd remembered, as Keefer squealed and patted him with her tiny hand as if to reassure him not to be afraid, Georgia's face washed in green and gold . . . look, Keefer, diamonds in the sky . . .

Of course he'd remember the appointment. How could he forget?

$\mathcal{H}$e had forgotten.

Faith was still dumbfounded when people forgot, just nipped out to buy nail tips at the Sam's Club when she showed up on their doorsteps for appointments planned months in advance. The same people who vowed tearfully that their rights to their children were more important to them than their own lives—and she did not, for a single instant, doubt this (the ownership of a child was elemental to the majority of people)—then spaced out on the very interviews that could support their case.

It should not surprise her. Even self-aware people were prone to avoidance. And the self-aware were not Faith's customary clients.

Gordon had been in the shower. She'd rung the buzzer politely, twice, then leaned on it, and then finally rung the other apartment. A fierce-faced woman nearly ripped the outer door from its hinges, spitting out a perfunctory "Yes?" When Faith explained her errand, the woman, who introduced herself as Judy Wilton, the owner of the house, quieted down and explained how fortuitous it was that she was there at all; she wouldn't have answered either except for having come home from the store to shower off the cheese smell from the store before her annual gyn checkup, a little more than Faith had needed to know.

Gordon opened the door in his gym shorts, thankfully not his boxers, with Keefer toddling naked behind him.

The stern faces of the two callers alarmed him.

"What's wrong?" he asked sheepishly.

"You're okay, then," Judy Wilton said, ruffling her spiky hair. "You didn't answer."

"We were . . . busy," Gordon said, "What's the matter? Were we making too much noise? We were in the shower."

"Evidently," said the other woman. "I'm Faith Bogert?"

He smiled and cocked a finger at her and said, "Here's looking at you, kid." But she saw the realization dawning in his face, even as he made his feeble joke, that this was the social worker and he had forgotten his appointment.

Judy Wilton, meanwhile, whirled and stomped down the stairs.

Faith reflected that people always said the same thing when they heard her name. "It's with an *e*, not an *a*," Faith said. She always said that. "No relation to the actor."

That had the effect of relaxing him. Faith noticed his shoulders sliding down from their protective posture. Good. "May I come in?"

"Of course, I'm sorry. Well, the *C* in my name is for 'Cooper,'" he said, blushing, suddenly aware of his clothing deficit, "not that anyone ever knows that. My dad was this big space buff."

Faith had no idea what he was talking about. But she nodded. "Parents," she said, with a practiced sigh.

Gordon swept a pile of laundry from the sofa to make room for her. He really was good-looking, Faith thought. The kind of man who never noticed her, who would see right through her if she walked down the aisle of the church stark naked. She was practical about men; her mother had seen to that. She didn't even send prayers after the ones who wouldn't be worth the effort. Pretty boys never went the distance; she'd known that since middle school, before she'd ever heard of a narcissistic personality. She stifled the reflex irritation with herself for having felt so fat that morning that she'd resorted to her stirrup pants and a tunic—stirrup pants were like a genetic marker for women who had something between their neck and their knees that they wanted to cover.

Never mind. This guy was where he should be. He wasn't paying more attention to her than to the little girl. He didn't let the baby run past him out into the hall. There were stairs out there. He was probably a good guy.

Her job was to find out whether he'd be a good father.

Faith had been carefully named (her middle name, to her despair, was Angel). She'd been carefully raised by a mother few people thought had the gumption for it. That she'd gone to college at all, much less become a psychologist (and there were people who hadn't thought she'd had the guts or the genes to do that, either), was a by-product of her own rearing. The single daughter of a single mother, she'd turned out better than anyone in Plano, North Dakota, had expected. That was a factor in her getting this job, a weighty job. She was only a twenty-seven-year-old whose ink hadn't dried on her Ph.D., still in her postdoc supervision. But her boss gave her cases they called A Gees, their private code for "anybody's guess," evaluations mandated by nasty divorces or investigations into charges of neglect. Faith had already seen much during her internships, public and private—a pregnant ninth-grader with a baby and fifteen possible candidates for the lucky sperm; grandmoms who went to play bingo and left six-month-olds asleep, watched over by Dobermans who bit the sheriff's deputy after she forced the door. And worse, much, much worse. A nine-month-old with gonorrhea of the mouth. One perfect five-year-old—the object of a feral struggle between two divorcing parents—who could tap dance like a Mouseketeer but screamed whenever she saw a cigarette.

Faith's mother had been poor, a waitress literally until the day she died three years before, struck head-on by a drunk while driving home from work. Faith had not only the credentials, but the chops. She could see past dirty hair and ragged pajamas to identify love unlearned but devoted, and past Baby Gap clothes to dirt that would never show in a photograph. She understood her prejudices and guarded herself against them.

She'd already visited the busy, sparkling interior of the Cadys' condo—mermaid wallpaper already going up for Keefer; the older girl's room plain white, no attempt to impose any decorating ideas on a teen, good job, there—it had turned her heart, she couldn't deny. And Delia, who ran her own cosmetics business from the house. Faith admired her skill in making more money than her husband while still keeping up the impression of a wife at home, so important to both of them.

Delia was probably a little too organized, the kind who offered a coaster before the guest accepted a drink. But Faith knew Delia would offer the same drink to a bum or a senator. There was something in Delia of Faith's own mother, that same combination of deep pride and caution. She had no illusions about the advantages of the two-parent family. All a child really needed was the absolute love of one relatively sane parent.

Craig didn't really loom large in the Cady family unit. Craig was a little uptight. His relationship with Alexis Tyson, the child of his wife's previous marriage, who lived with them except for two weeks each summer when she went to visit her motorcycle mechanic papa, was clearly a source of strain. The girl's room was the typical cyclone scene, and Craig winced when he opened the door. Craig might have stayed at home with his folks just a couple of years too long—thirty-five was pretty late for a first marriage. And yet, despite their shared devotion to religion, neither Cady insisted that Alexis attend Cornerstone Community Church with them on Wednesdays and Sundays. The girl had no interest in Sunday school—"Why would anybody want more school?" she'd asked.

It was a sort of garden-variety rebellion, a lot less harrowing than others she could have chosen. Delia and Craig seemed to know that and took care to drop her off at the pool or the library with her own cell phone for emergencies. This pointed to a welcome flexibility that didn't always go along with a big emphasis on organized religion, as well as an untutored wisdom: After all, the great majority of premature sexual experimentation took place when the parents of young teens were at work.

Both Craig and Delia would come up a little high on the inventories for obsessiveness. She would explain in her report to the guardian ad litem that the Cadys' results on the MMPI-Inventory II weren't exactly reliable, but no cause for alarm—they would not only be "faking good" the way everyone did who wanted the child, filling in all the most virtuous circles on those endless questions, but they would actually be "too good." As born-agains, they would have to be less suspicious about their fellow men than others.

For Faith, the most telling point in the Cady evaluation had been the play observation. That couldn't be faked. Delia was a real mother who knew that playing with a toddler basically meant following the little person around, offering a sponge when the chubby fist closed determinedly around a fork, changing activities every ninety seconds, hanging loose when the kid kicked over the blocks. The outlets were covered but the cabinets that held the Tupperware were open.

Craig had done the right thing, too, during playtime. Nothing. He'd held back. He'd had no idea what to do with Keefer, so he'd watched his wife. The Cadys had no children of their own, he'd confided, because Delia's health was delicate. Delia Cady had some muscle weakness, and suspected MS, which had disabled her mother's sister. Faith would have bet it was stress.

Gordon's house was also neat and safe, if not exactly

child friendly. There were half-filled glasses of water sitting around and a gymnasium's worth of bats and rackets and golf clubs . . . yikes, and a jockstrap. The outlets in use were in plain sight at baby eye level, though the ones not in use had plastic caps.

Still, Keefer wasn't yet in residence full-time.

Gordon began to show Faith around. He seemed very proud of the dog bed.

Faith had to smile.

She didn't smile, however, when Gordon twice let his arm brush her shoulder for a trace of a second too lingeringly. He was checking her out, trying to figure out if she was unmarried and susceptible. Perhaps unaware that he was doing it at all. Faith offered to hold the baby while he got into some clothes.

"I don't know if she'll go to you."

"Well, they usually do," Faith told him, taking Keefer and turning, in one motion, to point out the robin tending to its nestlings in the fragile birch outside Gordon's living room window. "Lookee. Baby birds," she said, and Keefer—what a doll she was—made peeping noises.

"I'm surprised," Gordon said. He's disappointed, thought Faith.

"Well, better get dressed before she decides against it," Faith instructed him. He emerged in two minutes, still mostly wet, but at least decent.

"I'm sorry I was still in the shower when you got here," he began. "It's right on the calendar. But she was up all night. She got a cold at the Cadys' house. I know that's prejudiced of me. I feel like, whenever she's away from me, they don't look after her as well."

"What did you do about it?"

"Well, I can't kill them."

"I assume that's a joke."

He'd given her a sharp glance. "Of course. The Cadys are

good people. They just don't know the Keefster very well."

"I meant about her cold."

"There's a routine. You have to feed her buttered noodles. That's her comfort food. And then, I put her in the bed with me . . . that's okay, isn't it?"

"Plenty of people have their kids sleep in their bed with them."

"And then we do the chant."

"The chant?"

"Well, I make this noise, like a little motor. And then she starts to make it, too. And I pet her head. And she falls asleep. Of course, then I can't move."

"Move?"

"Well, then I have to stay there with her. So she doesn't roll out. Like, last night, I was going to do some lesson plans, but I didn't put them by the bed before she fell asleep. And the chant can put me to sleep, too. I'm just a sleeper. So, I guess that's how I forgot. Though my mother did remind me last night at the fireworks."

"Did they scare her?"

"Nah. Nothing scares her," Gordon told Faith, with a sniff of pride, "except when you hand her to someone she doesn't know." The previous year, Gordon said, he and his sister climbed out on the roof with Keefer to watch the display over Rotary Park. "My sister and I used to sit out there and talk in the summer and flick the butts . . ."

"You're a smoker, then?"

"No, I don't mean . . . cigarettes. We were kids. You know, in college. We weren't . . . smoking when we were out there with the baby. We were just watching the fireworks. The other . . . What I was talking about was years and years ago."

"Ahhhh, yes."

"And it really wasn't a hundred times. I didn't do the drug thing much. Neither did my sister. Really."

"I'm not thinking that," Faith told him warmly.

"Good," Gordon let out a long breath. "Keefer, Keefer. Your mama loved you." Hearing her name, Keefer toddled over and leaned against her uncle's knee.

"Oh, gosh," Faith sighed, going for empathy, enlisting his cooperation, "we have a million miles of ground to cover. And these things." She took out her sheaf of forms, the MMPI and the MCMI-III, the sentence completion sheet. "This junk takes hours to do. Who's going to watch the baby?"

"Uh, well, I am," said Gordon, his eyes popping. They were truly gray. Most people, Faith had observed from having to observe so many, described misty, changeable eyes as gray or green if they'd been to college, and blue if they had not. It was a weird artifact.

Few, however, no matter how they described them, really had gray eyes. She hauled her gaze back to the folders.

"I'm afraid this stuff is something you really have to concentrate on," Faith apologized. "It's like the SATs. If you even get a mark in the wrong place—"

"I'll end up saying I prefer killing animals to building birdhouses," he said. "Or dressing up in women's clothes and making phony nine-one-one calls."

"Something like that. It's a personality inventory." Faith made quote marks in the air.

"I only have one."

"What?"

"Personality."

"Let us be the judge of that," Faith replied, walking the line.

"I'll call my mom."

"Is she . . . at work?"

"She's home because it's summer. She's a teacher. We're both teachers. My dad was a teacher, too. Now, he's a vitamin butcher."

"A . . . butcher?"

"He sells vitamins. Like, to all the health-food stores on

the planet. Sort of helps . . . plan them. He works at Medi-Sun." Gordon picked up the phone and called Lorraine, who said she'd be over within ten minutes.

"Okay. We'll just do a couple of things while we wait," Faith went on, "stuff I have to cover. Turn on the big lights, you know."

"Serious business."

"The most serious."

"Shoot."

"You're adopted," she'd said, when they sat down, Keefer in a diaper and a onesie planted with her musical blocks between Gordon's feet.

"I . . . I was adopted, yes," he acknowledged. Faith picked up on the tense.

"Of course," she said.

"I mean, as my mom always says, you know, it's not a life condition."

"Of course. What I meant was, do you think that's going to give you any special insights into raising Keefer?"

"Well, sure. My parents always told me certain things. . . . Like, you were so wanted we had to . . . you know, go out of our way to get you, to have you . . ."

"And . . . well, that's not true for Keefer."

"No. Yes and no. I mean, I could have done the same thing as Caroline Nye and Alison Nye, Ray's sisters.'"

"In choosing not to try for custody . . . but they already have families—"

"Caro doesn't. And it's still selfish."

Faith could see him panic, wish for an air hook to reclaim the last word.

"I don't mean selfish. I mean, she's their brother's child, too. But Caroline is apparently getting a divorce, and Alison, I don't even know Alison. I guess they have their reasons."

"Do you wish they'd shown more interest?"

"No. It's not like I want the competition."

"Did you always intend to adopt Keefer?"

"I guess so. Sure."

"Still, raising a baby is a big deal. And facing a custody case."

"Yeah. I guess it's a big case now, for sure. I hope they pull out of it and it doesn't get that far. It would be a disagreeable business. Delia and Craig are nice people. Not exactly people I'd hang out with but . . ." Gordon scanned Faith's face, which she'd composed to look impassive yet interested. "Still, I mean, this isn't my top idea of how to spend a summer."

"What is?"

"Oh"—Gordon leaned back, stretching out golden legs— "traveling. I used to work for this outfit that took families or corporate types on sort of semiscientific cruises. Really, vacations. But you'd end up seeing something . . . not like the Epcot Center."

"Won't be doing much of that now."

"No," Gordon sighed, "I guess not." Faith waited, giving him room for the obligatory follow-up, that Keefer was worth it, of course. It didn't come.

"I'm hearing that maybe this is all kind of overwhelming."

"Well, it is kind of overwhelming. Not Keefer. I've always helped out with Keefer, because . . . her mom, my sister, was sick, and her dad was . . . away a lot of the time. We didn't blame Ray. He played golf. He was just starting to make it pay, you know? Georgia accepted it. She wanted that for him."

"But the whole parenthood thing. It's huge." Faith leaned forward, making a deliberate, visible effort to set her clipboard down beside her, as if she might neglect to take notes.

"Well, yeah. Being a parent. It's . . . like full-time all the time. No overtime." Gordon laughed. "I guess I had it kind of easy."

"Not everyone would say that."

"How so?"

"Well, being adopted . . ."

"There's no . . . you know, there's no difficulty with being adopted."

"But there are issues."

"All I hear about is issues, these days."

"Well, it's one thing to think about that kids don't ordinarily have to think about."

"Are you adopted?"

"No."

"Well, how do you know what people think about it?"

"The literature. It's known."

"Who does the literature come from?"

"I don't get you."

"Well, it comes from psychologists who were . . . studying people who were already having trouble with something, or else they wouldn't have been talking to a psychologist, right?"

"No," Faith said, "just ordinary, well-adjusted, normal adoptees, too."

"I mean, look at that. That word. *Adoptees*. It's like you had a limb removed or something."

"Well, it's a word for a way of being—"

"It's a word like, you know, back when people started calling people 'adult children of alcoholics.' Then, it was just shortened to 'adult children.' Well, everybody gets to be an 'adult child' sooner or later, right?"

"I guess. But Mr. McKenna, the point is, I'm trying to learn what you hope to help Keefer understand about her background."

"Well, it's not like my own situation is. Or was."

"How so?"

"Well, I am her birth family."

"I see what you mean. Though, not technically."

"Well, now I'm not following you."

"I mean, yes, you've known Keefer since she was born, but you are not a member of her biological family, since—"

"Her mother was my sister. I don't see how much closer you can get."

Faith backed off, sitting back in the chair, trying to give him room.

"I know what you're saying, but Georgia and I grew up together. I was there when Keefer was born. I guess you could say I know firsthand everything you could know about being adopted and everything you could know about Keefer's birth parents, and so . . ."

"And so?"

"And so," Gordon said, revealing a smile of unnerving evenness, "I'm perfect."

Then, the doorbell sounded, and Faith thought, we'll see. We'll see.

CHAPTER ten

*A*t least the other shoe had dropped. Any more pussy-footing around might have driven Lorraine over an irretrievable edge. Even Mark—who still maintained that he would not surrender to bitterness—could not contain his disdain for Craig and Delia after they made it clear they wanted to adopt Keefer.

To take Keefer, a child they barely knew, from the people who had raised her and, thus far, raised her well.

The outrage. To describe the Cadys, Mark had used phrases he had never used for anyone else in their three-plus decades of life together—"deceitful finger-pointing" and "hypocritical ironies."

And when it came to Diane Nye, though Mark no longer said anything, his silence was ominous.

Lorraine could no longer think of Diane Nye without a wince of humiliation. When Lorraine had finally lost it, she'd said things to Diane Nye that made her ashamed. But Diane had been the one who turned up the flame.

She and Mark and Gordon, with only the occasional small teakettle shriek, had gone about all summer long with a tight lid on the simmering kettle. They'd pretended to be strong and showed one another concerned, contained faces. They went out of their way to help each other out. Nora made only the slightest comment one day that the lavender was full in, and no one had laid a sweep on Georgia's grave, and everyone knew how much Georgia loved lavender. By sundown there was a foothill of lavender, their gently moving petals, to McKenna eyes at the plateglass picture window across the street, a profusion of violet butterflies. Each one of them had taken on the obligation to do it, out of consideration for the others.

In all their dealings with Greg Katt, they remained courteous, hoping not to come off as hysterical. True, lately he seemed to pull a new gremlin out of the custody hat with each phone call, each meeting, each pleading. True, he seemed bent on senselessly frustrating them by requiring them to witness endless proceedings at which they never spoke and barely understood what was going on.

They avoided people outside the family, and people outside the family avoided them, as if the freakishness of the McKenna disaster challenged ordinary interaction and might possibly be contagious. Natalie Chaptman, Karen Wright, Sheila Larsen, and others from the church abandoned their program of bringing over casseroles. Lorraine's formal thank-you notes made it seem as though friends were demanding more of the McKennas by helping than by leaving them alone. Mark and Lorraine, sometimes with Gordon and Lindsay, had begun eating Sunday dinners out at the farm with Nora and Hayes. The head of the table was saved specially for Keefer's high chair, even when Keefer was in Madison with the Nyes. Nothing was said to inaugurate a tradition. They simply were asked one Sunday, went, then went again the next. By the third Sunday, they were expected.

Privately, they burst. One bashed the hard bag. One beheaded the rhododendrons. One stood at the bedroom window in her room, watching the lazy moon rock onto her back, while on the chair lay an album open to photos of Georgia in Ojibway war paint at the county fair, Georgia with two teeth missing and her parakeet, Rhoda, perched on her head. One bit a pillow and cried hard, secret tears.

It was not Diane's intention to blow the lid on all the restrained anguish. But that was the result.

To begin with, Lorraine couldn't believe the gall. Diane came on her own to pick Keefer up for a weekend visit. This had to be on the advice of counsel. Either that, or the woman was a nitwit. She had to know she was like fresh kill in the lion's den.

After that day, Gordon said he wished they had some kind of pneumatic tube through which they could whoosh Keefer back and forth, and goofy as that sounded, Lorraine knew exactly how he felt.

Keefer was to be available to her paternal relatives for twice-monthly visits at 5:00 P.M. on Fridays. It was more like 2:00 when Diane showed up.

Lorraine had been at her desk in the living room, halfheartedly concocting a pastiche of fall lesson plans from successful no-brainers of previous years. Before Georgia's illness, she'd given herself the shakes brimming over with new ideas for upcoming terms. Her last years of teaching were to be her most daring. Mark had even begun helping her knock together a little darkroom in an unused closet in the art room so that she could do a three-week unit on black-and-white photography. The *National Geographic* photographers who were working on the woodland people's dig had donated three perfectly serviceable old cameras. One guy was even ready to show Lorraine the rudiments of hand-coloring photos. Imagine the gifts the kids could make for their parents!

But now she would only do her best.

She would earn her pension.

At least the early days would be easy. She'd do things like face-and-vase exercise, for training the sides of the brain to truly experience their reverse connection to the hands, asking the right-handed kids to draw a profile of a face on the left side of the paper, facing the center, and then leading them through the left brain, gradually teasing out of them the awareness of how their right brains could "feel" shape and line in a non-verbal way. She'd teach self-collages. Word collages. Scrapbook collages. Pinch pots and then thrown pots . . . art-school stuff. It would not be easy. It would murder a part of Lorraine to sleepwalk through her teaching. Lorraine had just gotten up to treat herself to peppermint tea and a Percodan when the doorbell rang.

It had done her heart good to see that Diane looked ten years older.

And had gained weight.

Hey, sweetie, Lorraine called to Georgia's spirit, look at that big roll of dough over the waist of her Puritan shorts. Bet those shorts weren't from the children's department.

"Hello," Lorraine had said. "Are you early?"

Diane merely shrugged.

"Well, Diane," Lorraine said then, "what are we going to do for three hours?" Trade recipes, she thought? Forget we're embroiled in a bitter lawsuit and discuss new fall fashions?

"I never know how long it's going to take to get to somewhere," Diane explained. "You-all seem to be fixing the roads all the time, and all the roads go in circles."

Suddenly and utterly, Lorraine understood the sense in which her students used the phrase "Whatever."

Diane offered to wait until five. She had to take her cleansing tea, after all. Or she could sit outside in the car.

Lorraine was flabbergasted. "Forget it," she said, "you can take Keefer early."

Lorraine had the car seat, so Gordie couldn't bring Keefer over. She suggested Diane follow her in her own car, but Diane said she was sure she'd get lost. Diane assured her that "the kids," by which she meant Delia, had everything Baby needed, a whole other set of toys and clothes (Diane-type clothes, Lorraine assumed, shiny patent-leather Mary Janes with no arch support, and teeny golf togs with flag and alligator embroidery, shelves of pouting, sultry, hideously buxom ballerina Barbies, pink plastic purses with toy lipsticks like sticks of lard, terrifying videos like the one Keefer brought home, about a family of cucumbers who cried because their daddy was run over by the wheelbarrow). Lorraine had seen the smudgy Polaroids tucked into Keefer's diaper bag, tucked in as if to taunt her and Mark and Gordie with the largesse of that good ol' Southern-fried Christians-R-Us upbringing. Fuming, Lorraine thought, why had Georgia, her finely strung, impatient daughter, ever suborned that Delia, anyhow? Because she was lonely, Lorraine answered herself, lonely and away from Lindsay and them and all the things of home, away from Gordie off on one of his goddamned save-the world joy-sails, stuck on a sand spit, hungry for company and inclusion. That had forever been Georgia's tender heel—wanting to be wanted.

Before they left, Lorraine called Gordon, warning him not to forget the flannel shirt of Ray's that Nora had stuffed to make a pillow Keefer called "Day-doe." Throw in her plain wooden blocks, too, Lorraine added, and her duck-family puppets. Let them see what toddlers ought to play with.

"She'll be happier if she has the same things every day," Lorraine told Diane. "I'm sure Delia knows that."

"I'm sure she knows best," Diane agreed, with exasperating complacency.

They'd set off, Diane perched rigidly on the passenger bucket as if she were on a roller-coaster ride. Lorraine caught a profile instant of Diane's slack, powder-pale expanse of chin, its pert previous architecture still evident but wistful, like a ghost who doesn't know about its demise, and she felt soiled, sorry. No good would come of a verbal broadsword battle between old broads, each with their favorite swords. Lorraine could have demolished Diane— "Thank goodness, you've gotten your appetite back, Diane"—but it would have been too easy.

Then Diane said, "Don't take it out on Delia. Say whatever you want to me. I know that you're unhappy about how this has turned out."

"You can hardly say things have 'turned out,' Diane," Lorraine replied, deliberately staring ahead, braking a little sharply, aware that Diane's head bobbed, "There's been no decision made. And no matter what happens with Keefer, this is still an awful time for me. What's going on between our families only makes it worse. Because my daughter is still gone."

"And my son."

"And your son. Neither of us can replace . . . our children with Keefer."

"It's a family issue."

"It is, but the family at issue is Keefer's family. It's not what's best for you and Ray or Mark and me. It's not even what Ray and Georgia may have wanted, at any given time. It's what's best for Keefer. We all have to think of it from her point of view."

That sounded wise. Wiser than Lorraine felt. For all she knew, she had just put her mouth around a barefaced lie. In truth, she considered this battle her homage to Georgia half the time. She often thought of Keefer as Georgia's miniature.

"I hope you aren't going on about this as a personal thing, Lorraine," Diane offered.

"It's entirely personal, Diane. That's all it is."

"It's not. It's a matter of law. The law is the law."

"The law is the law? There's been no crime committed. No one's breaking any law."

"I'm really not free to discuss that."

"Oh, good," Lorraine snorted, "let's not discuss it." She'd been angry by then, and should have, she thought in retrospect, let it drop.

But Diane persisted, "All I was meaning to suggest was, I

hope you don't think that we, or that the kids mean this as any reflection on you-all, as people."

Lorraine slumped. She did know that. "Of course, we don't think it's meant that way. And, by the same token, Gordon doesn't mean this as a reflection on you as people, either. He just wants what's best for Keefer."

"If he does, then he will come to know what we already know. And I hope you'll come to feel the peace of God in that way, too, Lorraine—" Diane had clearly been inhaling Delia's vapors along with her cleansing teas—"because if this weren't the way it was meant to be, God would have sent a message."

"What if he has, and you can't read it?" Oh, shut up, please, Lorraine reprimanded herself. She imagined Greg Katt sitting in his office over Tree's Company Antiques, his ears getting red and hot as she blithely bandied words with an adversary who was probably wearing a tape recorder. No, Diane couldn't have organized herself to record a conversation. Diane was incapable of buckling her own watchband. Mark suggested that Florida women had lost the gene for autonomous dressing through natural selection during the antebellum era.

Or, Lorraine thought, was all that dependency just a social ruse? What if Diane was here by design? Recording the conversation on advice of her attorneys? Katt had regaled them with the strange things people did during custody battles.

"Diane," Lorraine said cautiously, slowly turning onto First Street, "I don't know what God thinks about it, but I know we're trying to do what we think is the right thing, just as you are."

"But you have no idea how we feel!"

"How you and Ray feel?"

"All of us! Keefer Kathryn is our flesh and blood, Lorraine!"

"And ours, too, Diane."

"But she's not." Diane's carefully roseate lips met with an audible pop, a cartoon representation of sudden ruefulness.

Cold sweat broke out below Lorraine's breasts. She considered whether she would actually hit Diane. Diane was larger, but Lorraine was fairly sure that she was stronger. Instead, she stopped in the middle of the deserted street and turned full to face the passenger seat.

"What did you say?"

"Nothing. Let's go get Keefer Kathryn."

"What . . . did . . . you . . . *say*."

Diane sighed a windy sigh. "You force me, Lorraine. It's not fair. You hear? It's just that she's not really your flesh and blood. Even if you feel that way. I know you loved Georgia, but she was an adopted child. Keefer Kathryn is a Nye, Lorraine."

The children had once, without Lorraine's knowledge, filled paper cups with freshwater snails at the beach on Hat Lake. By the time their swim was over, they'd forgotten their treasures, which they'd left in the stifling backseat of Lorraine's car on a breathless August afternoon. Two days later, she'd opened her door to a stench so potent it was like a shove in the face. Lorraine reeled back, literally having to stumble to the trash cans to throw up as the garage filled with the overwhelming reek of decay. What Lorraine felt, when she'd smelled that smell, was rage. She felt precisely this way now.

Diane had not noticed. Her accent grew deeper and wider as she rounded each bend of logic: Lorraine had never experienced a child growing in her body, and all that meant was that Lorraine could not see how a child could be a part of you. "We've tried our very best to understand, Lorraine," she said. "But now you-all are going to have to understand the facts of life, the way things are in the real world."

"The real world," Lorraine said, her voice suddenly calm.

There was another Lorraine, a Lorraine damp and quaking, throwing open drawers and clawing out underclothes, tossing them overhead with clawed hands, delving for pill bottles, cracking the bottles, scrabbling for the contents. But that was another self, over there. The other Lorraine, who was driving the car, was looking down on Diane from a great height.

One thing was clear: Lorraine needed her wits about her. Every wit. She would never take another pill living in a world among such dangerous fools. She would do what she should have done months ago. Cut out even coffee. Take gingko to sharpen her memory. She would train like a mental marathoner.

Diane jibbered, "Delia is just like my own daughter, and Delia is unable to have children, but do you think she would go to China or Peru or somewhere and adopt someone else's baby? She would not do that. She would just as soon not have a child. And Craig? He feels just the same way. They're willing to take Baby into their hearts because she is blood, Lorraine! They would not consider adopting a child who was not of their own blood. That is why this happened in this way, Lorraine. This is not our ill will. It's family."

Lorraine had serenely parked the car and begun moving Keefer's car seat. She had not answered Diane, though Diane kept talking; Lorraine could see her jaw working up and down. When Gordon walked out onto the front stoop with Keefer, Lorraine kissed the child, then silently walked past her son and went up the hall stairway into his apartment. She picked up the telephone and dialed Greg Katt and insisted on speaking to him instantly.

After they'd finished speaking, she went home and flushed every pill in her house, all the bigs and the littles. She kept only a few painkillers, thinking, superstitiously, there might someday come a time when she had a pain she really needed to kill.

"She said she would see that woman in hell," Gordon later told Tim Upchurch, as they drove through the dark toward their morning tee at Blackwolf.

"It sounds like it was quite a brawl," Tim said.

They'd stopped to grab a bite after softball, earlier in the evening, and Church had come back from using the phone, grinning, saying road trip. A member down at Blackwolf must have died or something—because, surprise!—they had a tee time at seven in the morning. Pleading a stroke of heaven-sent luck, pleading his one day to play golf of the entire lost summer, Gordon broke a dinner date with Lindsay, who was distant. Gordon tried not to notice. He was excited, primed. He would be good. He would feel as Ray had always told him it was possible to feel, no matter how long you had to furlough. There was no need to fear the first day out. It was like sex, it was like riding a bike; the hands did not forget. Church, wild as a cat under the sprinkler, would be firing them everywhere but down the center, terrorizing small woodland creatures and marketing executives parking their Beamers in the parking lot. It would not matter. Gordon would forget all about babies and lawyers and just play the game.

They had no idea where they were going to sleep, certainly not at the inn in Kohler, where a room cost what Gordon paid every six months for car insurance. They would figure that out later. Serendipity was the essence of a road trip.

"My mom said she'd see that woman in hell, and that the Nyes didn't understand anything about us, and then she called Katt and we went over and officially filed my adoption petition. At like, five o'clock. The clerk was madder than hell. And then she said she and my dad were going to go camping. Camping! The last time they went camping, I was like, ten."

"Jesus. Did she say why?"

"Why the adoption or why camping?"

"Why Diane in hell," Tim said, glancing covertly around him before opening the bottle of St. Pauli Girl he'd nested between his legs. The highway was jammed with people in

SUVs, all driving in the opposite direction, desperately heading north to camp and fish on the last long weekend of summer.

"She didn't tell me why they were going camping. And she didn't tell me what led to the fight. I was afraid to ask. My mom has a temper. She always had a temper—"

"Well, Diane is an excellent bitch."

"This brings it out in people."

"What did she mean, Diane didn't understand anything about you?"

"About our family."

"Ray was great, though."

"He was one of the greats."

"How can people be so different from their folks?"

"I am."

"Not so much. You and your folks are superclose. I don't mean so much you're like them, I mean you *like* them. I always thought that was weird, when we were kids, you were like, no, I'm going to stay home with my father because we're going to do an experiment to turn cabbage red or something. You'd stay home even if they didn't make you. Instead of going to the fort or something."

"We did stuff that was fun. I used to think everybody paid as much attention to their kids as they did to us. But, you weren't there for the great moments of Dad . . . like the time Georgia and I washed the basement stairs with the garden hose. This was my idea. I told her there were drains in the basement right at the bottom of the stairs, so the water would go right down—"

"You flooded the basement."

"We flooded the yard. We flooded the Dwors's yard next door. The water got so high it went right out the window wells. We were upstairs, like, watching *The Brady Bunch*."

"He got mad, huh?"

"Georgia and I were down there swabbing until four in

the morning. And then, when I got in bed, there's Dad, shaking my shoulder. We have to go over and pick up everything for Bob and Mary next door. Right then. Not the next day. Sometimes he's as tight as a clam."

"You can be like that."

"Not so much. I'm more like my mom. I say too much."

"About some stuff. But I don't know. You can be . . . aloof."

"So Lindsay tells me," Gordon sighed.

"You kiss him, though."

"My dad?" Gordon hadn't remembered that. He did kiss his dad on the cheek or the forehead, practically every time he saw him. "I guess I do. Don't you?"

"Don? Kiss old Don? Can't think of the last time. The sisters do."

They drank in silence. Church rummaged in the console for Echo and the Bunnymen and seat-danced a little. "So what's this all mean for you and Lindsay?"

"What?"

"You going to do the big deed, then?"

"Get married? Hello! One thing at a time."

"But you're together—"

"We . . . play house. I'm like, I love you, Lindsay, you're the best there is. But she wants . . . more."

"It seems like the two of you could be parents together. Keefer loves Lindsay."

"It could be a whole lot worse," Gordon said, then swiveled at Tim's groan. "What's up?" Church didn't answer, simply absorbed himself in rubbing at a knot of pine sap on the lip of the window. After long minutes, Church muttered something about Diane, and Gordon felt guiltily obliged to grab for the fluttering end of conversation.

"They're all going to try to make it hard for us."

"Why? It's not like you're going to take Keefer and move to Alaska."

"Well, they look at Keefer, and they see Ray . . . she's all they have left of Ray."

"I don't think she looks like Ray. I think she looks like you and Georgia. It's like looking at Georgia, when you look at Keefer."

"Georgia, yes. But me? My sister didn't look like me. Church, we were adopted. We don't have a genetic relation."

"Right. I never think of you guys as adopted."

"What does that mean?"

"I mean it . . . like a compliment. You're just McKennas. You remind me of your folks. Don't you think of it like that?"

"I do, but not because there's some kind of big deal about being adopted. In mouse studies, if a mother mouse is given a litter she didn't give birth to, those babies grow up to parent in the same style as the mother who raised them, not the one who had them. Some things are learned. Some are built in. You'd be surprised to know what's learned."

"Like what?"

"Well, like a bird learning to sing. They don't just do it."

"Huh," Tim drained his beer. "Still, you read these things about people who search for their real parents—"

"Their birth parents."

"Right. And they always say they love the people who raised them."

"But I wonder what's going on underneath. If they're making such a big deal about it. I guess I wondered a little when I was a kid." Gordon wondered, for a moment, what Keefer was doing. Probably saying the Congregationalist Rosary. "But frankly, I'm getting kind of tired of hearing about it. Especially now. It's like you have to make excuses if you don't have this big neurotic thing going on. The psychologist who came got off all over the place on it. It's like she wanted me to say, 'But I don't know who I am!'"

"Well, Keefer will know. She won't really be adopted. Because she's already yours."

"Yeah. But she'll be adopted."

"Not really."

"Yeah, really! Church, get a clue here. It's not that big a deal for her to be adopted . . . losing her folks, yeah, the way she did, that's a big deal, but . . ."

"But it would be weird to think of Keefer being *really* adopted, like by strangers."

"But they wouldn't be strangers, if they adopted her."

"My brother Kevin used to tell me I was adopted, because I was the only one with brown eyes, and it was like this . . . I used to cry about it when I was a little kid. He said, well, Mom and Don only took you because no one else wanted you. The police brought you over. And anytime they want, they can come and take you back. It's state law."

"And you were scared. Like you didn't belong where everyone else belonged."

"Right."

"Well, that's just it. People think you go around sweating that stuff all the time if your parents adopted you."

"But I bet there are families like that."

"There are people who hate each other who stay married for forty years, too."

"Like my grandparents."

"But they enjoy it."

"True."

There was a restaurant. Tim drove past, then circled back.

"What kind of joint is that?" he asked Gordon.

The sign said, FINE DINING IN A MUSICAL SPHERE. Gordon looked closer. It would once have said ATMOSPHERE. For the past few miles, as they neared the town, Gordon had been scanning the roadside for a place to eat, to ask about somewhere to stay, where he could get hold of a beer to chase the faint buzz upon him from the pair they'd brought. The long, low building they finally spotted was so jammed, cars and trucks straggled along the shoulder.

He consulted his watch. Nine-fifteen. Probably a band. They ventured inside.

He would have noticed her anyway, even if he hadn't recognized her from somewhere. She wasn't beautiful, but she had that kind of what-the hell body, dark tan, shirt too tight, jeans too loose, that would always make him think of Liza. She was dancing with four friends, all women, as if she were trying to unscrew herself from the floor, one long, fluid, endlessly repeating Mobius. Men would sidle up, and she'd just throw back her head and laugh and turn back to her girlfriends. When the band broke, she combed back her sweaty hair and walked up to Tim and Gordon.

"May I have my drink?"

"What are you drinking?" Tim asked.

"Ice water, and it's behind you." Now that she was closer, Gordon could see she was older than she had appeared across the room. He glanced at her hand. Rings, but only on the index fingers, at the first joint. Tiny, sculptured hands. "I know you. From Tall Trees, right?"

He nodded, measuring. How much older was she? Five years? More? There were tiny scallop shells of lines at the corners of her eyes. Obviously, she worked out. Everybody worked out. It was ridiculous. Everybody looked thirty now.

"Well, are you?"

"From Tall Trees? You bet."

"City of bait shops," Tim put in.

"I'm not. I'm from Merrill. We have a chalet," she gestured at her friends, who were making a big elaborate show of delivering a foaming pitcher to their table. For his benefit, Gordon thought.

The one blonde was very cute. But taller than him. "We're at the golf outing. For the firefighters," said the lady with the ice water.

"Your husband is a fireman?"

"I am."

"Get out of here." Tim was baffled. Gordon, too. The woman was like, five-three. She rolled up her T-shirt sleeve. Biceps like a boulder.

"Where are you staying?" she asked.

They told her: the car.

And then the rest of the women joined them, pulling her away. Her name was Alicia Rafferty. Rafferty, Gordon thought. He knew a Rafferty. Somewhere. He and Church sat down with them. The woman treated for beer. The band, which was called Midlife Crisis, started up again. She pulled Gordon out onto the floor. Thank you, Georgia, he breathed, for teaching me the swing. It ended with them offering to let the two men sleep on the floor at their chalet, if they promised to be good boys. Alicia got in the back of Tim's car, guiding them past the little proper postcard of a downtown, out a long forest preserve road to a bluff overlooking a steep cliff. Lake Michigan growled and sighed below them. The sky loomed close, stars throbbing.

The lights weren't out ten minutes when she came for him. "Come outside," she'd told Gordon, "I want to show you something."

She was a rogue, just dragged him up the bluff and, without a word, stepped out of her jeans. She had to be older. Girls his age either went at it like they were going to devour him or acted as though it were some big gift to even open their mouths, but she treated him delicately, teasing him with feather touches inside his thighs, then along the upper ridge, squeezing with those strong, competent little hands. And then she lay back, laughing, as he got ready to return the favor, to show her how it was done, Jurgen's best lesson, pretend it's sippin' whiskey, he'd told Gordie long ago.

Then he stopped. Like an exploding lightbulb, he'd remembered where he saw her name. On his class list. She was a relative of one of his students. A sister, a cousin.

A mother.

"Something I ate?" she laughed. Then, she sat up. "Do you have a cigarette?"

"I don't smoke," Gordon told her.

"Neither do I," she said.

"Don't take this badly."

"Uhhh, okay."

"I just don't have the . . . heart for it. You're gorgeous and sexy and all that, but . . ."

"I'm older."

"That is definitely not the problem."

"We don't know each other."

"I'm a biology teacher. Kelly Rafferty is going to be my student in the fall."

"That's my daughter, but it's okay, and I'm single."

"And so am I. Well, sort of. There's a really nice person who'd be really hurt by what I was thinking of doing right now. And I'm also . . . in a position."

"The lawsuit."

Gordon was shocked. She's known exactly who he was.

"That's right," he said finally.

"You're in father mode."

"All the time now."

"What's she like?"

"She's pretty great. She's the funniest kid. She just started being able to walk backward, you know? Gets this smile on her face, like it's this big accomplishment to go backward? I taught her to make that beeping noise . . ."

"Like a truck backing up?"

"Right. Little kids can do the same thing over and over . . ."

"Until the end of time . . ."

"And she still thinks it's hysterical. I can't help but laughing, too. She has the personality of a tank, you know? The other night, I found her in the bathroom and she was just whomping on this tube of toothpaste. It was everywhere. And she looked right at me and said, 'Dory! Ick! Mess! No, no Dory!' As if I did it . . ."

"Sounds like you're raising her to think like a guy."

"I hope not," Gordon said. "If I am, I can't help it."

"You must love her."

"I love her more than . . ." Gordon said, surprising himself, "anything on earth."

"I like that in a person," Alicia had said, and then yawned. "Do you mind if I put on my knickers here?" She'd raked her hair and then offered her hand, which Gordon took, gently. "Does my kid get straight A's out of this?"

"Nope."

"Do I get a friend?"

"You sure do."

"Well, you can't have too many friends in this long life," she said.

When he'd gone to the bathroom and she'd disappeared up into the loft, where her friends were snoring, Church had surprised him by unrolling himself from a blanket and sitting up. "What did she want?" he asked, something clenched in his voice that Gordon couldn't identify.

Gordon decided to take it light. "She . . . wanted to show me something."

"And you wanted to show her something."

"It wasn't like that. We mostly just talked."

Tim threw the blanket off and slipped out the front door. Gordon could see him in black profile, his face set against the lightening sky.

Jesus Christ, Gordon thought.

Tim Upchurch looked deep into the frenzy of stars and thought about Lindsay Snow. His gut was sour. He imagined his heart dividing like a hollow chocolate, neatly, in halves.

Mark McKenna lay on his pillowed arms and thought of

his daughter. Beside him, in their tiny tent, Lorraine slept more deeply than Mark believed she had in months. He'd been surprised, but hopeful when Lorraine came barreling up out of the basement with the tent and bedrolls. It was to the handkerchief beach on Spirit Lake, the place no one else but they ever seemed to discover, the spot they skinny-dipped on moony nights when they were young, where they took Gordie to watch a great horned owl feed her nestlings, carrying the children from their beds after midnight one mild spring night so long ago. In the tent, Lorraine and Mark had made love for the first time since Georgia's death. He had not felt the desire, and had not, in any case, felt good about mentioning it. It had been Lorraine who let him know, with the familiar wordless cues of a mate, that he would be welcome.

It was because they were away from the house, he supposed. Its restraining web of memories. And for long moments, he had managed to let himself forget, to be caught in the scented tangle of Lorraine's still-supple limbs, her skin looser, fallen, but no less soft to his hands than the first time.

Now, he felt terribly sad. All mammals felt sad after sex, but it was more than a physiological letdown. They had done so well, all their married life, at keeping the kids in perspective relative to their own union. They had given each other time. Even when Georgia was possessed, at fifteen or sixteen, they had managed to keep the circle of their respect and comfort intact. He had never told Lorraine a lie, except once, when he said that there had been another woman before her. A small vanity, from a shy man. That had been the only untruth he had told her until he'd said that he was grateful that it hadn't been her—Lorraine—that he had lost.

And that was a lie. Though he had set more store, as his sister would say, by Gordon, Mark McKenna's daughter had been the radiant center of his life. All the comfort and cohesiveness he had taken and given growing up close to his brother and sister, that mattered greatly. His . . . passion would not be too strong a term . . . for Lorraine, for his work, all this combined could not approach the might of his attachment to Georgia.

This had not been how he had believed it would transpire. Fear, real fear, had overtaken him when he finally agreed with Lorraine's desperate wish to adopt. More than most, he knew that genetic characteristics were not suggestions, but destiny. They were a map, with all the points of interest clearly marked. The Minnesota twin studies had proven that twins raised in separate adoptive homes—the barbarity of that, separating twins for adoption!—still chose similar jobs, parted their hair on the same side, developed the same ailments within months of one another. He had known, with complete certainty, that the nature versus nurture debate was specious, that a child's upbringing could only enhance or detract from that child's predestined development. An adopted child would be unlike him. That child would be a mystery. Talents, personality quirks, diseases.

Diseases.

But then Georgia had been placed in his arms by the foster parent who'd been caring for her. The placement coordinator from Catholic Social Services had been late. A half hour had passed. An hour. Finally, Mark had insisted that they put the baby in the car and leave. What if there had been a problem, and they intended to take her back? They'd been driving up the road, on the way home, when they passed the social worker driving in the opposite direction. They'd had a few laughs about it. The foster mother, the placement worker, and Lorraine, at least. Mark had not laughed. He could only see Georgia, examine Georgia's auburn fuzz, her piercing black eyes, her tender limbs.

He recognized his Georgia, his child.

He had forgotten an enormous fact of primate biology. The nature versus nurture debate was specious, but not for the reasons he had supposed. Georgia was who she was, and he who he was. But it was his nature to nurture her. Had anyone suspected how bewitched he had been, how unable to think of anything except seeing her, laying his finger against her skin?

Lorraine's joy over the baby verged on madness. It poured from her like scent. She had walked home from the library the day of the call from the adoption agency, her arms loaded down with a stack of child-care books, and forgotten for two days that she had left her car in the parking lot. She assumed it had been stolen and didn't care. With quarts of washable latex, she'd painted the walls of Georgia's room in huge splashes of raspberry and gold and metallic blue, so much color that her sister, Daphne, whose husband was a neurologist, worried that the baby might get overstimulated.

Lorraine hadn't even cared whether Mark took to the baby. She chose her name. When he balked, asking, "Don't you think the name is a little much?" Lorraine became short with him.

"Your mechanic named his baby Juniper," she'd said, pouting. She had planned since she was sixteen to name her baby after Georgia O'Keeffe—and by God, she was going to name her baby after Georgia O'Keeffe.

And it had been the most perfect name. Mark could not imagine another girl so unique and impossible to diminish as his child. Two years later, his son was born, on the day man first walked on the moon. They had not even known of Gordie's existence on the summer night that they, like all their friends, woke to the alarm and watched the grainy telecast, a drowsy Georgia sprawled across their laps. But six weeks later, even though Gordon Cooper hadn't been part of that particular mission, Mark had borrowed a leaf from Lorraine's book and named his son for someone famous and accomplished, and to commemorate the scientific historicity of his birthday. It was fanciful instead of practical.

How their names suited his children. Soft and hard variations of the same letter, they were like handmade shirts, instantly and perfectly fitting.

He had traveled for work until Gordie was almost a year

old. Longer than Mark would have liked. It had taken him time to reposition himself at Medi-Sun so that he would do more R and D. But wherever he was, whatever client dinner or other obligation lay before him, he would set aside everything to call home at six, just after Lorraine would have cleared the dishes. If it was a Thursday or a Sunday, he'd wait just a few minutes longer, to catch them after dinner and before *Bewitched* or *The Munsters* came on. There were times his wife hadn't had much to say. Two under three was quite a feat, and women didn't hold down full-time jobs and full-time families back then. Lorraine's job was always demanding, and she simply would not do things halfway. Even having Mary Dwors happy to care for the children in those early years and someone to help with the cleaning and ironing didn't make up for another parent. Mark was never unaware of how much sleep Lorraine surrendered to keep it all rolling when he was away. By the time Georgia was four, he'd come in off the road for good. Years later, they would look back and marvel at how they'd ever managed.

Mark felt the calls had helped. They were an anchor. When Georgia first began talking, he would ask for her, and she would grow wistful, no matter what her mood had been like in the moments before he called—"She was throwing her foam blocks at the baby and he was pretending to fall over just now," Lorraine would tell him, exasperated. "She was fine, Mark. This is Sarah Bernhardt over here. Tell Dad how much fun you were having, Georgia."

Mark would coax her, "Georgia? Georgia on my mind?"

"Daddy."

"My Georgia."

"My Daddia."

"Are you happy, Georgia?"

"No, I am sad."

"Why are you sad?"

"Because you are not with me."

"Soon, I will be with you."

"You aren't with me."

"Soon."

"Why aren't you here?"

And he would carefully explain, in language she could understand, how Daddy's job was getting vitamins to people so they could stay strong and healthy and not get colds that were too bad, even in winter. And still, she would say, "Daddy, I am sad." He did not once disbelieve her. He thought it was entirely possible that a happy life could contain enormous sadness, and he didn't think children's emotions were any less noteworthy than adults'. For a small child, the walls of the room were the boundaries of the universe. He would sit, in Phoenix or Milwaukee or Trenton, and imagine him and Georgia, each immured in the restrictive enclosure of their separateness, the wall of distance between them.

He had accepted, when Georgia became ill, that however long his life lasted, ten years longer, or twenty, he would be a man living on the other side of the wall from his own heart. The spunk and resolve Lorraine brought to their struggle over his granddaughter made him want to stand up and applaud his wife's courage. But he had no taste for it. He hoped that his distance was not felt. He hoped he could do his part.

The Nyes were wrong. He knew that much.

He knew very little else.

He was certain that no intelligence survived death.

So he did not at least have to live imagining Georgia's grief because he could not be with her. His chest filled with tiny, insistent pulses and he gasped. He wondered with vague curiosity whether he was having a heart attack. But no, he was only, finally, crying, tears hot along his cheeks, down into his ears.

"Mark?" Lorraine stirred, not quite waking. "Are you okay?"

"I miss my baby girl," he managed to say, holding himself still, trying not to alarm her.

"Monday," Lorraine sighed. "She'll be home on Monday. Go to sleep."

$\mathcal{G}$o to sleep, Gordon urged her. Gotosleepgotosleepgoto-sleep. He dared not cough or breathe or even shift the pillow to a more comfortable place between his knees because he believed . . . no, he knew, that Keefer could hear his thoughts.

Why was there so little research on this phenomenon? If he thought of nothing except sleep, then Keefer would slip over the edge into sleep. If he let his mind drift, if he began to think about skiing, or tomorrow's lesson, or an itch in his groin, or the pucker around Alicia's navel when she dived for the set on her volleyball team (he'd joined, insisting they treat each other as friends only, and she'd trumped him, asking him, with genuine bafflement, what he was talking about), or about how much he wanted a ginger ale with ice, then Keefer would stir.

It would begin with a single whimper, like a puppy on its first night home. Then would come silence, during which Gordon would plead with the universe, and one in every five times—he had counted it up—Keefer would sigh, insert her thumb upside down high in the back left corner where her grueling molars were sprouting, and collapse like a deflated wind sock back down onto her dog bed. Gordon had tried, for Lindsay, to describe the joy he felt when she fell back to sleep. The security of knowing that when the sun came up, he would not be desperate, wild, his eyes so dry they literally clicked open and closed. It was holy, a gift from above, one more night when he would not have to have watched the middle forty-five minutes of *Fast Times at Ridgemont High* or *Batman and Robin*, while he stroked Keefer's restless little feet with one thumb.

For a time, at first, she had slept overnight so well that Gordon felt as though he were on steroids. He could do fatherhood! Totally! Let Faith Bogert come. Let 'em all come. What was all this whining about never a moment to yourself? Why did the single parents at school always look like hell? "She's down at eight," he would comment, trying to stifle the sniff of pride he felt coming on, "and she's out for the night."

But then the molars peeked through, and Keefer woke up at night with a wail like steel on steel.

The first time, terrified, Gordon had called his mother, who asked him to hold the telephone close to the baby's head so that she could hear the quality of the cry. "She's just fussing, Gordie," Lorraine said wearily. "Now, let me get some sleep. I have to work tomorrow."

But Keefer wailed on, and Gordon finally wrapped her in his Brewers warm-up jacket, tying the sleeves in front in a way that kept Keefer both warm and immobile, and drove to Trempeauleau County Methodist. The resident who carefully thumped, eyed, and palpated Keefer was Asian, a young woman.

"You are her father?" she asked.

"Yes, I'm her uncle," Gordon answered.

"She's your daughter?" the young woman asked again, and Gordon thought, shut up, shut up, you spoiled overcerebrated brat, and he also thought that this was exactly the sort of woman who once would have, by now, been providing him accidental occasions to brush her breast against his arm. Single parenthood, he had discovered to his disgust, was not the chick magnet he'd believed it would be. When Keefer dimpled and kept her barrettes in, he had to beat the bruistas at the Perk Place off him with a stick. But when she whined, or threw herself facedown on the floor, kicking both her Weebocked feet until she puked, women were grateful to find him invisible.

"I'm her uncle. I'm adopting her," Gordon explained. "She lives with me, so de facto, yes, I'm her father. My sister, her mother, died last spring."

"I'm sorry. But I have a good reason for asking."

"Health insurance? She's on my parents'. I have a copy of their card, and a letter."

"I'm not a bookkeeper."

"Oh, right. Well, then, shoot."

"I want to know how much you know about the teething patterns of toddlers."

"A fair amount. I'm a biology teacher."

"I'm talking children, not dogfish sharks."

"Fine."

"So, you know why she's in pain. Pain equals crying. Restless sleep."

Bitch, thought Gordon.

"I'd be glad for restless sleep, Doctor. We're talking no sleep. I know she's getting a back tooth, but I didn't know it would affect her like this. . . ."

"What happened when she cut her front teeth? Was she bothered?"

"I don't know. I didn't live with her then. Her parents, my sister, was alive then. I think she was pretty little when she got her first ones."

"Well, this is considerably harder for her. Molars are bigger. And she's bigger. More sentient. Aren't you, honey?"

"Tell me about it. I mean, she never sleeps. She . . . never. . . . sleeps."

"Most parents of young children get far more sleep than they actually think they're getting. It's more of a misperception, because the sleep is so broken. I know it seems impossible, but everyone goes through this."

"Do you have kids?"

"Nooooo," the young woman, whose name tag read Michelle Yu, answered. "If she were truly sleep deprived, she'd have some physical . . . she'd show it."

Thank you, Yu, he'd thought, as she dismissed him with some sample packets of Tylenol syrup and he headed home for the dawn patrol.

Day after day, he caught himself nodding in class. The kids noticed. One of the endless procession of Reillys—this one named Dennis—woke him by turning the volume to the max on the CD player he kept in the lab. The opening riff of "Layla" blasted him literally off his stool.

"Tempus fugg-it, Mr. McKenna," the kid said.

Gordon forced down his desire to slug the kid and joked, "Reilly, I'm an old man."

"No, my brother's your age."

"Ahhh, yes, Sir Ryan Reilly. We survived fifth grade together."

"He says you were the big ladies' man."

"In fifth grade? I didn't know which end was which. I'm a Catholic, too, you know." Laughter. Relief. Perhaps they'd forget he'd nodded off.

"No, here. Right here at good ol' Wildwood. Says you plucked more roses than—"

"Whoa there, big fella. We won't be doing the mating dance in here until Thanksgiving." More giggles. Good. From the syllabus, they knew "the mating dance" was a genetics exercise. "And as for me, I'm in the army now. The parent army."

"Did you get married, Mr. McKenna?" said Kathleen Zurich, little vixen in the pom squad who sat right next to Kelly Rafferty.

Rafferty.

God.

"No, I didn't get married," he finally answered.

"Accident?" Laughter. "Lady got you in trouble?"

"No, I'm adopting my baby niece. My sister and her husband died."

"Oooooh. I know about that. It was on TV."

"That's right, and now I'm raising a baby. The most fabulous baby in the world, except she's nocturnal. I can't believe how much stamina your parents must have. How many of you guys are there now? Ten? Eleven? How do they do it?"

"Every which way, I guess. . . ." Reilly shrugged. More raucous laughter.

"What I mean is, I'm asleep on my feet with one kid. How do they manage?"

"They drink," the kid howled.

Gordon didn't drink. He quit softball with only three games left on their schedule. When Lindsay came over, he begged her at the door to take Keefer out so he could sleep for an hour. When she came back—Lindsay swore she'd been gone two hours—he'd drooled all over the couch. On Saturday nights, when Keefer was with his folks or the Cadys and Nyes, he had no strength for anything but takeout and a movie, through which he slept. In his mirror, he was sure he saw licks of gray at his temples. His patience with the ordinary guy's stuff of life was slim.

He'd almost got in a fight with a guy at the Wild Rose one night. There were two of them, business twits probably invited here by Medi-Sun, sucking up expense-account cocktails in their seafoam green muscle-man sport coats and Clark Kent specs.

Twit One started with a loud, meant-to-be-overheard account of some office skirmish, "Look. Heywood is over. He will never recover. I understand his need. But he's posturing. It isn't going to fool anyone . . ."

"You speak the truth," said Twit Two.

Behind the bar, Katie Savage, the bartender, rolled her

eyes and made a "down, down, boy" motion with her palm. Did Gordon look as disgusted as he felt?

"I'm struggling with the same things in my setting," Church began, affecting an English accent. "Ernie Blodgett can kid himself, but he'll never paint hydrants again. He's a broom man. That's the reality. When he tried painting hydrants, he was simply out of his depth . . ."

One of the twits next started on his boss's daughter. Gordon couldn't believe his ears. "And now she's let it be known to old man Vanderwood that she wants a real princess wedding, no expense spared—"

"And she's a dwarf?" guffawed his corporate twin.

"And so is the guy she's marrying! We're all expected to attend this very solemn occasion."

"Well, at least they can save on clothes. Get them at the Baby Gap. Get a Barbie's Dream House and they're all—"

Gordon lost it. "Do you know what dwarfism is?" He snarled in the guy's face. "Do you know that people who have congenital dwarfism sometimes don't live past forty? Do you know the courage it must have taken for those parents to raise their girl to believe she could live her life as a normal woman?" Twit Two made a dismissive motion, as if stroking an invisible violin. "You fat bastard," Gordon hissed, "are you a father? Are you?"

"Come on, Squirrel," Twit Two muttered. "Let's leave Bob and Doug here to their cribbage—"

"Squirrel?" Church crowed happily. "Squirrel? Jesus Christ, Gordie, don't mess with a guy named Squirrel! And who are you? Bullwinkle? I'm Boris. Moose and Squirrel must die!"

Then Kate was between them, holding on to Gordon and the bigger of the assholes, by the fronts of their shirts. "Next beer's on me, buds. If you just get back to your . . . cribbage here. Come on, Gordie. You'll never see these jerks again in your life."

Gordon got so hammered he had a gauzy recollection of

burying at least part of his face in Kate's bosom. He hoped he had not done wrong. Kate had been his friend since sixth grade, when she brought her father's *Playboy*s to him and Kip Sweeney in their tree fort.

But Gordon could gain no ground against his weariness. Up at five, he felt like Santa Claus heading out the door: book bag, diaper bag, briefcase, elf in stocking cap. All the way out Q to his aunt's, and thank God for that. At the beginning of the year, he'd asked Lorraine what they were going to do about Keefer's daytime care.

"Well," Lorraine asked him, shrugging, "what do you want to do?" He'd been sure she was putting him on. Didn't she already have a plan? How was he supposed to intuit what kind of childcare situation would be best for an eighteen-month-old who also happened to be the subject of a custody battle everyone in the goddamned town seemed to know about? He was righteously pissed.

"I don't think she should go to a day-care center," Gordon had said.

"I also don't think she should go to a day-care center," said his mother.

"She's had enough change in the past few months."

"I agree."

"And plus, the only day-care center is that born-again place, the Rainbow Club. It always sounded like a topless bar to me. How come Catholics don't have day care?"

"Catholics have grandmothers."

"Are you going to quit, then?"

"Quit my job, Gordie?"

"Yes. Quit your job. Take a leave of absence."

"I took a leave last year."

"Then, quit."

His mother had lowered her reading glasses. "Gordie, I most certainly am not going to quit my job. In case you haven't noticed, we are running up substantial bills around here—"

"Well, Keefer's insurance maybe could pay for some of that."

"They're our bills, not Keefer's. Even if that weren't illegal, I wouldn't do it. And, anyway, there's no money, because they're still investigating the accident."

"How long can that take?"

"I don't know."

"I still think she needs to be with one of us."

"Then you quit your job. I make more money than you do. I'm two years from being able to take early retirement, Gordon."

"Mother, I can hardly quit my job. I'm adopting a child, in case you haven't noticed. How do you think the judge would regard unemployment as a factor in my suitability?"

Lorraine sighed. "You have a point."

"And, so. . . ."

"Well, she can stay with Nora, I guess. For the time being. They're picking, though. Nora can carry Keefer on her back in a sling. Like a Pearl S. Buck novel."

"Bradie's out there. She just cooks and stuff during the day."

"We can't just assume they'll take her on."

"Aunt Nora would do anything for Keefer."

"Well, call and ask her then."

"You."

"You call and ask her. You're the one who wants the favor."

"Favor?" What the hell was wrong with her, Gordon wondered? What had he done?

In the end, Nora had offered. But that only meant that Gordon had to get up in the middle of the night practically, if he didn't want to go to school unshaven and smelling of Happykids Blueberry Cobbler. A couple of times each week, Mark volunteered to drive Keefer out to the farm on his way to the plant. Gordon didn't know why his father couldn't manage to do it every day; he was a vice president, after all. He didn't start work until an hour that was practically late afternoon in Gordon's world. But Mark insisted that he needed his run three mornings a week.

Run.

How come he didn't get a run?

Gordon's father would certainly outlive him.

Gordon was so out of shape and skinny his legs felt like sandbags the few times he could get up enough gumption to drive over to Merrill and play volleyball. Even looking at the shapely butts of Alicia and her teammates didn't energize him. He'd shown remarkable restraint with Alicia, though it had helped to learn that she was thirty-seven years old. Still, he wished perversely he could boast about it to Lindsay. Lindsay helped him often, but it still didn't feed the bulldog. When Lindsay did Keefer's wash, he still had to pick it up and put it all away. He spent almost every night folding teeny shorts and dresses and socks. Keefer had at least seven hundred socks, no two of which matched.

Teaching, which had always been a breeze, had turned to stone. It had been easy to be a hotshot at work if all you had to worry about was your own care and feeding.

Keefer had been still in her sleep period when the term began. But within two weeks, he was out of luck, and out of patience.

What biology was mostly about, he'd said one day, was reproduction.

They who reproduce best laugh last, he'd said. They get to keep the marbles.

"In the beginning," Gordon began, "before dinosaurs, before worms, before cats, before the guys who design the little silver strips on CD packaging, before DNA, even before Mr. Reilly here, there was RNA. Ribonucleic acid. And these RNA guys were pretty limited in what they could do for fun, back around four billion years ago. The planet was probably pretty new then, and nobody knew where the good hangouts were—"

"Where did it come from?" Reilly, of course.

Gordon would later review the tattered ribbons of that class day and admit that it served him right. He'd needled the kid, because Dennis was linked in Gordon's back brain to the dumbass older sibling, Ryan, who'd once tormented him about adoption.

"RNA?" Gordon asked now.

"Yeah, where did it come from? Because, if cells can only come from other cells, where did the first cell come from?"

It was actually a decent question. "I don't know. But we can presume that eventually these substances changed so that there was a bold new way of reproducing, a little more sophistication—"

"Like dinner and a movie first." This from that big blond soccer jock, Kye Olstadt, a really sweet kid.

"Right. And once it tried and failed and tried and failed and tried and failed for a billion years or so, one of these RNA guys invented DNA."

"I thought James Watson and Francis Crick invented DNA." Reilly again. "And, news flash, Watson thinks man couldn't have evolved from a single-celled creature so fast. Had to be aliens."

"What he meant," Gordon said, "was that it was possible that there was a life form that may have originated on a planet other than earth, like a supervirus. Not little green men. And, you know, evolution is just change. And it can happen really rapidly. Look how quickly bacteria become resistant to antibiotics . . . there's microevolution taking place in front of our eyes every day."

"Darwin's theory of evolution was wrong," Dennis Reilly said. "I have a cousin in Georgia who can get excused from class when they teach evolution because his family doesn't believe it."

"That hardly counts as a place," Gordon said. He did not want to go down this path, particularly in his febrile, combative state of sleep deprivation. Why didn't he start this year with ecology—nice, clean streams, big, bad polluters, sweet, smiling dolphins—like the other biology teachers? He was stubborn about starting with evolution because he had this hunch that every human being was most concerned with himself or herself, and so he'd use the rise of self as the bait to set the hook of fascination in a student. And yet, he knew from last year that it was a mined path, where at any turn he could tread on the belief systems of any number of small-town folks. He did not have the strength today. The room was stifling. The kids all looked to be a gathering of the recessive gene pool.

"Well, some people think Darwin was wrong," Gordon replied patiently, thinking, as he spoke, stupid people. "Some people think he did a pretty good job with the tools he had at hand a hundred and fifty years ago."

Reilly persisted, "But there's this one period of time, and it's only like ten million years, when everything supposedly evolved from bacteria to complex animals. If you're talking billions and billions of years—"

"It's called the Cambrian Explosion," Gordon said, "and, well, look at the AIDS virus. It was around in a limited way for forty years, but it wasn't until after 1980 that it began to really take off—"

"That was because of airplanes," Kye Olstadt chuckled. "The guy who spread it all over was a stewardess."

"And where's the fossil record of the missing link? The chimpanzee thing that decided to become a human?" Reilly asked.

"I'm not no chimpanzee," said Gunther Woffling, who, Gordon would have sworn, had been asleep five minutes before.

"Well, no, but you're ninety-eight percent chimpanzee," Gordon told him.

"The hell I am! I'm not no goddamned monkey!" No, Gordon thought, as the Woffling kid began loudly slamming his books together and shoving them into his backpack, you're an insult to chimpanzees.

"Class isn't over, Gunther," Gordon said quietly.

"If all this is true," Dennis Reilly added, "then why aren't chimpanzees evolving to be more like humans?"

"Because," Gordon sighed, "they're good at being chimpanzees. Look, let's get back to Gunther's point. If you were a little kid and you made a drawing of a man and a drawing of a chimpanzee, they would look almost alike, right? At least more alike then a drawing of a chimpanzee and a chicken? What does that tell you?"

"Well, why aren't lizards evolving to be more like humans?"

"Because they don't need to! Human beings aren't the most evolved species on earth."

"They are! They can think!"

"In fact, there are probably bacteria on the floor of the Atlantic Ocean more highly evolved than human beings . . . because they've had more time."

"You're saying a human being is no better than a bacteria?" Woffling again.

"Not better at being a bacteria! Look, you guys, evolution is not a theory. It's a fact. The theory part is about how exactly it happened, because we weren't there to see it happen. I don't know how. I'm not a Presbyterian minister. I'm not a cell biologist. I'm a science teacher—"

"Do you believe in God?" Reilly asked, adding, "Einstein believed in God."

"Maybe God created evolution," Kelly Rafferty sang out, "to give us something to do."

The buzzer sounded. There was a God.

Gordon dropped his head on the shelf of his cupped hands. "Read chapter four for tomorrow," he blurted. As they all thundered out the door, he could hear Gunther declaiming to all and sundry that he wasn't no bacteria, and if a man wasn't better than an ape, why was a man made in the image of God. There'd be a nice phone call from Mrs. Woffling tomorrow. And then he noticed, felt, a presence next to his desk. Kelly Rafferty.

"Mr. McKenna," she said shyly, "my mom told me about—" about that night at the lodge, Gordon thought; my career sinks slowly in the west; this is the end; no more worries about day care—"about your little baby . . ." Gordon's heart resumed ordinary rhythms. "I can't baby-sit in Tall Trees because I bus. But Melinda Gallo and Kathy Zurich baby-sit all the time. And they said I could tell you they'd help you out, because you seem kind of tired."

"How about two days a week after school and Sundays?"

Kelly blinked. "Well, I'll ask them."

Gordon had to ask, too. He had to ask Hart Rooney whether it violated any policy, however obscure, to ask one of his students to baby-sit for him. Rooney had smiled, looking not one day older than he had when Gordon mowed his lawn. "Why, Gordon," he said easily, "I never had a baby-sitter who didn't go to this school. Where else would you find teenagers? Just be careful they don't get into the beer or drive your car."

And so they came, Melinda and Kathy, his saviors, his baggy-pants saints, Wednesdays and Thursdays after pom practice, and took Keefer to the park or helped her make towers of her blocks, for two hours, while he unplugged the telephone and threw himself across the first horizontal space he could find. So began another short, deceptive period of peace.

Before the night of the bloody nose.

Keefer had been tantrumming. What started it? She'd figured out how to work the nozzle on his shaving cream and he'd let her squirt it into the bathtub a couple of times, but then she'd started squirting it on the walls, on the floor, and he'd taken it away and given her one of her puppets instead. She hit the ceiling. Or more correctly, she hit the floor. Dropped to her knees in the bathroom, screeching, and then slipped on the shaving cream and went down on the tile, and he saw the blood. "Oh my baby, my baby seal," he'd cried, snatching her up, cradling her against his shirt. The blood wouldn't stop. Holding her in one arm, he fumbled to knock some ice loose from the glacier in his freezer, grab a towel. Keefer was in full cry when he heard a knock at the door. Three knocks. Sharp and loud.

"I won't hesitate to call the police," said Judy Wilton.

"What?"

"I just want you to know that I won't hesitate to call the sheriff, or call the welfare," his downstairs neighbor went on. "Look at her!"

He looked at her, at them. He was holding a baby whose face was smeared with blood, who was screaming and pounding on his equally bloody chest with all her might. "Judy," he soothed, "she's having a tantrum."

"This is not normal. I hear this all the time. That baby crying as if her heart would break. I don't know what you have going on here—"

"She wanted the shaving cream. She was playing with the shaving cream." Of course he was lying, that was what Judy Wilton thought. And he began to feel as though he were, indeed, lying. "This isn't what it looks like. She's just mad. She fell and got a bloody nose."

"I'm not going to let you do this to a child."

"Do what? Judy, I love Keefer. I've never laid a hand on Keefer. You know that. You see us together."

"I hear you together. I hear how that child cries. I see the women parading in and out of here at all hours."

"What?"

"That Snow girl. And those college kids."

"Those are my students, Judy. They're my baby-sitters. Lindsay has been my girlfriend for years, and Jesus, Judy. Get a life of your own. What, do you sit down there making a list about who comes into my house?"

She'd given him one brief, bitter nod. An hour later, Sheriff Larsen hit the front-door buzzer, looking as though he were about to bawl.

"Now, Gordo, I don't want you to get all in a sweat here."

"She called, didn't she?"

"She called."

Sorrowfully, the sheriff explained the procedure. When an accusation of suspected child abuse was filed, no matter if the person in question was Dale Larsen's own mother, he was legally bound to alert the county. That didn't mean anything bad would happen, but a social worker would come over and have a chat with him—

"And then there'll be a record of that in some file, right?"

"There'll be a record, Gordon, to say the charge was unfounded. It happens to a lot of people, Gordon. Neighbors say things out of spite. People think they're seeing something they're not seeing—"

"And what if it means the judge says I'm a child abuser and I lose Keefer because of it?"

"If the charge turns out to be unfounded, then that's the end of it. A judge is legally bound, just like I am, to consider that investigation complete and valid, see?"

"I didn't hurt Keefer! She bumped her nose on the floor trying to get the shaving cream!"

"Judy said there was all kinds of mayhem up here all the time."

"That's because she's a crazy old bat who probably has microphones on the ceiling so she can have some diversion besides cutting up chickens for her father. She probably bites the heads off the chickens. Do you know her?"

Dale Larsen did know Judy Wilton. Knew for a fact she'd had a tempestuous lesbian love affair with Liz Kildeer, who used to be the women's tennis pro up at Fidelis Hill, and that deputies had been called out to this very house more than once to quell some pretty intense sobfests and fisticuffs. He hated like hell to do this to Gordon, but the law was the law. And the social worker who dropped by the next day spent a compassionate fifteen minutes with Gordon and Keefer, assuring Gordon afterward that he saw no evidence of any abuse or neglect of this very loved child, who obviously trusted her daddy.

But Gordon remained certain that Faith Bogert would know about the complaint, would know and would use it against him in court, and even when Keefer began occasionally sleeping through the night, Gordon would never have slept at all if it hadn't been for the sedatives his mother seemed to suddenly have in unlimited supply, which he used only once in a while and with terror, fearing Keefer would wake crying and he would not hear her, but Judy Wilton would.

In fact, Faith Bogert did not know about the complaint, not until much later. What she did know, when she arrived for the second observation, she saw things for which she would not have needed an MMPI or an MCMI-III, though the tests had validated her impression. She knew that Gordon was a highly functioning and seemingly optimistic person, who exhibited no overt pathology, with elements of what Faith would have described, if pressed, as characteristics of a mildly narcissistic personality, which was not in and of itself a problem. No more a problem than the fact that the Cadys' test results were utterly unreliable, because their evangelistic Christian beliefs led them to a trust and belief in human goodness way off the scale for an ordinary person. The husband had a rather elevated score for aggression, but that was no big deal. Police officers, for example, often scored way too high in righteous indignation, which in another person, might signal paranoia.

Still, as she watched Gordon try to lead the baby back to her blocks until she finally leaned over and delicately bit him on the leg, Faith wondered whether Gordon's self-centeredness—no, his self-involvement—would prevent him from making the kind of sacrifices a single parent would have to make, that her mother had made. He was an I-guy.

And a busy little bee, too. The phone kept ringing; he let it pick up. "Hey, Mr. McKenna, it's Molly and Kathy, and we're ready to start getting those straight A's in Bio. Ready to hit the bed?" And twenty minutes later, "Gordie? Honey? Lindsay. Call me when she's gone, okay? I'm going crazy." And five minutes after that, "It's firewoman Rafferty. You going to get that cute little butt out here for the tournament on Sunday? I think we can take all of them. Call you later."

Red-faced, Gordon had hastened to explain, "Those are my baby-sitters. I sleep when they're here. That's what they meant. And my volleyball teammate."

Faith simply said, "Don't worry about it. Everybody's life is complicated."

"I'm dying of thirst here," he'd told her then. "Want something?" He checked the refrigerator. "Got beer. Got water. Got frog blood. Got Pedialyte popsicles. How about Yoo-Hoo?"

"Thanks," she said, "but no. I'm trying to quit."

She did look thinner, Gordon noticed, but still wearing the unfortunate stretch pants. Red this time. But . . . hell. He'd dressed Keefer specially, carefully—with much singing and anguish, dangling Georgia's tinkly ankle bracelet in his teeth to distract her while she writhed like a python—in a cute little dress his aunt had sewn, each button a letter of the alphabet.

Now, she proceeded to pull the buttons off, one by one.

"Damn it, Keefer!" he yelped, without thinking.

Faith Bogert glanced out the window. And reached into her bag for a pen.

CHAPTER *twelve*

The emotional hurdle for any judge was to avoid getting a swelled head. Ego was a snare Emily Sayward believed made people stupid. It was probably more poised to trip her up, Emily reasoned, here in Trempeauleau County than it would have been in the Supreme Court of the State of Wisconsin, because her presence as the word made flesh was so visible. All she had to do was stop for a root beer—or worse yet, a *beer* beer—on any street from Wausau to Morehouse to Conover to Tall Trees, and she parted the waters. Conversation shushed as if she'd waved a wand, only to close behind her in ripples. "It's the judge," she imagined them saying, "the lady judge," even though she was only one of three. Emily prayed that the attention would have the sole effect of making her more careful and methodical, and she was careful by nature.

What didn't help was that Emily Sayward was . . . cute. The face and form that gave her so much pleasure in her personal life was an annoyance in her profession. Since she'd left her family-law practice to come here, and especially since her appointment, something about her size compared with the psychic space of her role didn't fit. Her robes looked like a costume. Her lipstick emphasized her habit of catching her underlip between her teeth as she was thinking hard.

Emily and her husband had come to live in their cabin on stilts, on Hat Lake, three years before, when Jamie, on a whim, applied and somehow won the job of general counsel to Medi-Sun (having an Hispanic mom had not hurt, Emily and Jamie privately believed). It was no robotic corporate stamper's job. Vitamins and herbals were not the health candy people believed they were; and now that boomers were chugging handfuls of them daily, there were lawsuits of substantial proportions—the woman who chalked up her psychotic episodes to Valerian, the middle-aged man whose hopeful experiments with ManPower had prompted, or so he alleged, a perpetual and painful erection, and the cancer patients who had desperately forsworn their radiation and opened their arms to the health-food store. Disclaimers and directions were invisible to people, apparently. The work had demanded all that Jamie, a skilled and compassionate litigator, had to give, and the salary and stock benefits gave the Saywards more freedom and security to raise their son than they had dreamed of back in One-L, as they'd tried to visualize their futures over Ramen noodles by candlelight.

Emily began as a county prosecutor. She had put Tom Collins, an unfortunate name for a woebegone drunkard, away for twenty years, revoked his driving privileges for life, and imposed an irrevocable condition of absolute sobriety upon parole. It had been a popular decision. Though Tom Collins was a man with hundreds of distraught and influential friends, the Redmonds' lives had been erased. Just six weeks after the Collins trial, the conservative governor—no particular chum to Emily's liberal leanings—had appointed her to fill the deceased Judge Crabtree's unexpired term. Two years later, Emily cut her long hair to a brisk bob, taught herself to feel incomplete without a blazer, and ran on her own. She won.

But she knew her age and shape still made her look winsomely boyish. When the expressions of even habitual druggies and wife beaters she was sending to Wayadega softened as they listened to her, Emily could barely contain her chagrin.

She had a wooden cigar box under her bench so her feet would not dangle above the floor.

On the night before she was to hear the case of Keefer Nye, Emily walked the lakeshore, checked three times on her peacefully snoozing five-year-old, and finally called her father. Emily's father Arthur Sayward was also a judge, a New Hampshire judge, which her mother, Peggy, insisted made him a judge with a grudge. Peggy often said her husband's opinion was that jurisprudence should never have extended beyond the original thirteen colonies. Arthur's advice was never offered unsought, but when offered, was accepted into his daughter's cupped hands with reverence. Arthur's axioms, Emily's husband called them.

Her father listened without comment as Emily explained how the petitions had come bustling into her chambers the previous night, a full hour after Emily would normally have gone home, the petitions of both sets of grandparents to withdraw their requests for permanent guardianship. Then, the Cadys' request for permanent guardianship and their motion to dismiss Gordon McKenna's petition to adopt his sister's child on grounds that Gordon—because he was an uncle to the child only by adoption—did not meet the standards of the section of Wisconsin law that allowed a streamlined adoption process for stepparents and immediate family members. After that, came the volley from Gordon's lawyer, requesting a separate hearing on his petition for adoption and asking to bar the Cadys from the process altogether, because the Cadys were the ones who were not immediate family, but only second cousins to the child, and thus had no standing to object to anything at all. These on top of the Cadys' earlier petition for guardianship and Gordon's petition to adopt, which had followed the Cadys' in a matter of days.

Everyone's contentions turned on the fragile axis of little Keefer Nye. One little kid robbed of her parents—suddenly cast as a central symbol of survival for two families—propelled by the selfish and yet understandable hunger of her elders' needs into a hornets' nest of competing claims.

There was not a bad egg in the crate.

These families had been through so much trauma; everyone in the county, everyone in Wisconsin, for that matter, had heard something of the McKennas' Sophoclean tragedies. They needed, at least, closure. They needed finality, a place to start to start over.

She could give them that.

"I'm going to hear them all together, Father," Emily said. "They'll want to separate, but this thing needs to be brought under control."

"I think that is wise, Emily."

Emily glanced through the hall arch at the briefcase she'd dropped beside her bed. The documents within seemed to shake and clamor, demanding she attend to their opposed urgencies.

"Consider what you're being asked to consider, Emily," her father cautioned her, after they'd traded assurances of the health of everyone under both their roofs and compared weather conditions in Wisconsin and New Hampshire. "Try to keep your vision trained on the issues right in front of you. You must, of course, be mindful of the circumstances that may proceed from your ruling, but those circumstances are not what you are being asked to predict or to control. Nor are the strong feelings of the families involved, however moving they are."

Her father always spoke for the record.

"And I know that you are not fearful of the possibility of being reversed—"

"I'm not fearful—"

"But it has crossed your mind."

"Daddy, it would cross your mind in this circumstance, too."

"It always crosses my mind, Emily. That's what I was suggesting. Mindful, but not fearful."

Emily recalled, with a sigh, the old law-school joke about there being two courses of action in life, one right, one legal. Her father interrupted, "What might distress you as a human being must not distract you as a judge."

"I know," she said, "but I can't help but think of how this family is going to suffer—"

"Do you want to run it past me?"

"I do, but I'm . . . I'm going to run it past Jamie, and I don't think I have the strength to do it more than once."

"You'll do exactly what you need to do. I know that."

She and Jamie sat on their back deck, parkas thrown around their shoulders against the chill that fell fast these late fall nights, their mugs of coffee warming their hands as the hot strong contents went cold.

"Here's what I'm going to say," she replied. "I'm going to say that while this interpretation might not be one that I would have agreed with personally, the distinction between relatives by blood and by adoption is one that the legislature has made, and while I don't know why the legislature made that distinction, it is there and I must abide by it.

"If people don't agree with the laws their representatives have made—"

"They should address their legislators to change them," her husband completed the thought for her.

"Yes, and then I am going to go straight ahead, and do what I can to see that this child has . . . there's no point in prolonging these things, Jamie, beyond the limits of fairness. The issue is not whether every adult with an interest gets a chance to be heard down to the last phrase and clause—"

"It's not going to be that simple. To be heard. They're going to go nuclear—"

"Not for long they won't," Emily said sharply. "Not in my courtroom."

"I know," Jamie said, pulling her head down onto his shoulder. "No one would want to be the one to do this, Em, but you are the one to do it, if that's any comfort."

"It isn't."

"You're going to catch hell."

"I know."

"That doesn't change anything."

"It doesn't change anything."

They sat up late, watching the moon veil and then reveal its sumptuous golden face. Emily drank all of her coffee plus a second cup, and still slept as though she'd downed six shots of tequila instead.

The next morning, the benches along the marbled hall of the Trempeauleau County Courthouse filled like church pews at the peal of Sunday matins. Everyone except his family and the Nyes, Gordon thought, looked bedraggled and sad. He spotted a guy he'd gone to high school with, a hotshot halfback on their team; he wore a flannel shirt over a tee that read "Cat's Claw Ammo," and his Fu mustache was stained brown at the corners of his lips. When he caught sight of Gordon, he touched the brim of his ball cap and then gathered up one of the skinny little girl children who swarmed all over him, who all appeared to be the same age, all wearing bright, sleeveless summer dresses, though it was nearly Thanksgiving, and Gordon had welcomed the chance, that cold morning, to put his suit jacket on for the ride. Someone, Gordon thought, had once said—who was it? Thoreau?—to beware occasions that required new clothes. He had worn a suit more often in the past six months than in the previous twenty years of his life combined. Today was just trying, wrangling. He looked forward in time to the day he would be back here, to formally become a father. Katt said soon. Breezy Cindy had approved his home study. All was in order. How would that day be? In a suit again, or maybe not. He and Keefer weren't the suit type. But Lindsay would be here, for sure. His cousins, his aunts and uncles. He imagined that this moment, formally adopting Keefer, would be how a man would feel on the day he married someone he already knew very well, like Lindsay; though an official seal would be imprinted on something that already existed, the thing itself would saunter along as it had before, comfortable, unchanged. Gordon felt a surge of longing for Lindsay, who'd taken the day off and was at his place with his aunt Nora and Bradie, cooking frantically for lack of anything better to do.

He saw that Big Ray, huddled on a bench down the hall in front of another courtroom, was only wearing a golf shirt. It would be hard to imagine Ray being able to find a sport coat around here that would fit. The guy had put on so much weight, and it was the kind of heft that didn't sit well, straining against his shirt and pants as if his clothing hadn't had a chance to catch up. Diane paced in front of a bank of windows at the far end of the hall, with Delia Cady and, Gordon assumed, a gaggle of suits who were their lawyers. Craig was closely examining the wall. The kid Alexis, who seemed to have grown into a real young woman over the summer, suddenly waved to him. He waved back.

When the McKennas' own legal troops arrived, there were introductions all around to Stacey Kane, the adoption expert from Madison, a willowy blonde with peek-a-boo hair. She was all angles and gestures, strung so tight Gordon thought that if the hall were quiet, he would hear a tone, like the thrum from a struck tuning fork. Katt explained that Stacey had, by good fortune, been freed up this morning to lend her powerful voice, one of long experience with adoption and the meaning of adoption in families. They would need her. "This is not going to be a slam-dunk," he told the McKennas, "but we are going to come out of here just fine."

His parents' new lawyer, a pleasant-faced older woman called May Hendrickson, bustled from the elevator; she'd been downstairs filing her request that his parents' guardianship be set aside to make way for Gordon. The Nyes, she said, without preamble, had done the same thing. Then, to Gordon's surprise, she marched up, shook his hand, and then hugged him.

Lorraine murmured, glancing at the Nyes, "They can't really mean that thing about Gordon having no standing."

"They're grasping at straws," Katt told her, "They're nitpicking at some outmoded language."

"It's based on something that was clearly not what the legislature intended and which has never been used to deny any person who was adopted any part of their rights as a full family member," Stacey Cane said, without stopping to draw breath, "and it also just doesn't make any sense. The law is made for people, people aren't made to fit the law."

The draggled people were filing into the other courtroom. His old high school acquaintance saluted as he passed. Then the hall was so still Gordon could hear the harsh caw of a crow outside. Since Diane's explosive visit, almost eight weeks ago, no member of the Nye family—except Alex, just now—had exchanged a single word with a member of the McKenna family. Even Nora, who'd taken on the role of the pneumatic tube designated to physically carry Keefer to the car when the Cadys came to pick her up, had learned to bite her ever-ready tongue. Details of Keefer's preferences and needs were relayed in terse notes from Lorraine and went unanswered by Craig and Delia. The wacky duel of motions hadn't helped. The very temperature in the corridor seemed to be dropping. What were they waiting for, Gordon wondered? And then the guardian ad litem, Keefer's very own suit, showed up and smiled and nodded at all of them; Gordon had forgotten her name. He could not help thinking that not even one full season ago, all these same people had fallen into one another's arms, all flaws acquitted in the press of bereavement.

"Where is Miss Keefer?" Katt asked, breaking the silence.

"Home with Nora, her auntie Nora," Lorraine said.

"Good," Katt nodded, but his gaze coasted past them, at Faith Bogert, the psychologist, who strode briskly past, saying, "Good morning, all," and motioning for the attention of the guardian ad litem. There was a sudden shuffle and clack at the top of the stairs and Upchurch, in his maroon Trempeauleau County Public Works shirt, appeared. Gordon's first thought was that something was wrong, that something had happened to Keefer.

"Are you okay?" Tim asked Gordon.

"I'm okay."

"I could stay, but I'm guessing they won't let me in."

"Tim," Mark McKenna took hold of Upchurch's shoulder and hand, in a warm, brief parody of a wrestle, "Tim, I'm glad you're here."

The bailiff pushed open the doors. Lorraine took Gordon's hand.

"How long will this take?" Upchurch whispered.

"Not so long, I guess," Gordon said.

"Gordo?"

"Yeah?"

"Well, I got your back."

Gordon, who could not speak, nodded and made a thumbs-up. It was beginning.

She was a tiny woman, the judge, doll-like in her voluminous robes. And as she nodded at all of them, Gordon saw her catch her lower lip in her teeth for a moment. Something deep in the fiber of his nerves crawled along the back of his scalp.

The clerk read, "Case 0886896, in the interest of Keefer Nye. Appearances?"

They all spoke up in turn: "Appearing are Raymond Nye,

Senior, and Diane Nye personally and by attorneys George Liotis and Benjamin Malone."

"May Hendrickson here, appearing on behalf of Mark and Lorraine McKenna. The McKennas are present."

"Gordon McKenna appears in person by Stacey Kane and Gregory Katt, attorneys."

"Mary Ellen Wentworth appearing on behalf of Delia and Craig Cady, who are here in person."

"Victoria Linquist, the guardian ad litem, and Faith Bogert."

"All right, we're all here," Judge Sayward began, her voice as small and unassuming as her looks. "And we have a bundle of various petitions to consider. In fact"—she pulled out a pair of reading glasses—"just this morning there has been filed with this court a stipulation from Mark and Lorraine McKenna and Diane and Raymond Nye that their petitions for guardianship be withdrawn and dismissed. Is this correct?"

"It is, Judge," George Liotis said softly.

"And there is the petition of Lorraine and Mark McKenna for temporary guardianship to be continued, with the same provisions for visitation by both sets of grandparents, during the interim until the final decision is made in this matter," added May Hendrickson.

"But scheduling grandparents' visitation," Judge Sayward said, "will require a separate date, and given that we are not entirely sure what is going to be happening with the remainder of these matters . . . can counsel be available at the conclusion of these proceedings? Or give the clerk a phone number where you can be reached, to set that date?" Then, over their murmurs and nods, she said, "Let's get down to what's left here. The petitions of the Cadys and Gordon McKenna. The other parties may leave now."

Greg Katt motioned to Lorraine, who shook her head briefly and violently, but then, led by Mark's hand on her arm, made her way up the aisle, half-turned to stare beseechingly back at Gordon. He had to shake his head to dismiss her face from his mind. Diane and Ray, by contrast, jumped out of their seats and hurried out.

"With regard to those two petitions," the judge continued, "these came to the court late yesterday . . . evening. One is a motion to dismiss the adoption petition. The other is a motion for a separate hearing and it also seeks to bar parties who lack standing. Do all counsel have copies of these motions?"

Katt said, "We do, Your Honor, but the record should reflect that we only got this fax at almost six o'clock at night."

"Well," said Judge Sayward, "that was late. But there we have it. Mr. Katt, what position are you putting forward here, on the motion for a separate hearing and to bar participation?"

"Your Honor, it's simply this. It's obvious. Under Wisconsin law, and here we're referring to forty-eight-oh-two in conjunction with forty-eight-ninety, the Cadys do not fall under any of the classifications referred to in the statute for a relative who may file an adoption petition at any time."

"Which are, yes, a parent, grandparent—"

"A stepparent, brother, sister, nephew, niece, aunt or uncle, or a first cousin. A petition can be filed for adoption at any time if one of the petitioners is a relative of the child by blood, without the customary six-month waiting period, because presumably that child has an already existent bond with the relative in question."

"Correct."

"And Delia Cady is a first cousin . . . ?"

"Not of Keefer Nye, Your Honor," Katt interjected smoothly, "of Keefer Nye's father, Raymond Nye, Jr., which makes her a second cousin."

"Yes," Judge Sayward said, glancing at Gordon, "I know that."

"And we refer to the case attached, in which the court ruled that the three children's grandparents lacked standing to object."

"But the parental rights had been terminated in that case," the judge said, "and the children subsequently were to be adopted, so the grandparents' connection to the children was through the parents whose rights had been terminated. That's not at all what we're talking about here."

"Well," Katt said, "our point is, why are the Cadys here? As second cousins, they do not meet the test of relatives."

Judge Sayward leaned back in her chair, and seemed to Gordon to square herself, to increase in stature. "So you're saying they're not relatives by blood, as defined by the statute. That is the basis of your motion."

"That's right," said Katt, but he glanced behind him hurriedly, uncomfortably, as if sensing an approach. "To quote from this case, only those who have a legally protectible interest in the adoption have standing to object to another person's petition to adopt."

"Miz Wentworth?"

"Judge, in our motion, which was in response, we indicated what is true, that Gordon McKenna does not have standing here because he is not a blood relative. There's the relative definition in forty-eight-oh-three but then under forty-eight-eighty-five, the statute specifies a blood relative. And my clients do have a legally protected interest, contrary to what Mr. Katt says, because they've filed under the guardianship code. And, if you will permit me, they filed at least two weeks prior to Mr. McKenna, so if the two proceedings were going to be segregated, I believe ours would come first, because we filed first."

"All right. Miss Linquist?" the judge turned to the guardian.

"Well, as I am here to protect the interests of Keefer Nye, I have an interest in the court's ruling on whether Gordon McKenna is a relative by blood. He is adopted. So there is no biological connection between Mr. McKenna and Keefer Nye. His sister, the child's deceased mother, was also adopted. I think it is a question of law that needs to be cleared up."

"On that issue, Mr. Katt?"

"Miss Kane is going to speak to that issue. I . . . I didn't know we were going to plunge into both of them at the same time. But . . . only people who have standing to adopt a child also have standing to *object* to someone else adopting that child. As per the case we cited . . . the Cadys have no right to petition."

"And they are not trying to petition—to adopt. Only your client is trying to do that. Miz Wentworth, the Cadys were aware that Mr. McKenna was adopted?" the judge asked.

"They were, Your Honor, but they did not choose to bring up that fact until they were forced to do so in order to respond to the appellant's wish to get them out of the case altogether."

Judge Sayward lowered her glasses and studied first Gordon, then the Cadys. "And so each side is challenging, by the same definition no less, the other side's standing. The wisdom of Solomon is strained."

Katt spoke up, "And they're trying to use a case in which children who'd been adopted tried to inherit money from their biological grandfather, but Your Honor, even then, the decision said adoption is intended to effect a complete substitution of all rights and other legal consequences . . ." He cleared his throat and continued, in a lower register. "It's an insult, is what it is. To cook this up the night before a trial. It goes against everything in our code where they define minors' families; all those sections referred to adopted children in the same way as natural."

"That's all well. But my question is this, Mister Katt. Why does forty-eight-ninety not say a relative, but a relative by blood?"

"I don't know."

"Well, I do know. The lawmakers we have elected, that you have elected, are making a distinction. They're saying that at least in this particular situation, expedited procedure is to apply to a relative by blood. Why didn't they just say a plain old relative? Do you have an answer, Miz Kane?"

"Judge," said Stacey Kane, placing her hand on Gordon's

shoulder. "This is offensive. This is the most offensive motion I have ever encountered and I have been involved with adoption work for nearly all my professional life. Now, presumably, the Cadys want to adopt their . . . godchild, Keefer. How can someone who wants to adopt a child do so by trying to abridge the rights of another adopted child, this child's very own uncle? After they've adopted Keefer, would they turn around and say, well, now *we're* not your relatives, because you're adopted? It's insane."

"No one said Mr. McKenna is not a relative," Emily Sayward told her. "He's not a *blood* relative under the statute he tried to use to adopt this child, which would have given him an advantage over the Cadys." She pressed her lips together and tapped the papers on her bench.

"But he is specifically to be treated as if he were a blood relative. All the statutes make it clear. Gordon and Georgia have all the same rights and standing they would have if the McKennas had given birth to them. They were raised from the time they were babies. The reason this statute exists is to get children in situations like Keefer Nye's quickly and expeditiously into the arms of those who know them best and love them most. And that is Gordon. Gordon, who cared for his sister while she was dying and helped his parents raise this baby and has raised her mostly on his own since then."

The judge squinted. "I thought that the grandparents were the principal guardians here."

"They are, but for the purposes of getting the child adjusted to the home that everyone believed she would have, she has been spending time with her uncle."

"I see," said the judge. "I see."

"And Gordon McKenna has submitted to a home study by a qualified agency and he has been approved as eminently qualified to adopt Keefer."

"All right. I think this is clear. If the statute said relative, and didn't refer back to the relationship being by blood or direct affinity, Mr. McKenna would certainly be a relative.

But it doesn't say that. It says 'by blood.' I can't ignore what the legislature has said. The legislature made that distinction, and I may not like it and you may not like it and certainly the petitioner here before us will not like it, and yet it's there. The distinction is made between just any relative and a blood relative." She sighed. "And of course, the Cadys don't meet that definition under the statute in question, either. And so they would not have standing to file for adoption, either, not at this time."

She looked down at her hands. "And so, since neither of the parties has the standing on this adoption, I am going to dismiss Mr. McKenna's petition at this time. That is denied."

Stacey Kane gasped.

"Judge, Judge," Katt spoke up. "Now, would you consider staying your order so that we can take an interlocutory appeal while this case is pending? Keefer has already been in the care of her grandparents, spending large amounts of her time with both her maternal and paternal grandparents and everything has been going well—"

"I hear she's been living with her uncle," the judge replied.

"And she has been in the care of the Cadys as well," Katt snapped. "The Nyes are permanent residents of the state of Florida."

"Yes, and?"

"Well, this is a pretty simple issue," Katt continued, visibly forcing himself to summon an easy smile, as if they were all old friends who could relax and make short work of this little obstacle. "The Court of Appeals could take it up quickly, and what if you were to grant the Cadys their guardianship and the child went to live with them, and then we were successful on appeal, and we'd be right back here where we started on Gordon's adoption—"

"Let's ask Ms. Wentworth," the judge suggested.

"Can Gordon McKenna remain for this?" Katt asked.

"He can remain, but not participate," the judge said.

Gordon nodded. The muscles in his legs were quivering, and he could not have stood unsupported even if he had wanted to try. He could think only of . . . blood. Red blood cells were the only cells in the human body that did not contain DNA. Blood? Blood, at least much of blood, was not the storage unit for the entwined chromosomal ladders that matched criminals to crimes or parents to . . . children. Blood. Blood like a painted fan on the windshield of the ruined car. Blood on the shredded sleeve of Georgia's purple and gold shirt, a shred of fabric bouncing gently on the surface of Lost Tribe Creek. He turned in desperation away from the hubbub in the room. . . . He looked out the huge cathedral window of the courtroom.

"I believe that my clients should be allowed to proceed. . . . back and forth between grandparents, one family unit here, one in Madison . . . harm in so much discontinuity . . . one home, one family . . ."

And another voice, the guardian ad litem—the guardian! "I represent Keefer. And while she has been in loving hands, she is not in a healthy situation . . . the venue dispute, that simply took more time . . . this is a little child . . . the appellate level could take months, two, three, more . . . Dr. Bogert's recommendation is that the Cadys are the more suitable couple. She has spoken with all of the family members, and many friends of both have said the same thing, he's a single man. He lived with his parents most of last year, and then he has had two separate residences since that time . . . their own home . . . Delia is a stay-home mother . . . a sister of her own . . ."

There was a beech outside the courtroom window. With their bronze leaves and peculiar trunks, they reminded Gordon somehow of banyan trees. Blood. The trunk. The torso. Carotid artery. Right subclavian. Brachiocephalic. Brachial. Pulmonary artery. Venae cavae. Limbs. Branches. Shoots. Capillaries.

Stacey Kane was nearly shouting. "This is a serious issue,

Your Honor. To say an adoptive brother isn't as good as a brother by birth undermines the whole foundation of the ideal of adoption."

Katt added, "Then we will file a petition for guardianship, Judge. My client will file a petition for guardianship, just as the Cadys have, and proceed with the required—"

"I would object to that, Your Honor. There would not be appropriate notice under the statute. And they were the ones who objected, when we all came in here, that we hadn't given them appropriate notice."

"I think," the judge said, "that we are going to proceed with the petition that is now before us, rather than allow any other petitions to be introduced. It is too late for that now. Mr. McKenna had months to decide what he wanted to do, and he chose to proceed with this particular kind of expedited adoption petition, rather than the ordinary kind that this court would have been unable to question."

"Judge, to complete the record," Katt pleaded, "we did not have time, since . . . I was only by coincidence in my office when this motion you have just granted, to dismiss Mr. McKenna's adoption, was faxed to me."

"As was I," the judge replied dryly.

"We have not been able to prepare adequately for this motion. We have not been able to find the law we know exists to support our position," Katt begged.

"Then you can appeal," she said.

"And we will, with all due respect, appeal, and our appeal will clearly state that the Cadys knew since they met Gordon McKenna and his sister that they were adopted . . ."

"That's not true," Wentworth pointed out. "I only became aware of it days ago."

"But it was clearly stated, in the report you have from Dr. Bogert!" Katt cried. "It's all over the place in that document, about my client's belief that as an adopted child, he would be uniquely qualified to teach Keefer about the meaning and importance of adoption. Your Honor, filing this motion at the eleventh hour was a maneuver."

"I've heard you and acknowledge your concerns," Emily Sayward said, gently, "but I'm not granting a stay. This child needs to be home. If you do appeal, and if the Wisconsin Court of Appeals finds me in error, we'll be back here with the petition again. But that could take too long a time. A very long time. We will proceed with the other matter now, the petition for guardianship by the Cadys."

"Will he be here?" asked Mary Ellen Wentworth, "I mean, will Mr. McKenna be present during this action. He's not a party to it. He has no petition before the court. He's like any of the other relatives out there in the hallway. It seems, therefore, that he has no reason to be present with counsel."

"Are you suggesting that there is some statute that says this man should not be present? Are you suggesting that?" Gordon, catching her tone, sought her eyes and saw the pity there. "It . . . and I'm looking at the forty-eight-two-ninety-nine, the court may allow any person at the proceeding who has a proper interest in the case. He has indeed a proper interest." She looked down at Gordon. "He is her uncle. Though not by blood. Our family code provides no legal weight for love. It's not prosecutable. It's not quantifiable. It's not concrete. And yet, it is real interest. Now, let us proceed."

When the doors with their brass half-moons opened, and the Cadys rushed into the arms of Diane and Big Ray, Gordon reached out and drew his mother by the hand until she stood in front of him; and his father, Church, and the lawyers followed, a circle, a huddle, the natural formation of a herd.

"It's not over," Katt told them, "I want you to know . . ." He removed his wire rims, and scrubbed at his eyes.

"Gordon, what did she say?" Lorraine laid her cool hand on Gordon's forehead. "You're burning. Honey, what did they say?"

Should he let Katt explain? Let Kane finish? Would the

facts speak for themselves, as he had believed his whole adult life? Facts, pressing forward, the uncontrolled variable, obliterating the truth, regardless of harm. He had not counted on the uncontrolled variable.

Georgia, he thought, his voice and her voice merging, growing faint.

"They said I'm not Georgia's brother," he told his parents. "They said I'm not your son."

CHAPTER *thirteen*

$\mathcal{N}$ora truly believed sometimes she did have eyes in the back of her head. When Rob was tiny, he'd come creeping into their room to peek under the pink foam rollers she used to sleep in. Nora had first dreamed bugs were crawling on her and then awakened with a jolt. "Did I poke you in the eye?" Rob whispered. He'd been all of four.

Still, at this minute, Nora could all but see, without turning away from the sink where she was rinsing the supper dishes, that Hayes was only pretending to read the *Bountiful Farmer*. Their son Marty had him interested in this idea of starting an organic co-op. People would buy shares in the spring, and each week throughout the growing season, someone (her, if she knew how these things went) would bring around fresh produce and jams to the members. They'd have to be certified organic, though, that was what the richies wanted, but organic wasn't going to be a problem. Hayes all but powdered his land's butt every day—as had her father and his father before that.

It wasn't that Hayes was reading, jiggering his chair the way he liked it, so he could prop up his big feet in their monkey socks. It was that he was awake at all. That meant something was on his mind. As the days got shorter, Hayes got sleepier and sleepier, just like a bird. By seven o'clock, he'd be snoring at the dinner table. Nora would crack open the farm's account books across from him and carry on whole conversations with her sleeping spouse. "So what do you think of Barbara Quintero running for governor, Hayes? Think a woman has a chance? You think Robin Yount's going to take the job as coach? Remember the Brewers back in eighty-two? Or was it eighty-three?"

Nora washed her hands and wiped them on the back end of her jeans. Bigger every month. She couldn't get the fourteens zipped anymore. She turned to Hayes. "Want some coffee, honey? I could drink a cup."

"I do, Nory," he said, carefully pleating the page, closing the magazine, setting it to one side. "I'd like a cup."

Definitely strange.

Hayes was not only awake at 8:00 P.M. but agreeing to stimulants and using the name he hadn't called her since their courtship. Could be feeling frisky. Not that she would mind. She'd never had a child that wasn't conceived in winter, the only time, it seemed, they ever did more than pass each other on the stairs. Lately, though, she'd been in town more than here. The days since the funeral bled into one another until you lost track entirely.

November, the short, dark month, was nearly over. Those people would come to take Keefer for good early in December, unless the lawyers figured out a way to stop it.

She went to Cleveland Avenue now every day, to mind Keefer and to hit the phones like the marines landing at Normandy. It hadn't taken Mark any time at all to see they needed another phone line. Gordie had taught Nora how to use the e-mail. Wasn't anything to it, for a woman who'd disked fields and put together bicycles from kits. Gordie and Lorraine got on the computer or the phones as soon as the school day ended, and Lindsay came after the store closed. Even Mike and Debbie were there when the reporter from *Newsweek* came. The fellow spent three hours, drinking five cups of coffee, asking them every possible question imaginable.

The Cadys wouldn't even talk to him, though Ray's sisters did. Greg Katt was so excited about the story in *Newsweek,* he'd told Nora, that he'd subscribed.

Why should those Cadys talk, Nora thought, as she measured coffee? They had what they wanted.

She sometimes thought that all the calling and e-mailing might be wasted, and then they'd be sorry they hadn't spent more time just cuddling Keefer and singing to her.

"Nory," Hayes said then, interrupting her thoughts about the letter they were planning, with a color photo of Gordie and Keefer with Pearl's newborn kittens, the heading on it "Do You Believe Adopted Children Have Equal Status with Biological Children?"

"Come and sit down, Nory, I want to talk to you."

He had prostate. She knew it. He'd been to see their doctor the previous week, the new doctor, Eve Holly, Hayes griping about having a woman put her finger in his rump. Well. Prostate was curable.

"Nory, I want to talk to you about this business with Mark and Lorraine."

Thank you, God. Nora let herself slump against the ladder back of her chair. "Hayes, you scared me to death. I thought you were going to say you had prostate cancer."

"Prostate cancer? I just had the Eve Holly special, the big checkup." He twirled one thick finger in the approximation of a spiral staircase.

"Well, I thought you were trying to keep it from me, with . . . the trouble and all."

Hayes stood up from his chair like an old penknife opening. He was only ten years older than Nora, but he acted like ninety some days. Still, he did the work of a man of thirty. She leaned over and kissed his lower lip. Hayes blinked.

"Nory, I don't know quite how to say this, because I don't

want to hurt your feelings in any way. I mean that, Nora." He measured four sugars into his coffee. "Now, Mark is a good man. I've always liked Mark. And Georgia was the sweetest thing on earth, God rest her soul. But what's done is done now. That judge is not a judge for no reason, Nora. She understands what's best for that child."

"What are you talking about?"

"Nora, I can't say that I disagree with her. Gordie is a good boy, a fine boy. But he's a single man. He has no more business raising a baby girl than our Rob or our Marty. Can you imagine Marty raising a baby girl?"

"Hayes, he's wonderful with Keefer. And, anyhow, what would you have done with our boys if I'd died?"

"Why, I'd have married Phyllis Cladley the first chance I got."

"Well good for you, Hayes. Are you suggesting that the judge made that awful ruling because she thought the baby would be better off with those people from Madison, those cousins?"

"I'm not saying that's all there is to it."

"Well, what are you suggesting?"

"The bottom line of it is, I don't want you involved."

"With the appeal? With the law change? Why? This is our family, Hayes."

"That's just what I'm saying, Nory. I care about those kids same as you do, but the law is the law. Think if it were your own child. Your own farm, say. Would you want some kid no one knows where he came from to inherit our land? Would you want it to pass out of our family forever?" He gestured, as if to encompass the horizon. "Things should stay in the family they came from."

"That's ridiculous. What if all our boys were gone, God forbid. What if Georgia was the only one left, what if Georgia hadn't died? Would you be upset if that land went to Georgia?"

"Yes," Hayes told her firmly, "yes I would." His eyes watered briefly, and then he said, "No. I wouldn't." He rose from the table slowly and blew his nose on one of the dish towels. "It was dirty anyway," he said sheepishly, when she glared. "See, I'm putting it right in the hamper."

"Well, you can take it right out of the hamper and wash it yourself, too."

"Georgia was one of a kind, Nora. But those people in Madison are that baby's kin. They're her kin the same as Mark is kin to our boys. They'll know things . . . about her. That we'd never know. They can give her a way of seeing where she came from."

"She came from Tall Trees, Hayes. Just like you did and I did."

"And there's no way you're going to convince any of those guys in Madison that they have to admit they're wrong!"

"I think we will."

"You can't fight city hall, Nora."

"I think you can, Hayes. If you couldn't, there wouldn't be a family farm left in Wisconsin."

"Don't mix apples and oranges, Nora."

"Hayes, you saw them that day. It was like Georgia'd died all over again. That baby's all they're living for, the baby and Gordie."

"But this is not about them, Nora. It's about us. People are talking. Not everyone in this town appreciates being slapped all over the front page of the *Milwaukee Journal*. *Newsweek*. The Blood Relative Case. The Blood Relative Case. It's all you see. Lorraine crying and saying, 'They are my blood, they are my flesh and blood. The blood in my brain gave me the emotions to love them . . .' I know she means well, but there are those who don't think that kind of attention is . . . appropriate."

"Who?"

"Lots of people."

"Name one."

"Well, the principal for one. The high school principal. You know he's got a big mouth, Lorraine. He always has. Heard at Hubble's the other day he's considering writing a letter to the editor."

"Have you seen the letters to the editor, Hayes? In the *Messenger*. They're all in favor of us. They all say it was horrible, what Judge Sayward did. We got seventy e-mails, Hayes, on Mark's laptop he brought home from the plant. Even parents who had their own children with no problem at all think this is awful. They're all for Gordie."

Hayes just stared at her, impassively. "Well, it's going to ruin us, Nora. It's going to ruin us, and you have your own family to think of."

"Ruin us?"

"You out all hours of the night in town. Lorraine running up street and down alley. Gordon—Gordon's a school-teacher, Nora! Do you think people want their kids being taught by some guy in the middle of this ugly thing?"

"Stick to the point, Hayes. You said it would ruin us."

"Well, you're never here anymore. I'm likely to die from Bradie's cooking."

"You don't look like you're losing any flesh."

"And the worst of it is—"

"Go on. Say all of it."

"Well, this idea Marty has. And the farm going as good as it is. People are going to be pointing fingers, Nora. Saying, those are the ones stirring up all that stuff over that baby. And that young couple? The ones with the fancy sign?" She'd seen it, THE JOHNSTON-ENGLISH FARM. "They're going to start a vegetable store and they're going to have coffee there, too, and antiques, and who knows what all else."

"So you're worried they're going to take away our business."

"Selling to restaurants pretty soon. My clients."

"You grow beautiful things, Hayes," she said soothingly. "No one would want Sungolds or Yellow Pear tomatoes from anyone else. They're just not like ours. Or Moons and Stars melons. Or the white asparagus—"

"I'm not the only one who thinks so. Your own son thinks the same way, Nora."

"Marty?"

"Yes."

"Well, Hayes, the day I start letting Marty Nordstrom run my life you can get out a shovel and—"

"What about me? I've been your husband for twenty-nine years. Oh yes, you don't think I remember how many. But I do. And I say it stops. Now. It's not that I don't wish them well. Hell, I wish them all the good in the world. They've suffered enough. And I'm not saying you can't help out with Keefer . . ."

Nora felt as though she'd been blown back by a great wind, blown back through the open window over the sink, up the meadow where their Holstein had grazed with her bull calf last spring, so reminding her of Georgia and Keefer, the little bull wide-eyed and gawky, over the thistled ridge down to the pond where the river birches seemed to brace themselves like delicate elderly ladies making their way down to wade.

This was her home. Every April, she took the big rake and ventured out into that mucky water and drew the mustard-colored fans of water lily, festooned with algae, toward her, filling her wheelbarrow, spreading that rich, wet vegetative paste around her perennials, her irises, and her ferns, hostas and lilies of the valley, which sprang up gratefully weeks before her neighbors' did. She cooked and canned and hoed and chased the flies and rubbed liniment into Hayes's hands and her own, beat the ridged mud from boots and overalls, hung them on the carousel in the sideyard to dry. She wrote out the disheartening checks to the bank and the water utility, fed the cats and caught and held them to give them their shots, taught Bradie how to use two knives to cut butter into flour for a crust, sliced the cool green stems of tulips and wrapped them in wet newspaper for the urns on the altar at church. In her mind, she was blown up onto the rise they called Deer Park, because the does nested there with their newborns—Nora would cook venison but would never allow Hayes or the boys to shoot a deer on their own land—where the boys had flung themselves on their sleds when they were little, where you could stand concealed among the evergreens and watch the lights punctuate the dusk, count them out like musical notes: the Romans, the Cladleys, the Zurichs, the Rooneys, the Wofflings. Where on a lucid day, you could see all the way to Snowmounds, the misty glaciated hills hunched in a ring. She and Hayes planned to build a cabin up there one day, and take their ease, while Dan and Marty ran the place. They planned a porch that wrapped around the cabin like an apron, with Adirondack chairs in a row.

In the decades since Father Barry had pronounced them husband and wife, Nora could not recall a time she had overtly disagreed with Hayes. He had never raised a hand to her, or to the boys, no matter what kind of loony stunts they pulled. He had never belittled Rob for his sorry grades, or rebuked Marty for starving himself practically to death that one summer over the Rooney girl, and it was he who insisted they set aside something every month for all the boys to get on their feet when they were older. She had not told Hayes in so many words that she loved him for . . . since their silver wedding. But she loved him as she loved her flowers and her mated cherry trees and Easter mass, not with the sharp, anguishing delight she felt for her own boys and Georgia, but with the enduring appreciation only refuge could provide. She could not imagine living without Hayes any more than she could imagine standing on thin air.

And so it was with a heaviness in her chest that she said, "I'm going to do this, Hayes, and it isn't that I don't care about your feelings. I'm sorry that you feel like you do. But I'm going to do this whether you like it or not. And I do not think it will have any effect on our farm. But if it does, that would not stop me, either."

He'd said nothing. He gripped his coffee cup in both hands, and Nora could see his knuckles bulge.

"You're set on this," he said finally.

"If I did not do everything I could to right this wrong, I could not face Georgia. God hates a coward, Hayes."

"God hates a fool, Nora."

"Are you suggesting I'm a fool?"

"Yes," he answered slowly, "but I will not say a word against you."

Gratitude filled her so that she could not speak. She touched his hand, then his thick arm, and they clung together.

Later, Nora pulled open the drawer where she kept her wedding nightgown and her slips and slid out Georgia's sweatshirt, which she folded against her belly and rocked and rocked. They could not stop now. There was no way to stop now. They'd come too far.

She wished she could have been there at the courthouse.

When they heard the news, she and Lindsay Snow knelt next to the dog bed where Keefer lay sleeping with her shirt pillow. Mad things had zigzagged through Nora's brain, like she and Lindsay should just pack up the baby and get on an airplane, fly to Hawaii. When Lindsay got up and locked the door, Nora didn't even have to ask why. Menace seemed to prowl the innocent snow-dusted street outside the Victorian. They stood at the window, waiting for Lorraine and Mark to come home, and when that hatchet-faced Wilton woman, the one who'd sicced the sheriff on Gordie, glanced up, they drew back, pressing themselves against the wall. Mark and Gordie drove up a few minutes later, saying Lorraine had gone to get her hair cut.

Nora thought Lorraine had finally lost her mind.

But when she showed up, two hours later, having marched into the Style Inn and demanded a blunt cut, Nora had to admit her sister-in-law looked different, freshened, somehow stronger. Ready for battle.

The next day and the next, when the reporters converged and photos were taken, Nora thought, Lorraine's no fool. In her blazer and checked wool slacks, Lorraine was proper, precise, businesslike, like a model from the Land's End catalogue, not a banshee in a shawl, all straggles and loose pins. The kind of person you'd trust, just from seeing her, as she distributed copies of a picture of Ray and Georgia holding Keefer, copies she'd had printed up overnight at the Sam's Club. The man from *Newsweek* came on Saturday, and *CBS News* on Sunday, and she and Marty and Dan watched in awe that night as Dan Rather spoke the McKennas' names, though, of course, not Keefer's.

A machine that ground on under its own power seemed to have been set in motion by that first phone call. Nora had actually been the one to suggest calling their state representative. Lorraine and Mark, who'd voted only in presidential years, had no idea who he was. But Nora knew not only Phil Kay's name, but where he lived. They'd phoned him at home, and Lorraine recounted the conversation. "I'm shocked," he'd said. "That's practically impossible." He promised to search out the history of the statute first thing Monday and determine whether the legislative intent had been to discriminate between family members who were adopted and those who were not. He'd been headed out the door when the phone rang, he told them later, and would ordinarily have allowed the machine to pick up, but something had told him he needed to take the call himself.

Lorraine, who looked to Nora as if she did not sleep a minute that first weekend, drafted a letter she said she intended to send to every newspaper she could think of, in Wisconsin and beyond, to TV stations and the National Organization of Adoptive Families and the president of the United States. They all toiled over it, striking those phrases that Lorraine liked but Mark considered inflammatory, including "hideous injustice" and "corrupt judicial system" and "people Keefer scarcely knows."

"It's not true that she scarcely knows them," he said. "She knows them well. And you have to keep in mind, they are acting on what they believe is right. They weren't attempting to pull the rug out from under us."

"I think they were," Lorraine insisted. "If they were so determined to keep Keefer in the family, why didn't one of the Nye girls want her?"

"I know that much," Gordon spoke up. "Caroline's getting a divorce. And Alison . . . I think she pretty much does what her husband says."

"But you don't know for sure," Mark reminded him.

"I don't know anything for sure," Gordon had answered meekly, "not anymore."

Where else would they post their message? Lindsay Snow suggested adoption agencies and the windows of stores. Hadn't they done just that with the golf outing to raise funds for cancer research? Natalie Chaptman brought an updated list of parishioners from Father Barry's secretary, and those were added to the list. And in church that Sunday, Father Barry read a portion of the letter from the pulpit. "Gordon is determined to affirm that he and all adopted children are proud of their heritage and consider themselves an equal part of their family units. As it stands, this law not only denigrates one family, but also the caring, nurturing institution of the creation of families through adoption, a bond that goes deeper than blood." He asked for prayers for the McKennas, the Nyes, and the Cadys, and for Judge Sayward, "who must be guided by conscience."

After the service, the Soderbergs' oldest boy, the one they called Corky, came up and said that the monks and several others had approached the bank where he worked with contributions for, as he put it, "the defense." Should these checks be sent to the McKennas? Did they prefer to set up a fund?

The Monday after her set-to with Hayes, Nora had shown up at Mark and Lorraine's at dawn. An hour later, Gordie, his eyelids raw and puffed, came in carrying Keefer. Painfully, reluctantly, Lorraine and Gordie got ready to drive to school. Both of them considered calling in sick. Mark had reminded them it might cast them in a bad light, if they didn't carry on as usual.

Nora was alone, with a phone in one hand and Keefer on her hip, when Phil Kay called.

The lawmaker said that his office had turned up no reason to believe that the law, written in 1959, had intentionally discriminated against adopted children. Kay then explained that similar cases from around the same period all agreed in substance that upon adoption, the rights of an adopted and a biological child converged. And so he would propose an amendment, so that the law would read "by blood or by adoption." It was his feeling that the language had been an oversight, that legislators assumed, as the McKennas had, that once a child had been adopted, that child became a full, blood relative, even if not literally.

They could expect the legislature to consider it within a year, or at the most, two.

"A year?" Nora gasped. "But we only have six or seven months until they actually adopt Keefer."

"I know," Kay said miserably, "but if you could get a stay—"

"The judge isn't going to give us the time of day," Nora told him.

"I'll do the best I can," the assemblyman told her. "I'll think this over every which way."

She thanked him. And she thought, it can't take years. Laws were changed all the time over tragedies. In California, it seemed like they changed laws once a day. Phil Kay wasn't the only representative in the world. She'd call the senator. . . . What was his name? Hammersmith? Nora was full of refreshed zeal when Gordon and the others came home, but actually speaking Phil Kay's words—a year, two years at most—punched a hole in her enthusiasm. They all looked shrunken.

Gordon lifted Keefer out of her high chair and carried her out into the hall, holding her against himself while he slipped her feet through the legs of her purple snowsuit and into her bumblebee boots. "Mama," Keefer said, waving to her grandmother and aunt.

"She means they're going to the cemetery," Lorraine told Nora.

"Good Lord," Nora breathed, "you think that's okay for her?"

Lorraine shrugged, "No, I guess it'll scar her for life. But I probably don't care about that, because I'm the hysterical old woman who's determined to put her own greed ahead of her grandchild's welfare."

"That was one letter, Lorraine. Which they didn't even have the guts to sign their names to."

"Maybe it is better for her. Maybe we're all so warped by the grief . . . maybe she needs a new start."

"Well, I don't think you should give up. The worst thing that could happen is that another family will never have to go through this."

"Nora," Lorraine sighed. "You're a better person than I am."

"No, I'm not."

"You are. Because I guess I'm not thinking of all the other families who could go through this. I'm only thinking of her. And I'm not even really thinking of her so much as I'm thinking of us. That letter writer, whoever she was, said Georgia asked *every* person who came to see her to take care of Keefer. I never thought she wanted anyone to do that but Gordie."

"Look at them," Nora mused.

Snow had begun to fall, huge, wet flakes tatting against the front window. The only speck of color against a milky sky was Keefer's bobbing snowsuit. "Isn't she just the picture of Georgia? That tough little way she walks." Prickles like a bolt of electrical current shot up her forearms when Lorraine pushed the drift of envelopes they were stuffing onto the floor.

"That's just it!" she said. "That's just it, Nora. No one ever thinks of family any way but that very way!"

"Whatever do you mean?"

"She looks like her. He looks like him. You're the picture of your father. Mark's the image of his grandmother!" Lorraine ranted, "Don't you hear yourselves?" Nora was struck speechless. "Every time Mike's boy Matt walks in the door, one of you says, 'There's little Mike, right there!' And then someone says, 'But Pete's got Debbie's eyes.' And then someone else will say, 'No, really he looks more like Debbie's sister.' It's like this is an endlessly fascinating subject. Even if you saw them the week before, someone has to comment on how much more they look like someone in the precious family . . ."

Did she do that? Nora tried to collect herself.

"No one ever meant anything wrong by it," she finally said.

"But how do you think my kids felt? You know how they felt? They felt excluded; I would see Georgia look away . . . Georgia always wanted everyone to love her. She was always trying to please people, whether it was me or her lousy friends or teachers. And Gordon, he doesn't look a thing like either of us. It was just so ignorant. Do you know what that Dr. Slater's wife said to my son? When her boy was on the soccer team with Gordon? Not that I could ever imagine old man Slater being able to father a mouse, and how she could even sleep with a guy sixty years old."

"*We're* sixty years old, Lorraine," Nora said, struggling to keep up.

"Well, we weren't then! And she was always such a snooty bitch. She walked up to me and Gordie after a game and said, 'Evan wants you to tell him why Georgia doesn't look like Gordon, even though they're brother and sister. And I've just told him that adoption was a very nice thing some people do for children who don't have homes.' I didn't know what to say, Nora. And you know what she said to us, then? She said, 'Well, Georgia could be yours, but Gordon sticks out like a sore thumb.'"

"I don't believe that," Nora said. "Though Doc Slater was always a horse's ass."

"Oh, Nora, it's like that for everyone else, the whole world is just a mirror, and people just want their kids because they're a reflection of themselves . . ." And then she added, "It was why we never came out with you."

"What?"

"We kept to ourselves, Mark and me, because we just couldn't stand it. It was as if nobody cared what the kids were doing at school or how they were growing, like the only value a child had was his McKenna chin or his big Nordstrom feet. It was like we'd brought something new into the family, a treasure to us . . . and nobody cared! I think it was half the reason Mark was against adopting. He knew you guys would never accept it."

"Our parents maybe, Lorraine. Old people set in old ways. When a woman couldn't have children back then, she just accepted it. I don't think our parents ever knew an adopted child."

"But you're not old and set in your ways, Nora. We grew up in the fifties. People understood it as a fact of life when we grew up. We didn't mind being different, but we minded having our kids' faces rubbed in it all the time."

"That was why?"

"Yes."

"We thought you didn't like us."

"Didn't like you? That's outrageous, Nora."

"It is not, Lorraine," Nora said, thinking, in for a penny, in for a pound. She was trading more cross words in twenty-four hours than she had in the previous twenty-four years. So be it. "You always had a way about you, of saying keep your distance—"

"Don't you see why, Nora? Even now? The whole world feels exactly the way you do. Judge Sayward feels that way. The legislators do, too. They think we feel like our children are . . . just guests in the house for eighteen years."

"How could you think I felt that way, too?" Nora stood up. Lorraine opened her mouth to speak. "If I felt that way, Lorraine McKenna, why would I be here?" Nora thought of Georgia's orange sweatshirt, its arms animated, lifting, outstretched. "Georgia was dearer to me than my own life, Lorraine. Maybe you think Hayes and I are dumb hicks, and if I ever said things that hurt her, I'll take that with me to my own grave. But if you think we ever set out to hurt you, or my brother, or your children, then I'll get up and walk out that door and take my ugly ways with me. And if you don't mean it, you'd better accept that there has been hurt on both sides and enough of it for a lifetime to go around."

Lorraine turned away, and looked out the window. "You can't even see the cemetery, the snow is so thick," she said.

"But it's warm out. They're fine," Nora replied. "It is coming down, though. Look funny going up, wouldn't it? Remember how Rob used to say that?" Nora thought if she didn't try to joke, she might cry, or run for the door.

"Nora," Lorraine said suddenly, "I never thought you were a dumb hick. You're the smartest hick I know."

Nora snorted.

"And more than that, you're . . . you're my friend. You're my family. If I didn't think that, I'd never have been so rude to you as I was just now. And Georgia loved you . . ."

"That's okay, Lorraine, that's enough."

"No. She loved you as much as she loved me. You made her feel part of the family, Nora. You have to forgive me. I'm not . . . I don't know how I can—"

When the telephone rang again, Nora answered. She was the most composed, though her ears still rang with the words of Lorraine's wrath and sang with the words of her respect, words she'd been fearing and hoping to hear for thirty long years.

So the words she heard next were at first confusing to her, like an extension of the conversation just completed, as if she'd wakened from a dream with dream narratives still in her head. It was Phil Kay's aide, a young woman whose voice chirped and tumbled as she explained that she, too, was adopted, as were her two brothers, and that this could happen to her, too, and to her parents. And that Representative Kay had a very unusual idea, which might not work, but he was going to try to tack the amendment onto another bill related to adoption . . .

Then the two of them, Lorraine and Nora, were running out into the snow, across the street to the cemetery, both shouting for Gordon, and it was Nora who got there first and was the one who was able to say, "Phil Kay is going to introduce the amendment now! Before the Christmas break in the legislature!"

"When?" Gordon asked, tearing off his cap. "When?"

"A week from Thursday!" Lorraine cried. And the three of them snatched up Keefer and whirled her around among the frosted monuments with snow filling in the carved clefts and swirls of names and dates. Nora would think later how mysterious it was, the way they gave Gordon the news right at that time, and right in that place, Georgia not a foot away.

CHAPTER *fourteen*

The last time Gordon had walked through the state capitol had been his eighth-grade graduation trip. He and Church and Sweeney had barely been able to hold their eyes open, caught in the otherworldly state they'd attained from spending most of the previous night throwing ice cubes from their seventh-floor room in the Park Towers at the heads of the girls sticking their heads out on the sixth floor.

He felt not entirely different when he and his mother arrived at the dot of eight on the morning Phil Kay was to present Assembly Bill 600 to the legislature for approval. Giddy with delight on the night they'd first learned about the possibility, they'd been quickly sobered by a phone call from Greg Katt, who said he'd managed to schedule a hearing to halt the petition for adoption the Cadys had filed and to stop Keefer from being transferred to their care until the court of appeals could take up the case. He hadn't had much hope. Judge Sayward would be on the defensive, Katt warned, and she had already refused, in substance, the same request.

But that, Mark had insisted, was before all the publicity.

"Judges don't like publicity, particularly of that kind," Katt replied, as they all listened in on the extension. "I imagine she's feeling the heat," Katt went on, "but we've got a shot, and let's give it our best." The hearing was set for Thursday morning, he said.

But they would be in Madison to see Phil Kay make his presentation to the legislature on Thursday morning.

Did they dare ask for another date?

Did they dare risk the passage of the law by seeming unappreciative, by not turning out in person?

Did they dare miss the hearing with Judge Sayward and risk giving her the impression that they didn't care what she decided?

They would compromise; Mark would stay home with Keefer. Gordon and Lorraine would rush home as soon as they'd finished testifying at the state capitol.

Gordon had no idea what testifying would involve, but it sounded like something that would fall beyond his realm of aptitude. "I'm not a word person, Mom," he'd dithered as they drove down, past the necklace of small towns that clustered on the periphery of the highway. "You tell them the story, and I'll just sort of stand there supportively."

"The whole world already thinks I'm crazy, Gordie," Lorraine said, "Even my friends have told me we should stop giving interviews because it sounded like we were trying our case in the press."

"I'm going to have to write everything down."

"It's your life, Gordie. You don't have to write anything down."

"I can't ad lib like you do."

"You ad lib in class every day. Just picture yourself talking to your class."

He had shared a room with his mother for the first time since he'd been a teenager, and when he finally did manage to fall asleep, Lorraine first worked him with her snoring, then sat up and turned on the lights and began rummaging through her bag of newspaper clippings.

"Mom, give me a break," he'd finally groaned, and the

light snapped out. A few minutes later, he heard her rustling through the closet. "What are you doing now?"

"I'm going for a walk," she'd said.

"You're not going for a walk in the middle of the night in the downtown of a city you don't even know," he'd told her.

"I'll be just fine, Gordie."

"You can turn the light back on. I don't care."

They'd ended up watching MTV all through the small hours, Lorraine keeping up a running commentary on the disgusting treatment of women in modern music, the images of torture and sadism and simple misogyny, until he wanted to suggest they throw some ice cubes out the window for fun. At the stroke of 6:00 A.M. they called his father, waking Keefer, who'd cut her finger the previous night when she'd smashed a jar of Lorraine's moisturizer on the bathroom floor.

"Was it a bad cut?" Lorraine cried, making the sign of the cross in the air.

It had not been serious, but had bled, Mark reported.

"And where were you while all this was happening?" Lorraine asked. He'd been watching Keefer, Mark told them mildly.

"Watching her cut herself?" Lorraine snapped.

"Settle down, Lor," Mark told her.

Everyone wished everyone else Godspeed.

Gordon still hadn't written anything down and was nauseated by seven, when they were the first people to venture into the hotel dining room. Though the bill dealt with provisions that would hasten children's transitions through the foster-care bureaucracy in the hopes of more easily securing adoptive homes, all the media could talk about was the Blood Relative Case. The McKennas had flipped to all three channels the night before Lorraine and Gordon left for Madison, listening with surreal calm as blond anchorwomen intoned, "Adoptive families all over the United States will turn their eyes to Wisconsin tomorrow, as our state may become a leading voice on behalf of adopted children, affirming that they are equal in every way. But for one family, the prospect of an amendment to Assembly Bill six hundred has a heartbreaking personal meaning. And for the McKennas of Tall Trees, Wisconsin, that story began agonizing months ago . . ." The past days had annealed the wince all three of them first felt when they saw their home videos displayed as feature footage; but Gordon's father still hit the mute button when Georgia's voice came on, reading *Green Eggs and Ham*. They couldn't bear it. Perhaps Georgia had been right. For Keefer to see her as she had been then would be a cruelty, like some bathetic Victorian ballad about angel mothers and rose-wreathed graves. Even with the sound extinguished, they all knew when the piece turned to "the controversy," because the camera zoomed in on footage of Delia and Craig.

Finally, a little before eight, Gordon waited for his mother to straighten her stockings in an echoing corridor off the main rotunda. He studied the dome, the Renaissance-style ladies who floated in vegetal splendor on the ceiling overhead—Wisconsin, flanked by Miss Lake Michigan, Miss Lake Superior, Miss Mississippi, each voluptuous goddess holding some romantically rendered object of commerce, such as lead, or tobacco. The reporter was practically on his back by the time he noticed her, and it irked him that his shrug of alarm was being captured by her camera jockey, a bearded giant in an Outlaws leather cap.

"I just saw you on TV," Gordon said, and when the woman grimaced, he thought, Gee, she's probably never heard anyone say that before.

"I just saw you on TV, too," she told him. "I'm Joy Bell, from *Channel Four News*?"

"Right."

"And you're Gordon. What do you think will happen here today, Gordon?"

"I have no idea," Gordon said, possessed by an urge to

wave to his father back home. "I mean, we hope that the assembly will consider this bill very carefully, because it means a great deal to a great many lives, not just ours."

"And Mrs. MacNamara"—the woman wheeled around as Lorraine stepped into the rotunda—"you're angry, too?"

"Mrs. McKenna," Lorraine said. "And what am I angry about? On the contrary, I'm just grateful that our assemblyman, Phil Kay of Merrill, took it upon himself to speak for adoptive families everywhere. As he says, this should have happened long ago."

"Then you'll be able to adopt your niece, Mr. McKenna?"

"That's a long process. We are in the process of appealing Judge Sayward's decision, and that could take months, and then only if we're successful—"

"Thanks so much," the reporter concluded.

"Another piece of incisive journalism," Lorraine grumbled. She'd been out of sorts when the previous Sunday's *Milwaukee Journal* featured a two-page spread under the words "Family Bound by Loss, Shattered by Love," which quoted Lorraine as feeling "hatred" toward the Cadys.

"I never said that," Lorraine told Gordon, astonished. "I said I hated what had happened, that I hated Keefer having to go through all this. I'm going to call that woman." But the reporter had left a message the following morning, cheerfully swearing that she'd checked her notes and was sure of what she'd written down, and by the way, look for an interview in the afternoon paper with Raymond Nye, Sr.

"We don't feel any hatred at all, toward any living soul," Big Ray was quoted as saying. "We just know what's best for this little girl. And the court knew what was best for this little girl. I don't really think it had anything to do with adoption at all. We wanted to carry out the wishes of our boy, and his wife, too, who wanted the same thing. We have proof of that. And that's all we've done. End of story." A photo of Big Ray, a doleful beagle, and of Ray laying down his putter at the Knockout so long ago.

That day in school, Gordon's boss remarked, "Knows how to stir things up, doesn't she?" And Gordon, caught by surprise, nodded.

Now, clinging together like children in busy traffic, Lorraine and Gordon made their way to the Assembly chambers, where outside the chambers Phil Kay and a dozen other representatives quickly surrounded them, wishing them luck, expressing their support. Kay introduced them to one after another indistinguishable light-haired man. These were the legislators who had crafted the language of the original bill, onto which the Kay amendment was tacked. "And now, nobody cares about all those months of work," Kay announced cheerfully. "All they care about is your family's part!"

"We'll make sure we never forget that the whole bill is meant to make families like ours easier," Lorraine told him. Gordon thought, My mother should run for something.

And then, Phil Kay led Gordon into the Assembly chambers, up the center aisle to the front of the room; the microphone was adjusted for him, and terrified that he would belch, he waited for Phil Kay's introduction and began, "My sister Georgia named her baby daughter after me, in a way. When I was a little kid, I knew my sister's full name was Georgia O'Keeffe McKenna, with two *f*s, but I couldn't pronounce her first name, for some reason, and so I . . ." He glanced at his mother, and saw her ghost of a nod, and continued, describing Georgia's illness, Ray's suffering, and the number of times Georgia had made him promise to look after Keefer and help Ray look after their baby. "I know she said that same thing to many of her friends and relatives. But it's different . . ." He breathed, tried to right the wobble in his throat. "It's different when someone is your big sister. I mean, you do what she says, right?" Faint laughter. "When it's your only sibling who asks something like that of you, you take it seriously. And Georgia was my sister, no matter what any judge says. Or any law. I hope you find it in your hearts to make the language of the law plain, because this period of our lives has been . . .

very hard. And it would frighten me to think that someday Keefer might have to go through something like this herself.

"Anyhow, nothing that happens here today is going to mean I will be more my parents' son than I am right now. I'm Mark McKenna's son. I'm Lorraine McKenna's son. By law and by blood, too." He sat down. Lorraine nudged him. Gordon shot back up. "Thank you," he said.

Phil Kay pointed out the big light boards that dominated the two front corners of the chambers; each of the boards had all ninety-nine representatives' names and a red and green light next to each of their names. Green, he told them, signified a yes vote, red . . . it was obvious. The Speaker of the House rose, and called for a vote on Assembly Bill 600, those in favor and those opposed. As they watched, the board came to life, with first one, then ten, then fifty, then what appeared to be hundreds of green lights.

And only one red.

Phil Kay was pumping his arm, and Lorraine leaned her cheek against Gordon's chest. And they were engulfed by backslapping, as they attempted to make their way into the aisle, toward the exit. As they passed, one man stood and began to applaud. All of them stood, the sound of their hands like a hard rain. "Well done!" someone called.

"This is just the first step," Phil Kay told them, as they emerged into the glittering street, "but it's a good one. The Senate will take it up next. I don't anticipate problems there. And I can assure you I will do everything in my power to urge the governor to act with the utmost speed. Merry Christmas, you guys!"

Driving through worsening weather on the interstate helped Gordon keep his anxiety quelled, but he caught himself wondering, as they passed the Dells, and Plainfield, and Stevens Point, what had happened at the appeal. Why hadn't they called Dad? Finally, they were turning onto Cleveland Avenue. Gordon looked for the sounds of a celebration. Horns. Hats. Bells. But nothing moved except Mary Dwors, who waved hello as she poked her head out to grab her newspaper. His parents' house was still, the blinds full drawn.

He almost wept with relief when Mark came to the door with Keefer in his arms. Someone—Nora he suspected—had wound her feathery hair into two pigtails secured with elastic ties. One red, one green ball on each. "I can tell by your faces," Mark said wearily, "that it went great."

And they could tell from his face that on this end, in Judge Sayward's courtroom, it had not.

"The judge did grant a stay," he told them, "but she refused to change the guardianship order. That means the Cadys are going to take her. Now, Lor," he said as Lorraine made a grab for Keefer, "this isn't all bad news. The judge ruled that they can't move to adopt her until the appeals process is completed. And we get visits with her, one weekend a month."

"When are they coming?" Lorraine asked.

"They should be here now," Mark sighed. "Delia just phoned."

"Not today," Lorraine said, raising her voice to a wail. "Not today! Not today!"

"Gordie," Mark said, "there's a drawer up in our room. Bottles of pills. Bring them down."

"Which ones, Dad?"

"Any ones, son."

"They're all gone, Mark. They're not there anymore. Well, almost all. And anyway, I don't need anything," Lorraine said, patting Keefer, who was patting her grandmother's back as well, and with her other hand gently scrubbing at the streaks of mascara on Lorraine's cheeks. "Don't worry, Keefer. Everything is all right."

They watched the hands on the clock stutter, and jump. A quarter past three. Three-thirty. Gordon thought, with a surge of hope, that the weather might have impeded the Cadys' progress. Perhaps they'd turned back.

They all heard the thumps of the car doors slamming, and Craig Cady stood on the porch.

"She won't go to you," Mark told him mildly.

"Yes, she will," Craig said, offering his arms. Keefer cringed.

"Aren't you going to put her into her snowsuit?" Lorraine asked. "Why would you take her out into a snowstorm without a snowsuit?"

"Okay," Craig was florid, sweating, miserable. Gordon almost felt pity. Craig called back over his shoulder, "Alex! Alexis!"

It did the trick. Catching sight of the red-haired girl, Keefer began making patty-cakes, showing all her white tooth nubbings, blowing kisses. "Should I take her, Craig?" Alexis asked. "Should I take her, Mr. McKenna?" she asked Gordon.

Together, he and the girl teased Keefer into her snowsuit. He could hear, behind him in the kitchen, Lorraine's voice, edgy, shrill, "Aren't you going to take her bed? Aren't you going to ask what her favorite toys are? What she eats, for God's sake? Are you going to drive back to Madison in this weather, with this child you love so much?"

"She has everything she needs," Craig said. "Don't make this worse than it has to be. We aren't trying to harm you people. We pray for you."

"You pray for *us*!" Lorraine snapped.

"Alex," Gordon whispered, "go out there for a moment and tell your . . . dad that I . . ."

"He's my stepdad," Alexis replied, also in a whisper.

"Well, tell Craig I want a moment with her, alone."

"He'll think you're going to run away with her, like they did in Florida."

"I'm not going to run away with her."

He had not envisioned how he would do this, accomplish this, actually part with her. And he told himself that this was foolish; he was not giving up Keefer. Today, in victory, they had taken the first steps toward a change that would have to carry weight with the court of appeals, even though he knew the court's members were charged with a challenge to the law as it existed at the time of the hearing, not as it might exist in the future. Regardless, he reminded himself, Georgia had regarded Delia highly enough to ask her to be her matron of honor. Surely, they would treasure Georgia's child. Ray's child.

Keefer was squirming, scrabbling at her snowsuit trying to scratch her itches. Gordon took one of her palms and kissed it. She pulled it away. He put his hands behind his back. "How many duckies back here?" he asked, first holding up one approximation of a beak, quacking vigorously. Keefer pointed at the door where Alexis had gone. "Okay, Keefster," Gordon said. Think now, right now, he told himself. "Now, I love you."

"Dory," Keefer said precisely.

"Dory loves you, so much." The baby immediately raised both hands over her head and waggled her fingers. "That's right. So big."

He saw the Band-Aid, a tiny green strip in the shape of a crayon and remembered his father's account of Keefer's cut, the night before. "Let me see the boo-boo, Keef," he said, and pulled the Band-Aid off. Keefer yelped. The cut had been significant, but had almost healed. Kids had the immune system of titans. But in the corner, where the scab had not quite congealed, one bright pinprick drop of blood welled.

Tenderly, Gordon lifted her tiny finger and placed it against his tongue.

CHAPTER *fifteen*

"*T*oday, we mate," said Gordon.

The class tittered appreciatively.

"You're mine, Reilly," Eddie Carlson cat-called. "You're all mine!"

"I must have Kelly!" Kye Olstadt croaked.

Gordon mused, as Kelly Rafferty's face crimsoned from the nose outward, whether Kye did have her, on a regular basis.

She looked exactly like her mother. Alicia had turned out to be one of the world's kindliest friends. She had sent him, through Kelly, a thick bunch of Gerbera daisies, bright as parrots, when Senator Hammersmith offered to sponsor the bill in the state senate, where it had passed and not just passed, but unanimously. With any luck, the governor would sign the bill before the appeal was heard. Both the senator and Phil Kay had written the governor, urging him to quick action.

All the news was good.

As a result, he was wildly apprehensive.

In atonement, out of some arbitrary zeal, he'd tried to become Mr. Chips—patient, jovial, the complete teacher. A matching pledge grant, in effect, for his aunt's novenas, his mother's bonzai national and international correspondence, her festival of superstitious gestures. Lorraine avoided looking at the rind of the new moon over her shoulder through window glass, whisked hats off any bed, walked backward out of the house if she had to go back in for something she'd forgotten and made a parody of rapping her knuckles on wood and touching them to her lips. She was his Grandma Lena to the fourth power. But without Keefer, for all of them, there was nothing much else to do but be superstitious and brood. At night, strumming, Gordon worked on Eric Clapton and Phil Ochs songs, but would end up torturing himself by playing "Puff, the Magic Dragon."

He had what he'd always craved, all the solitude in the world.

Though they had counted on having Keefer for Christmas, Delia had called on the morning before Christmas Eve and informed them tersely that Keefer had an ear infection. It was her opinion that she needed to stay "home." Keefer was just beginning to grasp the idea that Christmas meant candy and toys. "Because we believe that Christ is the reason for the season," Delia had told Gordon's mother, "we don't do Santa or very many presents or anything. But at least she'll be able to go to the service, and it's so wonderful, the children's choir dressed as angels, it's really glorious." It would be acceptable, Delia had further told them, for the McKennas to take Keefer for a few days during the week after New Year's Eve. Keefer needed to be home for the family New Year's celebration, at church, in Madison.

Lorraine had—politely, according to her own account—reminded Delia that classes resumed that week, so that she and Gordon would be working every day.

"Well, let's just wait for next month, then," Delia replied. "She can come in February."

Furious, Lorraine had phoned Greg Katt. Lay low, he'd advised. Lay low and be cooperative. He said Stacey Kane and Charley Borchart were about to file the briefs for the appeal. No waves. Think ahead. Be the most easygoing people on earth.

So, Christmas had been subdued, to say the least. The piles of presents that customarily overwhelmed the tree and burgeoned out into the hall were diminished when they'd mailed Keefer's packages to Madison, and her stocking at the fireplace, knitted at her birth by Nora, hung limp, compelling all their eyes, a palpable reproach. Gordon had always found his mother's Christmas mania extreme and embarrassing as they grew older and passed the developmental phase of naked greed . . . past the age of, say, eleven. He'd longed for a time when his mother would not ask them to watch while she moved the three kings— Georgia, as a child, had called them "the wiseguys"—a fraction of an inch closer to the stable, hand-carved in Hungary and blessed by obscure holy Hungarians. He'd longed, during college, and after, for what he imagined a Manhattan type of Christmas, adults sipping expensive champagne and nibbling oysters, exchanging a few but very elite items made of chrome. But his mother and Georgia favored shirts silk-screened with unearthed family photos, stocking caps with jingle bells, enough sports equipment to outfit his own gym.

Of course, damned luck, he missed that now, that excess, and was thankful for the chance to drive through the woods and over the hill to Nora's, where he and his male cousins had thrown a football around the side yard after consuming thirds of every class of cholesterol-enhancing cuisine. They had guzzled Labatts, sworn mightily, laughed at the dogs, behaved, in short, like people from Wisconsin, and Gordon was not pretending for one moment. Screw the chrome Christmas. He'd felt safe, counted in.

That night, he'd slept in his old bed at his parents' and dreamed of Keefer as a grown girl, fitting long, strong fingers down the seams of the pigskin, his own hand helping her form the fit. When he awoke, he woke to thinking of how it was for her in the morning, how he'd turn from shaving to see her flipping Rice Chex out of his cereal bowl, using the spoon as a catapult, and how he'd no sooner clean up the Rice Chex than he'd catch her washing the windows with baby wipes, and he'd no sooner get those back into the box than she'd try to walk in his shoes and fall, wailing. Her face, when he dared tell her "No!" was pure opera; Keefer would collapse to her knees, hands on cheeks, mouth wide open in the silent cry, and for an hour later, even after he'd given back the wipes, she would refuse to look at him. Mark had called Keefer's determined ignoring of her elders "shunning." He said that defiance was the picture of Georgia.

Gordon's place was his own now, but he'd lost the lazy luxury of bachelorhood. He'd once cleaned as a single guy cleans, to prevent the origin of species, not to pass the white glove test. Now, in the early days since Keefer's departure, he found himself unable to stop making sure that all the surfaces two feet above the floor were spotless. Keefer had possessed the baby's knack for finding subatomic particles on any surface to pluck up and ingest, and he eagle-eyed everything as if she were still there and vulnerable.

After a while, though, the second law of thermodynamics took over. Gordon was depressed. His tuner for the guitar occupied the middle of the coffee table, along with a six-pack of bottled water, along with the watch his parents had given him for Christmas, his electric screwdriver, a threaded needle and the rent shirt it was intended to mend, several sock bombs he rolled to pitch at the plastic hoop he'd desultorily mounted above his front door, a paper carton of grotesquely aged vegetable sub-gum, papers to grade—weighted with a can of antifungal powder. Laundry lived on the couch, clean to the left, dirty to the right. He no longer had to sweat the pixie rushing in the door to make joyous confetti out of his T-shirt and boxers. Rare, under-the-bed sweeps turned up wrenching relics, the tinkle bracelet that had belonged to his sister, one blue-and-green Baby Botte shoe, a sock with tweety birds marching around the ankle, the Barbie whose brittle blond hair they'd put in corn rows one Saturday night.

The energy he could muster he gave to his students. He'd given them a quarter of what they deserved.

"Everyone should have four cards," Gordon told the class, a few days after they'd straggled back from winter break and recovered from vacation lag, "two marked big *A,* two marked little *a.* Shuffle the cards and place them facedown." He switched on the CD player, "Love Shack" by the B-52's.

"Now, take the top card off your stack, and let's breed. Select your mate," Gordon instructed.

The boys lurched toward one another; the girls clustered instinctively. "Okay, okay," Gordon said. "Pick your partners. And remember, no one can breed with the same person twice. It's the experience that counts. Come on, people. This usually doesn't take that long, especially at your age." Over the boom of their released laughter, he told them, "As you know, each of these cards represents an allele. The genes that dictate a specific trait, such as brown eyes, can occur in two or more alternative forms, called alleles."

"Proximity is the most dominant force in attraction," Carlson said to Perry Kistler, "and we've lived on the same block for years, Kistler. I think we're meant for each other."

"Let's reveal what you've produced—or reproduced— here, scholars," Gordon tried to joke. "Just looking around, I confess I feel a little concern . . ."

On the first round, the cards had distributed themselves fairly evenly, as he'd known they would. "What are we seeing here, Mr. Carlson?"

"Well, my offspring are big *A,* big *A* . . . that's homozygous dominant," the boy said. "Not that there's anything wrong with that. . . . it's just the way some people are." More laughter.

They proceeded into the second round. Barry White on the CD player assured his sweetheart that they had the staying power.

"You got any Steppenwolf, Mr. McKenna?" one of the boys shouted. "I'm dying with this music."

"No, it's good," another guy chided. "Soft rock reminds me of getting my braces off."

"I don't understand this," Kathy Zurich mourned.

"That's not what I heard!" the Woffling kid teased.

"No one understands it," Gordon told them, during a pause. "The science of genetics is like the theory of relativity in that there are so many detours and apparent contradictions that it's difficult even for biologists, and I hasten to point out I am not one, to get their minds around it. Even Gregor Mendel, who was the father of what remains the basis of all genetics, even Brother Mendel—"

"A hip-hop guy," Carlson said.

"No, a monk, even Mendel gave up in despair when what worked with yellow peas didn't work with other plants on which he tried the same method of hybridizing. He quit and became an administrator."

"You should quit and become an administrator," Kathy said. "This is way confusing. Do I have to do the calculations if I baby-sit for you extra?"

The class fell silent. Gordon heard a siren's brief whoop from somewhere west, near his parents' house.

"Shut up," Carlson said.

"Well, I'm sorry," Kathy whispered. "I wasn't thinking. I forgot she was gone."

"Don't worry about it," Gordon went on. "Now, you know that among all species, human beings are the only creatures to which natural selection does not apply. In other words, humans keep bad genes going. And I'm not necessarily referring to you, Carlson." Laughter. "No, people, now listen. A good example is a baby born with PKU, phenylketonuria, a disease that means a vital conversion of amino acids can't take place. If it isn't converted, the child's metabolism will be all messed up—that baby would be retarded, and then die."

"That stinks!" Melinda Gallo meowed.

"That's what perinatal researchers thought, too. So now, practically the first thing that happens after a baby's birth is a urine test for that condition, that defective allele," Gordon told them. "And if it's there, the baby can be given a special diet and therapeutic support through all its life, and lead a normal life. So what happens?"

"It grows up," Carlson said.

"He or she grows up and mates"—Gordon nodded—"and eventually there'll be a pairing with another individual who possesses the recessive allele, and it will manifest again. And so, genetic traits that should have vanished go on. Now, at one end of that spectrum, you get some wonderful things out of this, like the great physicist, Stephen Hawking and Ludwig van Beethoven, who was also disabled . . ."

"And at the other end, some other things like Carlson," Kye Olstadt said. "Are freckles on the recessive gene?"

"Let's proceed to the third round now. You should be noticing some changes in the distribution," Gordon continued smoothly. "More of your offspring are carrying recessive genes for certain traits, even if their actual appearance, their phenotype, doesn't reveal that. But they are capable of passing on those traits . . . beware." He turned on "Patience" by Guns N' Roses.

"Impressive herd of CDs there, Mistah McKennah," said Dennis Reilly.

"I'm sooooo dominant!" from Kelly Rafferty.

"Listen, Olstadt, nobody said anything about love," Ben Jones said.

"Say you'll call, be sure to say you'll call," Gordon reminded them, falsetto.

"Here come the offspring! I'm in the delivery room now! Where's the placenta?" Reilly asked. "Speaking of placentas, where's yours? My brother Neal said you had a real one. Did you get it from the UW?"

Gordon balked. "I wasn't going to use it," he said. "Let's finish all the pairings and then we'll talk." He had, in fact, prepared a biohazard bag to dispose of the placenta. Keeping it had seemed like a lark at the end of last year, and now it seemed like a blasphemy. Half of that ruddy-colored, once vital, now only illustrative former organ had nourished Keefer. Half had come from his sister. He watched the kids, giggling and exclaiming over their cards, and then, slowly, opened the freezer and lifted out the placenta, in its steel roasting pan, and set it on the slate lab tabletop.

"Last year, when my niece was born," he began, "I asked my sister if I could keep this. Hell, I didn't know if it was against the law or something. But she said sure, why not? Some carnivores eat the placenta. Some people, too, but not in Wisconsin. Lots of cultures customarily keep all kinds of relics from a birth, like part of the umbilical cord—"

"Yish," said Kathy.

"Well, yeah, pretty gross," said Gordon. He uncovered the placenta, which, even frozen, seemed to glisten. "But this is the sustenance of a baby's life. This is how Keefer grew, entirely dependent on my sister's body, and yet entirely separate. At no time during gestation does the mother's blood ever mix with the baby's. Anyway, I wanted to preserve this for my classes to see. But now, my . . . you know that my sister died." Twenty-four heads dropped in unison. "It's okay. I know that some of your folks must have talked about it with you. You saw the TV news."

"That you were adopted," said Dennis, "by Mrs. McKenna at the middle school."

"But not last week. I was adopted when I was a baby," Gordon said. "My mom is the only mom I've ever known."

"Do you know your real mom?" Kelly Rafferty asked.

"I don't know her," Gordon said. "But it was from her, and my birth father that I received this . . . bad hair and these very excellent legs."

"Was your sister adopted?" Dennis asked.

"You know she was, Den," said Gordon.

"I didn't. I thought only you," Dennis insisted. "I can't imagine being adopted. With our family, it's always, like, there's a Reilly. That's gotta be a Reilly. We'd know you anywhere, you're Bill Reilly's kid."

"That's something I've never experienced. And I never will, unless I ever have kids of my own. And in fact, though, as we've seen right here, you can be the genetic product of both your parents and not look anything like them," Gordon said, "which is what you can all think about tonight when you're doing the math."

"I think it sucks," the Reilly kid said, suddenly.

"What?"

"What happened with your baby," he said, "it sucks big-time."

"What did you say then?" Lindsay asked him that night as they lay spoon fashion, in his bed. Lindsay more often than not stayed over now, Gordon no longer having either the urge to stray or the absurd inhibition to shield Keefer from his nocturnal proclivities. And Keefer was so rarely, anymore, around. He'd given Lindsay a key, and she would come directly from work, and they cooked together—*hi, honey, hi, honey, how was your day?*

"I couldn't say anything," Gordon told her. "I guess I just nodded or something. I hope the kid knew I appreciated it."

"He gave you so much flack before."

"He's a good kid, though. Definitely the genetic high-water mark of all Reillys."

"Does it make you think, teaching all that stuff, about what your own kids will be like?"

He felt Lindsay's back stiffen when he said, "I don't know for sure if I'll ever have kids, Lins."

"Why not? Gordie, you're beautiful."

"You're biased, goofer."

"No, I mean, you have the best genes."

"I guess I think about Keefer. And if I get to raise Keefer . . ."

"And?"

"Well, how she would feel, if we . . . I mean, if my wife and I, if I should get married, would feel about me having a kid who was biologically related to me. I wouldn't want to hurt Keefer. I know that's nuts."

Lindsay rolled out of the bed, and he noticed the faint line where her bikini had covered the crack in her butt before she shrugged into one of his shirts. She sat down cross-legged on the foot of the bed, her pale red pubic thatch visible between her knees. Hills, Gordon thought, thickly forested with evergreens, had always reminded him of pubic hair. "I think it is nuts, Gordie. You wouldn't have felt any different about Georgia if she'd been born to your folks."

"I was jealous, when I was little, that she looked like my mom."

"But you say you're like your mom."

"I am like my mom, in personality. Maybe because I was jealous. Kids are like any other little animal. They'll push and root and find their niche in the unit. If they're not the biggest, they'll be the quickest—"

"I think you should have your own babies because—"

"What?"

"Because what if you don't get her back?"

"I have to think we're going to get her back."

"And you're going to just be you and Keefer for the rest of your life?"

"I didn't say that."

"Well?"

"Well?"

"Well, what about me?"

"You mean, you want to have kids."

"Of course I do."

"That's something we're going to have to discuss—"

"Fine. Let's discuss."

"Not now. I've got a stack of labs out there I have to grade—"

"Now is a fine time."

"Lins—"

"Who's Alicia?"

He felt a tingling in his jaw, his shoulders. "Alicia?"

"When I came in, there was a message from her on the answering machine."

"You listened to my messages?"

"No, she was leaving the message right when I walked in."

"She's the mother of one of my students."

"Well, she asked if you got the flowers."

"She sent me some flowers with her daughter, when the bill passed the Senate."

"And she mentioned the volleyball team."

"You know I play on a volleyball team sometimes. Christ, Lins, it's the only exercise I get anymore. I'm starting to look like pictures of my grandpa Kiss. The guy had legs like matchsticks. My dad can probably bench more than I can at this point."

"There was . . . she said 'cutie.'"

"She's just being nice."

"Did you date her?"

"No."

"Did you date her, Gordie?"

"No! We've hung out a couple of times."

"Hung out? Did you sleep with her?"

"No!"

"Did you fool around?"

Lie, he thought. Make it easy. Don't lie, he thought then. Make it easy.

"A little, once. Drunk. A long, long time ago. I stopped because I was involved with you and I didn't want to trespass on what we have. Okay, Lindsay?"

"How much do you expect me to overlook, Gordie?"

"What does that mean?"

"It means, do you want me to say it more slowly, how much do you expect me to overlook?"

"Lindsay, nobody forces you to be with me. I assume we're both here because we want to be."

"All through college, I was your vacation fuck. You think I didn't know that? And summers. If you were around—"

"Wait a minute here. Wait a minute. Neither of us ever expected that we were having an exclusive relationship then."

"But that's what I wanted, and you knew it."

He'd known it.

"Well, we are now," he said. Lame, even to his own ears.

"So what's going to happen to us?"

"I've thought about that, Lins." He hadn't thought about it, but it became clear to him, as the words formed. "It depends on what happens with Keefer."

"How?"

"Well, I guess if I get to keep Keefer, I'll stay here, in Tall Trees. Maybe buy a house. Keep her where she can see my parents and my aunts and uncles and my cousins, and the Nyes, too, of course."

"And if it . . . goes wrong?"

"Then, Lindsay, I don't know what I'll do. But I can tell you, I'm going to want to . . . take off. Go work for Enviro-Treks again. Or find some hilltop in Montana and be a hermit who collects botanical specimens—"

"All alone?"

"That's how I think of it, yes. But it's probably crazy." He lay back on his pillow, on Keefer's "Queen of Everything" pillow, which he'd taken to keeping in the bed. "Maybe I'd go back to school."

"For what?"

"My doctorate. Maybe in cell biology. I think about, you know, my sister, and her cancer. People don't just get breast cancer at twenty-six unless they carry a gene for it. Which could mean that Keefer could be at risk for it. She's already at risk for it. And the human genome project is under way, maybe I will work in research . . ."

"And you'd have to go to school alone, too."

"Not necessarily. But since when would you want to leave Tall Trees, Lins? You almost fucking starved to death in college because you missed Laura and your parents so much. And pretty soon, Laura's going to have kids, and you're going to want to be with them, too."

"I would leave for you."

"Think that over, Lins. Don't just say it."

"I thought that if you get Keefer, you're going to need me, Gordie. A girl needs a mother—"

"So thought the psychologist, that dumb bitch."

"A girl needs a mother, Gordie. And I would be a good mother."

"I think you'd be a great mother, Lins. But think about whether you'd be satisfied raising my kid? Just my kid?"

"You make this impossible. You're leaving if you don't get her. You're going to be practically a . . . monk if you do get her. What is my choice?"

"It's not fair," Gordon pulled Lindsay down beside him, and her gorgeous hair spread like silk threads over his chest; there was no more luxurious feeling. He remembered Keefer's delight in rooting her tiny, box-shaped feet in his own hair. Keefer. What was she doing now? "It's not fair, and I'm not asking you to wait. I change my mind about stuff every day now. I can't plan and I can't project. There's the appeal next week and then the time it's going to take to wait for the decision. If I were a decent human being, I'd tell you to get up and take your toothbrush and leave me to rot."

"Yes, you would," Lindsay told him, pouting. She struggled out of his arms and leaned on his bedroom window, studying the spangling of frost on the trees. He breathed in the scent of her leg, of their sex. Maybe all this talk of solitary specimen collecting was romantic horseshit.

"On the other hand," he ventured, "maybe Keefer would love having a brother or sister. She's crazy about that kid of Delia's . . ." Perhaps there was even logic in it. If he reproduced, a child of his would grow up with Keefer as he and Georgia had grown up, a representative of his genetic endowment alongside his sister's. And those children's children would carry forth his sister's traits and his own, their adoption being, then, a sort of clumsy macrometaphor for the double helix—unrelated strands notched with genetic messages looped loosely round one another in a braid generation after generation.

Lindsay flung herself across him, straddling him.

"Is that a yes?"

"Lindsay, you look like Lady Godiva."

"Is it?"

"It's a definite maybe, and I feel like a piece of shit making you settle for that."

"Oh, Gordie. Gordie, my Gordie," she crooned, nuzzling him, wakening him.

It was time, he guessed, to make someone happy. If you made someone happy, like the old song said, maybe you would be happy, too.

CHAPTER *sixteen*

$\mathscr{T}$he governor was a small, powerfully built man whose hometown, he told Gordon and his parents, was no more than ten miles from Tall Trees. Ever spent a summer shearing Christmas trees, he asked Gordon, who answered, yes, sir, many. Hot work, the governor nodded, chuckling. They sat down in their assigned seats under the seal of the eagle amid the luxe expanse of Wisconsin cherrywood paneling at a table crafted from Wisconsin black walnut in chairs Lorraine assumed were padded with Wisconsin foam rubber. Jungles of cables and tent cities of tripods crowded the door and spilled out into the hall as the governor signed Assembly Bill 600, turning first to Gordon to hand him a pen embossed with his name and the seal of the state, then to pass one to Lorraine, to Mark, to Senator Hammersmith and Phil Kay. In chairs against the walls, Tim was wiping his eyes, Nora and Lindsay were sobbing outright. Two months and three days had passed since that first phone call, the one Phil Kay had felt summoned to pick up on his own.

"Are you a Republican?" one reporter asked, as Lorraine and her family made their way into the hall.

"No, a very indebted Democrat," Lorraine answered. "This is a great day for all adoptive families, all families period. There are people all over the country who are going to sleep better tonight."

"And will this law make it easier to resolve your own custody dispute over your granddaughter?"

"It's not my custody dispute," Lorraine said. "It is our son, who is . . . well, who nobody can doubt now is the equal of her 'blood' uncle, who hopes to adopt Keefer Kathryn Nye. But we're going to stand beside him every step of the way."

"Gordon"—a woman with corkscrew black curls that reminded him of Georgia's untamed childhood do, worked her way to the front—"Is this law going to affect the appeal?"

"We don't know anything for sure," he said, "because, you probably know, the appeal will deal with the decision Judge Sayward made before the law was changed, not taking into consideration the way the law—"

"Thanks," she smiled.

"You went over the limit of the sound bite," Mark told Gordon.

On a whim, feeling like stalkers, they drove past the Cadys' spruce-colored condo, straining for a glimpse of Keefer. There was a pink playhut in the backyard and signs of a wooden swing set under construction. "It's a pretty neighborhood," Lindsay said, and they all glared at her.

Delia and Craig had known full well, Lorraine assumed, that the bill would be signed into law today, Friday, the same day that their first visit with Keefer in two exhausting months was to commence. Lorraine had sent a note; they would be in Madison on business; they would be happy to pick Keefer up at noon and spare the Cadys a two-hour drive. Delia had left a message. No, Keefer's time with the McKennas did not begin until that night—the Cadys would bring Keefer up on Friday night, as per the stipulations of the visitation agreement, and they would pick her up on Sunday afternoon. Routine, she added, was important for a child. They would be surprised, the message continued, how Keefer's language had taken off. She was using three-word sentences almost overnight, and saying "Daddy" and "Mommy" and "Lexie" clear as a bell.

Until that moment, as she played and replayed the message, Lorraine had not thought that Delia was mean-spirited. She had believed her righteous to the point of fatuousness, but not unkind. But she caught herself trying to reframe, reclassify incidents with her son-in-law, Ray. Even Ray bordered on boorish in his insistence that Georgia be . . . obedient. No, that was wrong. Ray had adored Georgia, and it had been her daughter who gratefully assumed the role of devoted servant. Honey, want a piece of pie, it's homemade? Honey, let me change her; she's sopping, no you don't have to bother with it. Honey, let me unpack for you.

Lorraine sharply stopped herself from following that train of thought.

No, there was no real malice in Delia, or how could Lorraine live knowing that she had the daily care of Georgia's child, the responsibility to wash her and feed her and rock and read. Hadn't the psychologist's report noted Delia's patience, her serenity? Delia was not a carbon copy of Diane, that smothering, pushy, self-pitying . . .

On Saturday they would celebrate, all together, on Cleveland Avenue, the passage of the law and Keefer's second birthday, which, though it did not fall until March ninth, would also not fall on one of the McKennas' designated weekends.

They arrived home soon enough for Lorraine to teach her afternoon classes, but when she arrived in the art room, she was stunned by the silence. All the kids were there, but bent busily over their sketch pads, and Lorraine knew enough about seventh graders to look for ominous overtones in any kind of quiet. Without a word, Lorraine's principal, Linda Fry, nodded at Lorraine and took her leave. Gingerly, Lorraine approached her desk, where Linda had set up a mannequin, draped in scarves, for the unit in figure drawing they'd begun the previous week. Not a peep from even one of them, though the little Rooney girl couldn't help but flash a full-metal smile at Lorraine. Something was wrong. Something was up.

"Attention," the public address system, never state of the art, crackled and guttered, "attention, students and faculty of Tee Tee Em Ess. We have an important announcement to make." Linda. The kids were stealing out of their seats. "Among us right now is a woman of history. A woman of courage. A woman whose love and devotion has today single-handedly changed the law of the state of Wisconsin to protect the welfare of families and children everywhere. Let's all proceed—in orderly fashion, please—to celebrate Assembly Bill Six Hundred and our own art teacher and lawmaker extraordinaire, Lorraine McKenna!"

The kids galloped from the room, tugging at her arms, taking her hands. The banner reading "Way to Go, Mrs. M!" stretched from one end of the basketball court to the other. Not only were her fellow teachers there, but Dale and Sheila, Nina and Bud, the Wiltons, the Soderbergs and their banker son.

And when Lorraine finally arrived home, there was Nora in the doorway, beckoning Lorraine to a kitchen that looked as though a florist's truck had unloaded its entire capacity on the table, and under the table, Keefer, who said, "Nana! Peep in poddy!" Keefer, whole and pink, thinner, but clearly healthy, carefully unpacking her dentist Barbie, her pilot Barbie, her Mozart blocks, her firetruck that made horrific blatting noises and flashed red and yellow lights, each for their amazed admiration. She was no longer interested in playing with the duck puppets. "One, one," she told Nora with a pout, pushing them away, and though Nora was momentarily crestfallen, she responded with a hoot when Keefer twisted her chubby fingers together and nodded, urging Nora, "Itty bitty, itty bitty." The "Itsy-Bitsy Spider" was the last thing Lorraine remembered saying as she drifted off with Keefer between Mark and her in their bed, and she awoke from a dream of Georgia climbing the drainpipe, tapping at the window, Mom, let me in, let me in . . . but it had begun to rain. Lorraine crept from the bed and to her desk, where she began to write a letter, "Dearest Keefer, What a year you've had! You have gone from a baby to a big girl who can talk and walk and only wears diapers for sleeping! You know many songs. You have been spending lots of time playing with your family, Delia and Craig and especially Alexis, and we are all excited to have you here with us tonight. The people who will come to your Tall Trees birthday are Gordon and Lindsay and Rob and Bradie and Aunt Nora and Uncle Hayes and Tim and his brand-new puppy named 'Taxi'! Isn't that a funny name for a puppy? Things have happened this year that Grandma and Gordon and all your family will explain to you when you grow up, but everyone loves our Keefer. . . ."

The cake fiasco was the only blot on the next day. Keefer had been tired, Gordon having insisted on taking her to the park to haul her around wobbling on the wee, double-bladed ice skates he and Lindsay had given her, along with a full set of the Madeleine books that came with a blank-faced, blue-felt-coated dolly. They'd all watched with amazement as Keefer used a grownup fork to carefully twirl and delicately munch at her spaghetti, and marveled when she'd held out her hand for a napkin to dab her lips. "Uckies," she'd gravely explained.

What Nora wanted, when she hauled out the gargantuan double-chocolate cake with strawberry jam mortared between each of its three layers was to snap some of those tot-plunders-cake photos. But Keefer, though her eyes widened at the sight of the sparkler candles and the gooey roses, would not touch the cake with her fingers. She'd gestured, pleadingly, for a fork. "Go on, Keefer," Nora urged her, "dig in on it. We don't stand on ceremony here."

And finally, experimentally, Keefer had dipped one fingertip into the frosting and licked it. They'd all cheered. "Mommy?" Keefer asked. Everyone glanced around, as if expecting Georgia's wraith to have materialized in the kitchen. "Mommy?" Keefer said again, her little face collapsing into boo-boo mode.

"She means Delia," Gordon announced, disgust curdling his voice. "What she wants is Delia."

Nora leaned over and slapped a dot of chocolate frosting on Keefer's downturned tulip of a nose, and the baby roared, jerking her head back from Nora's hand, pushing hard at her high-chair tray, drumming her heels on the foot rest. "Uckie!" she screamed, and began to gag, and if Gordon hadn't gotten her to the sink in time, she'd have heaved all her spaghetti onto the floor. As it was, she spit up only a mouthful or two, Gordon managing to distract her by squirting cold water onto her wrists from the hose nozzle on the faucet.

"I'm so sorry," Nora begged them. "I'm so sorry. I didn't mean a thing by it."

"Nora, she's always had a mind of her own," Mark said. "Don't even think about it. She's tired is all she is. Worn out. All these new faces . . ." No one said a word, but the import of the sentence rang in the room like a blow. And by the time everyone left, Keefer was asleep, curled with one fist clutching Gordon's shirt, on Lorraine and Mark's bed, and neither had the heart to move them. Mark bunked on the couch. Lorraine alternated napping on Gordon's old twin, and pacing.

Lindsay and Gordon had a regional tournament for the co-ed volleyball league they'd both joined and had to leave for Wausau late Sunday afternoon. Mark had reluctantly agreed to meet a group of Japanese investors at Medi-Sun for a tour. Lorraine was eager for the short time it would give her alone with Keefer, before Nora drove out to make the formal transfer to the Cadys. But Lorraine had just begun to read, "In an old house in Paris, that was covered with vines . . ." when the doorbell pealed, and pealed again, and again. Craig Cady stood on the porch, a shivering Alexis beside him. The child was in a T-shirt and a skirt, no coat on her at all, and Lorraine's reflex was to open the door and lead both of them inside. "My wife is ill," Craig said. "She's sick, and I think she needs to see a doctor."

"Should we call an ambulance," Lorraine asked, "or the sheriff?"

"No, I just need to get her to a doctor quickly," Craig stammered. "Mrs. McKenna, I know that I shouldn't ask you for anything, given what we've . . . given how things are, but can you please, please tell me how to get to a hospital . . . ?"

"Methodist is only about six blocks from here, Craig. You take Cleveland to Main and Main to Third. Turn right on Third, it's about a block, you can't miss it."

"Come on, Alexis," Craig beckoned, and then seemed to notice the girl's unwonted shivering. "Mrs. McKenna, can she stay here?"

"Of course," Lorraine said, "don't worry about it. Just leave her right here with Keefer and me. We'll be just fine, won't we, Alexis?" Craig shut the door and dashed back to his car.

"It's Alex," said the girl. "I guess so."

"Lexie!" Keefer trilled, and the red-haired girl swept the baby up, jigging with her around the kitchen.

"Let's rock around the clock, Keefe! Let's do the hand jive!" Alexis sang. Keefer's head tilted back with shut-eyed bliss.

"We were reading," Lorraine said uncertainly.

"Okay," Alexis said, setting Keefer down on her feet, "let's go read. I read to her all the time. I read to her every night, don't I, pickle-toes?"

"Tory, tory," Keefer urged, pulling Alex into the living room.

"That's her name for my son," Lorraine explained. "She calls Gordon that."

"No, that's her word for 'story,'" Alexis told Lorraine. "She means, tell her a story not from a book. I tell her stories not from books. I tell her about this mouse child, his name's Eddie, and he got apart from his litter when he was just a newborn baby, and he was raised by the rabbits, so now he's a mouse that goes hop, hop, hop, and he feels bad because his ears aren't growing like his brothers' ears . . . what kind of manger scene is that?"

Lorraine was abruptly aware of how many Christmas decorations she'd simply never managed to take down. The tree, when they'd finally gotten around to it, had been a veritable skeleton. She tried to see the ancient manger through Alexis's born-again eyes. The one at their house probably featured a Mary and Joseph who looked like June Carter and Johnny Cash. The carved figures in Lorraine's crèche were unpainted, primitive, the faces of the kneeling kings seeming to emerge organically from the knots and burls of the wood that made them. "It's Hungarian," Lorraine explained. "It's from my grandmother."

"I know where Hungary is," Alexis said. "World geography. In the mountains, the Oral—"

"Carpathian Mountains," Lorraine said. "What is the matter with Delia? Does she have flu?"

"She gets sick," Alexis shrugged. "She gets pain and shaky, from what's wrong with her."

"She has . . ." Lorraine prompted.

"She has MS, we think, but it's more . . . it's more than that right now." Alexis studied her chewed nails. "She'll be okay."

"You must be worried about her."

"No, she gets better after a day or two. It's like a spell or something."

"Does she have to stop working?"

"My mom? Not if there were a hurricane! God! My mom would work if they were like, building a highway through our house. All the nail ladies would die without her. She does the chancellor's nails. She does facials, too. For professors. Girl professors."

"From the university?"

"Yep. French manicure for the chancellor. Every week," Alexis's eyes swiveled back to the mantel. "I think that thing is kind of cool-looking."

"You can take it down if you like."

"Mary looks a little . . . damaged."

"Oh," Lorraine laughed, "those are marks where Georgia gnawed on her when she was a baby."

"Your girl."

"My daughter, yes. Keefer's . . . mom."

"Can I see her picture?"

"Right there," Lorraine said, pointing to Georgia, beaming in her high school graduation gown, Gordon beside her, laughing at the camera.

"Gordon's handsome. He looks like a movie star."

"He hates when people say that."

"Well, he does."

"He. . . . hates it! Anyhow, it's just his smile that makes people think that. Lots of teeth."

"Well, I hate it when people call me Carrot Head."

"You'll be glad when you grow up that you have that hair. Red's really in now. Gordon's girlfriend Lindsay has beautiful red hair. Georgia tried to dye her hair red about ten thousand times when she was your age. And the Hungarians, the Magyar people, well, this probably isn't true, but it was said that when a child was born with red hair, the gypsies considered her a goddess, the flame-haired child."

"Huh," said Alexis, settling on the couch beside Lorraine. "Go ahead."

"You'll just be happy, about your hair. It's a woman's crowning glory, my grandmother Lena said."

"Now, that's in Transylvania, right? Hungary?"

"The other way around."

"Where Dracula came from."

"So they say."

"And did kids tease you?"

"About . . . ?"

"Did they call you Dracula's daughter?"

"As a matter of fact, when I brought in some of my grand-mother's ceremonial dance clothing, yeah, they did. For weeks, it was 'Leeenaaah, ve vant to bite your neck.'"

"Who's Lena?"

"Lena was me. Back then. I changed my name in high school to Lorraine."

"Because of the Dracula bit?"

"No, because I thought a person named Lena should have three chins and a big hind end. It was just such an . . . old-country name. I changed it after my grandma died."

"Awwww," Alexis said. "I'm sorry she died. I'm going to change my name, too, though."

"To what?"

"To Alex."

"But it already is Alex."

"No, it's really Alex-isss. Which I hate."

"But that's a pretty name. It was the name of the last czar of Russia, a little boy whose mother's name was Princess Alexandra, the czarina. And she was murdered, you know, with all her children, even the little prince, Alexei, by the revolutionaries. . . ."

"Oh," Alexis said, "I didn't know that. That's cool. So, do you have a radio?"

"Yes, we do. You want to hear something?"

"Do you get Zee One Oh Four?"

"No, that's just in Madison, I guess. We have a station that plays oldies. Like, the Beach Boys."

"Umm, no, that's okay."

"What do you like?"

"I like Annie Lennox."

"That's pretty sophisticated."

"Well, there are pretty severe limits on what I can listen to."

"Right."

"They have the God station on all the time. Oh, Jesus, touch me. Oh Jesus, thanks for everything. I can only listen to rap when I have my earphones on in the middle of the night."

"Some of that rap is pretty sick, anyhow."

"It's totally sick. It's like, 'I want the world to suck my—' "

"I know, I know. I teach seventh grade. I've heard it all." Keefer woke and whimpered.

"Can you get her a washcloth to chew on? She likes to go to sleep chewing on a washcloth. Mom won't let her have the bottle 'cause she'll need braces."

Lorraine went to fetch a cold cloth and Keefer chewed beatifically, snoozing.

"Well, so, go ahead with the story," Alexis urged.

"It's not a story."

"The one you were telling before. About the red-haired girls."

"It's not really a story."

"Well, don't you know a story?"

"I know . . . one."

"Tell," Alexis said. Keefer inserted her thumb high in the left corner of her mouth. "Someone's getting sleeeeeepppppyyy."

"Well, there was a poor woman, in my grandma's stories, everyone was poor, who had a beautiful daughter, a beautiful daughter with red hair that was the envy of all the other mothers in the country," Lorraine began. "And it was said that this girl, by virtue of being the flame-haired child, possessed magical powers. Girls who wanted to woo a man to fall in love with them would come and ask to purchase a locket of the daughter's beautiful hair, to tuck into their sweetheart's pocket, and . . . oh, mothers who wanted to have babies and couldn't have babies—"

"Like my mom," said Alexis. "She only ever had me, with my dad. He's Jack Tyson. But now we have pickle-nose—"

"Uh, well," Lorraine said, "well, all those women would come to touch the girl's beautiful hair to their tummies, so that they would conceive a child, and in hopes that this would also be a flame-haired child, a lucky child. Of course, this was fine with the poor mother, because she needed all the pennies people gave her."

And then, Lorraine continued, as Keefer's eyes drooped and finally closed, there was a great famine in the land. The lord who ruled the land, Lorraine called him Vlad Dracul, for the sake of flourish, summoned his gypsy soothsayer to give him wisdom on the plague that had savaged the crops and dried up the cows' milk and poisoned the fish in the streams. Seek out the flame-haired girl, the gypsy wise man advised. Only the flame-haired girl can heal the land. Fill this girl with your son, the soothsayer promised, and when that child is born, the mountains and rivers will bloom with new life. The lord sent out his minions, who listened to the tales of the country folk and finally came to the poor hut where the flame-haired girl lived with her poor mother. They seized the girl and brought her before the lord, who instantly summoned his priests and married the girl, who wept bitterly for her mother. Though the lord was rich and powerful, he was also cruel. He gave the girl, Sofia, jewels and fine clothing and all the food she could hope to eat, but the girl wept and begged for her mother. She would not eat the food, and as the lord realized that Sofia would soon have a child, in desperation, he summoned the mother from her hut to attend to her daughter.

In due course, Sofia gave birth to a beautiful baby son, and, just as the soothsayer had promised, the rivers and fields sprang back to life. Sofia, seeing the lord's joy, begged that her mother be allowed to stay forever with them in the lordly manor. But cruel Vlad refused. He was envious of his flame-haired wife's love for her old mother, and he banished her, back to her hut with only the clothes on her back. Mad with grief, Sofia stole away one night with her baby son wrapped in warm blankets, away to her mother's hut, where they ate their crumbs of cheese and drank goat's milk to give them strength, and then they began their journey down the tributaries that would lead to the great blue Danube River in Buda-Pest, where they would shelter among the many people in the city, and raise the baby away from his cruel father.

"Of course, the lord Vlad got wind of it," Alexis urged her on.

"He did indeed. And he sent for that gypsy soothsayer, who told them only a witch whose dark powers were stronger than the flame-haired girl's powers could bring his son and his wife back to him. The witch, given a pouch of silver, transformed herself into a great, black bird, a raven, and flew over the land until she spotted the girl, her mother, and the baby boy struggling along in the mud near the riverside."

"Did they get away?" Alexis asked. "Did they shoot her?"

"The witch, assuming her human form, appeared before them—"

"In a puff of smoke."

"Probably," Lorraine said. "And she cawed, in her witchly voice, for the soothsayer, who was riding nearby on his great black war horse, and who came thundering to the riverside, and scooped up the baby prince and commanded the girl to leave her mother and return at once to the castle."

"And she refused," Alexis said. "I wouldn't leave my mom."

"She refused. She said, in Hungarian, which I can't speak—in fact, you know, a real scientist once thought the Hungarian language was so different from all the other Eastern European languages that he believed the Hungarian people were descended from Martians! My daughter, Georgia, was also Hungarian, even though we adopted her, and she used to like to think she was from Mars."

"What did she say?" Alexis demanded.

"She said she was from Mars, that she was dropped in the yard by a spaceship, or did she say that about Gordie? I forget—"

"I mean, the princess Sofia."

"Oh, well, the princess said, 'I will stand rooted to this spot until you return my child. I will not move. I would rather stand on this spot for the rest of eternity, than see my child raised by that evil man.' And so the witch changed the princess into a tree. Right there. Into a river birch tree, a delicate white tree. And the witch and the soothsayer brought the baby back to the castle. Well, the girl's mother wept so piteously for so many long days that another witch, a good one, heard her cries. And seeing the mother's grief, she quickly transformed her into a willow tree, so that she would always be able to stand by her daughter's side and shelter her. And that's why you always see the river birch with the willow tree beside it, the weeping willow, alongside the river."

"That is the most depressing story I ever heard," Alexis said. "He got the baby?"

"Yes, he did. And yes, it's pretty depressing. Hungarians are only happy when they're dancing or doing chemistry experiments. There are a lot of Hungarian scientists. But every Hungarian who isn't a scientist is pretty melancholy. My grandma never told a story that didn't have a sad ending. You know, Georgia felt the same way about that story. She used to tell me, let's pretend the baby boy had magic powers and he went back and changed the girl and her little mommy into people."

"Her little mommy?"

"She called me that. Little Mommy."

"You are kind of little."

"Do you want something to drink, Alexis? Alex, I mean?"

"I'll have a Coke."

"We don't have any."

"I'll have a water."

They sat side by side listening to the electronic ticking sounds of the kitchen clock, and when Keefer woke, they watched the Munchkin parts of *Wizard of Oz,* until finally Craig arrived. It was nearly ten.

"I don't know how to thank you," he said. "She's much better."

"Is the baby going—" Alexis began.

"Everything, everything is okay," Craig told her, sternly. "And yes, let's all get going. I'm sorry we kept Keefer up so late. We're going to have a sleepyhead on our hands in the morning."

Lorraine kissed Keefer, who peered over Lorraine's shoulder muzzily, asking "Dory . . . ?"

And Alexis said, "Yeah, we heard a really good story, huh. Craig, I have to tell you this really sad story about Dracula . . ."

Lorraine had closed the door with some difficulty, against the stinging wind, when she again heard knocking. It was Alexis. "My mom said thank you for taking care of me, although I am almost fifteen," said the girl, whom Lorraine noticed with relief did own a coat and had put it on.

"That's okay," Lorraine said.

"Maybe I'll come back and visit you sometime."

"That would be nice, Alex," Lorraine replied, thinking, oh, good Lord, your mom would love that suggestion.

Instead of going back inside, Lorraine plucked her shawl off the hall tree and stood on the porch, watching as Craig and Alexis got Keefer settled with her sippee cup, Delia slumped in the passenger seat. The car pulled away, its tail-lights brightening at the stop sign, then dimming, then disappearing. A slight, sandy snow had begun, and the tinted coach light at the end of Lorraine's walk made a rosy halo, which put Georgia in mind of the O'Keeffe poppy, petals warm and eager as a human face, but its center the chilly blue of an embryonic moon.

Her son finally asleep, Emily Sayward huddled in the corner of their couch. Jamie set the VCR to play the tape they'd recorded of the Friday night news, which they had meant to watch all weekend, but had not managed, with the back-to-back urgencies of shopping, cooking, and minimite hockey practice. In silence, they watched the governor signing, Lorraine's brimming eyes, Gordon's elated smile, the snippet of footage of Ray and Georgia cradling their infant in her baptismal gown. No one—not one of their friends, not the ladies in the soap shop who drew aside whispering into a corner when she walked in to buy a basket of bath goodies for her mother's birthday, the checkout girl in the Safeway who slapped down the CLOSED sign as she approached, the young man at the public works department who told her tersely he would get to it when he had the time after the whole block's worth of banked snow was somehow dumped in an impenetrable wall at the end of the Saywards' driveway—no one had spoken a word of overt criticism about her decision. After glancing at a few of the dozens of letters her clerk had handed her, Emily had asked that the letters be filed. When Jamie told her he would request an unlisted number, after the hang-up calls began, Emily had insisted they wait, and the calls had dwindled, then stopped altogether. She read the newspaper quotes from the McKennas and was relieved that she did not take them personally. Their rage was directed at a symbol, not an individual. Had it not been she, it would have been Aaron Kid or Kendall Crowell. Either of her colleagues would have made the same call.

Jamie held her close as they watched the closing moments of the report, the reporters' banter; how astounding it was that a single word could change a family's whole future, and how they certainly wished that poor family well.

"So there you have it," Jamie said. "Are you okay? It doesn't necessarily mean that the appeals court—"

"Yes, it does," Emily told him, "but I'm ready for that. The little girl is where she should be, with the Cadys. And also, it was bad law, and it needed to be changed."

$\mathcal{T}$hey waited.

An appeal involving a child would be "expedited."

Childhood could neither be deferred nor extended.

The request for an appeal was accepted by the Third District Court of Appeals before Christmas, and Greg Katt told the McKennas that briefs filed late, even by an hour, could result in the entire appeal's summary dismissal. In short order, then, over the course of the period specified for each, were filed an appeal from Gordon, a rebuttal from the Cadys, and an amicus brief, on the McKennas' behalf, by representatives of the American Association of Adoption Attorneys. Not until early in May, after the amendment to A.B. 600 had been signed into law, were all of the briefs completed and presented.

Once all the briefs had been filed, a panel of judges would review them, and it was promised that the forthcoming answer would be "expedited." But the review of the original decision, and the hearings that preceded it, the appeals and the history of laws governing the status of adopted children, would certainly take many weeks. It could take many months. If one of the panel of three judges was ill or was on vacation, the deliberations would stop and resume only when the full panel was reassembled.

Keefer was two years and one month old. Then she was two years and three months old.

They waited.

At a garage sale they passed on Friday evening in Madison, when Delia's continuing illness prevented their driving Keefer to Tall Trees, Lindsay spotted a tricycle that sported red and yellow pom-poms extending from each molded rubber handle. It had huge, old-fashioned inflatable tires, and a seat in the shape of a western saddle. At first they were suspicious. It had appeared as one of those garage sales more humiliating to attend than to host, where people sold five of their shirts and a few old bottles of makeup. But the bike was sound, and a stunning bargain at ten bucks. They bought it, Keefer babbling, "Me bikey, me bikey," all the way home. Once the trike hit ground, she could not be pried from the seat. Even after her bath, she screamed for one more ride, and Lindsay took a photo of her, stark naked except for her bike helmet, furiously pedaling in a circuit from the bedroom, around the couch, back to the foot of the bed. Gordon worried about the photo, even when Lindsay upbraided him for paranoia. The cheapest and fastest photo prints were made by the little Kodak shack, but who among the town's other thousand souls would see the snapshot Lindsay was calling "naked biker chick"? They let Keefer ride until ten, gave her disgustingly sugared cereal she ate daintily with a spoon, then nestled her in her dog bed, for which she had grown nearly too leggy. She turned up quizzical eyes, patting the sheepskin lining and asking "Pretty?" Very pretty, they'd assured her, and it was Keefer's good bed at Dory's. He'd been about to suggest Lindsay mosey when he caught a view of the two of them, Lindsay stroking Keefer's hair, like a Mary Cassat in the frame of his closet door. When Lindsay'd begun to gather her things, he'd taken them, taken her in his arms. They woke in the morning when Keefer placed one of her fingers in Gordon's nostril and said, "Dickens, hi, dickens."

The following week, Gordon received a wedding invitation from Carl Jurgen's parents. The honor of his presence was requested at the marriage of their son to Pearson Corcoran, the daughter of Dr. and Mrs. Haven Corcoran of Boca Raton. Still under the impression, even as he dialed, that he meant to congratulate Jurgen, Gordon called his old friend, got a machine, then a call back the next night. They spoke of nothing, at first, their parents' health, Jurgen's imminent graduation from law school, and then, inevitably, the case. Jurgen had been watching the developments closely, and keeping in touch with Diane and Big Ray both when they were in residence in Madison and when they spent time in Florida. Both elder Nyes were battered by the conflict—family things seemed so simple to them, Jurgen explained.

"But you knew it wouldn't be simple," Gordon had suggested then.

"I could see it coming, yeah, Bo."

"And you told them how it would be. You helped them figure out . . ."

"Well, I was never their legal advisor, if that's what you mean. But both Dad and I . . . we could hardly refuse to try to help them find the people they needed. I thought for sure that Alison's hubby was going to cave in, so that they could have been the ones to step forward. That would have been the best solution all around."

"It would have? How do you figure?"

"Well, kids more or less the same age, a sister instead of a cousin, you know. And Alison and Andy live more of a, well, moderate life socially than Delia and Craig do."

"You mean the church thing."

"I suppose it's not a big deal."

"Carl, it's a big deal to me."

"I know that, Bo, and it stinks. It's lousy. But there you have it. You couldn't have been too surprised. Gordie, you're not quite the settling-down type. Not from what I know of you. Amazes me that I am. Pearson's great. Great backhand.

Great back end. Smart as hell. You know, I only met her three months ago. Our first date was Easter, ever so pure. Which, speaking of that, how's the lovely Lindsay? You two still cooking?"

"I want to finish talking about the other thing . . ."

"Okay. Fine, fine. But I don't ever want you to think that we felt anything negative toward you, or your family. It's just, Gordo, it's just always been clear . . . Ray was a real close-in family guy, Bo. He would never have been able to rest knowing his baby girl wasn't going to be raised with all the, oh, the trappings, the ways . . . he was always so out of place, up there. We have a way of life, Gordie, and it's not like you-all's way. Might sound strange. But everybody in Jupiter seems to know everybody else in Jupiter—"

"You know a lot of people in Spanish town?"

Jurgen stopped. "I mean, in the area where we grew up."

"So you don't know everyone in Jupiter, just the people who hang out at the country club. The Beaumonts, and the . . . the Cabots and the Lowells and the Rockefellers . . ."

"Gordie," Jurgen began to laugh. "What the hell are you saying there, Bo?"

"Can you even admit the possibility that my sister felt the exact same way about her hometown? That Keefer had two parents? That we have our ways, and our trappings, and even if we're not the kind who slobber all over you and call you 'honey, sugar, doll' every five minutes, we feel just as close to one another?"

"I'm sure you do." Jurgen made his mellow voice formal, remote.

"And so you certainly can admit the possibility that even Ray, at least at one time, felt sure that Keefer would be happier and more secure among the people who knew her best?"

"I know he had a grateful heart for all you did for Georgia," Jurgen answered evenly. "Now, Gordie, maybe we better just get this conversation on an alternate track. Because you and I—"

"And he was my friend."

"He was your friend."

"And you were my friend. You were my friend. You were closer to me even than Ray was. I thought you might demonstrate some loyalty. I thought if you couldn't demonstrate some loyalty, you might at least demonstrate some neutrality."

"Gordie, I don't want to have this conversation."

"Carl, I don't want to have this conversation, either. Or any other one. Ever."

"I don't think you're always going to feel that way. We go way back, Bo. I expect you there to help me hoist the—"

"We go way back, Carl. But we don't go way forward." And Gordon put down the telephone receiver, juggling it and bobbling it as if it were something scalding, his hands in a brain-stem tremor like his grandpa McKenna's. Maybe he'd got Parkinson's, he thought. No, he and Pop McKenna were not blood relatives.

They waited.

Nora had never noticed how little work there really was to do on the farm. Even in planting, it had begun to function, not without her, but without the constant, watchful attention she had grown accustomed to giving. Certainly, some of that was due to the fact that the land in asparagus was mature now. The asparagus did everything but jump up into the boxes by itself. Marty had quit his day job to work with his dad full-time, and they spent evenings huddled over Extension pamphlets on free-range chickens and sustainable agriculture. The appeal seemed to be taking forever. How long did it take intelligent people to do what was right? she asked Hayes one night. "I'd sure hate to be somebody on Death Row," she'd murmured.

"We don't have a Death Row in Wisconsin," Hayes grunted.

"I know that, you old crab," Nora retorted stoutly. "It was a for-instance." But kindly though he had been about the case since the night of their argument, Hayes was still not all that keen on discussing it.

Half at loose ends, Nora volunteered to take over the presidency of the altar guild from Helen Wilton and spent hours in the jeweled, dusty silence of the nave, planning elaborate themes for the Sunday services that would incorporate the wild flowers and even the lacy weeds with cultivated blooms. She scoured garage sales for vases, urns, old milk bottles, dried silver sage and statice, grape vines and cattails. Only when Father Barry commented that he was afraid he might trip over a planter during communion did Nora scale back her ministry. Still, she drew out her afternoons at church. So few people came into Our Lady of the Lake during the day that Nora had no reason to feel self-conscious about her overalls or her perm growing out like duckweed. She sometimes lost herself in a prayer that took her like a sleep. She prayed to Saint Jude, the patron of lost causes, not because she feared their cause was lost, but because insurance never hurt. She prayed to Saint Anne, the benevolent grandmother, Saint Therese, the Little Flower, for her well-known interest in children, to Saint Catherine of Sienna, because she believed in taking action and was criticized as obsessive, to Saint Anthony, the patron of adoption, Saint Nicholas the Martyr, because of that awful story about the little boys he brought back to life after some psychotic butcher tried to pickle them, to Saint Thomas the Doubter, and to Saint Fidelis because he was local.

In her reveries, she asked God for assurances of his continued interest in the appeal, though she could not be sure that whether the fullness of grace she felt replenish her was God's answer or the echo of her own supplication. During those times in her life when she'd tended toward complacency, Nora had turned to the shorter, more humble forms of prayer, her favorite, "Not my will, but thine," but she could not quite abandon herself to that now. God needed specifics, as there were undoubtedly millions storming heaven at any given time, and only the one divine judge.

Lorraine would have welcomed an interval of stark, staring madness. By the magnitude of her losses, she was owed greater latitude for weakness and eccentricity. But her life offered no room for a breakdown. Their thirty-fifth anniversary fell in May. They dined, on a gift certificate sent by an anonymous well-wisher they could not find to gratefully refuse, at a fancy seafood restaurant in Merrill. Offered Chilean sea bass in a thyme reduction sauce, Lorraine agreed she certainly could use one, but the server only gave her a baffled smile. Over the course of the next two weeks, school was drawing to its close, with its festival of final projects and exhibits, the culmination in the students' work on the gifts they would offer, the sculptures Lorraine was keenly aware hold pride of place for parents long after the children themselves had made homes of their own.

And the machine that spread the news about the outrage now proceeded of its own momentum; Lorraine pulled along with its progress, posing for photos for magazine stories prepared months before, pulled to respond to a request from *Redbook* that she write her own first-person narrative—all she would really have to do, the editor who called insisted, would be to write down the facts; someone would massage the facts into a story, but even writing down the facts had taken a week of nights at the table with Nora busily looking up facts and dates Lorraine could not remember.

At a seminar in Wausau on integrating art into other sections of the curricula, which took up one whole day of the Memorial Day weekend, when they had Keefer, Lorraine was approached by a woman who first asked her to sign a copy of the column on the case that had appeared in *Woman's Day,* and then condoled her on losing her "adopted granddaughter." The sheer glass wall of ignorance daunted

Lorraine, who nonetheless took time to carefully explain that she had not adopted her granddaughter, that adoption had fused their lineage before Keefer was ever born. Patty Roe of the American Academy had called to tell them that there was indeed not one, but thirty references to "blood relatives" in the Children's Code, and that it was her belief that the law would not truly be sound until each of them was amended. Greg Katt no longer charged them for his thrice-weekly telephone calls, sharing details of the opposing side's arguments, the points their side rebutted, the questions from the panel of judges. The McKennas now owed Greg Katt and his posse more than $40,000, the hope of a new trial with all its attendant costs still ahead. Quietly, Lorraine and Mark visited the Soderberg boy and remortgaged their long-since-paid-for home on Cleveland Avenue.

Lorraine kept hats off the bed, and shoes off the table. She carefully closed her umbrella before stepping inside her front door. During the long evenings in May, she set herself the task of clearing out Gordon's and Georgia's teenage memorabilia, but was sidetracked almost immediately by one of Gordie's college biology textbooks. She carried the book down to her work table. Using a root charcoal and a handful of nubbin-old pastels, Lorraine began sketching what would be, by August, a series of fourteen, vastly imagined magnifications of the shredded gossamer of a sickle cell, a tumor cell, a healthy erythrocyte. She would call them "Cell Lives."

Retirement, Mark realized as they waited, was receding further and further to a distant horizon for him. That was fine. Medi-Sun employed chemists in their seventies, took pride in their embrace of older colleagues. Though Northern Mutual had come forth with the $500,000 premium, it would be ninety days before the check arrived. Through their attorneys, both sides had agreed to permit Great Wisconsin to manage the estate until a final decision was reached. During meetings at work over a bizarre legal claim—a woman who'd blamed her diverticulitis on the four thousand milligrams of C she'd ingested every day since 1985—it slowly dawned on Mark, piecing together various references and comments and mental snapshots of the yearly Medi-Sun picnics at Fidelis Hill with the peculiar atmosphere in the conference room, the anxious glances some of the managers sneaked at him when the corporation's lawyer spoke, that one of their counsel, Jamie Zavara, was actually the husband of Judge Sayward. Mark's first instinct was to disarm the young man—it was a small town; they were coworkers. But the man's manner, his avid, almost greedy intelligence, put him off. Thereafter, he quietly informed his boss, he would communicate with the legal division through memoranda.

Dale Larsen called one night and invited Mark to join him, a few of his deputies, Bud Chaptman, and Hart from the high school for a few hands of poker. Mark went and gratefully consumed more than his share of beer. He'd offered muzzily to walk home, but Dale, who had, Mark noted, tipped more than a few himself, drove him slowly home in the cruiser. Dale urged his wife to include Lorraine in her bunco night, but Sheila felt too shy to approach Lorraine, whose new haircut and forceful public face only rendered her more intimidating to acquaintances who'd considered her demeanor perfectly nice, but regal enough to give an ordinary person pause, before any of the events of the year began. Dale began to see how a single event of ordinary grief opened bystanders and made them generous, but an enduring misery of crisis hardened and repelled. Marooned by their own exigency, the McKennas probably needed the welcome interference of friends more than they had during Georgia's illness, when well-wishers had tripped over one another on the path to the door of the house on Cleveland Avenue. There was the assumption that people who got on TV were sufficient unto themselves, Dale ruminated.

He nagged his wife to call on Lorraine, at least ask her to

lunch. As a man, he felt that he could not do that without causing talk, the kind of rumors that would be more damaging for the fact that they would be true. Dale Larsen's heart went out to Lorraine, but too far, and it was a bittersweet reckoning to admit to himself that people in their fifties were not, after all, beyond the nonsense of secret crushes. When Sheila finally rolled into bed one night tossing out the intelligence that Lorraine had agreed to a lunchtime pep walk, Larsen seized his wife in a bear hug, and it was after midnight when they finally parted to den in the accustomed hollows of their respective sides of the bed, lingeringly, gasping, each of them privately grateful and confused beyond words by the resurgence of passions they thought they'd left in the birthing room with Trina long years before.

On the night that they watched a Tom Brokaw special report entitled "Thicker than Blood?" Emily Sayward and her husband discussed, briefly, the idea of moving back east and starting a practice together. The discussion had not been much more than desultory. Jamie loved his job. And Emily loved the safe, quiet sixties life on Hat Lake they could give as a gift to Emory, their son, who would begin school in the fall. Later that same night, as they undressed in the dark, presumptive current between them, Jamie had suggested it might be time for another child, a little brother or sister for Emory, and though Emily emphatically agreed, dispensing with the cervical cap that very night, she mentioned the next morning her concern that she was thirty-eight now. What if she could not become pregnant? What if there were issues? And when Jamie, busy replacing a rotten deck board, replied that they would adopt—that no one in Colombia had ever heard of Tom Brokaw—she had refused, irrationally and pettishly, to speak to him for a full day.

In late May, at Sandpiper Reserve, in the final hours of a tournament dedicated to Raymond Nye, Jr., and to benefit

Keefer Kathryn's scholarship fund, Big Ray's left arm tingled, then went numb, and over fear from that, he supposed, his heart began to gallop, and, in a little beverage cabana off the ninth hole, he'd vomited. Haven Corcoran and Lee Jurgen bundled him into the car, over his faint protests, and by that night he was ensconced in a private room at Tampa Memorial, where the next morning, he underwent angioplasty. Too much bacon and eggs in there, the cardiologist gently chided him, pointing at Ray's gut. Lose the golf cart and walk from this day forward, the doctor further added.

That night—when Diane arrived home from Wisconsin, wringing her hands and imploring him not to die, she couldn't take any more, not one single thing more, she was going to have one of those lives where one tragedy toppled over into another tragedy and another tragedy—he'd quieted her down and taken her hand and told her what he'd been thinking about when they'd run the icy liquid into the vein, and that was Gordie McKenna. "Now, don't get yourself in a swivet, Mother," he soothed her gruffly. "I just have a notion we ought to be in touch."

"Be in touch?"

"When I was lying there, in that room, never knowing if I'd ever see another sunrise, I got to thinking about the first time Ray brought Gordie to the house. You remember? It was Caroline's wedding. And the two of them came up here at five in the morning, getting me out of bed, saying, 'Dad! We're going to have us some beer and eggs! Beer and eggs, that's what you need, Dad!' Both of them in those big shorts the surfers wear, Ray jumpin' up on the bed, you screamin' . . ."

"Ray, what could that mean now, honey?"

"It's that . . . when I thought I was about to die, I thought, Diane, Baby is right where she ought to be, except . . . and it's a big except, one of our own girls should have wanted more than anything else on earth to raise our son's only child. That's the truth and you know it is, Diane. And Gordie did. He was a good boy then, and he's a good boy now, Diane, and my boy, my boy loved Gordie." Big Ray breathed carefully. He could not get over the notion that his body was made of some friable material, like Diane's hollow crystal cats. "Here's what I'm saying. I want you to write to Gordie and to his folks and try to make amends. I'm not saying we can ever make amends, or even that we'd do anything differently if we could. I want Keefer Kathryn to grow up a Nye. But I also want to rest easy on my own conscience, Diane."

"Lorraine McKenna would never allow—"

"And if you don't write, when I get up out of this bed, I will."

The following night, she had brought him the letter she had begun to compose.

One early evening, Tim Upchurch glimpsed Lindsay and Gordon walking Keefer along Main Street. Each of them had hold of one of her hands—step, step, big swing. He'd been about to brake and wander over, when some unaccustomed reluctance brought him up short. He had just braked then, and watched. Step, swing. Step, swing. The baby's hair was long and wavy, like Georgia's. Lindsay's gaze on Gordie was a sun. Tim saw his fist connect with his best friend's perfect, big, white front teeth. He would have treated her so well. He would have fucking treated her like a princess. Tim watched them vanish around the corner by Hubble's. They were a family. He had no place with them.

Out at the edge of the subdivision, the fire department was conducting a practice burn on one of Ryder's ancient outbuildings, a corn crib, Tim believed. He thought he might motor out there, perhaps catch sight of that yummy mommy Alicia they'd run into up at Black Wolf. Gordie evidently hadn't taken the bait after that first night. It wouldn't be the first time Tim had been in the position of scavenging Gordie's leavings. But Gordie's leavings were better than anyone else's. There was that. And no thirty-plus woman would be interested in Tim for anything more meaningful than a night of energy. Well, what was so bad about that? One night of energy was something Tim could definitely get invested in.

Greg Katt waited like a man who knows he has two court-side tickets to a play-off game in his windbreaker pocket.

If he had ever felt more confident during the course of his professional life, he could not recall it. He rose every day at dawn and embraced his wife and kissed his little daughters, then jogged slowly, even through the blessing of a warm rain, and drove to work singing Aretha's greatest hits. For this, the most-watched, most publicized and most heartfelt case he might ever argue, he could have felt no more game. No fear. Only daring.

It would be a walk in the park.

They would go down. They would be rubble.

The amicus brief prepared by Rob Greenbaum and Patricia Roe, representing the Academy of Adoption Attorneys, built an elegant historical house with a door that opened wide to admit Gordon McKenna. Excluding Gordon constituted a complete contradiction of all the other statutes that made up 48, the Children's Code, which was one of the most thorough in the nation. Rob and Patty quoted from the section "effects of adoption," a scant two paragraphs from the now notorious 48.90. After adoption, the bond between the parent and child was to include "all the rights, duties and other legal consequences of the natural relation of child and parent."

They bore down harder: Even before the amendment, had Ray and Georgia Nye been bad parents, whose rights had been terminated by law, Gordon would have been among the immediate family members entitled to immediate placement of his niece, with no waiting period. How could common sense prescribe a different set of rules for an uncle whose sister's rights had been tragically, through no fault of her own, terminated by death? How could common sense allow the same chapter that defined adoptees as exactly legal in status omit adoptees from the definition of "relative"? The brief examined other laws on the books: People called up for jury duty, for example, could not be related "by blood or marriage" to defendants or attorneys involved with a trial. No auto insurance policy could exclude from benefits persons related to the policy holder by "blood or marriage."

And so, was state law intended to prohibit families from getting car insurance for their adopted children? Could the prosecuting attorney's sister, if she were adopted, get on a jury and help push along the conviction her brother was trying for? Was that logical? In any universe?

Even the United States Supreme Court, in 1977, had given the opinion that "adoption, for example, is recognized as a legal equivalent of biological parenthood." No statute should ever be construed to degrade common sense. The legislature, in the Children's Code and in countless other instances, had clearly intended for adoptive children to be included in every possible definition of family. The omission had been oversight, that inclusion perhaps so obvious that it might not have occurred to the lawmakers at all.

He'd focused on the specifics. And in his brief, he dismembered the whiny preoccupations of Wentworth and the guardian ad litem. Wentworth lovingly recounted the history of the Cadys with Ray and Georgia in Florida, how they'd planned to buy a duplex and live side by side forever, that they had specifically, in naming the Cadys godparents, "a role to which Craig and Delia gave utmost allegiance," actually conferred on them the traditional role of godparents as prospective guardians. Wentworth attacked the McKennas, claiming that "little K.K." had been sheltered by the Cadys from the "firestorm" of national publicity "orchestrated" by L. M. and her unnatural obsession with her "adoptive" grandchild. Wentworth condemned Gordon's attempt to "tactically outmaneuver" her clients using the expedited adoption procedure and concluded smugly that this "presumed advantage" had blown up in Gordon's face. In a footnote, Wentworth prissily noted that Judge Sayward had rebuked Gordon's team throughout the hearing for trying to one-up the Cadys instead of considering the best interests of little K. K.

And though the best interests of Keefer would be served, Katt went on with exultation, when they first reviewed their documents during discovery, that was not at all the point for which they had been summoned in the first place, at all! Gordon had never even been given the chance to present his side of that very issue in a court of law, since the court had ruled that Gordon had no standing to petition to adopt his niece. And why should Gordon have not attempted to use every advantage?

Katt addressed that. It was ludicrous. He was the child's *uncle,* now by indubitably signed law even a moron like Wentworth could not misinterpret. "Gordon was the sole surviving sibling of Georgia, Keefer's mother, and his deceased sister's dying wish was for Gordon to care for her child," Katt wrote. To deprive Gordon of any part of his status as Keefer's only maternal uncle was to deprive Keefer of her very heritage.

Dr. Bogert's recommendation of the Cadys was based solely on the bias that sprang from every section of her report, the psychologist's belief that a female child of tender years should have a mother. It was not Gordon's—Katt quoted—"loving and positive" relationship with Keefer that she doubted, but his inability, as a single male, to cope with the developmental needs of a female child. And yet, Katt reminded the court, the Wisconsin legislature had specifically noted that "any unmarried adult," not merely a woman, might adopt a minor child.

"The only issue before this court is to determine whether Gordon, adopted as a baby, has the legal standing," Katt had written, "under Wisconsin Statute 48.90, to petition for the adoption of his niece. Should an 'adopted' uncle be denied the same opportunity a 'natural' uncle would certainly be afforded?"

The only reason Gordon had not moved sooner to adopt Keefer was so as not to seem to interfere in the venue dispute by both sets of grandparents. His hesitation was prompted by family loyalty, not by indecision or by reluctance. Resoundingly, Katt had, in his final brief, sliced away at their feeble assertion that the adoption statute intentionally discriminated against adopted relatives in "procedural" matters of law, though not "substantive rights."

No court in the land, certainly not the courts of the state of Wisconsin, had ever upheld that it was "appropriate to discriminate against an adopted person, provided that the discrimination is limited to legal procedure."

Show him one example, he dared them between the lines.

Wait and hope, Mary Ellen Wentworth comforted her clients, when they phoned her, Delia especially distraught over the Tom Brokaw show. Every day that Keefer Kathryn lived in their home was a good day, a day for their side, she advised. Whether or not Judge Sayward's decision was overturned, whether or not a new trial went forward with Gordon able to present his petition, Keefer was growing older and more bonded to her mother, father, and sister. With the passage of each new day, any judge would become less disposed to interrupt her healthy adjustment. Don't worry, Mary Ellen told them. The delay actually works for us. Nothing will ever overrule the child's best interests.

Mary Ellen's brief did not reflect the rancor she felt toward that fanatic witch, Lorraine McKenna, whose self-seeking fervor had forced them all through the hoops of a three-ring media circus. The McKennas might win, but they would not prevail. She and Victoria Linquist were utterly in sync, equally propelled by determination and disgust.

* * *

June third, the anniversary of the accident at Lost Tribe Creek Bridge, was the last day of school, which ended for the term at noon. After lunch, Nora and Lorraine cut a double armload of lilacs from Nora's yard and bought a couple orchid stems at Every Blooming Thing and drove to the bridge, where they leaned together over the shining segment of repaired railing and dropped the stems, one by one, into the gossipy current of the stream. A breeze came up, and kept blowing the flowers back into their faces, out onto the shoulder of the road, once onto the highway. The two women ran to recover them. "That's Georgia," Nora laughed, "she always wanted to get things stirred up."

Even Lorraine had managed a fragile smile by the time Greg Katt drove up in his car, slammed on the brakes and staggered toward them. Tears were streaming down his face.

"Better go home and stock up on gummy bears, Grandma," he said. "I think you're going to have a little girl running around soon."

The Court of Appeals had reversed Judge Sayward's decision, on a vote of two to one. A new hearing must take place. It was, as Nora later said, a whole new ball game.

CHAPTER *eighteen*

*N*othing would ever make them forget that interval, when there was glory.

They accepted congratulations as though they'd purchased the winning lotto ticket, then misplaced it, then found it in the pocket of a shirt destined for the Goodwill. Lorraine felt eyes approve her passage through the stalls at the outdoor produce market on Fidelis Hill, through the library, up the steps of the municipal pool building, where, after a year's sloth, she'd begun taking a water aerobics class with Karen and Natalie. This, she thought, must be what it is like to be a movie star, the bath of approbation—first startled silences, then small murmurs of recognition.

Yes, she thought, as she nodded in receipt of the smiles, we are the ones you recognize from the news.

We are the ones who won. We are the good guys.

There would be a new judge, probably Aaron Kid.

Greg further told them that he would henceforth tremble at the mere mention of Judge Sayward's name. Getting a judge spanked, no matter how resolutely impersonal both parties endeavored to behave, was playing with matches. Interviewed for ABC, Katt told Lorraine, he'd tried to be as gracious as David might have been, bending over backward to give all the credit to the design of the slingshot. Had this ruling not been provoked by the McKennas' tragedy, it would inevitably have arisen from another family's loss. That Gordon would now have the status to be heard was no recompense for that loss, but did offer the balm of justice, the rare sense of having been at law for a reason beyond profit or punishment.

In the town at large, the victory spread like water under a door, mouth to phone, desk to desk, fence to rolled-down car window. For years afterward, people would tell new acquaintances how it had been that night with a kind of swagger not quite that reserved for low brushes with celebrities or being an eyewitness at historical tragedies, but close enough for a town of three thousand, north of Stevens Point. Heard of the blood-relative case? The one that was on *60 Minutes*? Actually, they said, we know that guy. They'd seen him with the little girl, in the soap store. One of their boys took science in his class. The grandpa was that guy who used to talk about deer and bird feeders on the radio? Remember him? And they had that golf outing, too. Andy North came, yeah, that was right, because the baby's father was a big-time golfer. Semipro. They would remember running into Mark or Lorraine or Gordon at the Dairymaid the day after or the week after the Court of Appeals sent down word. You know, they'd say, it was the art teacher's son. The Supreme Court said, in the decision, that her son was as good as any other kid and no one dared say otherwise. Yes, it was the Supreme Court, the telephone versions reported to daughters whose husbands had been transferred to Seattle or San Antonio.

Were you there, people asked each other, referring to the Friday night party, which started with a few hamburgers grilling on the McKennas' front lawn and drifted out over to encompass the Dwors's house and the street until it seemed that all the fireflies in Trempeauleau County had birthed multitudes in front of the house on Cleveland Street. Was it true, a few people who had been out of town asked, that couples waltzed in the cemetery, like black-cut paper dolls against a stainless sky? Did anyone get in trouble for that? Who was the guy who showed up with a violin? The husband of that wild girl, the sheriff's daughter? You had to be there to understand how it was, others would say, because it was as if a party began without an invitation sent or a phone call made, a gathering that seemed reconstituted from long ago, not long ago in Wisconsin, but long ago, when the Woodland people now lying still in their plundered tomb on a rise ringed by new roads and backhoes were alive and congregating. You had to be there to see how it was, the first long night of June giving up its extravagant bath-warm air, the heavy, creamy scent of peonies in first bloom, people nipping back to their houses for casseroles they'd popped in the oven an hour before, someone carrying a keg all the way from the Wild Rose on Oakwood Street, down Main to Cleveland, someone else appearing with a cake covered in flowers, the blue-white veil of moonlight, the stars that fell, the children who fell asleep on lawn chairs, their chins iced with frosting and petals.

Some would recount how they saw Craig Cady arrive that night, squealing too fast around the corner, sitting with the windows of his Jeep rolled tight while the skinny teenager with the magnificent hair carried sleeping Keefer up onto the lawn and delivered her into Lorraine's arms for her weekend visit. Some would invent words Craig said, words of the John Wayne genre, "You haven't heard the last of this!" or "It's not over yet!" though Craig had in fact not even turned his head to look at any of them.

The florist at Every Blooming Thing and the office manager at the middle school would be among those who slid a thumbnail down the spine of a magazine four months later, cutting out a story from *Ladies' Home Journal*, a story they would post on their refrigerators for reasons they could not even explain to their husbands or children, a story naming Lorraine as one of the previous year's twenty Women of Valor, women never to be underestimated, the profile of Lorraine under a headline that read, "Out of Love, Law . . . Her Daughter's Legacy," an honor that would mean a dizzying trip to New York for Lorraine and Mark, a check for a thousand dollars to the National Association of Adoptive Families, and lunch at the Four Seasons at a raised table only two seats from Oprah.

Lorraine had danced with Mark that night on their lawn. She did not remember how many glasses of wine she drank, but she did remember having told Mark that she was going to let herself feel happy for one entire night. Guests, friends, neighbors simply seemed to materialize. She met Stephanie Larsen's sexy husband, a Latin kid with that hair the color of hot tar, hair that begged to be rubbed between finger and thumb, and wilted with laughter as she tried to fit her arms around Stephanie, who had the girth of a sequoia and wobbled on her feet with her pregnancy like a dog on an old ladder.

Then Sheila came strolling along.

"Twin boys!" Sheila said. "It's twin boys I'm going to be a grandmother to. I'm going to be grandmother for the first and the second time the same day!"

"I feel like I'm trying to carry two buckets of water without losing my balance," Stephanie laughed, "and I'm only eight months! Even if I don't go to term, the doctor says they'll be fine. They have to be huge! We're going to name them Daniel George and Diego Dale; Dad hates it, he says they'll sound like lounge singers. But I couldn't name a baby Dale! For a first name! I mean, come on! And I couldn't name a baby George for a first name, even though, you know it's meant to be for Georgia . . ." Her great brown eyes sparkled precariously. "I want him to be named after Georgia." Lorraine's own eyes brimmed. "I dreamed the other night that I saw Georgia climbing up the standpipe to my window, and I wasn't scared. It wasn't like, oh my God, there's a ghost! It was like I'd been waiting for her to get there. And then, the dream changed around, and I was out there climbing up with her, like I could do that the way I am! But I looked down and we were both of us, like sixteen again. . ."

This sweet, restored, bygone Georgia whom Stephanie had encountered was wild and windswept and roaring with health, unconquered by the rain that pelted cold around them. "'We won't fall, Stevie,' she told me, that's what she used to call me, when I wanted to be fragile and little and wear floaty dresses like Stevie Nicks. 'We won't fall.' And we made it all the way up to her window, but it was locked, so we climbed on the gutters, kind of scrunched over to your window, which we did do, in real life, a few times, and it was open . . . and we sort of fell in on your sofa, that used to be right by the window?"

"It still is." Lorraine coached her on. "Then what?"

"And she said, 'Okay! We're safe.' That was the end of the dream. And I called my sister the next morning and said, 'Trina, that appeal is going to go through. It's going to be fine. It was a sign.'" She massaged her belly with its obscenely distended pancake navel and nodded sagely.

Tim Upchurch stationed himself next to his cooler on wheels, passing out St. Pauli Girls to everyone who passed. About a dozen Reillys of various denominations piled out of a car, the high school kid jumping on Gordon's back, and Gordon going right along with it, though the kid made Gordon spill a full plate of Swiss steak on Lindsay Snow's lap. Later accounts, passed along to those who missed the party, always mentioned that the coral dress Lindsay wore when she came back outside after the spill had belonged to Georgia Nye.

Lorraine had given the dress to Lindsay to keep.

She and Nora bounced Keefer on the bed in Lorraine's room while Lindsay changed, talking to them through the open bathroom door.

"I hope it fits you, honey," Lorraine had said. "Georgia was much bigger than you."

"No, she really wasn't," Lindsay, muffled, answered. "She was so short she looked as though she weighed more, but we were exactly the same size, even after Keefer was born. We both had the big butts and no boobs." Lorraine heard a gush of water in the sink. "I'm sorry, Lorraine," Lindsay said then. Lorraine saw a crease of worry cross Nora's face.

"No, I'm okay, I'm really okay," Lorraine told her sister-in-law, and raised her voice. "Is that true, Lindsay? You always look so slim—"

"I only weigh about ten pounds less than Gordie," Lindsay said. "He made me get on the scale one night. He practically had to lift me on it, and I was screaming, like, no, forget it! But he said you should tell the person you're close to about everything, and that a woman's weight was the last bastion of intimacy—"

"So, you two," Nora said then, "what's up with you?"

"What do you mean?" Lindsay trilled. "Nothing."

"Oh, I don't think nothing. I think plenty," Nora murmured.

"We're not, like, making plans or anything." Lindsay said, "My dress is shot, Lorraine. It's toast."

"Just needs a little stain spray," Nora called, slapping her knees beneath the cuffs of her khaki shorts. Nora wore a white shirt, closed to the topmost button, and pearl earrings. She'd gone formal on them, Lorraine noticed, amused. "Do you have stain spray, Lor?"

"In the cabinet over the washer."

"Come on, Keefer!" hollered Nora, "ponyback ride!"

Lindsay emerged from the bathroom, tendrils of her red hair nearly indistinguishable against the rosy fabric.

"That looks wonderful on you," Lorraine said. "You can have it."

"It's Georgia's," Lindsay breathed.

"No, I want you to wear it. Will you wear it? I mean, more than tonight, if I give it to you?"

Lindsay reverently stroked a fold of the gauze. It was really a pretty dress, Lorraine thought, a smocked yoke and a skirt that twirled. Georgia had worn it to Keefer's christening. "I'll love to wear it," Lindsay said quietly, "but you don't have to give it to me. I can have it dry-cleaned."

"It bothers me that I never gave you anything of Georgia's," Lorraine said, leaning back on her elbows, reaching for her wine glass, which she remembered, abruptly, she'd left outside. I'm tipsy, she thought, I could say much too much. But she continued, "Georgia considered you one of her best friends, Lindsay. I guess I just always thought I'd give you some of the things . . . some of her things . . . if you and Gordon . . ."

"You know how much I love him," Lindsay told Lorraine, sitting down beside Lorraine on the bed, reaching out, withdrawing, then reaching out again and lightly taking Lorraine's hand.

"I know," Lorraine said, "and I know he loves you."

"I don't know about that. I get the feeling, sometimes, that he's looking over my shoulder, trying to see what else is out there. I don't mean other girls. Though that, too."

"He's got quite a knack."

"He does." Lindsay looked about to weep. "But I don't want to talk about my craziness. We're probably happier together right now than we ever were when we were kids."

"The thing with Gordie," Lorraine said, sitting up, swaying, steadying herself, "is that you have to let him be the one who comes to you. This is how he is. He's like . . . some deer in the forest or something. You can chase him all day and you'll never get him—"

"Do you think I chase him?" Lindsay withdrew her hand, glancing about her, as if fearful of being overheard. The man who was playing the violin—who was he?—had begun to play "Georgia."

"I don't think that at all," Lorraine comforted her, "It's just a manner of speaking. I only mean that while Gordie seems pretty devoid of the kind of male-pride thing you're starting to see in young men again, which seems to have sort of skipped a generation with Mark, thank goodness, not that Mark ever would have been a macho man anyway . . ." I'm machine mouth, she thought. Shut up. She had never before discussed anything more weighty than Susan Lucci's quest for an Emmy award with any of Gordie's female friends. No, that was not true. She had talked many times with Lindsay about the most pitiable details of Georgia's illness. She had discussed the case with Lindsay, even revealing her irrational hatred of Diane Nye.

What she had never discussed, she thought then, was her son. She had never talked with a girlfriend of Gordon's about Gordon. And she had never discussed a girl in any real detail with Gordon. Of course, she knew about his legendary eloquence in the clinches. Georgia had made sure of that. And Lorraine and Gordon were close enough that he would have brought her, as he'd brought her his snails and snakeskins, the husk of a love that had burned his wings. She'd expected it, the brokenhearted confidence, long distance, expected to be able to offer soothing words and affirmations. She had even planned it. She would never even have suggested that what Gordon had experienced had been trivial. She would have shared her belief that all love was significant, and failed or flourished on by degrees, and often through no fault of either of the partners . . . but it had never transpired. With Georgia, yes. The only way Lorraine was certain she had never failed her daughter was in having been a resolutely loyal listening force through dozens of deceptions and snubs, from male friends and female. Gordon had simply never seemed fazed. She'd no sooner master a capsule history of a mentioned woman than he'd blithely refer to someone else entirely. How many times had she even met girlfriends of Gordon's? Six? Five? That little surfer girl in Florida, the one with the most extensive collection of navel jewelry in captivity. The woman from EnviroTreks, the zoologist, who'd had shorter hair than almost any man Lorraine had ever met. She tried, and failed, to summon images of others. Hopeless. They were forms blurred in the swirl of the revolving door. Susan. Andrea. Taylor. She was sure about Taylor. Or had it been Tyler? The girl from Apalachicola. Courtneys and Lisas and Lizas, Susannahs and Susans. Emily? No wonder poor Lindsay despaired. But then, her son, despite all of his experiences, losses, and responsibilities, was only twenty-five years old. At twenty-five, Mark had actually felt his teeth chatter when a woman breathed on him. Some people were late bloomers in one way, if not in another. Gordon was really only a boy.

The thought satisfied Lorraine immensely. She did want her wine. She patted Lindsay's hand.

"Just enjoy each other," she said. "This is a time to enjoy each other." Lorraine tried to ignore Lindsay's crestfallen look. Time enough, Lorraine thought, to be a mother-in-law again, if it comes to that.

After everyone had drifted off that night, and Keefer was tucked into bed with her water ba-ba and her Day-doe pillow between her and Mark, Lorraine, restless, had got up in her nightgown and made a sweep of her lawn, picking up paper napkins and stray cups, allowing herself pleasure in the air on her nearly naked flesh. She'd raised the hem of her nightgown, letting the breeze stir up over her hips, her heavy breasts. If she had not thought she might frighten Mary Dwors, who suffered from insomnia, she would have let the breeze carry her across the street, between the brick gates of the cemetery to Georgia's grave, where she had often sat, to cry or to read the classifieds. She had sent her thoughts on the wind instead. We've got her, honey. We've got her.

This was the pattern revealed. The missing piece placed. The torturous bridge that connected this house with that cemetery was complete. The piece was Keefer, the daughter of their daughter, who hummed when she walked and slammed the ground, hard, with her heels, because she liked the rhythm of the vibration, who did not drink her water baba, but slept with it under her neck like an orthopedic roll. Keefer, the word that spelled Georgia down and Gordon across, the answer to the question that had been God's. A grave and enormous question—are you up to this?—had been presented to her to swallow in unbearable portions. Scalded, stung, kicked, awakened when she would have preferred to lie numb, dragged to this place, Lorraine's feet touched down on the other side of the understanding with a quickening of her legs, an agility suitable to God's tested message carrier. She raised her gown high over her thighs, so that she could be more like a leaf offering no resistance to the wind and the moving darkness of grace. She would see it all through. She would see all of it and ask only for the strength to understand it. She felt the phantom touch of Georgia's baby foot, the toes wiggling and seeking in the hair on the crown of her mother's head. Lorraine nearly spoke.

It was nearly dawn when she awakened Gordon, who had fallen onto their living room couch, and told him, "You have to buy a house."

"Now?" Gordon asked. "What are you talking about?"

"You don't have a real bedroom for Keefer. She's two. She can't go on sleeping in the closet."

"Mom, what am I going to use for money for a house? And anyhow, what does it matter where she sleeps?"

"The Cadys have a whole . . . fairyland for her, Gordie," Lorraine continued, sweeping her hair back ruthlessly, snapping off ends that had become entangled in her reading glasses. "I've been reading the classifieds. I circled some things for you to look at."

"Now?" Gordon asked. "Mom, I'm dying here. I didn't mean that. I mean, the last time I drank so much beer as last night, I was in college. Why didn't somebody stop me? Tim was like the beer pusher. It feels like a truck ran over my head. I'm sorry. I didn't mean that. . . . do you have an aspirin, Mom?"

Lorraine flew from the living room and bounded up the stairs, rummaging for the one, last, ancient pill bottle. The light in the bedroom was too dim for reading small print, even with her spectacles. Was this Demerol? Dilaudid? Gordon was healthy. It wouldn't kill him. Keefer and Mark were snoring in unison. Good. Lorraine had never felt more wide awake. She plopped the single pill into Gordon's palm.

"Juice," he muttered. "If I drink water, I'll puke. I mean it. Where's Lindsay?"

"She went home hours ago."

"How did I get on the couch?"

"I guess you walked."

"Let me sit up," Gordon muttered, and Lorraine gave him her hand, her hand of amazing, soaring power. "Okay. Here. I'm drinking this juice. This is a big aspirin . . ."

"It's extra strength."

"Okay. Mom, it's not hardly even light out. What are you going on about?"

"It's that you need to buy a house. Or at least, we need to look at houses. There was this little farmette I read about, right here, now it's on Hat Lake—"

"I can't live on Hat Lake. Emily Sayward lives there."

"It's a big lake, Gordon."

"I can't afford a lake house—"

"It's like, fifty or sixty thousand—"

"Then it has to be a hellhole."

"Well, okay. There's a bungalow, it's brick, on Mission Street. That's right behind the middle school, Gordie. Keefer could walk to school."

"She can't even talk yet, Mom."

"Well, she could walk someday. You have to be planful, Gordie, honey."

"I know. I am very planful."

"Brick is nice. Warm in winter. Cool in summer. It says . . . may I turn the light on, honey? It says, wooded lot. And three bedrooms. Tile floors."

"Mom, if they're reduced to mentioning the floor, it's got to be in crummy shape . . . and what does it cost?"

"Eighty thousand."

"It might as well be eighty million."

"We can figure something out, Gordie." Lorraine tapped her teeth with the earpiece of her reading glasses. "You can get an FHA loan. Dad and I got an FHA loan. You can only get them for the first house you buy. You get a great interest rate, and you only have to put down like a thousand bucks."

"Maybe thirty years ago, Mom. You can't put down a thousand bucks on an Airstream now."

"I think you can. I think you can get this . . . homestead thing or something. I'm going to make some appointments, to just look——"

"Don't you think that would be . . . tempting the gods, Mom? You know, putting all your chickens in the same basket?"

"You know we're going to win now."

"I don't know anything. Except I think I have to lie down. My head is going around like the mechanical bull ride . . ."

"That's just the meds."

"Mom, I've had aspirin before. I think I have a fever or something."

"Gordie, you have to pay attention here. That woman, that Faye, the psychiatrist. . . . she's going to evaluate us all over again . . ."

"Faith."

"Fay, Faith, Fate, whatever . . ."

"She's a psychologist."

"Gordie!" Lorraine surprised even herself by grabbing his ear. "Listen to me. You have to show how confident you are that Keefer will remain with you. That's what the Cadys did. They just went ahead. Enrolled her in Sunday school. Put up wallpaper. That was how they edged us out."

"Well, okay. I hear you," Gordon sighed. "You can make an appointment to look at the mission——"

"The house on Mission. It's a good street name, isn't it? Not like Bluebird Hill Parkway or something? The address is Eleven Eleven. Those are good numbers, Gordie. That's the make-a-wish number, remember?"

"On the clock," he nodded, fumbling for a pillow, burrowing his face in its fullness.

"Because she's going to be making an appointment with us, probably any day now. That's what Greg Katt said."

"Okay, Mom," Gordon agreed, "houses. Houses and wallpaper."

In fact, however, Faith Bogert decided to hold off even on approaching the McKennas until after a good, long visit with Delia and Craig in Madison. To make sure she was at her best, she drove down the night before, staying at a massive old bed-and-breakfast inn just above the university boathouse on Lake Mendota. Before dinner, Faith took a pep walk, following the instructions of the nutritionist she'd visited two weeks and four pounds earlier: Jog for two houses, walk for two houses. Intervals burned fat more efficiently, the counselor had told her, and though Faith was almost sure that a guts-out run would burn fat faster than anything, she had pretended to go along with the woman's certainty. She did not yet have the capacity to run a full block anyhow, having spent far too many summer days curled up with a book instead of clenched on her living room floor, doing sit-ups on the AbMaster she'd madly purchased one late night from the Shopping Channel.

Delia's appearance, when she opened the door, shocked Faith Bogert more than she could effectively conceal. Delia had applied makeup carefully and more skillfully than Faith would ever have been able to do herself—the blending of blush was Faith's Waterloo. A cheesy pallor put lie to Delia's wide, welcoming smile, her brisk offer of iced tea, her proud display of Keefer, decked out in a white tea-length dress with pink covered buttons, each button in the shape of a rosebud. The same blossoms decorated a bow that caught up a strand of Keefer's cottony auburn baby's hair.

"How do you ever manage to keep that on?" Faith asked, extracting her clipboard from her tote bag. "I never met a toddler who'd put up with it."

"Well," Delia said, "well, first, we dress her up for church every Sunday, so she's become used to taking care not to spoil her best clothes. We get lollipops for that, don't we, Sugar-Face?" Keefer leaned blissfully against Delia's knee. "And the other thing is, well, my little secret. A beauty-school trick."

"What?" Faith asked, more to conceal her scrutiny of Delia's bloated face than from any real curiosity. What was the matter with Delia? She'd always been a large woman, but large in the sense of robust, never—despite the MS she suspected she had (though she'd told Faith it had never been confirmed)—with the look upon her of any sort of ill health. Now she was massive. Was Delia pregnant? Faith, under the pretext of examining Keefer's hairband more carefully, leaned in closer, getting up to seat herself on the ottoman near the sofa where Delia half-reclined, her legs, sculpted red shells of toes crammed into white sandals, splayed as if to hold her erect. "What's the big secret?"

"I glue it on," Delia giggled.

"You glue it on."

"I glue it to just the tiniest little piece of her hair. I use nail adhesive."

"Doesn't she try to pull it out?"

"Not more than once!" Delia said, with a gleam of triumph. "It didn't really hurt her. Of course it didn't, right, Keefer Kathryn? Just tugged enough on her little noggin that she learned to leave it alone."

"Well, how do you get it out?"

"Just snip it off. It's just the teeniest itty bit of hair."

"Aren't you afraid you'll make her bald?" Faith heard the nervous octave in her voice and deliberately breathed in slowly, lowering her tone. She could not make out whether Delia was pregnant or simply . . . huge. The woman had gained thirty pounds easily. She must weigh well over two hundred. For one nasty and repented instant, Faith felt for the newly emerged contour of her own rib cage.

"We don't dress her up so often it would make any difference," Delia assured Faith, leaning back, straining to pull Keefer up onto her lap. There. Faith scrutinized the motion. She was pregnant. No. Delia was packed with new flesh all over, not only through the abdomen. "Their hair grows so fast. And they don't ever dress her up. I'm working out monkeys from her hair for days after she gets back from up north. I don't think Gordon ever puts a brush to it."

"I know he does," Faith said mildly. "I've seen her little comb and brush set at his place."

"Anyhow, he's a man. Right?" Delia loosed Keefer, who began fiddling with the roseate buttons. "Sugar, you leave those buttons alone now. You heard me. Alexis! Will you please bring me her board puzzles? The big ones?"

The teenager, taller by inches, appealingly sloppy in jean shorts and a bathing suit top, banged in from the deck where she appeared to have been sunning. A burn that already looked wrathfully swollen shared space on her narrow shoulders with a bright white pair of strap marks. "Ouch," Faith said warningly, "looks like you need some sunblock."

"I don't even feel it," Alex told her amiably. "I just move from the back to the front with the sun every day. It goes away. I get tan. My dad's part Indian."

Delia snorted. "I don't know what part you mean," she said sourly.

"He is, Mom. You know he is."

"I take it you don't mean Craig," Faith said. "He looks pure Irish."

"Her dad in North Carolina, she means. Jack Tyson."

"Are you planning to go see your father this summer, Alexis?"

"Alex," said the girl, carefully removing two puzzles from a stack on a low shelf. "Come on, Keefer-Weefer-Poo. Let's get these trucks all back in their houses. Yeah, my dad says we're going to the races in Daytona." Another snort from Delia. Alexis took note of it, then seemed to ball it up and sail it out of her consciousness. Good for her. Delia apparently had no idea of the rage that putting down a child's absent parent could engender. Well, few people did.

Faith smiled. The girl's manner with the baby was balm on the chafed memory of the dozens of angry runaways, sullen shoplifters, habitual ungovernables who'd left a sad trail through her files, rich truants who blamed everything on their parents, poor truants whose parents blamed everything on their children. This girl was good medicine for this baby. Faith took up her pen. "So what is it we're calling this young lady with the roses on her dress these days?"

"Craig's mother made it. She's coming to visit for a couple of weeks real soon."

"And Craig?"

"He couldn't be here. We're both sorry. Meetings. You know, he's had to miss so much work. But they're really behind him. They keep telling him, you just work on keeping that baby—"

"Well," Faith said, circling back, "so I noticed. You use both her names."

"We're slowly, slowly trying to work our way around to calling her Kathryn," Delia said. Faith noticed the drizzle of sweat on her lip. "She's named after my granny Kathryn, you knew that. My grandma and Ray's."

"And after, well, the name Georgia chose for her."

"It just doesn't sound right on a girl. The two, together, that's all right. At home, we use two names a lot. You know, like Billy Bob? But Keefer?"

"I like it," Alexis chimed in, not inappropriately. "I like girl names that sound like boy names. They're cool. I'm having my name legally changed to Alex."

"That's for you to decide when you're older," Delia said. Faith was struck again by her patience. "I'll hope you don't change it, but it's going to be up to you. And names are like houses. You can move, and then move again."

Faith nibbled at the proffered banana bread.

"How are all of you doing this hot summer?"

"Well, I haven't been as well as I'd like," Delia admitted ruefully. "I'm feeling this heat, I can tell you. And me a Southern girl."

"How's the baby?" Faith asked quickly. Now, the bait was on the water. She would rise to it or not.

"She's doing fine. Nothing bothers her," Delia said smoothly. So. Perhaps she really was just obese. "We try to keep things very quiet for her. No TV. And definitely," she smiled ironically at Alexis, "no MTV."

"My mom's got a blocker."

"Best twenty bucks I ever spent."

"I have to get my fix of MTV at my friend Liesel's house."

"I can't control what other parents let their kids watch," Delia said. "And I like Liesel, she's a nice girl. But I think those messages, all that. . . . sexual, you know, and not a healthy sexuality . . ."

"I have to say I agree," Faith said, jotting briskly. "So what's going to happen if the court on the retrial decides in Gordon's favor?"

"Well, I pray that will not happen. But, we are prepared to face it, Doctor. My husband and I will do everything within our power to keep Keefer where we believe her parents wanted her to be. But we will go on either way. We'll be able to accept it."

"That's good. That's a good way to keep your hopes up," Faith said. "So Craig is equally committed to the long haul?"

"We both believe we know what's best for her. We know that the love of two good parents, even if they're not the ones God gave you originally, can heal a lot of hurt."

"And you're open to helping her come to terms with . . . her questions?"

"If she has any, yes."

"What fun things do you two do together?"

"We try to have a standing date every other Saturday night. I have to say, Alexis is a wonderful baby-sitter. And she doesn't charge too much."

"I meant you and Keefer."

"Oh, we play all day. We play beauty parlor. We play house, though with all this weight I'm trucking around, I can't get down with her like I should. We play Barbies. I'm teaching Alexis to sew. We've made her some really cute Barbie outfits."

"And you're still working?"

"God willing, yes. Doctor, raising children is expensive. Not to mention the legal bills. And we'd like to get a bigger house down the line."

"So, things seem to be going well." Faith tried again, "Except you mentioned not feeling well?"

"Just my headaches. My aches all over, nothing so special, nothing I won't survive." Delia was a wall.

Faith took her leave feeling as she did when a run opened down the back of her stocking—irritated and exposed in a way that made no sense. She had learned to trust these instincts, but there was nothing here to see. Delia was clearly not sick enough to skip work. She was managing both girls well. Her mood seemed generally good. Perhaps Delia was simply one of those women, like Faith's own Aunt Mary, who ate their way through crises and fasted their way through good times. Not a particularly heart-healthy way to live, but crises would probably not be standard fare for the Cadys for too much longer.

A breeze had stiffened while she was inside, and as she stowed her tote bag in the backseat of her car, Faith noticed Alexis cheerfully hip-hopping her way out to the sunnier front porch, yellow earphones in place. Mad dogs and teenagers, Faith thought, as the wind snatched the loose pages of her notes and whipped them down and out through the gap of her open car door. She would be able to reconstruct, but wait . . . the pages had been trapped in a window well, blown flat against one wall of the concrete box. Faith sprinted and captured her pages and was turning to leave when she heard Keefer scream. It was a baby's angry wail, Faith ascertained quickly, coming from the open window just over Faith's head. She made a mental inventory of the house's plan, trying to keep her cool, as Keefer sobbed, "No, no! No wetty!" A jet of water. Delia's voice, low, not precisely threatening, but stern, very stern. "Mama said leave those buttons alone! And if you scream anymore, you're going under the shower, Miss Priss. Do you hear me?" Okay. What Faith was hearing was not a forthright abuse. She was hearing a fairly strict, Bible-bound Southern woman, probably suffering from a pounding headache, administering the threat of some fairly inappropriate discipline for a two-year-old. On the other hand, it was only a threat; Keefer was quieting down, Delia was making crooning noises. The shower was shut off. Delia had not struck Keefer. Faith had herself been slapped, only once, in ninth grade, the time when Eve Bogert caught her smoking behind the pool building with Jennifer Adderly.

Faith knew good, perfectly adequate parents who spanked.

She would get into her car and leave. But she would make note. It would all go into the report.

But before she could close the door of her car, she looked up, drawn into the steady gaze of the teenager on the porch. Alexis shrugged.

"What's with all that?" Faith asked her. This was not a great idea, buttonholing a kid.

"She doesn't hit her," Alex said.

"Does she lose it like that?"

"More now. Her nerves are shot. That's what my aunt says. Her nerves are shot."

"Do you get afraid for Keefer?"

"I don't like it. I don't like her to yell at her for something like pulling the stupid flowers out of her hair."

"So, this is fairly often?"

"No. Mom is usually pretty nice and peaceful. She's got to have it her way. But she doesn't lose it. It's just since . . . she's real sick from the baby."

"From Keefer?"

"From the baby she's going to have. She can't take any of her medicine or anything. She's like, her legs hurt all the time."

"You knew your mom was pregnant."

"I've just known for a couple of months. But it happened at like, Christmas, I guess, anyhow. They don't exactly describe their sex life to me."

"Nor should they," Faith said. She hesitated. Clouds were piling up over the lake, thick and threatening, and she had a long drive ahead. "Well, Alex, you think your mom's in the tub or whatever?"

"I think she's putting Keefer down. Keefer takes a one o'clock nap. Every day."

"Well," Faith said, "let me get around you there."

She raised her hand to knock at the door, to an over-whelming sense of déjà vu. This was the part where she would be as welcome as the plague. Faith was used to it. She was going to have to stomp a big hole in someone's day. She was going to have to talk, and talk long and hard, with Delia about her state of health and her state of mind. About private things that would ordinarily be nobody's business, especially a stranger's. Unless that stranger, like Faith, held a big piece of the puzzle that would make up a child's future, in her hands.

CHAPTER *nineteen*

"*I* am dismayed," Judge Aaron Kid said, pausing not even for the grooming rituals of greeting Gordon now saw as requisite to all members of the legal species. "I am dismayed by the way this case has been tried in the media."

He slid his reading glasses from his nose, folded them briskly, and pointed with them at the McKenna side of the aisle. "I am speaking of the media presence of your clients, Mr. Katt and Miz Kane and Mrs. Hendrickson. The guardians of the child in question have not given any interviews, so far as I can tell, nor have they sought to curry editorial opinion. They have been engaged in the business of raising this child, or else they are inclined to be very private individuals, which, in this setting, is entirely helpful and appropriate."

"But it is not quite true, Your Honor." May Hendrickson, the McKennas' attorney spoke up quietly. "In fact, the Cadys have given several interviews to local print media and to local television stations, and the child's paternal grandfather has been filmed for similar media venues."

"I am aware of that," Kid rejoined, "but these are drops in an ocean of ink. Your clients have consistently sought out national and international media."

"Excuse me, your honor, if I may point out," May Hendrickson said, "those media have sought the McKennas. Your Honor, this only makes sense, since it is the McKennas' interests that were abrogated in this case, so it was naturally assumed by the press that they would be the ones with a grievance to air."

"Mrs. McKenna, have you at any time contacted the newspapers?" Judge Kid asked.

"I can answer that," Greg Katt offered.

"I am asking Mrs. McKenna this question," Kid replied, "and she is entirely capable of answering it. Mrs. McKenna, have you at any time contacted members of the press?"

"Yes," said Lorraine, "months ago, at the beginning."

"And of course, that set the ball rolling. I have been doing nothing this past weekend but reading the history of this case as revealed through the documents of extensive and innumerable court procedures, and one thing that has become clear to me is that the court-appointed psychologist and the guardian ad litem have been the sole voices of restraint in this process, consistently drawing the attention of the bickering, litigating adults back to the critical issue of what is best for this child."

"With respect, Your Honor, may I speak to what may be an oversight?" May Hendrickson went on. "The guardian ad litem in the original action joined with Delia and Craig Cady by concurring on the initial ruling, that is, on Gordon McKenna's absence of status as a blood relative. So we have to presume that the guardian was biased on the Cadys' behalf. Indeed, she has been quoted in the press saying that the higher court's ruling would have no effect on the ultimate disposition of this case. That bias, I would suggest, throws into question whether this particular guardian ad litem can serve the charge as the eyes and ears of the court in this case."

"That may be so, and yet I see no reason why she cannot now fulfill that role. I'm looking at Victoria Linquist's comments about the necessity for legislative clarification. She says she *does* believe this to be an important consequence subsequent to the original ruling. She's not ignoring it. What we need for an effective conclusion is real cooperative effort among all parties to keep the emotional interests of the adults involved secondary to the needs of the child. And that also means the privacy of this minor child. I think that was the guardian's main concern." May Hendrickson nodded, her shrug and the slight upward cast of her eyes negating the message of the nod.

"There will be no more of this," Judge Kid said severely. "Formally, as of now, I am imposing an order to the effect that there will be no discussion with the press by any party to this action about any aspect of this action. There is no excuse for exposing a child's private and very vulnerable world to such unfair scrutiny."

Mary Ellen Wentworth spoke up. "Your Honor, the guardian ad litem and I are very concerned that the constant rehashing by the press of every aspect of this case creates an inflammatory and prejudicial atmosphere in which to carry out a trial. The Cadys have made valiant efforts to shield this child, even while they have been entirely aware that their refusal to join this media frenzy may have had an adverse effect on them with respect to public opinion. So I would ask that you be very specific in your order to include disallowing interviews about anything that has taken place since the death of Keefer Kathryn's parents, even if those interviews do not include the specifics of this litigation."

"That seems reasonable," Kid said. Unfolding first one leg, then the second, of his reading glasses, he carefully placed them halfway down the bridge of his nose. "Now, we have just spent fifteen or twenty valuable minutes here discussing a tertiary circumstance of this case, an unnecessary intrusion, no matter who brought it on, and that goes to underline my point, that it is a distraction." He jutted his chin toward Cady, toward Greg Katt. "Is that understood?" The lawyers regarded their shoes, like mourners asked to join in a silent moment of prayer. "Counsel? I can assure you that this court will not be affected, at least not favorably, by any amount of media criticism."

"Yes, sir," said Greg Katt, "though you must admit it was necessary, under the circumstances, regarding the deficit of the law as it was previously worded—"

"I am not describing the circumstances of the past, Mr. Katt, nor debating the merits or the demerits of a given law's prior or current wording. I am referring to what will take place before this court here from this day forward."

Gordon had not included any of this in his calculus, he thought.

The magisterial world Gordon had concocted after the reversal had been a world in which objectivities would arrange themselves on either side of a median, not a gulf, but something more. . . . symbolically summary, perhaps a table. The judge would sit at the head of this imaginary table. The judge would behave like a father who had to make decisions based on greater wisdom and experience; even painful consequences would be for the greater good. He would be kindly toward Craig and Delia, kindly (though maybe with a twinkle of approval) toward the McKennas. There would be a mopping up, a reductive setting on of seals, a paring of inconsequential concerns. What else could there be? If Gordon now was by both the spirit and now the letter of law her uncle, the Cadys' prior claims were insubstantial as the cordite smell of smoke after fireworks. Something had happened, something stirring and triumphant. Gordon listened to his lawyers and the Cadys' lawyers comparing their calendars, setting up a schedule for motion deadlines, disclosure of witness lists . . . like soldiers in island caves without radio contact, preparing for the next battle, not realizing the war had ended months before.

A new trial? Of course, why not five more trials? Why not carry this on until Keefer had her own law degree? Gordon had wanted to scream with frustration. It was like having to listen patiently as his first college girlfriend told him why the pyramids at Giza were not just structures but great big magnets.

But if this situation had been so muddled by everyone who got the chance, simplicity would now seem absurd. Why should the judge pay attention to a higher court? Why should he be eager to make right the clear and present wrong done the McKennas? This judge was human, subject to the same petty currents of ego and loyalty all people felt toward others of their kind. This judge would have to pee on the tree, too, make his own mark.

Real things would have no force. The unseen and nonsensical would have force, like pyramid power had force for goofy people. They believed it; it didn't matter that it didn't exist. If people believed in a force, the force would be enough to crush him. He would be crushed by something he would never be able to see.

Gordon remembered one breathlessly hot September night in Cocoa Beach when Ray, trying to cajole Gordon into coming out to the Sand Bar for margaritas instead of studying for an exam, had tried to explain to him the theory of relativity. He told Gordon how the great scientists in Denmark and Germany roamed together on seashores and in parks, using rocks and waves and the flight of birds overhead to ask each other their questions about reality and flux and time, and despite the amazing insights they came up with, scientists were still asking one another many of the same questions. Nothing, Ray told Gordon, was truly objectively measurable, because all things were made of particles and all particles were in a constant state of change.

I get that much, Gordon replied, deflated, wounded. And so, Ray went on, no sooner was one determining factor measured than it changed, and everything, including the nature of the entity doing the measuring, man or computer, was changed, too. If you tried to measure distance, speed made faces at you behind your back. Nothing could ever be truly real for more than a moment, and all variables must be reconsidered.

"Even this conversation is only real while we're having it, and you're having a different conversation from the one I'm having because you're confused about relativity and I'm not; but you will remember it more clearly because you're sober and I'm shitfaced." Ray concluded, "And if you wrote it down, it would be a third conversation, and if somebody read it, it would be a fourth conversation."

"Even if I understand the words you're saying, I don't understand what they mean," Gordon said. "And so this is a fifth conversation, a conversation that isn't really a conversation because only one of us is having it."

"Nobody understands what words mean," Ray said. "But Bo, that's not the point. There you go with the thinking again. What do I have to do to get you to stop it? Hit you one on the side of the head? All you have to be able to do is describe what you don't understand better than anyone else. The only person who really knows what reality is, is my cousin Delia."

And she was not in court, Delia. She was not here present, embodying the Cadys' reality, a reality of supercharged superiority because Jesus himself believed in their cause. Then there was the reality, according to the press. Judge Sayward's reality, and Judge Kid's. The Nyes' reality of genetic entitlement. Delia's biology, a curse when it had an impact on her vision, her headaches, her legs, and her balance, a hindrance when it prevented her from giving birth, but a great boon when it came to staking a claim to Keefer. His own biology, which gave him great teeth and funny hair and an estrangement from his parents he steadfastly maintained was not real, was now the paramount reality to everyone else. His discarded razor was only another piece of disregarded landfill plastic in his bathroom wastepaper basket until Keefer glommed it in her seeking little fist; then it was a lethal weapon. An open window on the warm night a blessing until a hornet passed through it. And in all these competing realities, Gordon would not be allowed to do what he could do best, be a photon tracking down the electron and illuminating its evasive presence. He would not be permitted to shed light.

Delia was ill.

She was ill and pregnant.

Keefer's "new mother" would be ill, not as her birth mother had been, but still sick, perhaps even after the birth. And deprived of the centering force of her own parents' love, she would now have to share the love she had come to rely on with another, younger sibling.

"These are not insurmountable obstacles, but they do not add up to the optimum atmosphere for Keefer at this time," Faith Bogert had written. "Delia Cady is under great stress, and that stress will necessarily have an impact on Keefer's emotional stability. It may not be a permanent, damaging effect, but it is a stressor." She'd also pointed out that Gordon's parenting skill had developed substantially, and thus he and the Cadys now could be considered equally positive candidates, though the McKennas remained Keefer's "psychological family of origin." Still, she'd balked at recommending Gordon outright. She made noises about all the adults in Keefer's life "working together toward many joint covenants about Keefer's care and experiences." And still, it wouldn't be perfect. Keefer would never, in Dr. Bogert's opinion, have an entirely traditional family experience, but would have "extended family patterns in common with many children in her peer group as she grows older. She would definitely need access to professional counseling as she reexperiences the losses of her infancy at each developmental stage."

Only Nora had been blunt enough, when they saw the report, to say plainly what they were all thinking.

"I'm sorry for them, but shouldn't this disqualify them?

Aren't they just going to put her through the same thing she already went through?" Nora asked.

Was he a brute, Gordon had thought, because his first hope was that Delia would be swiftly and irreversibly incapacitated? Disabled to the point that her active mothering of Keefer would be compromised? His mind scampered forward with fully developed projections, Delia interviewed by Tammy Bakker or someone, for JCTV, in a wheelchair for life, cared for tenderly by devoted Craig, who would say that he didn't mind that they'd never have marital relations again, Alexis brought to a conversion by her mother's courage, all of them rooting for little Jessica Sunshine, the miracle baby, born four months premature and cheerfully stumping along in her own little pink leg braces . . .

Would that be so bad?

Why introduce a wiry little roughneck like Keefer? Better off with Gordon, down among the unsaved.

Gordon's dark predictions for Delia had been the only thing that distracted Gordon from his fury over the pregnancy. It was a betrayal that filled his throat with acid liquors. It was a deliberate, sneering, personal insult, like finding Lindsay in bed with another guy. His baby was not enough for them. They'd wanted a big, selfish cowbird chick of their own—an even closer, more important blood relative—that would squeeze Keefer out. And yet this season! The baby was due in three months!

From the guardian's point of view, of course, this would be ticked into the ledger as another wonderful plus for the Cadys, another brother or sister nearer in age to Keefer than Alexis.

During the first hearing with Judge Kid, Alexis had sat on the floor at the back of the courtroom with Keefer, oblivious to Craig and the proceedings, her long legs in absurd canvas platforms making hurdles for the bailiff in his progresses. Keefer would venture one finger into Alexis's mouth; Alexis would pretend to furiously bite it off, Keefer would with-draw her finger with a pout of mock terror, then bell out her full, teeming, deep-voiced laugh. Every time it happened, they were all forced to smile, all charmed except Judge Kid, who finally, exasperated, suggested that a courtroom was no place for a child. Alexis, on a nod from Craig, carried Keefer out into the hall.

"It's encouraging that he seems to hate everyone else as much as he hates us," Lorraine said to Greg Katt later, over tuna salad sandwiches at Hubbles.

"He's just feeling the pressure," Katt replied, mouth full. "Kid's a law-first kind of guy. A real stickler for no leeway. He'll do the right thing. He has zero options. But, and I mean this, we certainly do not want to antagonize him with any further stories in the press."

"We won't do that," Lorraine said, aghast. "We haven't talked to anyone in weeks, unless you count our e-mails."

"Sit back on that, too," Katt told her.

"People write who are afraid the same thing could happen to them, who don't know the laws in their own states and are concerned about their own family's circumstances," Lor-raine said.

"Well, there'll be plenty of time to write to them when Keefer's on your lap," Katt said. "Just say you're busy with your own legal process right now. We get our ducks in a row, and we hope the Cadys don't appeal the appeals court verdict."

"Do you think that's likely?" Gordon asked, thinking of course it's likely, it's a virtual certainty . . .

"Not really. I think that if I was their lawyer, I'd advise against it. I think it would make them seem mean-spirited, if they did. If Wentworth is smart, she'll tell them to sit tight. And I guess they're in no shape for that."

"Well, it was her choice to get pregnant right now," Lor-raine snapped.

Katt looked embarrassed, and Gordon knew what he was

thinking. That his mother sounded as mean-spirited and obsessive as some people portrayed her. He'd wanted to hug his mother, to let her know that he understood she was just frazzled, not spiteful.

"I think we're fine," Katt said, leaning over to gather Lorraine's small, and Gordon noticed, scrubbed hand.

The scrubbed hand was a clue. It meant she'd been working on her art again. In childhood, when their mother was at work on drawings, they would complain not only because it distracted her from their all-important demands but because it coarsened the skin of her hands. When she came in at night to rub their backs, there were little cracks, irritating as emery boards, on the balls of her fingers. They would flinch away, annoyed. She would apologize. For one Mother's Day, he and Georgia had brought Lorraine a basket filled with one of every kind of moisturizer they could find, including udder balm. Now, seeing evidence of Lorraine's engagement with something in life apart from the case and her grief moved Gordon's heart to a silent cheer. Good for Mom. Good job.

Gordon himself had been unable to turn his anger outward, into energy. He felt genuinely, physically ill, and he knew it all stemmed from the subversive work of his emotions on his body. Headaches, menstrual cramps, nervous stomachs, he'd always considered these things in the same bag with "panic attacks" and "motion sickness." They were things anyone with the self-awareness of a cricket could overcome.

But he could not will himself to feel healthy. He'd begun to regret the scornful opinions he'd once held about psychobiological illnesses.

On the nights when Keefer was not with him, he lay horribly awake. Sometimes he could not relax even with the human security blanket of Lindsay, curled into a balletic sleep pose beside him. She was such a quiet sleeper, Gordon occasionally thought she'd stopped breathing, though both he and Keefer snored uproariously. He had such piercing, local headaches he felt as though he'd been battered on the side of the head with a garden trowel. He'd even asked his mom for more of her extra-strength aspirin, but she'd said it was a prescription, and had run out. When he tried to do something as innocuous as a hammer curl, his neck caught and clamored. He was losing even more weight, becoming chickeny, a scrawny light man, like his great-uncle Harold. Rather than endure such interfering wretchedness for life, he would have chosen to die.

Nothing helped. Not the eye mask scented with eucalyptus that Lindsay had brought from the store. Not the white noise of the fan he ritualistically placed near the head of his bed. Not water or Benadryl. He would drift close to sleep and then in would skip images of his Keefer. His combustible darling. Keefer, not there, but an apparition with a voice and a presence just beyond his reach. *Where's Dory's hair? Where is Kipper's hair? Dory's eyes, Kipper's eyes, Dory's funny tooth, Kipper's pretty tooth*. She was so fucking brilliant, and he wasn't just saying that. She had the strutting, assured presence of a tiny Atlantic City mobster.

"Whose scrawny little kid are you?" he would demand.

"Mine!" Keefer would cry, jabbing her round belly with her index finger, and then relenting, and nuzzling his shirt. "Mine Dory's."

He'd gotten up. A walk, maybe. He was too sore to really move, too restless to lie down. He could hear her chirps, her soprano variations and combinations: "Dory out dere! Whass at? Uh-oh. Baby go wah! Doggy go ruff!" He could feel her smooth cheek, an orb filled with freshest water, as she nuzzled it along his chest when they lay in bed mornings, the belly farts she made so exuberantly, the sly looks she had taken to giving him from the corners of her eyes, her head feathered with fox-colored tufts of baby hair that somehow refused to grow long like other toddlers', so that she looked like a punk rocker, the perfect globes of tears that spilled from her great marmoset eyes at will, the way she covered her face with the wings of his pant legs when they encountered a pushy stranger. He thought of Keefer and ended up stiff-armed over the toilet, bent double, heaving up nothing, especially not the dinner he had been too nauseated to eat. Steeped by proximity in his mother's absurd rituals, he slammed the window closed at the sound of a whippoor-will, racing thoughts like imps of kidnapped souls. He was too clumsy to strum, too jangled to read. Another day would come, and he'd have to face it dry-mouthed, reedy with weakness. He'd been unable to overcome the momentum of knowing he'd lose her. What he had to do was to construct a way to live without her. How could he live without her?

He would live, that's all. He would do many interesting things with his freedom and include her in as many of them as he could. He would be an important figure in her life.

He would die.

He would live, a pithed, cored old man in his twenties.

The Cadys would mark her, sacrifice her, transform his renegade darling into a compliant, lumpen Jesus-freak baby. She would shy from him. He would bore her. She would complain about the turpentine smell in his mother's house. She would grow up and wear mall bangs and tight T-shirts embroidered with Rich Girl in cheap sequins. She would marry early. She would never marry; she would be raped by the youth minister at the Foursquare Christian Church.

She would become a cosmetician.

He would die without her. He had never been alive before her. When Gordon pictured his life previous to the inheritance of Keefer, he saw himself in a series of muscle-and-fitness poses, a buff mannequin with a hyperactive, grinning dick.

He could give Keefer up, with dignity.

He would eliminate his rivals. He would find a way to crimp Craig's brake lines with pliers. He knew nothing about cars. He would plan a field trip to the State Hygiene Lab, and, while his students viewed gruesome forensic marvels, he would liberate a virus, a crumb of cyanide . . .

He would have to relinquish her, stand aside so that she could become someone else. He could do it. He had mourned Georgia. He had mourned Georgia and gone on.

This was a lie. He had not begun to mourn Georgia. He had not had time. He had been forced to shunt Georgia aside, for Keefer. In the unremitting struggle for what already was his.

He would lose them both!

How were such things accomplished? He thought of talking this over with his father, who seemed to have achieved a quiet acceptance. What reserves of character did Mark possess that Gordon had not inherited? Experience. He would come to it in time. An accumulation of wounds degraded the first gash. He would learn.

That hot night, his neck pain bellowing if he so much as moved his eyes, a weird belling in his left ear when he lay down, he'd driven to the ER at Methodist. And the doctor on call had been Michelle Yu.

"I thought this was stress, but now I think I have a neurological problem," he said. "I'm stroking out."

"Stress *is* a neurological problem," she smiled. "You look like the sicker brother of the guy I saw in here a couple of months ago."

"How do you remember me?" Gordon said, and then cursed himself for an egregious asshole. "I mean, you see hundreds of people every week."

"You're thinking it was your good looks?" Doctor Yu smiled, rubbing the face of her stethoscope in cupped hands before placing it against Gordon's breast. "Well, let's just say I remembered. And that I'm an avid late-night viewer of CNN. You've got quite a pulse going there for a guy your age. Ninety-five, resting. How's your daughter, formerly your niece?"

"She's my niece again," Gordon began.

"How so?"

"We're breaking up," he said, and began to cry, gulping grateful sobs that forced his head down, as though he were a diver with the bends.

To her eternal credit, she did not try to put her arm around his shoulders or even pat his back. She'd hitched one tiny hip onto a metal stool and said, "Fortunately, what's out there is an old guy with a sore throat who's going to smoke no matter what kind of lecture I give him, and an older lady who makes the rounds of urgent-carecenter rooms to get painkillers for a back injury she suffered when Jimmy Carter was in office."

"You weren't born when Jimmy Carter was in office," Gordon said.

"I was," Michelle Yu told him. "I'm thirty-five, Mr. McKenna."

"You are? How come you look so young?"

"Ancient Chinese secret. I've been at this for a while. It takes a couple of semesters to become a doctor."

"Right. I considered doing that."

"Too intense?"

"Too much math. I'm sure you use calculus daily."

"Yes; in fact, constantly." She'd smiled.

"Well, I couldn't hack it."

"But you are a scientist."

"Only to people north of Stevens Point, like my friend Tim says."

"So, as I was saying, what we have is a waiting room full of people who've induced their own ailments. In fact, everyone here tonight has what we'd call emotionally aggravated physical complaints."

"Me, too, you mean."

"I mean, you have a sleep deficit."

"How do you know?"

"By the circles under your eyes, and by the fact that it's

two in the morning and you're here talking to me instead of sleeping."

"Right."

"I could do an electrocardiogram. I could do some labs, because you could have mono. But in the absence of fever, sore throat, vomiting—"

"I vomit. I'm a great vomiter. But nothing comes up."

"Persistent nausea."

"At night."

"Any other kinds of . . . dysfunctions?"

"Wouldn't know," Gordon sighed, "I have the romantic life of your average retirement-home resident."

"You'd be surprised by that, I think. You should hear that guy out there with the cigar throat tell stories. I think that what we're talking about here is a healthy guy under an unhealthy amount of pressure. Who needs sleep and surcease of sorrow—"

"My sister would know what poem that was."

"Your sister, who's dead—"

"A year now."

"Buddy, I'm going to give you . . . about, um, ten Alprazolam. That's more or less Valium . . ."

"I don't think I need ten."

Doctor Yu rolled her eyes. "I don't mean ten at once, Mr. McKenna. I'm going to give you what should amount to a couple of weeks' worth of guaranteed uninterrupted sleep. . . . Do you use any form of sleep medication now?"

"No medication whatsoever. Except," he blushed, "like Nutra-Gen. Muscle potion, you know."

"Training for the Iron Man?"

"No, just an idiot."

"Now, you'll need to be careful with alcohol when you take one of these. Start with a half, and don't do it when you're getting ready to fire up the John Deere; this is all on the label."

"And it will make me sleep."

"It should. You should feel drowsy in about an hour. And get some decent food."

"I can't face food."

"Not even Kung Pao tofu?"

"I wouldn't know Kung Pao tofu if it was hanging on my leg."

"Well, I will introduce you to it. I'm off in fifteen minutes."

"Tonight?"

"I eat every night at this time."

"Where do you go to eat at this time? Around here?"

"My house," she said. A look balanced between them. "I'm not inviting you to have sex with me, Mr. McKenna. Though it has crossed my mind, this would not be the time or the place. You just . . . I've read about what you're going through; I made the connection with the little girl who didn't have an ear infection, and now you're the one who's losing sleep. I thought we could eat a midnight snack, which would not include me."

"You're going to cook?"

"Ancient Chinese secret," she said. "I buy it from Hurry Curry in Wausau every night on the way to work and then I think of it all night, just waiting for me in that little silver-lined bag in the fridge."

They did just that. They ate tofu in her elegant, spare, totally white apartment, fetchingly decorated with dried branches and constructs of rock and driftwood. "I thought doctors were rolling in money," Gordon said.

"First-year residents are rolling in debt," she explained.

"This is very kind," he told her, finding that it was possible for him to eat in the company of another. "This is impossible to understand."

"Not for me. I was adopted."

"But your last name—"

"I'm the only Korean orphan in America to actually have been adopted by Chinese people."

"So you don't have . . . all the stuff you're supposed to have?"

"All the anxiety about my roots?" She twirled her silver chopsticks, then made them into a cross. Gordon was using a fork. "Dave and Sherry Yu are as Chinese as lox and bagels. We're Episcopalians. Our favorite holiday is Thanksgiving. They gave me dolls from Korea. But I'm a New Yorker. I only have the custom chopsticks because I don't like the taste of the wood kind. And I fight with my dad every time we spend more than three hours in the same apartment."

"How'd you get here?"

"UW Medical School. I like it."

"I think sometimes of going back for my Ph.D. Research."

"Yeah, well, I love my dad more than anything on earth. From behind, when I walk, I'm a little Dave Yu. He's . . ." She looked away from him for an instant. "He's my heart. I love my dad. I love . . . my dad."

They turned to their food, embarrassed by the size of the emotion in the small room. "So, I wish you good luck. That's all."

It was nearly four when he left. At the door, he leaned over and kissed her cheek, inhaling her scent of wooden tongue depressors and honeysuckle. "Thanks," he said, and then put his hands on her waist and kissed her again, with intention.

"You have a girlfriend," she said.

"You're psychic, too?"

"You do."

"I do. But right now, I wish that I did not."

"But right now, you do."

"Thank you for the tofu, Dr. Yu. That sounds like the name of a movie."

"No fee, Mr. McKenna. For the tofu or the consummate wisdom."

"May I call you?"

"Someday, maybe. I'm not going anywhere."

He'd been asleep for no more than four hours, drooling blissfully in the arms of the tranquilizer, when his telephone rang. Lindsay told him, "Your mother couldn't find you this morning, and she called here. The judge is asking for a tele-conference, at two o'clock." Gordon asked for a moment, dropped the telephone, stumbled into the bathroom and opened his mouth under the faucet.

"Run this by me again."

"A mediation."

"Judge Kid?"

"He wants you and your parents, and the lawyers . . . where were you?"

"When?"

"Last night . . . when! Where were you?"

"Do you mean, was I with a woman?"

"Yes. Don't tell me. No, tell me."

He told her. "I was at the emergency room, Lins. For sleeping pills."

"Gordie, I love you," she said.

"I know," he said, "I know. And I love you. And I'm going back to sleep if I can."

"I'll call you at noon."

"Okay. You don't have to."

But she had called and had come to sit beside him as the red numbers on the clock toiled over to two, and Greg Katt phoned, putting him on hold while he got access to the con-ference line. Gordon could have sworn he felt the air change when the Cadys entered the line space.

Judge Kid was brief. "I want you people to meet. I want you to make a good faith and honest effort to work this out among yourselves, reach a solution like the family you are, for better or worse."

"We have made every effort . . ." Mary Ellen Wentworth began.

"Make more," Judge Kid said. "Listen. I am perfectly in

earnest when I say that it is not impossible that I could find that this child cannot thrive in an atmosphere of so much hostility. You communicate with notes, Mrs. Cady, Mr. McKenna. You ask your aunt to bring the baby outside when the Cadys come to visit—"

"That was agreed—" Greg Katt said.

"I want you to know that if you cannot reach an agreement, a third-party adoption is not out of the question."

"By . . . what do you mean?" Lorraine breathed.

"It would be stressful for her in terms of her adjustment, but Dr. Bogert assures me that she would indeed adjust, and the stress she is absorbing from this endless wrangling is not inconsequential, either."

"Your Honor, we need time to respond—" Greg Katt said.

"Take your time!" Kid retorted. "Take hours! Take days! The Cadys have assured me that they are not intending to appeal the higher court—"

"Is that true?" Mark asked.

"We are not going to appeal the decision," Delia said clearly.

"So you accept that Gordon is Keefer's blood uncle," Lorraine said.

"We also think that we know what's best for her," Delia said.

"If you know what's best for her, why are you putting Keefer through this?" Lorraine asked.

"We don't think we're the ones putting her through anything," Craig Cady said. "We think we simply want Keefer to have a stable, permanent home."

"You're ill!" Lorraine cried. "You're ill, Delia!"

"I'll get better, Lorraine. It's almost over, and what a blessing it will be for Keefer to have a sibling."

"This is the kind of thing I want you to consider together," Judge Kid said. "Am I perfectly clear on this? I'll expect to hear from you . . . this is Wednesday. By Monday. We'll get a conference call . . . Bridget?" He summoned his assistant. "Can I do a meeting on Monday at three?"

They waited, their breathing gusting over the line.

"At three on Monday. I wish you Godspeed." Kid's tone softened. "I mean that."

The McKennas tried that night to talk together, choosing a restaurant in Merrill, a quiet Italian place where they assumed no one would recognize them, until the owner came bobbing out of the kitchen, wiping the backs of his hands on his striped apron, telling them their meal was on the house; he'd seen them on NBC. They'd eaten quickly, then sat on the porch on Cleveland Avenue, letting the mosquitoes feast on their bare arms undisturbed.

"We can't give up," Lorraine said. "Greg says the judge is harder on people he knows have the best case. That's why he's being so hard on us."

"Maybe if we let him decide, he'll make that call," Gordon suggested listlessly.

"But what if he makes the other call? What if he does actually consider allowing Keefer to be placed for adoption?" Mark asked the night. The moon rose, dull and nacreous as an oyster, and dappled the treetops in the cemetery.

"We'd have some control, we'd see her," Gordon said.

"How can you say that?" Lorraine cried, leaping up from the stone steps. "How do you know that Delia would honor anything she promised? How do you know Diane Nye wouldn't talk them right into moving back to Florida?"

Gordon felt as if he certainly was dying. His hands and feet were chilled, cumbrous, despite the eighty-degree mug of the ten o'clock air. When he'd finally left his parents, he'd sought the salvation of the plastic bottle, along with half a joint Tim had given him on their last drive through the subdivision, then two bags of Cheetos and three bottles of Labatt. Still he'd been unable to sleep. Finally, he'd driven back to Cleveland Avenue. The grave was adorned, he knew, by Nora, with a spangled flag and the silvered cardboard representation of a firecracker. The firecracker gaped, unglued by the previous week's rains. Gordon disengaged it gently from the flag and pressed it flat, folding it to discard at the trash basket near the gates.

How the dead celebrate, he thought.

Long after midnight, he drove out Q to his uncle Hayes's farm. A light was on in the kitchen. He peered into the glass back-door pane. Nora was patching jeans at the broad single-planked table. He did not knock, but let himself in, and Nora did not startle or lay her large flat hand to her chest, telling him he'd given her a turn. She simply turned to him her tired, tanned face and said, "Honey, do you want coffee?"

"I don't know, Auntie. I don't know what I want."

"Well, I'll have a cup, then."

Gordon held the seat of his uncle's faded dungarees flat while Nora placed, then whipstitched a red patch. She was wearing a bright orange sweatshirt, and something about it reminded Gordon of . . . of church. He had thought as a child that his aunt Nora resembled the large, sad carved wooden saints that ranged along the outer aisle in Our Lady of the Lake. Especially Saint Michael. "That's Georgia's," he said suddenly.

"I wear it to sleep," Nora told him softly.

"I can't sleep," Gordon said.

"None of us is doing a bang-up job of that."

"Do you think he would actually take her and give her to someone and we'd never see her again?"

"No," Nora said, selecting another pair of jeans from her stack. "No, I think he'd catch his ass in a wringer if he did that."

"But he might give her to the Cadys."

"Actually, I think there's every chance he will do that, Gordie. I'm an old fool, and I never gave up hoping that there would be a miracle, and Georgia would get up out of that bed and walk away cured . . . but I knew, even as I prayed, she was going to die. And I had to admit to myself that a part of me was going to die, too. I had to get my heart ready to let that part of me die."

"And did you?"

"I guess I did," Nora said, "'cause I'm still here, breathing."

"How?"

"I think about . . . I know you don't hold with this, Gordie. But I think about the life of the world to come. And in my mind, that life is a restoration of all that you've lost in this life. Georgia. The baby I lost—"

"I didn't know you lost a baby."

"At seven months. A boy. Before Rob and Dan."

"Was he . . . did the baby have birth defects?"

"No, perfect. Just not for this world."

"I'm sorry, Auntie."

"I am too, honey. I'm still sorry, thirty years and more later."

"So what do I do?"

"When I can't sort myself out from the blues, I think, what really matters, Eleanor Jane? What will last?" She said, "Maybe you can ask yourself. What's the most important thing in the world to you, Gordie?"

"Keefer," he said. "That's easy."

"And the next most?"

"Georgia."

"And then?"

"My mom," he said, "and Dad." He hesitated. "And you."

"Don't have to say that."

"I know I don't. But that's true. You. My family. Much, much more now than before all this."

"Well, I say the same things. Hayes and my boys. And you and Georgia. But right up there, with them, Mark and Mike. My brothers. And Lorraine."

"But she's just your sister-in-law."

"No," said Nora, "She isn't. Of course, that's not what she might say."

She bit a thread. "She and Mark and Mike. Ahead of my mother and father. Ahead of everything except God," Nora went on. "No, that's not quite true. Ahead of God." She crossed herself, making a lattice in the air with her middle finger crowned by her thimble. "Because I don't know God."

"Okay."

"You're more closely related to your siblings."

"That's true genetically, of course. More than either to your mother or your father."

"Gordon Cooper McKenna. You know that genetics is not what I'm referring to. I'm referring to . . . being family. Even when we fight—"

"I never think of you and Hayes having an argument."

"We didn't used to. Now a week doesn't go by. But I think it's good for us. The fights we have. It gets your blood going. People are what tie you to this life, even when you want this life to let you go."

"That's how I feel, like letting it go."

"But you don't. Otherwise, you'd be out there running that car into a tree. Like Ray did. He cut the ties."

"The insurance company ruled it wasn't a suicide."

"But you know it was."

"I didn't ever really think about it much after it happened."

"I think it was. I think he wanted to let Georgia be free. And he couldn't cut the tie to her, from him. So he had to go, too."

"What makes you think that?"

"A stupid thing."

"Tell me."

"That they took out the car seat. And took the old car."

"Huh," Gordon said.

"But you're holding on to your life. You want to see

what's around the corner. In spite of how much this all hurts you."

"I guess."

"I know you do. You know you're going to heal. That is . . . the terrible legacy of being a person. But you're going to bear Georgia's witness, take the past you had with her and add on to it, and add on to it, and give that to Keefer. All except for that one part, that's gone. You can't ever replace your sister."

"No, I can't."

"You put her before Mark and Lorraine. And why's that?" Nora asked.

"Because, I never thought about it, a sister knows you better . . . you can let her see . . . things even your parents or maybe your wife . . . I couldn't fool her. My sister."

"So you would say, from a child's point of view, you need a brother or a sister?"

"Not need. But yes, it's the most important thing."

"Well," Nora said, "you sure you don't want some of this coffee? It's hazelnut."

On Sunday night, Gordon did a full circuit with his weights. He splashed his face, but did not shower. He sat down at the phone.

Alexis answered on the first ring.

"Speak," she said.

"This is Gordon McKenna," he said. "I need to talk to Delia. I need to talk to your mom."

"Mom!" Alexis shrieked.

He heard Delia say, with laughter beneath her voice, "Stop that noise right now," and when Keefer shouted "Mom!" as well, "This means you, too, Miss Kathryn," and then she was on the line, her "Helloooo" filled with Florida banjo.

"This is Gordon," he said.

"Gordon." The damper of Delia's hand went down over the line. "Hush now! Take them, honey." She was back. "Gordon, I don't think we're supposed to talk with you right now. I think Mary Ellen said we should meet tomorrow. I was going to call her tonight. The judge said we should talk in person."

"He said we were to work it out between ourselves."

"He meant our attorneys, I believe."

"Well, I'm tired of attorneys, Delia. What I have to say I want to say directly to you, in plain language and not in legalese."

"Gordie," she breathed, and the use of his diminutive disarmed him, "I know how you—"

"You have no idea what I'm going to say, Delia. There's nothing to be afraid of. Just as I have no idea why you've put my family through this, that having been said, I know that my sister treasured your friendship, and Ray loved you. And that's good enough for me."

"What do you mean?"

"I mean I will withdraw my petition."

"You will? But, why?"

"Isn't that what you want?"

"Of course it is. But, why now?"

"I guess . . . because I love her so much. I can't stand for her to be pulled in two directions anymore. And I know you're sick, and struggling, and for a good reason, to bring a baby into the world. For which I admire you, though I also hate your guts, in a way. But also because if there is any reason on earth why Ray and Georgia would have decided, together, in favor of you over me, it's because their child was a girl who needed a mother, and a child who needs a sister. I'm willing to let you be that . . . mother. I know you want to be. But I have conditions."

"Go ahead," Delia said evenly. "But wait just a minute. I want Craig to pick up—"

"No," Gordon interrupted her, "no, I'm talking to you, Delia. Not Craig. You're the blood relative."

"Okay," she said, and he liked her for a moment, when she continued, "okay, shoot."

"Her name is Keefer. Keefer Kathryn Nye. Not Kathryn. Not Kathryn Keefer, and definitely not Kathryn Cady."

"But the children—"

"You already have one daughter who has a different last name from yours. Have two. You're going to have a kid with another last name altogether, aren't you?"

"Okay. But I think that Ray—"

"Ray would want his child to have his name forever. I mean no disrespect to Craig. This is *my* gesture of respect for Ray. And her first name is Keefer. She's to be called Keefer."

"Okay."

"We want access to Keefer two weekends each month. Either me or my parents. And if I go back to school . . . in Madison"—Gordon hoped he did not sound as though he was making this up as he went, though he was—"I'll want her to stay over one night a week."

"That's being a stepfather, Gordon. Not an uncle."

"These are my terms, Delia. I'm not negotiating now. I'm not mediating. I'm telling you. This is how it has to be. This is what my sister would want for her child. She would want her to have more than a cursory knowledge of her McKenna relatives."

"Okay."

"Okay, what?"

"Okay, okay. I accept your . . . terms."

"We want her for a month in the summers."

"That's ridiculous. She's a baby."

"Okay, for two weeks. And then more when she's older. More if she chooses more."

"And what else?"

"Before I go on to what else, I want to hear you say you agree to as much vacation time with her McKenna relatives as she wants, barring the necessary things with school, and so on."

"And?"

"I want you to say you agree."

"I agree. Now, and what else?"

"You'll stay here."

"Here."

"Here in Wisconsin. In Madison, for at least five years, and here in Wisconsin forever."

"I can't promise forever."

Gordon massaged his eyes. No one could promise forever. "Okay, five years here, and then we work together to come up with a plan for Keefer if you should move."

"This is joint custody, Gordon. I don't even have this kind of arrangement with Alex's father."

"I'm not Alex's father. You've told everyone over and over that this isn't personal, that you have nothing against me or against my parents. We aren't getting divorced, Delia. We're starting a life of sharing a child."

"It might as well be a divorce."

"Suits me. Withdraw your petition and you can never see me again."

"Keep going, Gordon."

"There's only one last matter."

"Which is?"

"I will be the one in charge of Keefer's inheritance."

"Gordon," Delia's voice spiked sharply. "That's a no-go. That's not possible. We need to be the ones to make the decisions about her education, her needs, whatever they are."

"You can ask me about those things, and I will agree to any reasonable request. I will be more than generous."

"You're going to spend it on your parents' legal fees."

"I couldn't do that, Delia. Not that they don't need it. If my parents end up in . . . subsidized housing someday because of this, I'll never forgive you. But no, not a nickel of it will go to my parents or to me. And I want to make sure not a nickel of it goes to you, either. To Craig buying his own dealership. To a nice place in Florida for you guys."

"That's an insult, Gordie," Delia said. "That's a damned insult."

"Yes," Gordon said, "it is."

"Well, you are honest."

"I've never been more honest."

"I don't think I should make decisions like this without consulting Mary Ellen Wentworth."

"Okay. We will not be meeting tomorrow. See you in court."

"Now, wait. Don't get all twisted around the propeller. If you think that any of our interest in raising Keefer Kathryn—"

"Keefer. Her name is Keefer."

"In raising Keefer had anything to do with that money—"

"I don't think that, Delia. Don't make me even entertain the thought. Just agree."

"All right. I agree. Now, what else? Do you intend to come and live in our screen porch?"

"No, that's all there is."

"Gordie, thank you."

"Don't thank me. I'm not doing this for you, Delia."

"But thank you. This is the right thing."

"I pray to God it is, Delia. If it's not, if anything should ever hurt my . . . this . . . her. . . ." Gordon mastered his voice. "Anyhow. That's my piece. Said."

"Gordie?" Delia asked breathlessly, her thin voice thinner, "Gordie, are you still there?"

"I'm here."

"Thank you," she said. "Bless you."

Gordon replied, "I'm going to call my mother."

He hung up the phone. It rang. Gordon reached over and switched off the answering machine. The phone continued to ring. He did not answer it.

CHAPTER *twenty*

*W*hen small things went wrong, the child Gordon would comfort himself with the thought that somewhere someone was having the best day of his life. Someone had been drafted on the first round. Someone had gotten into M.I.T. Someone had inherited a bright red Sebring from an old lady he used to mow the lawn for.

As he began a slow circuit of his apartment, setting aside those things to bring, those things to give away, those things to store with his mother, Gordon attempted this. He sketched a memory picture of Georgia hurtling into the house, throwing down her backpack, bellowing, "I'm Emily, Mom! I'm Emily! I got the lead part!" He saw himself at four, a bright red moto-cross bike under the Christmas tree. Envisioned a man his own age, or older, getting news . . . I'm pregnant . . . I'm not pregnant . . . I got the job!

Rain rapped insistently on the bay window, and the thirsty, bedraggled August foliage rattled. Gordon found six of Keefer's seven hundred socks, one stitched with tiny blue cats all around the ankle by his aunt on her Singer. He found spoons from the period when Keefer would eat only yogurt, when he'd been so frightened that she would starve; he'd purchased a dozen rubber-coated spoons that he carefully lined up before each feeding attempt so that he could keep on shoveling, even when she threw one over his head.

He opened his drawers and his files from school and began to prune. Teacher of the Year. All District. His first year. His teacher's test keys, his plan for his mating-dance class. He made a note to himself: Secure a biohazard bag for the disposal of the frozen products in his classroom. Plants and frogs trapped in time by cold, their wonders transformed into maps. Vials of insect egg sacs. A human placenta.

People were trapped. When things were ending, the past blossomed. Everything past seemed better. The legacy of people.

When his father phoned, Gordon thought, oddly, this might be one of the last calls he ever received in Tall Trees. Mark said that there was an old colleague in Madison who had, at one time, collected derelict farmsteads he planned to rehabilitate and sell as hobby homes after his retirement from the faculty. And sure enough, the man was juggling three of them right now, and one only eight miles south of the city, a perfectly serviceable three-room house that needed only a couple of coats of paint and a good airing after the eviction of some renters who'd turned out to be more like squatters. If Gordon wouldn't mind ripping up some decent carpet that had been ruined by cat urine, Mark's friend would be entirely willing to let Gordon live rent free until fall. It wouldn't take that long for him to find a place, Gordon had ventured, touched by his father's munificence.

"Take your time," Mark urged him. "You need to find an apartment that you can stay in for a while. You want to make it nice for you and Keefer." He'd offered Gordon a loan, but Gordon refused. It was he who would have to help his father, down the line, with all the legal bills. He was sure he'd immediately find work subbing in Madison, even though the district was renowned around the state for its pricey clannishness. He was a man, and that was helpful, and he could sub phys ed and health as well as science. And a decision on the three-year doctoral program would be forthcoming by December. The forms, completed, lay on Gordon's unfinished secretary desk. In three years, Keefer would be looking at kindergarten, and the provision the Cadys had accepted—to remain in the Madison area for at least five years—would still be in force.

Though only a week of days and nights had passed since the last conference with the judge, he'd made his decision so quickly that all that was left for him to do was to pack up and leave.

Overnight, Gordon's immediate future had telescoped into a series of good-byes. Good-bye to his job; that had been easy. His relations with Hart Rooney had, he thought in retrospect, been traversed by unspoken resentment and obligation from the first. Gordon had put it down to a town-bound older man's natural wariness of a former student who'd returned glossed with some mildly surpassing accomplishments—Hart had been a science teacher himself. The necessary pressure on the school created by his frequent absences during Georgia's illness had been something Gordon hoped to repair after the conclusion of the case, and he had been comforted in the knowledge that his student and peer reviews were uniformly excellent. But Hart's palpable relief at his resignation lent weight to Gordon's suspicion that the aloofness between him and his boss had older, tougher roots, that it went back to the days when he'd outshone Rooney's own stodgy, replicant sons, one year older and one year younger than Gordon. It went back to Lorraine's not particularly covert resentment of Rooney's well-meant comments about adopted children. That series of nasty letters, without postmarks, making reference to serial killers who were adopted, had come from somewhere: Gordon knew that there had never been love lost between his mother and Laurie Rooney, Hart's shrill wife, who was the band director at the middle school. He would miss his classroom, its noisy, chaotic safety, and the daily interaction with kids he'd come to love, but he was glad to close the book for his own sake, and for his mother's.

The deal he had cut with the Cadys had broken her spirit, if not her heart. Nora had cried. His father had left the room. But his mother had said nothing. She had not disputed him, only looked up at him—she was so tiny—in a way that made him feel sorely the immensity of his role measured against the span of his immaturity.

And now he would have to tell her that he, too, would be moving away from her. Tell her, knowing that this last choice of his would complete the demolition of the familial village Lorraine surely had dreamed of—peopled with her children and their children—so long ago when first Georgia, then Gordie, came back home.

Coward that he was, he'd waited until a doleful dinner, a few nights after his conversation with Delia.

Lindsay and he went together. It was not a festive feast. All of them were picking at a pork roast with apple glaze in silence, Lorraine's and Mark's appetites no keener than their guests'.

Sure that one more hitch of the ticking clock would explode him into babbling hysteria, Gordon simply came out with it. Perfunctorily. *I'm thinking of going back to school, to Madison, to be closer to Keefer*.

Shock yawned in the room. Lindsay was obviously angry at being flanked by this announcement, which was news to her; his father was both constrained and yearning, his mother suddenly very busy gathering up things to take to the kitchen before dessert.

He was home alone later, after Lindsay had left frustrated by his feeble promises to discuss his rashness more fully, when the telephone rang.

"It's me," Lorraine said, and she would not have had to say another word; the volume of her injury was so distinct in her voice, in her breathing, that he'd wanted to slam down the receiver and run to her, as he'd run to her every day when he was small, entering the quiet house after school, frantically searching for evidence of her presence, her purse in its customary place on the ledge, her honeysuckle scent in the hallway, throwing himself at her midsection, the fear he felt all day when he was a first-grader, a second-grader, melting in the beatitude of her greeting, in the rapture of their reunion. Georgia, who considered the short bus ride home a rolling recess, an occasion to plan and bicker and carouse with other kids, would come home later, after the endless series of stops at the end of graveled roads to eject dozens of farm and lake kids. More days than not, Gordon would manage to elude the bus, running through the parking lot behind Wilton's, through the middle-school playground, holding his breath as he jogged through the cemetery so that he would get his wish, jiggling his pee-loud bladder on the curb as he looked both ways before rushing across Cleveland Avenue. Tell me every single thing that happened today, Lorraine would urge him, confidingly, and, over granola bars, he would lead her through his day, through his triumphs in spelling and in gym, his painful struggles in math, his suffering at the hands of the Reilly brat. It had been their protected time, the half hour before Georgia burst in, pulling them into the vortex of her demands and her energy. They talked and snacked, played long, archaically precious games, such as cat's cradle and jacks—Gordon still played a mean game of jacks—or she held his hand while he drew a thousand elephants, the curve of the elephant's ear that he could see, then a blind curve, with eyes closed, his hands taking over for his eyes, feeling the sweep and heft of the trunk, the tusk. They plucked overblown roses—"That's right, sweetie, above the three-leaf"—in the front yard in June and sang, old rounds and rhymes, "Waters of Babylon" and "Wren, Wren, Little Wren," and the old song that repeated, "Will you go, lassie, go?" the song about mountain thyme that played when Georgia walked down the aisle at

Our Lady of the Lake. They rooted out the outlaw dande-
lions, Lorraine teaching him the chin test for telling if a boy
loved butter, and searched for buttercups. They were utterly
content and contained, in ways that Gordon, as a horny, iras-
cible teenager would recapture only when he was fortunate
to get a sore enough throat that Lorraine would not only let
him stay home, but take a day of leave herself.

Georgia had been able to take his mother's love for
granted, but he had not. He had never been able to bear to
hurt her, and had been aghast at the casual way that even
good kids, such as Kip, shouted at their mothers, called them
"old bitch" behind their backs.

The construction of the family had plainly been intended
for Gordon to be Mark's child, his boon companion, a little
man doing complex male things at the side of his patient
elder mentor; and Gordon had certainly acquiesced, but it
had never been to Mark that he'd brought his treasures, his
granite wedge with its grinning slash of glinting mica, his
mummified mouse, and his nuggets of emotional pain. It
was Lorraine on whom he counted to examine and proclaim
or dismiss them, Lorraine whom Gordon strived to please.
Though Georgia reserved, with the stately assurance of a
firstborn, her space in Lorraine's lap, the eminence of her
drawings and certificates in the middle of the corkboard,
Gordon had believed all his life that it was he his mother
loved best. She might call Georgia her image, but Gordon
was her jubilee. He gave her the most ease, the most uncom-
plicated pleasure.

As he grew older, and ambivalent about his adoration,
he'd made his withdrawal from Lorraine careful, gratified
that it was not he, but Georgia, who made Lorraine cry, who
kept the line of light under his parents' bedroom door bright
late into the night, who picked at Lorraine until his mother's
temper detonated and Mark had to intervene. Until he'd
graduated high school, his mother had never, not once, forgotten to kiss him good night, reaching out, embarrassingly,

to turn up his chin and give him a peck on the lips or cheek even when Gordon, buried in a book, would have offered her the top of his head with a mere grunt of acknowledgment. When he was ten and brought her a muddy bucket of crawdads for her anniversary—he knew she'd loved lobster—Lorraine had made a big fuss, preparing a savory tomato broth she served that night over noodles. It had been Georgia who found the package of frozen lobster buried at the bottom of the trash can and brought it to him, pointing out how his mother had been unable to cook his crummy crustaceans and had deceived him. Lorraine had burst into tears, called Georgia a vengeful little shit, let Gordon stay up late, even though it was a school night, and watch Johnny Carson in his parents' bed. It was still one of his most cherished memories. And though he knew nothing could be more excruciatingly boring than watching someone else play golf, Lorraine had patiently trekked through the mosquito-plagued twilights at public courses every time he played, driven him to the Kwik-Stop for raspberry slushies on the way home, displayed his lame trophies on the mantel long after he would have preferred she box them. Until he had been a . . . parent himself, he could never have imagined how tireless Lorraine had been, always working, always making her art around their many urgencies, always preserving a radiant face for them.

That night, Lorraine had begun with tender questions, was he sure he wanted to move? There was his job. And what had Lindsay said? What about his friends? They would still have Keefer two weekends every month. Rendered mulish by her concern, Gordon had offered more certainty than he'd actually felt. Until then, the move had actually been only an idea, a possibility. But suddenly, he was certain he had to make a break. He was all there was left; he would be again that little boy, racing hammer-hearted and short of breath through the cemetery. And he'd wanted, with fully half his heart, to relent and be that boy, but he was irrevocably grown. "If I can't be her father, I want to be . . . sort of her stepfather," he told his mother. "Delia and Craig have no idea how busy they're going to be with a new baby and Keefer. I'm going to be there for her."

Lorraine had not argued. But Gordon could tell, from small, stifled sounds, that she was crying.

"Mom," he whispered, squeezing his eyes closed, hugging the phone with both hands, "Mom. I'm going to miss you guys—"

"It's like losing her all over again."

No, the voice in Gordon's head cried! No! Foul!

"You mean Keefer?"

"I mean your sister."

"But . . . I'm going to be around. I'll bring her up here all the time. And you and Dad can come—"

"Dad said we could move to Madison when we retired. He said we could get a condo, on one of the lakes."

"But you live here, Mom! You and Dad have lived here a thousand years . . ." That hadn't come out as he'd intended. It had sounded like a preemptory strike, a way to head them off from following him down there, something he almost felt but dismissed as his own fretful impatience. Why shouldn't they move down there someday? He'd like it. It was just exhaustion, playing hell with him. He wanted sleep. He wanted for this to be concluded. "Not that it would be a bad idea or anything. Take it one step at a time. You have a whole life here. What about your friends? And Nora and Hayes?"

"My friends are sick of me," Lorraine said viciously.

"Things are going to get back to normal."

"No, they aren't."

"Well, what are we going to do, then? Just all of us curl up and die?"

"You don't know how this feels, Gordie."

Yes, he'd thought, I do. I've lost my child, too, he thought. "Take it easy, Mom," he'd pleaded, his voice syrupy even to his own ears, patronizing, false. "Take it easy. It'll all work out."

"It's not that I don't want you to have your own life."

"I know."

"It's not that I don't want you to have what you want."

"Mom, you weren't like this when I went to Florida."

"That was a beginning, Gordie! This is an ending. This is an ending. I don't know how I'll feel without—"

"Without me?"

"Without you, and without . . . the quest. Everything I had, everything I was went into trying to get the law changed, trying to make it possible to keep Keefer, trying to do what Georgia wanted."

"I think that this is what Georgia would have wanted. She would have wanted me to be there, going to the school play, taking Keefer to the museum, you know?"

"It's just that I don't know what I'll do with myself. Your dad and I, we hardly talk anymore. I don't know him. Maybe you never know people."

Gordon had been blown back. His parents' small circle of reliance on each other's companionship had been the substructure of his entire life. He'd always assumed, watching them fold into one another, their backs turned to the outer world in the cozy declaration of their unity, that his folks rushed eagerly to one another when he and Georgia were gone. He'd overheard them, when he was in sixth or seventh grade, poring over travel folders Mark had picked up on the way home from work, chatting about bicycling through Ireland, backpacking in Italy, Lorraine pointing out with wry weariness that they'd started so late as parents, by the time the kids were grown, they'd be wheelchairing through Ireland.

"There were always so many things you wanted to do," he said after a pause.

"We wanted to," Lorraine sighed, "but it's not the same now. We can't just pick up and go on as if none of this ever happened. It's . . . Gordie, it's as if we were owed, and we ended up paying. We have a mountain of debt, and all for nothing. And we're not young . . ."

She sounded, Gordon thought in terror, whiny. Old. The burden of her need for him would devastate his resolve, and in giving in, he would give up, give up as she had. He could feel his very brain relent, softening.

He could not leave her. He could not leave.

He must leave. He must leave or they would all drown.

"I have to do this," he'd said.

I have to do this, he'd told Lindsay, the following night, a Friday, when she opened the door of his apartment with her own key to find him sleeping among his cartons on the folded pillow of Keefer's dog bed. He fought the instinctive pull to amend his statements, to make this somehow easier for both of them to bear.

When Lindsay sat down, sobbing, on a taped box, he wanted to enfold her, cradle her. When her weight collapsed the top, and she fell backward, floundering, the helpless, undignified splay of her legs vanquished him, even as they laughed together. Gordon wanted to strip her, bathe and smooth her, bandage her against the wound he had caused, pet her not like a lover, but like a father.

"I knew how upset you would be," she told him, patting at her tears with the heels of both hands. Gordon saw plainly how badly he did love her, how he would never see a redhead, her curtain of burnished hair divided by one innocent ear, and not think of Lindsay, his dear and clean and loyal Lindsay.

"It's not that I'm upset, though I am," he said. "It's that I have to change my whole way of living now. It sounds as though I'm running away, and maybe I am. And if I am, I hope I'll be enough of a . . . man to figure that out and come home. Come back."

"I'll wait for that," Lindsay wept. "It's not as if I haven't waited."

"You've waited way too long, Lins. Since we were kids. It's not as though we're old people, or anything. Maybe there was a time for us to get married, or whatever, and we missed it. I blew it."

"Or maybe it isn't here yet."

"That's possible. But I don't want to offer it as a reality because I'm not sure."

"Not sure if you love me?"

"Not sure if the way I feel is the way people should feel when they start a life with someone."

"How will you know? How will you know, in Madison? You'll be all by yourself—though, knowing you, not for long—"

"Don't, Lins. Don't cross us . . . what we have, with that stuff. Because that's not at all what this is about. I'm not saying it wasn't about that when I went to college. I'm not saying it wasn't about that ever. But it isn't now. This is first, about Keefer, and second, about me. What kind of person I'm going to be."

"You'll be all alone. You'll be all alone," she said.

"I'll be all alone and I'll be fucking miserable. But I think I need to . . . be miserable alone. In a way, having you and my folks has made it too easy for me."

"What will happen?"

"I don't know. Maybe I'll grow up. Maybe I'll realize I've already grown up. But I don't think, I just don't think marriage is in the cards for me, Lins. Not with you now, or with anybody ever. The way I feel now, I have one space in me, and it's for Keefer, and that's all I can handle."

"How can you know how you'll feel in six months? In a year?"

"I don't know. But I don't want to let you think I'm doing this . . . on a whim. Just for a while. As far as I know, right now, I'm going, Lins. I'm going for good. If I didn't think that was true, I would never hurt you like this."

She got up from the box, leaning on his extended hand. "May I touch you?"

"I'm here," he said, opening wide his arms. She sat on his lap, stroking his neck, until he felt himself begin to be aroused, and urged her to one side. There would be no farewell romp, though at the instant she stood, straight-backed, to leave, he desired her more than he had since images of her butt and her lower lip had frenzied his seventeen-year-old dreams. He pulled her back down, beside him. The light drained into a pewter afterlight—the days, Gordon noticed, were already diminishing; he could no longer pretend it was high summer. Neither of them moved to turn on the lamps. He asked Lindsay whether she was hungry. She asked if he had any wine. They drank a whole bottle of merlot, the last liquid he had in his fridge, and then slept, side by side, clinging together as chaste as a brother and sister. When Lindsay left in the morning, she had not wakened him to say good-bye.

That morning, he was sorting through more papers when he uncovered the folder of Georgia's his mother had given him. The one he'd noticed in her apartment, containing a thick envelope from an organization called Families United. He shook out the contents, and began to read a letter referring to Georgia's "initial inquiries" and "possible contact." The research carried out by someone named Blair Bell, had, Georgia would be happy to learn, uncovered some very interesting possibilities about Georgia's birth family. The last name "Kiss" was not uncommon in Hungary, but it was in the United States. It was the surname of cousins of her birth mother, for whom Blair Bell had no current address, only a work number from a hospital in San Diego. There, the personnel department had no record of future employment, but Georgia's birth mother, whose name was Hannah, had been a physician's assistant in 1988, and could well have married. Locating her would not prove difficult, should Georgia instruct Families United to authorize further inquiries. What was most compelling, the letter pointed out, was the ancestral surname, the name of cousins of her birth mother, and also the last name of her adoptive mother. The next steps should be exciting. The health information Georgia had initially requested would also be forthcoming. Blair Bell wished Georgia well as she contemplated her own path toward parenthood. There was an invoice, dated February 6, with the year of Keefer's birth.

Georgia had been eight months' pregnant then. Had she already felt sick? The head's premonition of the body's betrayal? Or had she simply, suffused with her own expectancy, longed for the ratification of the biological bond? Longed for deeper insights than her mirror's messages about the heritable forces she had unleashed to build the being that would be her child? The name! Gordon ripped the letter once, and with difficulty because of the thickness of the stock, and folded it to rip again. What could it have meant to Georgia, the possibility that on some removed rung of ancestry, her beloved mother was her blood relative?

What could that possibility mean to Gordon?

He could dial the 800 number.

He tore the paper again, into fourths. He needed it gone. To live with it among his things was untenable. Why? He was ready to hear the correct multiple-choice plug-in, announced quickly, but shrank from an analysis. At last, he stuffed the fragments back into the envelope. For Keefer. This key was Keefer's.

On the last day, he offered Judy Wilton his eggs and fresh vegetables, which she nodded at and received. Gruffly she told him, "I'm sorry about what happened last winter."

"No, you're not," Gordon said easily. "But you were wrong. You were dead wrong."

"I am sorry," Judy Wilton said, and to his fascinated horror, began to weep, with a caliber of snorts he hadn't heard since *Mister Ed*. "I really am sorry. I talked about it with my mother. And she said I don't know a thing about how kids behave. She said my sister and I screamed all the time. We screamed so much she would put us in one crib and go out in the yard and smoke my dad's cigars."

Gordon could not help it. The snapshot of Helen Wilton puffing a stogie overcame him, and he laughed.

"It didn't have anything to do with what happened, Judy," he said.

"If it did, I'll never forgive myself."

"Forgive yourself," Gordon told her.

There was no need to say good-bye to Tim, who was planning to drive down with him Friday and help him tackle the fabled terrors of the piss-permeated farmhouse, and he had no heart for a mock-rousing mustering of his old friends. He'd had enough of gatherings to last him a decade, and he set his thoughts on the week he would have in Madison to paint and fumigate and make ready for a week from Thursday, when he would have Keefer for a full four days, a gift Delia had offered on a postcard she'd written him earlier in the week.

A few days after the postcard arrived, Craig Cady had left him a message on his machine. Their actual filing for the adoption would have to wait. Delia had been hospitalized, at least for a few days' observation, and would probably be on bed rest for the duration of the pregnancy. He would have his hands full. They were both relieved, Craig's bluff, uncomfortable message informed Gordon, that he would soon be in town.

A drive out to the farm would have taken more stuffing than Gordon had left. He expected that even the sight of the farm, where a brand-new sign now proudly proclaimed HORIZON PRODUCE, HAYES NORDSTROM AND SON, would provoke such a sentimental response that he would be unable to leave it, in case it should disappear when he turned his back. So he sent flowers to his aunt Nora—aware that this constituted sending a case of coals to Newcastle—six white roses, for each of the children she'd loved, and an orchid for no reason except that he knew how the color purple always lifted her spirits.

The daylight hours on Friday were crowded with securing a rental trailer and loading it, tying down his bike, securing his guitar with a bungee cord in the bunting of Keefer's dog bed, wedging in his six raggedy boxes of books and pots, the same ones he'd packed to move from Florida to Tall Trees and from the slum to the Victorian—he was so green, Gordon congratulated himself wryly. He then made phone calls, to the biology department in Madison, to his mother and father—he knew she'd been at her water aerobics class; he'd timed the call to catch her out—letting them know what time he'd stop by, to the guys who were taking the sublet. He scoured the oven he'd never used and swept the floor. He sealed his keys in an envelope and closed the windows. Just before he closed the door, he looked back and noticed one last task and used his Swiss Army knife to pry the little plastic covers from all the outlets.

Just before six, he rattled up in front of his parents' house on Cleveland Avenue. There was a note on the blue stationery he'd read from all his life, which featured an ink sketch that was something of a cross between an open poppy and a plat map of a river, the stem of which formed the *L* in "Lorraine K. McKenna."

It read, "There are sandwich makings in the fridge. We are eating over at Nora's. Come by if you want. You said this is not a good-bye, so we're not treating it that way. P.S. Ray and Diane Nye have asked us to have dinner with them next Saturday at their palatial Madison estate. We are going, though they will probably poison our food. We will then visit you and Miss Keefer at your hovel. Be there, or you will be out of the will." The note went on, "P.P.S. Gordie, do not put up any pest strips in that farmhouse. They are dangerous to breathe, no matter what the labels say." It finished,

"I love you." She had inked out the "I" and replaced it with "We."

She signed "Mom," crossed it out, wrote "Mom" a second time, crossed that out, and wrote, "Mommy," but let the *y* trail down into a deadly cruel caricature of him, all teeth and cowlicks. Gordon removed the tack, put it in his shirt pocket and held the blue sheet to his nose. Its smell was not of his mother. It smelled like the Sharpie she'd used to draw.

The grave had been decorated with an abundance of late-summer flowers, mums and stargazers and tiger lilies—Nora was relentless; he was surprised she hadn't managed a UAW sticker for Labor Day. It was apparent, however, that no one had been around for days. The mums had been plucked featherless by the wind, and the lilies were parched in their empty Mason jar. Behind the stone, the scraggly small pine that had been wound with a sprinkling of white lights on a battery box had succumbed, the few remaining needles a toasty brown blanket on the ground. Georgia O'Keeffe McKenna. Raymond Jasper Nye.

Beloved Wife and Mother. Beloved Husband and Father.

Gordon easily uprooted the tiny, dead tree. It snapped in his hand. Under the needle drift there had been a litter of bulbs from the twinkle lights. He'd crushed them. They lay sparkling in the late-day rays alongside tatters of ribbons: yellow, violet, silver, which seemed bent on working their way into the earth, graftings for a bush that would bloom with memorial wreaths. All around the grave was festive, forgone litter. It looked like a fairground after the carnival had closed.

CHAPTER *twenty-one*

$\mathscr{T}$im called it the Hotel California because you could check out anytime you liked, but you could never leave. The first time they tried to open the doors from the inside, they discovered the old wood had swollen so tightly it took two of them to budge them.

For all that, Gordon's domain was not so bad. The appliances, set off in one corner behind a ridiculous red velvet drape, were startlingly out of keeping—a big, handsome fridge and a newer gas stove alongside a steel sink that roared like some subterranean beast whenever Gordon turned the faucet on. The kitchen and the shower wedged in under an unused attic staircase were surprisingly serviceable. All the appliances belonged to the damned hippie squatters, his father's friend had informed Gordon, and he would be switched if he let them take a damned thing out of the house before he got a goddamned rent check. Gordon was welcome to use them so long as he paid the utility.

The view from the front porch made up for the hot and cold running ants. It was staggering, a hemisphere of sky and tree that stretched to the shadowy gray scalloped rim of the Blue Mounds more than ten miles distant. Bats *krred* and swallows crisscrossed in the twilight, while he and Tim sat nursing bottles of ale and sore shoulders, tipped back on a folding chair and a single orphaned recliner. They'd spent two hours in pitched battle with the doors.

Patting the arm of the pink velvet recliner the squatters had left behind, Tim said, "This chair belongs here, Gordo. It really sets the tone, porch-furniture wise. A real piece of resistance. Confirms you as trailer trash."

Gordon agreed, "Right you are, my man. People will take me for an Upchurch."

"Where do you think people actually go to deliberately *buy* things like this?"

"Tall Trees," Gordon said.

Gordon's mother blew her top when she later saw it. Overstuffed furniture on the outside porch? She insisted he let them buy him a simple wooden Adirondack chair, at least. "This is like . . . a redneck," she told him.

"I like it, though. Probably the legacy of my blood relatives," Gordon told her affably. Lorraine grimaced. Had she been twenty years younger, she'd have given him the finger.

He had let them buy him a set of plastic plates with sections. As a child, he had liked keeping his peas separate from his chicken, and he thought Keefer might like that, too.

As the weeks passed, he came to rely on two polestars, Keefer nights and the view.

He and Keefer liked to sit outside watching the hills disappear, singing the batty-bat song from *Sesame Street*. That peace alone, on a fall night, was worth the rent, which was the steady ache in Gordon's back and arms from days—after he'd gotten work subbing—nights of scraping and sanding and painting walls thick with generations of gunk. It was archaeological, the layers of flocked fleur-de-lis, natty navy blue stripes, pink paint and white paint and paint the color of ripe pumpkins he unearthed as he tried to strike plaster without destroying it. Something had instructed his predecessors at the house in the doctrine of redecoration without regret. Even the exterior of the house had been sided insanely, blue aluminum right over the remnants of beige aluminum. When he thought about what might be under the beige, and suspected it might be asbestos, Gordon quaked. But asbestos was no danger to anyone unless it was disturbed. By the time anyone disturbed these walls, Gordon would be living in a sane, cheaply built apartment in some modern anonymous complex, where he would listen to the bathroom intimacies of people on the other side of his eighth-inch drywall, and they would listen to him having sex, if he ever did that. He did not expect it would be soon. He'd told Tim, only last week, he was sure that if he ever had sex again, he'd cry out his own name.

Four weeks melted. The walls were painted a serene, washable white Keefer could scribble on with her wax crayon sticks, something he allowed her to do without reproving her, fuck Delia's wallpaper. The hardwood plank floor that had underlain the piss-perfumed shag could have been refinished, and he longed to see how it might have looked oiled and shining; but this was not his house. He settled for sweeping. His mattress on the floor faced the largest of the windows, and he'd calculated that the sun hit his face full, waking him, a few minutes past six. He could work every day he wanted to work, and the pay, though not a king's ransom, would stand him well into a few months' rent, if he put away something. By the time that ran out, his student loan checks would have begun to arrive. He'd been accepted into the three-year program that would lead directly from his bachelor's to a capital *P* and a small *h* and a capital *D* behind his name. He had no idea whatsoever what he planned to do with his advanced degree once he had it. He trusted time to reveal. Substitute teaching had introduced him to morsels of everything, from leading self-conscious, complaining junior girls on a mile-long jog to grinning like a chimp at kids from Poland and Laos through four days of English as a second language.

What he missed was having students of his own, and he knew that he would have ample opportunity to teach, teach regularly, during grad school. He dreamed of resuming life as a student as well. He would welcome the routine of chapters and projects, labs and deadlines. It would make his days finite, predictable. From that imposed security, he planned to flex the muscles of his autonomy, to see how far they stretched before they caught.

Twice, and with utmost care, Gordon had written to Lindsay, breezy informational letters about his painting travails, about the entomological fauna that greeted him each night when he tried to sleep. When he came to the closing, he dithered. Love? Your friend? He'd finally settled on, "I'm thinking about you . . ." She had not written back, which saddened him. He checked his mail twice daily, hoping for a letter from her. Four times, he had lifted the telephone to call her, then replaced it after dialing the numbers. On nights when he woke chilled from a sudden turn in the weather, he ached for her clean, freckled, gently curving spine. Once, with a few beers in him, he had called Michelle Yu. But their first rush of greetings had subsided to empty air within a few minutes. He'd closed with a promise to look her up at Christmas, a promise that sounded halfhearted even as he spoke it.

He'd let Keefer color or build with blocks on the porch until darkness and the bugs drove them inside. He had no television, nor did he think one would work if he had one, and his library amounted to Georgia's old copy of *Wuthering Heights, Goodnight Moon,* and *Pat the Bunny*, which Gordon tried to edit every time they began it, deleting the references that bruised him, to Daddy's beard and Mummy's wedding band, though Keefer invariably led him back, insistently pointing to the pages he skipped until he read them. They counted cars, his niece gravely holding up one finger, then two. It took forever to get to ten, the volume of traffic, even at five in the afternoon, on his quiet country road outside Oregon, Wisconsin, as bustling as a Sunday midnight in Tall Trees. "That's a Dodge, Keefe," he would tell her.

"That's an Audi." Using her left hand, she would laboriously uncurl her stubborn ring finger to make three, then gleefully pop up her pinkie to make four, the goofy O of her generous mouth so like the signal face Georgia would make to mock an adult behind that adult's back that Gordon nearly cried. It had given him hope, the easy relief he felt the first time he picked Keefer up at Craig and Delia's. She had galloped out the front door, easily negotiating the steps with legs that seemed to have grown six inches since he last saw her, and leaped into his arms. She'd been out of sorts, lonely, Craig said, or so he supposed, with Delia in the hospital and Alex, who was now a sophomore, consumed with the rapture of her first real boyfriend and the chance to get away with almost anything she wanted to now that Craig had far more than Alex's curfew on his mind.

Gently, that first time, so as not to alarm Craig, Gordon had suggested that Keefer spend more time with him. His place was no palace, but he would gladly refuse the occasional job to have her more often. Warming up to it, he'd told Craig about the barn kittens that wandered over from the working farm next door. Keefer would love chasing them. Something in Craig's face warned him he'd gone too far. Craig's mother had gone back home, but she was planning on coming for a long stay soon. And Diane was usually free, between driving Big Ray back and forth to his cardiac rehab appointments. They were all fine, Craig assured Gordon. The baby, a boy, was due in two weeks. They were monitoring Delia closely, as her blood pressure was way up and the threat to the baby real. They could take the baby anytime, Craig said. He told Gordon that Keefer got a kick out of watching the heartbeat blips on Mommy's monitor. Gordon had been able to suppress his wince and wait until they were back out at his house before pulling the Jesus Saves T-shirt off over Keefer's head. The little shirts and pajamas he'd brought with him in Georgia's old doll trunk were tight and short on Keefer. But his mother had made a power sweep at Target when she'd arrived, buying Keefer a season's worth of clothing in forty minutes. They chose brightly colored waffle fabric mix-up-anyway tops and bottoms, like baby long johns, the kind Gordon favored, his laundry capacity now limited by his willingness to drive to the E-Wash coffee store, computer lair, and laundromat ten miles away on East Washington Avenue in Madison.

Over scallops, Diane Nye assured Lorraine and Mark were the good kind, flown in from her very own seafood merchant in Jupiter, Ray had made a stalwart apology for the pain his kin had caused Lorraine and Mark, and especially Gordie. Big Ray had aged ten years, the weight he'd piled on since the accident having deserted him since his heart troubles, leaving him looking more than ever like a sad hound whose jowls shuddered when he spoke, according to Lorraine's report. Neither of them had known what to say about Delia's dangerous condition, about the process of adoption Craig had suspended. They'd eaten hurriedly, nodded politely at the Nyes' bizarre offer to give Gordie any kind of help he needed in Madison, murmured agreement with Ray's vow to behave as grandparents should, stay out of the young folks' way, thanked Diane for the copies she'd had made of Keefer's recent baptism as a child of the Congregational Church. They had then joined hands and quickstepped for the door, rushing into the squalor of Gordon's dilapidated farmhouse, staying late, even though they had available their own perfectly comfortable and air-conditioned hotel room. Mark had expressed some concern about Gordon's locks, but was reassured when he realized that no one could get in or out except by main force. Lorraine had promised to mail Gordon a fire extinguisher. He had told his mother that such things were, indeed, available in Madison, too.

Gordon had no life.

The gym teacher at the school he subbed at most often, Madison Middle, was a hearty, deceptively delicate-looking blonde in her forties and had invited him to join her softball league, strictly pickup, though with some mighty moves out there. He'd gone once, his body delighting in the release of competition and exercise, his heart protesting at the absence of Sweeney and Church and the Wild Rose Chuggers. He paid for a two-week trial membership at a gym and watched herds of fetchingly flushed women in sports halters eye him from the margins of the track. After two visits, he had no spirit to return. He began taking long walks at night, observing that the darker the field, the fewer the bugs, rambling along the lanes between the contained bustle of subdivisions and the lonelier lights of scattered farmhouses.

The tiny dairy outfits just east of him and across the road were owned by twin brothers, big, rangy men who had to be eighty years old, so similar in every feature that Gordon had believed they were one person until he saw them together, one morning at sunrise, strolling past his mailbox.

One twin was called Ferris. His brother was Larry. One stifling Sunday, Ferris had shown up and announced himself with a smart knock and spent the day helping Gordon paint. "Just don't call me Ferry, is all I ask," he said, becoming quietly grieved when Gordon offered to pay him something. The house Gordon lived in had once belonged to Ferris's much older brother, Stuart. "He passed a few years ago," the old man told Gordon, and added, as if by way of explanation, "He wasn't a twin."

That first Keeferless weekend drained away fast, in a fury of rehab. With the practiced economy of a man who had moved often, Gordon shopped for towels and a shower caddy, a blind for the front window, sheets and a toothbrush. He bought Keefer a Barney toothbrush and cup.

On the second Keeferless weekend, he had to physically restrain himself from jumping in the car and driving north. Perversely, he promised himself he would not visit Tall Trees until visiting did not feel like running for cover. He spent the evening reading the dust jackets of books he could not afford at a mammoth Madison bookstore. Saturday yawned before him. He slept late and drank his tea on the porch, reading a letter from his aunt about the little monster costume she was sewing for Keefer for Halloween. Nora had been seriously drawn to a cute little devil pattern, picturing Keefer's delight at a rubber pitchfork, but she finally reckoned—and didn't Gordon agree?—that it would give the Cadys fits. He slept away most of Sunday, avid for the call that finally came, summoning him to a solid week of sub dates.

That Friday, after picking her up, he treated himself and Keefer to fish fry at the Avenue Bar. The phone was ringing when he pulled into the drive of the old house. He could hear it through the open window, but he didn't bother to rush. Once he'd disengaged Keefer from her car seat and thrown himself against the front door three or four times until it gave way, there would be no one on earth so persistent they would not give up. But the phone kept on ringing. Twelve rings. Fourteen. Gordon had no answering machine. He made a mental note to drive out to the mall and get one first thing. He was probably missing jobs. This very moment, his mother was probably sending Mark out to get Nora and prepare for a rescue mission.

He answered on the seventeenth ring.

"Oh Gordon." The voice was a watery blat, a wavering inhuman noise made by something that had endured mean damage, as if the oscillating structures that gave sound form had been wrenched. It sent a current along Gordon's forearms. "Oh Gordon, God help me." He did not know the voice. "Oh Gordon, Delia's in a coma."

It was Craig Cady.

Sweating, gasping, tearing a box of spaghetti open through the cellophane window on the front when he couldn't manage the top, spilling stiff noodles out onto the floor so that Keefer would have something to play with and not wander toward the cellar stairs, Gordon tried to piece together a chronology from Craig's gutturals and whimperings. Delia had given birth not long after five to a healthy baby boy. She had come through the birth exhausted but game, holding out her arms to her son, asking that he be named Hugh, after her late father. Craig and Alexis had left her in the care of the high-risk team, watching as the baby was weighed. Gordon couldn't follow Craig after that. It was . . . Gordon pressed the glow button on his watch. The misty underwater light told him it was only eight o'clock now.

What had happened in three hours that a university hospital could not prevent or intervene to repair?

And why was Craig calling him?

"Listen, Craig," Gordon said finally, "you have to find somebody to be there with you. Is Diane there? Is Ray around?"

"The wedding," Craig answered, his voice clotted with weeping, "the wedding is tomorrow."

"What wedding?"

"His sister. Caroline." Gordon had not known Caroline was actually divorced yet.

"Ray's sister? Are you sure?"

"They . . . Florida. I called . . . a big storm."

"And your mom, where's your mom?"

"All weather," Craig cried, "there are all these storms."

"Okay, okay, listen," Gordon soothed him. Listen? Just what the hell did he plan to say? At least Keefer was here with him, instead of reeling with Craig through forbidding, antiseptic corridors. "Where are you? I mean, it was the university hospital, wasn't it? Is Alex there with you? Can I just . . . talk to somebody else for a minute?"

"God help me," Craig wailed thinly, "God help me. God help me."

In the end, Gordon drove sleeping Keefer, still clutching a fistful of uncooked spaghetti, through the downtown night to the massive medical center parking lot, where Craig waited in the hollow of a lighted shelter near the main door. Alexis, violently shuddering, stood half hidden by her stepfather's bulk, a scarecrow in Craig's navy blazer. Craig needed to be back upstairs; neurologists were gathering for a consult. Alexis stayed with Gordon. From a pay phone, lacking any better idea, Gordon called his mother. Lorraine, probably lacking any better idea herself, said she was throwing on clothes, she would be down in a few hours. Gordon felt he ought to object, but could think of no good reason to deny himself the stalwart center of his mother's presence. The lights and smells of the hospital lobby, the artificial daylight through which children slid, squealing, in their socks, so wired they were oblivious to the haggard or rigidly masked faces of their parents, these worked a malign spell on his senses. Twice, he'd had to correct himself after calling Craig "Ray."

He suggested they might sit in his car, or take a ride. But Alexis said she hadn't eaten since breakfast. He and the two girls sat in a huge, marine blue cafeteria among doctors and nurses in smeary scrubs. Keefer and Alexis munched soggy french fries. Gordon downed two acrid cups of coffee. At midnight Lorraine and Nora burst through swinging panel doors, Lorraine carrying in one arm a six-pack of Diet Pepsi, and in the other three of Gordon's old team windbreakers. She opened one of the sodas for Alexis.

"Tell me what is going on here," she said.

"My mom had the baby and she went into a coma," Alex began, in a clear, small voice. She got up from her chair and circled the table, sitting down beside Lorraine and leaning into her breast. "She was really sick all week, and they said they had to take the baby out because the baby could die."

"So she had an operation."

"No, she started to have labor right after that."

"Gordie, was this caused by her multiple sclerosis?"

"From what Craig says, the thinking is that she had an aneurysm in her brain," Gordon told her, slipping into the bath of welcome exhaustion by the relief of her presence, "and that's all I know. I have no idea if it was related."

They sat for another hour, Alex and Gordon playing tick-tacktoe and hangman on paper napkins. Keefer fell asleep across Nora's lap. Lorraine suggested they find someone in charge and make inquiries, but Gordon balked, reluctant to search out their way to the obstetrical floor and accost a nurse. Who would they say they were? Ex-family?

Finally Craig appeared, flushed and tearful but coherent. Delia's condition was uncertain but critical. The baby was fine and weighed nine pounds. Delia had suffered from gestational diabetes. Delia may or may not have had a stroke caused by an aneurysm in her brain. No one believed Delia had ever had MS, but they were doing tests, all kinds of tests. He thought he would be able to drive Alexis home. He thought he would be okay to do that much. Alexis could probably care for Keefer.

"That's not going to happen," Nora told him firmly. "Alexis is a child whose mother is very sick, and you have to be here, and she can't be on her own at home."

"I guess you're right," Craig admitted, balling his fists against his reddened eyes like a huge kid. "I don't know what to do, is all. I don't think I should leave her. Leave my wife."

Lorraine pondered, tucking tendrils of her hair behind first one ear, then the other.

"Well, I guess we'll take them home, then."

"I can give you my keys," Craig said. "Gordie knows where it is."

"I mean home to Tall Trees," Lorraine said. "We'll take these girls home with us. You know my telephone number, Craig. You will call us when Delia is better. I suppose Alex needs her things. Do you need your things, Alex?"

"I have my period," Alex said softly, miserably.

"Oh, I don't mean those kinds of things," said Lorraine. "I mean your . . . your CD records and things like that. Not things we can pick up any old place."

"I don't need anything," Alexis said, "but I don't want to leave my mom."

"Craig is going to look after your mom. We're going to let him, so he doesn't have to worry about you guys. And this whole place is filled with people who are going to look after your mom and your new baby brother. Did you get to see him? Is he cute?"

"He's very cute," said Alexis, "small."

They turned as one to face Craig. Craig patted the side of Alex's face. Nora patted the big man's arm. All four of them staggered to the parking lot, Lorraine somehow organizing, on the way, an emergency sticker for Gordon's car, which they would leave behind. There was no question of him driving. There was no question of his going back to his place. Lorraine handed him her cell phone, prompted him to call whatever school he was expected at on Monday and leave a message that he'd been trapped by a family crisis. They bundled him into the back, with Keefer's car seat and her bag of water ba-bas and pull-ups. Alex sat on his other side. Both girls sank immediately, suddenly, into sleep. And even before they hit the highway, Gordon was dozing, as well. There came a dim awareness of changes in atmosphere, neon lights, another parking lot, the car door ajar, the key signal's tone, the radio blaring then sinking, his mother's voice, then his aunt's, excited chatter and sighs, all the familiar ease with which plans and routines were struck down in the path of fire, replaced by new imperatives about which there could be no question. There was no question that Alexis would be going to school. No question of him showing up for the job he'd committed to. The lights would burn in his farmhouse. No one would come to turn them out. Why was he leaving? Where was his part in this exodus? He could not question. He belonged to the clan who owned the territory of loss, were the masters of disaster, the postdocs of posttraumatic procedure. Who was he to question them?

Lorraine was shaking his shoulder. He was stumbling over the familiar hump of the doorstop at his parents' house, Mark holding him first by the shoulders, then close, in his arms. Water, gulped at the bathroom sink, from his cupped hands. His childhood bed, Keefer a damp bundle between him and the protecting wall. His aunt's hands, smelling of peat and pie, tucking a quilt around them.

Something had begun, had turned in space and accelerated, the McKennas' practiced gift for locating themselves at the epicenter of the most unaccustomed adversity. Gordon could not rouse himself. He drifted, wondering whether he should try to pray, if he dared pray for Delia's recovery, whether he would be struck dead. Bless me, for I have sinned. It has been fifteen years since my last confession, and even then I was making it up, just repeating what Tim told me to say; it was only to please my parents. A coherent statement of fears and hopes was too remote; he could not manage to escape his torpor. He heard his father's voice, Mark's even, sonorous voice, and let himself sink, drowned in guilty joy. He'd made it home safe, with Keefer's thumb like a plushy hook in the hollow of his ear.

It was afternoon when Gordon jerked awake, confused, shaken, overtaken by his own smell, pungent as cooked meat. He looked for the daffodil border from his apartment on First Street, the stippled wall of the farmhouse. But there was a framed print of the bridge at Saint Andrew's . . . his room, his boyhood room. Keefer was gone from the bed, but he could hear her chirping in the kitchen, asking for peanut body. Alexis, Lorraine cautioned him, when he surfaced, was still asleep upstairs on the daybed they'd installed in Georgia's old room. Craig had not phoned. Diane Nye had phoned. Even had they wanted to leave Caroline on her wedding day, they would be weathered in, at Tampa. Big Ray had been at her all morning to call the McKennas, call the McKennas, call those McKennas and thank those folks for looking out for those girls.

"Diane said she felt better knowing Keefer was with you," Lorraine told him, placing a bagel with peanut body on the tablecloth in front of Gordon. She made a move to pour him milk, but he got up with a small, settling gesture of his hand, finding a glass, pouring his own.

"What do you think of that," he said, after sitting back down at the table, "of what Diane said."

"I think it's a day late and a dollar short, Gordie," Lorraine told him.

"Mom, that's hard."

"Keefer is right where she should have been all along. And it's entirely possible, I don't wish Delia ill, Gordon, but it's possible that she could end up with—"

"That's wishing her ill, Mom," Gordon said, more harshly than he meant to. He wanted salt to toss, open umbrellas of his own to banish. "Delia will probably recover. She's probably awake now. It was probably some . . . swelling. Maybe she even had a stroke. But she's not dying, Mom."

"Good morning, Alex," Lorraine said forcefully.

The girl's blue eyes were shot red, rayed with dried rivers of mascara. "I need some help," she whispered.

"That Walgreens bag is right on the night table in the room where you slept, and everything's in there, toothbrush, some underthings. I left out an old pair of my daughter's sweatpants, and I'm afraid a shirt of mine is all I have. It'll probably fit you."

"Can I take a shower?" Alexis asked, cringing from Gordon. "Is my mom okay?"

"We're just finding out," Lorraine said. "Towels are in the closet next to the bathroom door."

"Allie, hi!" caroled Keefer.

"Hi, shortcake." Keefer planted a big smooch on Alex's knee.

Poor Alexis was a hostage, Gordon thought, a villager under fire.

Craig Cady called at four. Delia's vital signs were solid. His mother was en route. His voice had recalibrated into its customary cadences. If they would like, Alex could bring Keefer home on the bus. He would be forever grateful to them all. Nonsense, Lorraine replied, Mark would drive them all back—she turned to Gordon, treated him to a rueful, elaborate toss of her head—but not until tomorrow or the next day. Tomorrow, then. No, today is impossible, Lorraine said. Alexis was fine, both girls needed some good food and rest.

"Well," Lorraine said as she hung up, "they'll get the rest at least."

Just before they left on Monday morning, Lorraine, who'd wept on relinquishing her granddaughter, stirring Keefer into an impromptu tantrum, drew Gordon aside behind the burning bush in the side yard. She wrapped her arms around him and clung. "Gordon, I don't want you to think I have any rancor about Delia or any secret desire for her to get sicker."

"I don't think it's a secret, Mom." What was making him so cruel? His loathing of self for the self-same thoughts, expectations, fantasies?

Lorraine threw back her shoulders. "Gordie, I do not wish some poor soul to have to leave her newborn baby or spend her life paralyzed. And also, yes, I don't care whether she lives or dies. In a sense, I don't even know Delia."

"So if an innocent person dies, it's okay as long as you don't know her personally."

"I'll ignore that, honey. What I meant to say is that Delia is important to me only so far as her life has bearing on Keefer's life. And, to a lesser degree, on that poor little girl over there," Lorraine paused, glancing at Alexis. "That said, I would be an unnatural person, an unnatural grandmother, if I wasn't at least glad that the adoption hasn't been finalized. Craig Cady doesn't know our child."

Gordon felt a prickle of fear. It was his mother, not Diane Nye, who would do anything, who would stop at nothing. "Craig's lived with her for most of the past nine months," he said.

"He's not her father. He's barely even her stepfather."

"I don't want to dredge all this up now, Mom. I don't want to drag every turn of events back to the issue of the primary claim on Keefer. Keefer stands to lose somebody else she loves, you know? And that kid who just left her cereal bowl on your table loves her mother as much as Georgia loved you. She loved you even when she treated you like crap, which, if you recall, was only ten years ago."

"Gordie, I know that. It would be simpler if I didn't know that."

"Then give it a rest."

"But we have to be prepared to act, Gordie, in case the worst happens."

It would not be the worst for you, he'd thought, examining Lorraine's fervent, energized face. Even her skin seemed to have tightened, grown supple. She was no longer the bemused, absent woman who'd come to his house that weekend in Madison, who walked as if walking hurt.

It would not be the worst for you, and it would not be the worst for me. He was his mother's child, direct, blunt, impervious to contradiction, a heedless missile as she sped toward her goal.

For most of his life, her goal had been to love him. He would not have thought of trying to deter her. Now, he got one clear-shot look at the Lorraine people saw when they tried to deter her, to distract or placate her. Her style, her humor, her affectionate, right-brainy air of artsy exuberance, these had distracted him from the essence of his mother, which was the white-hot coal of the fully professed. He saw this Lorraine, and she frightened him. He kissed his mother's forehead and left.

Craig Cady had a full house. His mother was rocking the swaddled bundle that was Hugh, fresh from the hospital, the one tiny hand visibly dusty from the membrane bath he'd so recently left. An austerely tall man with an edifice of pomaded silver hair, wearing a clerical collar, stepped forward, cupping Keefer's chin, gripping Gordon's and Mark's hands in a crushing, soulful press. Craig Cady said, "This is our pastor, Reverend Whitehead."

The strangling sound he heard behind him was, Gordon realized, his father laughing.

"We'll keep you in our prayers," the pastor said.

"Thanks," Gordon said.

"Well," Craig ventured, "well, thanks."

"No problem," Gordon replied. "We hope Delia gets better every day. Just call old Keefer and me here when you need me to bring her by."

"I'm . . . well, Gordie, you don't have to take her anymore. My mom's here. I'm sure she'll want to see the baby."

"Has Keefer met your mom?"

"Once. But my mom's great with kids."

"I think I'll just keep her with me while all this is going on, Craig. You don't need a two-year-old bombing around, into everything, when you have a sick wife and a new baby and a scared teenager."

"It's okay."

"It's not okay. Keefer's coming with my dad and me to get my car, and then we'll be back out at my house in Oregon."

"Keefer needs to stay here," Craig said.

"I think, in this situation, what Craig is trying to say is that this family needs to draw strength from one another, Gordon," the pastor put in. "He wants all his children under one roof."

"Well, Keefer's not his child. At least, not yet. She's . . . his ward. And I am her uncle, and she's just spent two days beating up and down the highway. She needs a little time focused directly on her."

"Please, Gordon, let's not increase the already intense—"

"Craig," Gordon said, "I want to speak with you privately."

"I have no secrets from our pastor."

"But I do have secrets from your pastor, who is not my pastor, and I want to get this over with quickly."

They sat down together in the bedroom, each perched, at the end of the bed, on opposite corners of the mattress.

"Craig, Keefer is going to be frightened and needy right now."

"She needs to stay here. Your weekend is up."

"Craig, my parents and I just busted our asses for you."

"And I appreciate that. But I know that when Delia wakes up, the first thing she's going to ask after is her baby, and Alexis, and where Keefer is."

"Keefer's third."

"What do you mean?"

"She comes after your baby and Alexis."

"Gordie, Delia is . . . she could be . . . I can't handle your-all politically correct way of saying stuff."

"You have not said a single thing about your concern about how Keefer feels. When we came in the door, you didn't pick her up and kiss her, you didn't try to tell her that you missed her. You introduced us to your fucking shepherd—"

"Don't get all hot on me, Gordie. I warn you."

"You didn't give Alexis a hug and get your mother to let Alex hold the baby. You introduced us to your . . . pastor. And he was the one who said you wanted your family to-gether under one roof. You didn't say that. You just said you'd find somebody to take care of Keefer."

"Of course, I missed her," Craig blustered. "No, Gordon, actually I didn't miss her. I didn't miss anyone. I haven't slept in three days. I just laid eyes on my firstborn son, and my wife, who I love more than my life, is laying up in some hospital bed with a computer reading her brain—"

"That's my point. Keefer needs someone who can see her, who can get outside his own hurt to give her his love. That's not you, not right now. I mean that as no insult, Craig, be-cause I know exactly how you feel."

"Right, Gordie, you're the big advocate for families. You're so devoted to your family, all you could do for your whole life was screw every woman you laid eyes on, including coming on to my wife—"

"What?" Gordon was speechless. "What in the hell are you talking about?"

"At Ray's wedding. You were all over her."

"I was the best man, Craig, and she was the matron of honor. I had to stand next to her. We had to dance. I want to tell you that I will never say anything more true in my life than this: I never made a pass at your wife. I never wanted to make a pass at your wife," Gordon said, and added, "How long have you been thinking about this shit?"

"Your sister even said as much. Not about Delia. But about everybody else. It was what people thought about you."

"Don't bring up my sister. Don't say a fucking word about my sister. And, what the hell, Craig, all of you couldn't wait to suck up to Ray. It wasn't me who played on the Knockers. On a tour sponsored by a restaurant that specializes in ladies' boobs—"

"You know that joint has nothing to do with the tour."

"Yeah? Well, that's what everybody thought."

"Yeah, well you're the perfect man, Gordie," Craig muttered.

"I'm not at all perfect. I'm a fucking ex-science teacher who lives in a rathole—"

"Teaching kids evolution—"

Gordon stood up, sweating. "Teaching kids that man is not the perfect creation, but a frail creature in the process of change. Isn't that what your church teaches?"

"I don't want to do this." Craig covered his face. "I'm sorry. I'm not myself, Gordon. I'm not myself. You don't know how bad we felt about what we had to do to you guys. Just because you have to do something that's right doesn't mean it's easy. And now, all this. You don't know what this is like. The woman I love gives birth to this precious gift, this wonderful baby we thought we'd never have—"

"You had a wonderful baby already."

"But a son. My son. And then, she's cast down into the shadow, the greatest joy and the greatest grief, right up against one another."

"I know exactly what that's like," Gordon said. "It wasn't my wife, but it was my only sister. I watched her bravery when she gave birth to Keefer, and her fight to stay alive to raise Keefer and how she died trying, and I couldn't do a damned thing about it. I've never been a husband, so I don't know how that feels. But I loved Georgia as much as I ever loved any person."

"Gordon, I'm not questioning your love for Georgia. Or Keefer. Look, let's get back to the subject," Craig said, weariness in every slow breath. "We have custody of Keefer. We're adopting Keefer."

"But you don't really want her."

"Of course I do, Gordie. She's a great little kid."

"Do you love her as much as you already love Hugh?"

"I can't . . . you can't compare those things."

"Do you love Alex like you love Hugh?"

"Alex has a father of her own. Alex is Delia's child. I didn't even meet Alex until she was in, what, fourth grade—"

"Well, do you love Hugh?"

"I never thought I could love anything on earth so much."

"That's how I love Keefer. She is the kin of my kin, Craig. She's the flesh of the flesh I love. She's my own."

"I know that you think of it that way, and I admire you for it."

"You admire me? You admire me? As if it was a noble act to love the baby I helped deliver, that I helped raise? Do you really think I could feel any more connected to Keefer if I'd planted the seed? That there would be some kind of magic trick if the first cells that divided and divided until they were her came out of me?"

"You haven't experienced it, Gordie."

"You think you can know more about loving a kid in four days than I know about loving Keefer for two years?"

"Why didn't you say all this back then?"

"Because no one gave me a chance to say anything. And I didn't think I had to. I thought it was obvious."

"Someday you might have a kid of your own. I pray that you do. Then you tell me."

"I had a kid of my own, Craig."

"If that were the truth, you would never have given her up. You were the one who gave her up. But even then, you and I are not the ones who control these things, Gordon, not really."

"What is really? Is your reality the correct reality or something?"

"I'm a car salesman, Gordie. I can't do fancy talk about science."

"Okay, plain talk. You didn't want her. And you don't want her now."

"I wanted to have a child with my wife. Having a child who was blood related to my wife was almost the same thing. I wanted to do what my best buddy Ray wanted and fulfill the wishes of Georgia, his wife."

"But you didn't want Keefer, specifically. You said it was almost the same thing, as if Keefer was a reasonable facsimile of a kid."

"Don't be an asshole. You know I'm not saying that."

Gordon relented, "No, I do know that you don't mean that. You mean, she was as close as could be to the child you might have had together."

A baby who looked like me, Gordon thought. *A baby who was smart, like your father.*

"Exactly," Craig sighed, his massive shoulders slumped.

"But, see, I wanted her, specifically. I wanted this one child, who was already mine."

Shaking his head side to side with somber slowness, like a

bruin scenting a presence he did not recognize, Craig seemed to meditate. "I don't know how this all got started . . ." He looked beseechingly into Gordon's face. "I can't even see how I can live my own life, let alone these kids. I don't know what Delia is going to need. I don't know a damned thing."

Gordon felt a knot open and loose. "You poor bastard," he said, reaching out stiffly, grasping Craig's forearm. They pulled apart, and sat with their hands dangling between their knees until Gordon said finally, "Well, what you have to do is a thing I know how to do. You can ask me. I won't ask for a payoff. I won't ask for more days with Keefer, it's not like that."

"And I haven't even called Alex's father. He has to know—"

"Craig," his mother called from the living room, "it's the hospital!" Craig lumbered to his feet. Gordon followed him out to the living room, nodding to his father, who stood up, craning his neck to retrieve one of Keefer's red Converse high-tops from the coffee table, where it peeked from between lavish twin urns of silk lilies.

"What does that mean? A ventilator? Is that temporary?" Craig was asking, as his mother rocked faster, faster, faster.

Mark made a grab for Keefer, bobbled her wriggling rump, and knocked the shoe to the floor.

"What do you think?" Mark asked urgently, looking hard into Gordon's eyes, a look that was steady, young, ready to dare anything.

"Let's go," Gordon told his father, scooping up Keefer with one arm, pressing her face against his shoulder, turning the knob on the door with his free hand. "Leave it. Leave the shoe. It's not bad luck. It's not on the table."

CHAPTER twenty-two

*My name is Keefer Kathryn Nye. K. K. N. I live in Madison,
Wisconsin. I am almost ten. My birthday will be right before
spring vacation. I want to do paintball. My dad is saying no,
because it is guns, but it is not guns. He also says that all the
other kids would not be able to come, because their parents
would think they would get blind in one eye. Hugh got to do
paintball, and he is only a kid, but I guess it's different when
you are a boy.*

Is that fair?

*I am going to write the story of my entire life. I have all
night.*

My mother died when I was a baby.

*It's Tuesday right now. It's night. I had to take Monday
and Tuesday off for a medical emergency. My dad was out of
town. He went to a meeting in Kansas or California or
someplace. He never goes to meetings, so why now? He is
not a tenor, so they pay him peanuts. But he is going to get
out of school pretty soon. He says I am paying for his education, but then he is going to pay for my education. I would
rather have a mansion on Lake Mendota than his education.
My friend Alaya has a mansion on Lake Mendota with a
bowling alley in the basement. Our house is this big dump. It
has five bedrooms and a porch all around and seven birch*

trees. It looks much better on the outside than on the inside. But it is a rotten color. My father says it is shi-you-know-what bristol green. My dad's car used to be that color. We got it for the neighborhood, but we only have the chairs and couches we got from my grandma and grandpa. At least the bank doesn't own the chairs. We are going to get another house later. Even my aunt Lindsay says our house is a dump. And she is my best aunt. She is so nice, she would not lie about something like that. I don't remember my mother, because I was only a baby when she died. She was pretty famous. My grandma McKenna has a big book of pictures and stories about my mother, and one was in People *(not* Teen People*) and there is a tape that was on the old-time show that was like 20/20. I get to keep it when I'm twelve. My cousin Hugh's mom died when he was a baby, too, so we have gone through the same things. Once Mrs. Mallory said I thought I could get away with a bunch of stuff because I thought people would feel sorry for me because I didn't have a mother. This was a big, fat, stinking lie.*

I have to do two days of journaling because of this medical emergency. It makes up for everything I'm missing in homework, even science and math. I'm learning a lot of science here in the hospital. You bet! I'm the only one to help out. Okay, so first we went to the hospital on Monday, and we just sort of sat around, dum-dum-dum. Nothing happened. My dad called on the phone and said, read something. I said, like what? My dad says that if I don't learn to read for pleasure, he will have to get me my own shopping cart when I grow up, so I can push it up and down State Street with my little chihuahua sitting on top of the plastic gallon milk jugs. I know what he means by this, and it is not funny.

And so, now it's Tuesday, and I am out in the hall, because they won't let me in the room yet. I'm not sterilized. My dad died when I was a little baby, too, but not my dad now. It was Ray. I don't think I ever met him. We live in Madison because my dad has to always go to more school, more school, more school! It is ridiculous. I would quit school right now if I could, because I do not apply myself. I would like to ride a racehorse for my job. I am a pretty good rider, because I took lessons at Barnstable Ridge. Also, I am the shortest one in my class except for Ames Smith, which doesn't count because he has a wheelchair. He is a pretty good kid. He's coming to my birthday. He couldn't do paintball, though, because he can't stand up. He gives me rides in the wheelchair all the time because I only weigh fifty-two. My grandma always says, eat something. But she is short, too. Eating does not make you taller. My other grandma is a lot taller, and she can do the swan dive. But she has migrating headaches.

Hugh and me got in a pretty good amount of trouble in our lives. Actually, it was mostly my idea, but Hugh goes along with everything I say. He does everything I tell him to, even if I don't totally mean it.

Is that fair?

I would get sent to the counselor, which is how I met Miss Tyson. Miss Tyson! Ha! Ha! She was a training counselor. She was only in our school for one month, then she was going to move on to another school. She said they gave her the potential criminals. So she could see what she was getting into. Right away, she was calling my dad. Answering machine! What does she think, he's home? He has to work. But that was a long time ago.

> Miss Tyson: *So, are you taking away the little kids'*
>   *Mothball cards?*
> K. K. N.: *We traded.*
> Miss Tyson: *What did you trade?*
> K. K. N.: *Rubber bands.*
> Miss Tyson: *Rubber bands?*

K. K. N.: *Big rubber bands. The blue ones. I collect*
them. You could use them for a slingshot.
MISS TYSON: *Do you think that was a fair thing to do?*
K. K. N.: *It was like the pioneers trading beads with*
the Indians. For their furs and land.
MISS TYSON: *It was EXACTLY like the pioneers trading*
beads with the Indians, which is what makes it so
terrible! The first-grader parents are calling up,
and they are mad as hell! They are saying they paid
ten dollars for those cards and you ripped those lit-
tle kids off. You have to give them all back.

I don't care about the rubber bands, so there.

"Keefer, I didn't have a mother, either," Miss Tyson said.
I hate when teachers do this, but I sort of liked her because
she didn't treat me like a one-year-old. I was a brat, she
said. She ran away two times. She smoked cigarettes when
she was eleven. Like I care! You can get away with a lot
when people feel sorry for you, Miss Tyson goes. But you
don't really get away with anything because you can't get
away from yourself. LECTURE! Then she told me about the
bread in the waters, which was more interesting. If you put
bread on the water, it will come back to you threefold, she
goes. I was like eight, at the time, a lot younger, so Hugh
and I actually tried this. Now I know she meant, the bad
things you do will come back and be worse. My dad said the
law of karma was horse you-know-what. But it makes sense
to me.

So, after I was killed for the Mothball cards, my dad came
to school. We had a conference. I was sitting there when
Miss Tyson told me who she was. I think my dad already
could tell because he was staring when he came into the
room. She is pretty. She is a babe. She has a textured cut. She
said, "I am your cousin Alex."

I thought, right.

But she told me all about it. She did not know I went to this school, but Uncle Craig used to be her stepfather. Her real father's name is Jack. He is pretty nice, but he is not the marrying kind. After Delia died, she went back to live with Jack. They were bachelors, like my dad and me, except with a log cabin.

Okay! Miss Tyson used to practically be my sister! That was where all the Barbies came from. I still have all her Barbies. I'm too old for Barbies. But they're from the olden time and they could be worth something someday, my grandma Nye says. Grandma Nye has all her dolls from when she was little. The one with no arms is the most valuable.

We called up my grandma. My grandma, my dad's mother, that is. We both got on the extension. My dad was like, Can you believe this? It's Alexis! Then we called up my uncle Craig. My dad said, can you believe this? He said more than that, actually. Unprintable. I said, why didn't Uncle Craig know where she was all the time? My dad said he knew she was in Madison but not at my school. And he would not have known unless I got in so much trouble all the time.

I had a dream and I remembered when Alex and I took baths.

Dad asked Miss Tyson over to dinner and made the broccoli pasta, which is the only thing he can cook practically, but it's good for cancer. My dad probably cooked once in my whole life besides this time. When I was just little, like three, we had takeout every day. One time, he tried to give me some fried rice and he said it was Thai, but I said, this is not Thai, this is Chinese. My dad tells everybody this story, so why not you, too?

Hugh's mother had a disease. So did my mother, but she was killed when she fell from the bridge. They were different diseases. I used to think I killed her when I was a baby, by accident. Hugh actually did kill his mother, but it wasn't his fault. She died from complications. She had a fat artery in her brain. They had to have her on a breathing machine, but just breathing didn't get her better. Her brain was blown out. She would have been a vegetable. My uncle had two babies all of a sudden, me and Hugh, because my dad couldn't have me until they went to court and said he was in his right mind.

Alex went back to live with her dad and after a while she grew up. I never saw her again until now.

It's confusing!

Then she went to college in Madison, but we never saw her, because she lived on the east side. Also, we didn't have her phone number. She lived right near the guy who makes the sculptures out of car motor parts. So, I got in kindergarten. I used to call my dad by his first name. It was embarrassing. Alaya asked me why. I said because my dad used to be my uncle.

I mean it!

My dad and my mom were brothers and sisters. She adopted him when he was a little baby. And then, my dad adopted me when she died. Not exactly. After Delia died. Which is Hugh's mother, except that she is dead. First they lived right by us, behind the Orange Tree store. Now, they live in Oregon. Not the state, the town! Oregon, Wisconsin. My dad used to live there when I was a baby, but now we can't afford to. My uncle Craig sells Jeeps. We can't afford one! Hugh says he is going to get a horse, which is a total lie. He came over all the time to cook out. We went to see the Brewers. They stink. We went to Colorado rafting with Aunt Lindsay and Uncle Tim. They're the Upchurches. Two high churches. Uncle Tim always says he's going to steal me. But now they are having a baby so he won't have to. He has a dog named Taxi. My aunt Lindsay was in love with my father. My dad has a weakness for red-haired girls. But they were too young. When she got old enough, her and Tim got married. They lived in the same town. And we lived in Madison. My dad had to move to Madison to take care of me. That was how Hugh and me got to be friends, though he is only a kid. Eight. We have a big picture of me and my dad with the cake. It says, Keefer, All Ours. There was this big part grabbed out of the cake, which I did, because I was two. I got to go to Florida by myself when I was six. My grandpa Ray let me drive the golf cart. Alone. My grandma M. and Auntie Nora came down and got me for the honeymoon. They went to Ecuador. Now I can go there all summer, not Ecuador, but Tall Trees, if I want. I'm old enough. My grandpa M. taught me how to burn things with the magnifying glass, though it was Hugh who burned up the recycling. We were both killed then. He used hairspray. I said, don't, Hugh!

WARNING! DO NOT READ THIS NEXT PART IF YOU ARE UNDER SEVENTEEN!

The next time I got sent out in school was over Hugh's weenie. I was not in trouble for weeks. I had this idea. Everyone in third grade wanted to see a weenie. Big deal. So I would split the fifty cents with Hugh. Fifty cents for one look. It was a pretty good deal. Hugh was only in first grade. Hugh actually has a pretty big one for a little kid because I have seen two others. I won't say who, but their initials are D. R. and M. P. That's all I'll say.

Now, I'm back.

This next part is the exciting part. Alex was in transition. My dad was stuck up in the air. Then he went to Chicago. Okay, Alex was telling him on the phone, should I hold my legs together or something? It was snowing. I knew I would not even be able to go to school on Wednesday because we would probably get a snow day, which we have not even had one yet. It is global warming.

I forgot one part. Somebody, I will not reveal who, but it is Sarah Tanaka, told that we were selling looks at Hugh's weenie. I'm back in Miss Tyson's office. She says it is inap-

propriate. She says it is sex. I say, no, it is not sex, it is biology. I say, my dad is a biology professor, almost. She says, I know all about your dad.

Uncle Craig comes to school. I can tell he puts all the blame on me. He thinks Hugh is perfect because his mom died.

They got married when I caught them. My dad and Alex. I knew she was going to come over.

I threw up at Zoe Palisio's house and I wanted to GO HOME. Zoe's dad drove me home, and he had a new car. He gave me a towel to put my face in and he drove fast, and he said, run in, when we got to my house. Grandpa M. says dad is the nutty professor. He doesn't lock the door. So I did. Okay! There they were, no shirts. They didn't freak out. My dad said, are you sick, Kee? And I said, I'm sicker than a dog, Daddy. After I was in first grade, I said, are you my daddy? And he said, yepadep, no daddy except this daddy. So, I started calling him Daddy. I used to call him Dory. It was my baby name for him. We still don't have the same last name, but lots of kids don't. So, they were laying in the bed, my dad said, okay, Missy, get out of here. And I went out in the hall. He said, I love Alex. I'm like, duh.

She was dating a professional baseball player. Okay. They had to break up. A Madison Mudhen. That is almost a professional. They get paid. When my dad had to come to school like the hundredth time, he said, oh, what is his name? Alex said, Bob. They're all Bob. My dad says, oh yeah? She had to break up with the baseball guy, but she still plays baseball. The first time she came over to dinner, my dad had been at his softball game and he smelled, and Alex said, go take a shower. Dad said, I play hard. Slow pitch? Alex asked him. He said, yeah, do you ever play? Fast pitch, she said. My dad said, yeah?

My uncle Mike says my dad is robbing the cradle, but they

are really only ten years apart. My dad just looks really old because of his glasses.

Let's get back to the baby. The doctor looks at me, and he says, who is this child? Alex says, she is my kid, Keefer Kathryn Nye. The doctor says, okay. He says Miss McKenna, don't try to push until I tell you. I say, she's a Mrs. McKenna. Alex says, don't be scared, Keefer, because if I scream, it's okay. Well, she SCREAMED! I ran out in the hall. Then, I had to get sterilized again. I thought I would puke. Then I thought I would faint. I washed my face in the bathroom. The nurse, Jennifer, said, do you want to go back in?

K. K. N: Yes. Is the baby here yet?
JENNIFER: Pretty soon now.
ALEX: Christ, to hell, I'm dying. Damn!

We go back in. The doctor says, I see hair. I see pretty red hair. Push, Mrs. McKenna. Push. Push. Alex's face is totally purple. There's guts all over the place. Push, push. I think they are going to pop Alex's head off, but she says, between screaming, Don't be scared, Keefer. Don't be scared.

Wait a minute!

There's the baby!

She pops out like boom! She's very strong.

She's not that gross. The slime is natural. She's so big. She's like a big baby like Zoe's baby brother, only she's just a little born baby. The nurse Jennifer says, Big sister! Can you hold the baby? Oh, they let me hold the baby, my sister baby. I did not care about the blood. I kissed her right on the mouth. She sneezed! I was so sick of being a bachelor. Alex is all sweaty, but they wash her up. I let them have the baby so they can wash her up. We call grandma M. and she says, I can't stand this! There's like three hundred inches of snow outside this house. In Tall Trees. I come from up north. I asked Alex if we could call

Lindsay and Tim and my grandma Nye and her dad in North Carolina. All we got to call was her dad. Then she says, I'm going to sleep, how about you? I couldn't sleep. I was so excited. Alex says, Honey, find something to read. Don't turn on the TV. I just watch the lights. The lights are smooshed *under the snow. No cars. Well, one car. Just the pizza car.*

I was not sad. I was glad the baby had a mom of her own. I wanted my dad. I started thinking he might have a plane crash. It was a little creepy. I took some change out of Alex's purse and went to the vending machines. They had Pringles in little small cans. I like sour cream best.

I went back.

Alex wakes up to feed the baby from her boobs, sick. The baby already knows how to eat. She's very smart. Alex says, shnikeys, I'm a mother, what do you think of that? Then she says, Kee, I'm your mother, too. I said, step-mother. She said, no, I'm your mother because I take you as my child, like in the wedding. You don't have another mother so I don't have to share you. I said, well, you could adopt me, too. She said, can I sleep overnight first? She shut her eyes and told me she did not have a mother either. I told her to just use my grandma, because my grandma doesn't have a daughter. Get up here in bed with us, she says, go to sleep. We all fit.

My dad woke me up. I was dreaming about this swimming pool in the jungle where all the mermaid babies played.

I said, did we get a snow day? He says, yeah! We are go-ing to name the baby right now. I'll have to get back to you in a minute.

They had sort of a fight about it. My dad liked Georgia or Elizabeth. Who is Elizabeth? says Alex.

Then she said, No, she is Dory. Dory Delia McKenna. She said remember? He didn't remember. Then she says, about once there was a little girl who could not say her father's name. She thinks I don't remember what this means. But I do. They told me this story like one hundred times, about Georgia.

It is a kind of okay name though.

D. D. M.

and K. K. N.

My dad cries his head off. He is such a goofer. Why cry? Dory weighs nine pounds. My dad says, I have too many girls to love in my house. Ridiculous. I need a boy now, Dad says. Get over yourself, Alex says.

My dad says he is taking me home. Aunt Nora is already here. I said, what, has she got a one-horse open sleigh? But my dad says Aunt Nora could drive a dog team. I don't want to leave. Actually, I am pretty mad. After this whole medical emergency, okay! Good-bye, Keefer! But he sort of squeezes my arm hard. I yelled, ouch. The nurse Jennifer comes back in. Are we okay in here? It serves him right. She gave me this "I'm the Big Sister" T-shirt. It's okay looking. It's a little small. Most of the big sisters are babies. Alex says it's a crop top. The nurse says, she is the prettiest baby in the whole place. You are all redheads. I'm not a redhead except in summer. My dad says you both have to have the gene. Alex says, no, you don't. My dad says, yes, sweetheart, you do. That's my dad! Mr. Bossy!

We had to get going. The nurse Jennifer brings in our baby, all cleaned up. We had a bath, she says. Dad says, hurry up, Keefer, you are always the last one out. I say, I just want to see something once. Alex puts the baby down in the baby holder. She is sleeping. But she's smiling in her sleep. Her mouth goes up and down, up and down. She thinks she's eating her dinner.

Dad says, don't wake her up, but I kiss her anyhow. I say, Kiss me so you don't miss me. Dad just stands there in the door. He turns around and looks out in the hall. Then he comes over and just picks me up and puts my head under his coat. He carries me all the way to the car, which he will never do, even when I was little and totally had cramps in my legs at the mall.

   This is five pages, at least, both sides.

The End

May 24, 2000
Oregon, Wisconsin

Reader Group Guide

1. In whose home do you think Keefer would be happiest—
   Gordon's or the Nyes'? On what would you base your
   decision? What makes a good parent? What makes a
   happy home?

2. Do you think Mitchard's portrayal of Diane as a mother and as a born-again Christian is a balanced one? How
   does she make Diane a sympathetic character?

3. There are many kinds of single parents in the novel:
   Gordon, Delia, Craig (after Delia's death), the birth
   mothers of both Gordon and Georgia. How would you
   use this book to argue for or against single parenting?

4. Gordon is first introduced as a highly analytic person,
   one who thinks that "life could be lived like an experiment conducted in keeping with scientific method, that
   a certain set of results could be obtained and, once
   obtained, repeated." Eventually he comes to realize "the
   pressure of the human hand behind the instruments."
   How do Gordon's relationships with Keefer, Lindsay,
   his aunt Nora, and his mother bring about his own emotional development?

5. Discuss Gordon's decision to drop his petition to adopt Keefer. Was it the right one, given the circumstances? How much of it was based on his relationship with Georgia? How much do you think was based on the difficulties he would encounter as a single father?

6. Discuss how the phrase "a theory of relativity" touches on the novel's themes: family, heredity, adoption, and parental love, to name a few. Can you think of any other issues this title suggests?

7. Do you agree with Judge Sayward's decision to deny Gordon's petition for adoption based on his own status as an adopted child? As a judge was she compelled to give a literal interpretation of the law, or do you think she should have assumed that Gordon's status was the same as any other blood relative of Georgia's?

8. Discuss the possibility that Ray's and Georgia's accident was a suicide. How does it make you feel about Ray?

9. Where do you stand on the nature versus nurture debate? Do you think your personality has been determined genetically or by the situation in which you grew up? How do the characters of Georgia, Gordon, Alex, and Keefer support or contradict your beliefs?

10. In the last chapter, Mitchard offers us a glimpse of Keefer as a ten-year-old. Did she "turn out" the way you expected? How do you think Keefer would have been different if Delia had lived and become her mother?

James Schnepf

JACQUELYN MITCHARD is the author of *Twelve Times Blessed*, *A Theory of Relativity*, and *The Deep End of the Ocean*. She lives in Oregon, Wisconsin, with her family.

Books by
Jacquelyn Mitchard

The Breakdown Lane

ISBN 978-0-06-137452-4 (paperback)

"From our petulant, prideful heroine to her sullen-yet-saintly son, each character's complexities shine."
—*Washington Post*

Twelve Times Blessed

ISBN 978-0-06-171578-5 (paperback)

"[Mitchard] perfectly understands women's insecurities and the minutiae of daily spats. She wrings tension out of every sharp word and awkward hug."
—*People*

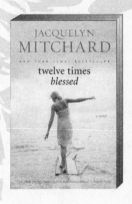

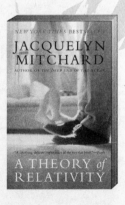

A Theory of Relativity

ISBN 978-0-06-083693-1 (paperback)

"Deft . . . complex . . . a powerful tale of a shattering custody battle. . . . Mitchard's gift is her ability to present her characters in a compassionate light, even when revealing them at their weakest moments."
—*Us Weekly*

Visit www.AuthorTracker.com
for exclusive information on your favorite HarperCollins authors.

Available wherever books are sold, or call 1-800-331-3761 to order.